If I Could Tell You

ELIZABETH WILHIDE

FIG TREE
an imprint of
PENGUIN BOOKS

FIG TREE

UK | USA | Canada | Ireland | Australia
India | New Zealand | South Africa

Fig Tree is part of the Penguin Random House group of companies
whose addresses can be found at global.penguinrandomhouse.com.

First published 2016
001

Typeset in Dante MT Std by Palimpsest Book Production Ltd, Falkirk, Stirlingshire
Printed in Great Britain by Clays Ltd, St Ives plc

A CIP catalogue record for this book is available from the British Library

ISBN: 978-0-241-20959-2

www.greenpenguin.co.uk

MIX
Paper from
responsible sources
FSC™ C018179
www.fsc.org

Penguin Books is committed to a sustainable
future for our business, our readers and our planet.
This book is made from Forest Stewardship
Council™ certified paper.

To Glenn and to Jocelyn

Time will say nothing but I told you so,
Time only knows the price we have to pay;
If I could tell you I would let you know.

– from 'If I Could Tell You', W. H. Auden

London, 1944

People fell from the sky. Some spread-eagled, some twisting and flailing, others drifting down as if weightless. Face after face after face passed her by, neared then disappeared into greyness. They were angels, falling from the angel roof. She understood she was to join them.

They were men and women and children. They were war dead.

She understood she was war dead too and reached out her hands.

Death is truth, they told her, falling.

Her mouth was caked in dust. Her throat was dust. Dust was in her nose. She took a breath and it was ashes. She coughed and there were knives in her chest. She couldn't move her arms, her hands, her legs, her feet. She could move her head a little. She tried to call out but her voice was shut up in her throat.

Someone else called. She heard their thin cries. It was dark.

Her mother told her she needed a little colour at her neck. Her mother told her that if she'd had her opportunities when she was a girl she wouldn't have thrown them away. 'Half a pound of anti-macassars,' said her mother.

She was pinned. She couldn't move her hands, her arms, her legs. Dust silted her mouth and choked her.

It was sunny and hot. The tide was out. She was walking down a shingle beach with a mermaid's purse in the pocket of her dress. The sea was sparkling.

Something shifted, tilted, gave way. A cavity opened up, a vacancy. From above came a narrow probing beam of light.

Someone groaned; something moved. She smelled gas. The light went out.

She was walking down a shingle beach with a mermaid's purse in her pocket.

Protect my family.

I

1939

Julia Compton was frightened, of course she was. The gas masks dangling from the hallstand in their cardboard cartons – hers, her husband's, her son's and their housekeeper's – lurched her stomach every time she laid eyes on them. Obscene things, rubbery and goggle-eyed. She couldn't remember much about the previous war – she'd been too young – only the maroons banging and bursting at the end of it. That did not stop her from imagining a miasma of yellow mustard gas creeping over the town, borne inland on sea breezes, settling into the furrows of ploughed fields.

That summer they all knew it was coming. The papers were full of it, the pubs and pulpits too. Appeasement had failed. Any day now the waiting would be over. Twenty years, and they'd scarcely got over the last one, people were saying.

For this reason she was as relieved as everyone else when a film crew arrived from London in the last week of August and gave them all something different to talk about. The great topic of conversation was why they had come. It was a small town on an east-coast estuary with nothing noteworthy about it. Trippers passed it by routinely; amateur painters tired of hunting for subjects and didn't stay long. What could possibly interest them?

Fishing, it turned out.

The news was received with surprise. You caught fish, you smoked them, you sold them. No one in their right mind filmed them. Somewhat later the penny dropped. Films about fishing must feature those who made their living that way. Women were

3

the first to realize this and the hairdresser on the high street found herself busy.

'What is it,' said Julia, 'that so attracts people to filming? Is it glamour, do you think?'

The six o'clock bulletin was over – no war yet – and they'd switched off the wireless. A pleated paper fan hid the summer hearth. On the mantelshelf: a green ceramic bowl of spills for the fires they would have to light soon, a brass carriage clock, an engraved invitation on stiff white card to a yacht-club dance propped against well-dusted ornaments.

Richard looked up from the newspaper and lamplight glanced off his face.

These days she often forgot how handsome her husband was – it was the same as the mantelshelf ornaments, familiarity cloaking their original appeal – but on this occasion it struck her as if she were seeing it for the very first time, as if he were a rare prize displayed in a shop window alongside bric-a-brac. He was nearing forty, eight years older than her, and age, which would eventually dim and blur her slight, dark prettiness, was only maturing his good looks, confirming them with a few crow's feet and a distinguished scattering of grey. Beauty was unfair that way: it treated men and women differently. The matinee idol, her mother had called him. He was a solicitor and oddly lacking in vanity.

She set down her sherry glass on a leather-topped coaster. 'Peter's been down at the quayside all afternoon watching them, along with half the town.' Their son Peter was nine.

'In his case, I suspect it's the mechanics of it.'

'The train-set aspect?'

'You have to admit it's rather impressive kit they've got.'

She laughed. 'You're just as bad as he is.'

He put the newspaper to one side. 'I think I might have secured a counsel for Perry Clayton.'

Two months ago Perry Clayton, who worked in the smoke-house on Brewer Street, had got into a brawl with a man who was sleeping with his wife and beaten him so badly he later died of his injuries. He was currently on remand awaiting trial at the assizes.

'That's good,' said Julia.

Harry, their housekeeper, came in to announce dinner was ready. Peter's footsteps pounded down the stairs as they went into the hallway.

'Walk, don't run,' Richard said to him. 'How many times have I told you? Don't they teach you that at school?'

By the time they sat down at the table, her husband's appearance had regained its customary normality. A phrase occurred to her: 'the institution of marriage'. She slipped her napkin out of its bone ring.

Julia tidied up the clothes her son had left on the floor. 'Have you brushed your teeth?'

'Yes, Madre,' said Peter. He was in his pyjamas, pushing his Hornby engine to and fro with a bare foot.

'Pop into bed then and I'll read to you.'

Peter bounced on the mattress and flopped back. 'Mr Birdsall let me look through the camera.'

Julia closed a drawer. 'Who's Mr Birdsall?'

'He's in charge of the filming,' said Peter. 'People who are in charge of films are called *directors*.'

'Are they,' said Julia. 'I hope you weren't making a nuisance of yourself.'

'Filming's ever so complicated,' said Peter. 'Like maths.' Peter was good at maths.

'Get yourself under the covers now.' She sat down on the edge of the bed and opened the book. *The Story of the Treasure Seekers*. 'Are you sure you want this one again?'

He nodded.

'*Being the adventures of the Bastable children in search of a fortune*,' it said on the title page. Underneath was her name in an eight-year-old's loopy letters. Peter never seemed to tire of it. Perhaps as an only child he enjoyed imagining himself part of a large family.

When he settled himself down she began to read. "'It is one of us that tells this story – but I shall not tell you which: only at the very end perhaps I will. While the story is going on you may be trying to guess, only I bet you don't. It was Oswald who first thought of looking for treasure. Oswald often thinks of very interesting things –'"

A satisfied chuckle from the pillow. 'He gives the game away. Right there.'

'He does, doesn't he,' said Julia, turning a page. This part of the day belonged to her alone and she took full pleasure from it. One chapter a night was the rule but the chapters were short and she allowed herself to be talked into a second. By the end of it his breathing was even and he had stopped interrupting.

Sleepiness turned the clock back a little – sometimes by as much as a year, which was when he had last willingly submitted to a goodnight kiss. Tonight he must have been especially tired because he reached up and hugged her with his thin, reedy arms, which allowed her to drink in his smell under the cursory face-wash. To be hugged by your child, was anything better than that? Or more bittersweet? For with a hug came a whole history of hugs and the reasons for hugs, along with a future when they would eventually dwindle to handshakes and pecks on the cheek.

Another week and he would be back at school. Her spirits sank. All mothers whose children have been sent away to board learn to endure the highs and lows, to post their anxious love in letters and parcels, to measure out the year in half-terms and holidays. Perhaps if they had been able to have more children she wouldn't have missed him quite so much when he was away.

'You won't die like the mother in the book, will you?' said Peter.

Julia knew better than to be worried by this. He was not morbid or anxious, only in search of rote reassurance. The question tended to come up at this early point in the story, before the motherless Bastables began their adventures.

'I'm not planning on it,' she said, stroking his hair, dark like hers. 'Not until you're a hundred.'

'At least.' She switched off the light.

It had been a beautiful summer. Stand in the garden, stare up at the cloudless sky and you would think nothing could be wrong anywhere in the world.

The next morning sun was streaming through the windows again. The house was quiet. Richard had gone to work and Peter had dashed off somewhere after breakfast. Julia was not about to interfere with the way he spent his time or tie him to her apron strings – that was bad mothering in her opinion – but still the hours to his departure counted down in her head with the same dread tick as the country's approach to war.

The Broadwood lived in the drawing room where the wireless was. After instructing Harry on the day's tasks and chores – or 'conferring', as she preferred to think of it – Julia selected a score from the sheet music in the canterbury and sat down to play. 'La Cathédrale engloutie'. It had to be said it wasn't one of Richard's favourites. He was more of a Bach man.

Debussy was deceptive. The refusal of the harmonies to resolve, the blurred, sonorous bass notes, the layers of voices, masked precision, each sound occupying its own rightful place. The piece demanded technique, control. Within a chord it was often necessary to play one note more strongly than the others to bring out the meaning, and the pedalling had to be exact, never forced. 'The art of pedalling is a kind of breathing,' so Debussy had said, and her tutor had often quoted. Then and only then you saw the scenes hidden in the music, heard the bells of the drowned cathedral ringing under the water, an elegy for lost faith or a testament to faith's survival; she was never sure. When she reached the tolling end she began all over again, the watery notes sliding under her fingers.

'Mrs C? *Mrs C?*'

Lost in music, Julia raised her head. Harry was in the doorway, smudges on her apron, thick stockings rolled down over garters. The old blind dog bumbled after her, banging into things. Today he was wearing a dressing on his head: this was the housekeeper's doing and would soon be banged off.

'You're wanted on the telephone.' Like many women of her generation, Harry regarded a ringing telephone in the same grave light as a telegram, and this was reflected in her tone. (Harry's preferred form of communication was on the astral plane; she was a spiritualist.)

'Oh, sorry, I didn't hear.'

'It's Mrs Spencer.'

Julia went out into the hall, with its wallpaper of tawny leaves and beeswaxed banister. Of all their circle of acquaintances, Fiona Spencer was the one she counted as a true friend, without entirely approving of her, it had to be said. Four years ago her husband had dropped dead one Sunday afternoon while washing his Wolseley. Since then she had taken on the draper's shop in town; a rather surprising step for someone of her class, means and background was the local opinion. Then there were the rumours of Geoffrey's philandering, which seemed to indicate some failing on her part, either in provoking the infidelities or in putting up with them. To which must be added the mildly notorious behaviour of her children, that of the elder daughter, Ginny, in particular.

All the same, Julia couldn't resist Fiona's vitality. She was the salt in her life. They also had the connection that they had both married older men, a fact that somehow made their own ten-year age difference less significant.

'Darling,' said Fiona, when she picked up the receiver. There was a pause as a match was struck, then a swift exhalation. 'I was wondering if I could entice you out today? Such glorious weather, pity not to make the most of it.'

'What about the shop?' said Julia.

'Early closing.'

'Surely that's Wednesday?' Today was Monday.

'In my shop it's whichever day I choose.'

Julia laughed.

'Seriously,' said Fiona, 'Miss Simmons will hold the fort. She's been dying for the chance to demonstrate her superior knowledge of cretonne.'

'What did you have in mind?'

'I thought we might have a little picnic down by the Martello tower.'

Julia weighed options. It would mean she would miss Peter when he came home for lunch. On the other hand, when he did he would eat as fast as possible and say as little as possible before scampering out again. Long hours stretched ahead. 'Yes, why not? That would be lovely. What shall I bring?'

'Nothing. My suggestion, my treat.'

The tide was out, far out, and the sky was a strong, clear blue with wisps of cloud towards the horizon. They walked along a path through the salt marshes towards the beach, past shirring reeds, clumps of purple sea lavender and shrubby sea purslane. Down on the flats by the estuary, redshanks probed their spiny bills into the drying mud and a man dredged for cockles. All along the shingle the groynes were exposed, the wooden posts, some rotten and leaning, like the serried rows of teeth in the gaping mouth of a vast marine creature. Over on the hill to the north were six black cannons, remnants of another war, a threatened invasion over a century and a half ago. Gulls screamed and swooped.

'Oh, look, here's a mermaid's purse,' said Julia, bending down. Mermaid's purse: the seedpod of a dogfish. The small matt-black pouch, which was ugly and vaguely menacing, had a pair of thin curving prongs at either end. Such finds were precious to her, tokens of good fortune, as were holey stones. She picked it up from the shingle, put it in her pocket and made a wish: *Protect my family.*

Fiona smiled. 'Ever the beachcomber. You look all of sixteen in that dress.'

'Untidy, you mean.' Julia brushed her hair back from her forehead.

'Nonsense,' said Fiona. 'Charming.' She herself was smart as a bandbox in a navy frock with a white collar and white dotted stitching on the bodice and down the pleats of the skirt. On her, navy was vivid: everything was against the blaze of her red hair.

Tortoiseshell-framed sunglasses, bright lipsticked mouth. No one in town dressed like Fiona; no one else could have carried it off, or would have particularly wanted to. (Julia thought her a little vain.)

'Let me take the hamper.'

'Darling. I thought you'd never ask,' said Fiona.

When they rounded the bay the Martello tower came into view. Squat, egg-shaped in plan, it was made of London stock brick long ago weathered grey. Similar examples of these Napoleonic defences were strung out at intervals all along the east and south coasts. The pointed end, where the wall was thickest, faced the sea. High above the ground was a door, which would have been reached by rope ladder pulled up behind the defenders. Had the need arisen in those distant days, they would have fired from the roof.

'Sun or shade?' said Fiona. 'If we can find any shade, that is.'

Julia shielded her eyes against the glare. 'The film people are here.'

'Are they?'

'Yes.' She pointed. A dozen or so men were grouped around a camera. One of them, tallish, fair-haired, was doing a fair amount of waving and shouting. Surrounding them at a slight distance was a small crowd of onlookers.

'So they are.'

'Did you know they would be?'

Fiona smoothed her skirt. 'I might have done.'

Julia said, 'You're outrageous.'

'No reason why we should miss out on the fun.'

'*Carpe diem?*'

'That sort of thing. Let's face it, it's all going to get pretty grim soon.'

'So Richard says.' And he had been one of the lucky ones, still stationed at his training camp when they'd signed the Armistice. Although by no means unscathed: a brother killed, and two cousins.

They crunched over the shingle.

'Which reminds me,' said Fiona, 'I must dig out my lease.'

Lease? thought Julia. Fiona's conversation was elliptical at the best of times. She had a tendency to drop you down in the middle of her thought processes. 'What's that got to do with the war?'

'Nothing whatsoever.'

Richard – solicitor – legal document – lease. That would be the way the dots joined up.

They had been making their way rather aimlessly in the direction of a small fishing boat pulled up on the foreshore, which, aside from the Martello tower, was the only other distinguishing feature of this broad stretch of shingle.

'Here?' said Julia, setting down the hamper.

'Good a place as any.'

Julia smiled to herself. Of course it was. They had a perfect view of the filming.

Like everything Fiona laid her hand to, the picnic was beautifully done. Dainty cucumber sandwiches, devilled eggs with a well-judged hint of curry powder, a sponge cake, dark juicy plums from the tree in her garden and a thermos of tea which they drank out of the proper china cups with which the hamper, with its neat leather fastenings, was equipped, along with proper china plates, cutlery and a cruet, all snug in its wickerwork interior.

By the time they had finished the onlookers had drifted away, leaving the film crew to do whatever it was they were doing, which appeared to be nothing at all. 'I must say, I fail to see what the fuss is about,' said Fiona, lighting a cigarette. 'It's like watching paint dry.'

'Mmm.' Julia leant back on the rug, licking plum juice from her fingers. There was a faint smell of creosote and a stronger reek of fish coming from the boat in whose lee they sheltered and the sun was warm on her neck and her bare legs. She felt buoyed up by the simple pleasure of eating in the open air, and by talking, although Fiona had done most of that.

'The shop's clean out of blackout,' Fiona was saying. 'Which is a pity, because that silly Lumm man came round yesterday and told me to put up blinds in the conservatory. Whatever for? We never sit in there after dark. The ARP training must have gone to his head. Now I'll have to do it with paint, and what will happen to my poor cuttings?'

Fiona talked as she breathed. It spooled out in ribbons. From the blackout she somehow got on to the topic of her daughters. Ginny, who had failed her School Certificate, was now sitting around at home all day lacquering her nails, playing gramophone records and writing horrid things in the diary she hid under her mattress. Her younger daughter, Avril, was turning out to be surprisingly good at science. Where had that come from? Mr Moodie, her next-door neighbour, had developed a religious mania and could be heard praying aloud in the garden. 'I distinctly remember from RE,' Fiona said, 'that the general idea was that one should communicate with one's Maker silently and in the smallest, most private space, which in my mind I imagined to be our old broom cupboard under the stairs. Not in plain view by the dahlias.' She broke off. 'Oh, here comes trouble.'

Julia sat up. 'Something happening at last?' Then she caught sight of Peter coming round the bay. He had that rapt, self-contained expression of the schoolboy on holiday. She waved at him and he carried on where he was heading, which was towards the film people. 'Peter!' she shouted. He briefly turned in her direction but didn't stop.

Fiona said, 'I recognize that look. I get it from Avril all the time. "Oh, am I related to you in some way? I think not." *That* look.'

'He's started to call me Madre,' said Julia. She missed him calling her Mummy.

'Better Madre than Mater,' said Fiona.

'Richard finds it amusing.'

'And how is the Sainted One?'

Julia prickled with irritation. Whenever Fiona mentioned Richard, there was always an edge in her voice: she couldn't imagine why. 'He thinks he might have found someone who's prepared to defend Perry Clayton.'

'I can't think of anything more depressing than defending a guilty man,' said Fiona.

'Innocent until proven guilty.'

'With all those witnesses?'

'If this were France he might walk free,' said Julia. 'Crime of passion.'

Fiona said, 'Well, thank God this isn't France. What he did to the Dowler lad was brutal.' There was another thermos in the hamper. She reached for it.

'Oh, I couldn't,' said Julia. 'I've drunk so much tea.'

'It's not tea.' Fiona uncorked the thermos and produced two glasses from the miraculous hamper. Poured. An astringent, oily, lemony smell.

'What is it?' Julia took the glass, which had been immediately chilled by its contents. She sniffed. 'Gin?'

'Cheers,' said Fiona.

A bit early for a drink, thought Julia, but she drank it anyway. Fiona had that effect on her. Even so, she wondered whether her friend might have a little problem.

The sea gargled stones in its mouth. The tide was beginning to turn and the shushing sound it made reminded Julia of what she had been trying to ignore for the past ten minutes. She squirmed. 'I'm never going to make it home.'

'Go behind the boat.'

'Fiona!'

'No one's looking.'

Julia laughed. 'What if they do?'

'They won't.'

Nelson said the white letters painted on the boat's side. She squatted and peed. The relief was enormous. Afterwards, she realized it was getting late, the shadows lengthening. Down by the Martello tower the film people were still doing, or not doing, what they had been doing all afternoon and Peter was still hanging about, watching them.

Fiona was sitting on the rug smoking. 'Better now?'

'Much.'

She held up the thermos. 'Have another.'

'I shouldn't. I really ought to get back. Let me see if I can winkle Peter away and then I'll help you pack up.'

Julia walked across the shingle in the direction of the sea and incoming tide, and the stones rolled around under her feet. Sun, air, gin, a little light-headed. For the moment: happy.

As she approached the tower she saw nothing glamorous at all about the proceedings. Close up they were a rackety-looking lot, dirty jerseys and so forth. One was consulting a clipboard; another was rolling up a tape measure; others were making adjustments to the camera, whose focus was unclear. Cabling snaked over the ground and a hum came from a black box she assumed must be a generator.

No one noticed her approach. 'What?' said Peter, swinging round, when she touched him on the arm.

'Don't say "what?", it isn't polite. Time to go home.'

As she might have expected, he dug in his heels. There followed a good deal of plea bargaining of the 'ten more minutes', 'five more minutes' variety, which was beginning to exasperate her, rub off her good mood, when she looked up and saw that the man who appeared to be in charge, the director she supposed, was staring at her. He was around her age, tall, thin, with a beaky nose and a lock of tow-coloured hair falling over his forehead.

She caught his eye. In that instant some odd connection was made, what she could only describe to herself as a meeting. It was shockingly familiar. New and jolting. Both at the same time.

'Your property?' He nodded at Peter. A mobile mouth, rather wide, rather full, rather sad, and a voice she could have sworn she knew, a voice that her body heard. It was as if he played a chord right through her.

'I'm sorry,' she said. 'I hope he hasn't been disturbing you.'

'Not at all.'

'You see?' said Peter. 'Just another few minutes. *Please.*'

Julia became aware of her breathing. She tore her gaze away. The man was still looking at her. Her skin told her that much. 'No, we need to go.'

'That's a pity,' said the man. He walked towards them and crouched down to speak to Peter. 'May I borrow your mother for a moment, if I promise to return her safely?'

It was almost comical how seriously Peter considered the question. After a time, he nodded. 'I expect so.'

'Good.' The man straightened up. That gaze again, that shared knowledge: what was it? 'I wonder if you would mind helping us out.'

'What do you mean?' She was trying and failing not to look at him. 'I'm afraid I won't be much use to you. I know nothing about filming.'

'All you have to do is stand over there.' He pointed. 'And look out to sea.'

'Over there' was directly in line with the camera. 'Oh, no,' said Julia. 'I couldn't possibly. I'm sorry.'

'It won't hurt.' The man put out his hand. 'Dougie Birdsall.'

She had no option but to take it. 'Julia Compton.' His hand was warm and dry, fingers tobacco-stained, nails bitten to the quick.

'And it won't take long,' he said. 'The light's perfect right now, but it's going.'

Julia felt stiff and starchy with self-consciousness. Yet something, perhaps the gin, was wickedly encouraging her to have a go, to step for one moment out of ordinariness. She glanced back to where Fiona was sitting by the boat and saw that she was reading. 'I thought you were making a film about fishing.'

'We are.'

'You want me to stand?'

'Yes. Simply stand and look out to sea.'

She caught his eye again. She couldn't help it. 'Should I be thinking about fish? While I stand?' For some reason, this struck her as funny.

This appeared to strike him as funny too. 'Think about whatever you like.'

It took more than a few minutes because they did it three times, the last time in close up. Turn over. Action. Cut. At the end he thanked her. That mouth again, that smile, that look.

'You've caught the sun,' said Fiona, marking her place in her book with a gull's feather.

Julia put her hands to her cheeks.

'They filmed her,' said Peter.

Fiona pulled down her sunglasses. 'Did they?' she said. 'I *am* jealous.'

'They filmed her,' said Peter.

'Who filmed whom?' Richard helped himself to carrots from the Crown Derby serving dish, a wedding present survivor. The light had shrunk, little by little, since they had sat down to eat. Julia, opposite, pushed food around on her plate.

'Madre. The film people filmed her,' Peter said. 'Down by the Martello tower.'

'Don't talk with your mouth full,' said Julia. She cut up the boiled beef into smaller and smaller pieces, wondering how she was going to eat any of it. She seemed to have lost her appetite. It would be the heat.

'Did they? How extraordinary.' Richard raised an eyebrow.

'I expect they might film me tomorrow,' said Peter.

There followed an interval of cutlery scraping on plates.

'Dad?' said Peter. 'Can we go for one more sail before I go back to school?'

'We'll see,' said Richard.

'Joe Seddon says that they'll stop pleasure boating when the war comes.'

'Joe Seddon is a mine of misinformation,' said Julia.

'Sadly not on this occasion,' Richard said.

Julia disliked the boat. She mistrusted open water.

Perhaps allowing herself to be filmed had been improper, she thought. Perhaps that accounted for how unsettled she felt. She set her napkin beside her plate and decided that tomorrow morning she would seek out the crew and tell them she'd changed her mind.

2

Whether the lighthouse was to be dimmed, or blacked out, or camouflaged was the talk of the public bar. 'Mark my words,' said Sam Binns, 'they dim it and there'll be consequences I wouldn't want to answer for. I wouldn't want to answer for the wrecks, for a start. And mark my words,' he said, 'there will be wrecks if that lighthouse is dimmed.'

Joe Seddon set down his pint. 'And then where's your herring? Speaking personal.'

The barmaid, by the pickled eggs, polished a glass. 'Oh, I see. So we're to carry on as per usual, are we? "Hello, Fritz!" You might as well say, *Coo-ee, we're over here!* We'll be bombed to smithereens.' Festooned under the tobacco ceiling were dusty glass floats, red, purple and green, drawn up in a shabby net under the matchboarding. Above the portrait of the King was a pair of Coronation paper flags, somewhat curled out of their original jauntiness. A few of the film people were drinking at a table by the door and from time to time the barmaid's glance rested on them: to no avail. She was regretting the money she'd spent on her hairdo. Not even her husband had noticed.

'What I want to know,' said Sam Binns, 'is how you'd go about camouflaging a great big thing like that. I mean, you can see it from Whitmarket. You can't tell me sandbags is going to do it.'

'They could paint it,' said Joe Seddon.

'I'd like to see that ladder,' said the barmaid.

One of the film people, coming up to the bar to order a round, broke a rule and stepped into the conversation; broke two rules, in fact, by revealing he'd been listening to it. This person, a plump, pimply lad hardly old enough to shave, explained that it was most likely that the lighthouse beam would be screened or narrowed in some way, perhaps with the use of dark cloth or hardboard, and that the timings of the beam would be coordinated centrally with shipping schedules. At the bar they listened in silence, not knowing that this information was a second-hand recounting of what the boy had been told earlier that day. When the pints had been pulled and carried off slopping to the table, they moved on to a subject that was more impenetrably local.

Eddie Grogan carried the pints across the pub with its sticky floor of dampened sawdust. Dougie was drawing, pencil describing great arcs across his sketchbook, a lock of hair flopping over his beaky nose. 'Here's the change, Mr Birdsall.' Eddie spilled the coppers on the table.

'Mmm,' said Dougie, without lifting his eyes from the page. 'Thanks for getting them in.'

The camera operator, Frank Moss, said, 'What's that you're having, Eddie? A ginger beer?'

It was obvious what Eddie was having. 'No, sir. Same as you.'

'Seventeen, aren't you, Eddie?'

'Eighteen in two months.'

'Well, if you don't tell, I won't.'

Eddie sat down. 'Went well today, didn't it? The filming?' Dougie glanced up and smiled. Talking about filming made Eddie feel like King Vidor, with his own canvas director's chair and cigar. He couldn't quite believe the luck that had fetched him up at the Unit: when he was eventually called up, as he was bound to be, at least he would have lived a little. 'Quiet, please'; 'turn over'; 'cut': these words he loved. They were a small crew – no sound recordists on this occasion – and he was the most junior member of it. But junior or not, one of the things you learned on the job was that you weren't necessarily the only one learning.

'Anyone know what the forecast is?' said Dougie.

'More of the same, by all accounts,' said Frank.

'That's a shame.' Dougie swivelled his sketchbook in front of Frank. 'This is the sort of thing we're missing.'

Eddie craned his neck. The drawing was of a harbour in storm conditions. You could taste the spray, hear the wind sheer in the rigging. Dougie'd pencilled an oblong over the top of it. Eddie had seen him frame his eyes with his fingers in the same sort of way.

'We could have filmed that in Grimsby,' said Frank. 'It was blowing a gale up there.'

'We couldn't have filmed that in Grimsby because it was blowing a gale,' said Dougie. Grimsby had been a bit of a disaster. There were lots of shots they'd missed at Grimsby. They'd got other shots instead.

'We can't be held responsible for the weather,' said Frank.

'Tell that to Macleod.' Dougie put on a Scottish accent: 'Ye'll just have to sit it out, laddie. A guid deal of filming is waiting.'

'Aye,' said Frank, 'it'll cloud over soon enough.'

They laughed.

Macleod was the head of the Unit. People called him McGod.

'How many cans have we left?' said Dougie.

'Four,' said Eddie promptly, feeling like the kid at school shooting up his hand with the right answer.

'Is that all?'

'We finished one filming the boat this morning and used up another two by the tower.'

'You got a little carried away there,' said Frank.

'The light was perfect.'

'The girl wasn't half bad either,' said Frank. 'Although unconvincing as a fishwife, I should have thought.'

'That's not why I shot her.'

'Oh, yes,' said Frank. 'I was forgetting your private collection.'

'Very amusing.' The truth was Dougie didn't know why he'd filmed her. But it was in the nature of his work to find images even if he was unsure how he would eventually use them. 'The camera loved her. You must have noticed. You were looking through it.'

'That's not all I noticed,' said Frank.

Eddie said, 'I liked the boat. *Nelson*. That was a nice touch.'

'Eddie,' said Frank with a wink, 'your mistake is to assume he knows what he's doing. There's such a thing as luck, after all.'

'Nothing to do with luck,' said Dougie. 'Everything to do with keeping your eyes open.'

'Coincidence, then.'

'I don't believe in it.'

'If you're going to bang on about surrealism again, I'm going for a piss.'

'Be my guest,' said Dougie.

'What's surrealism?' said Eddie.

'The chance meeting on a dissecting table of a sewing machine and an umbrella, someone once called it.'

'Oh,' said Eddie, none the wiser.

Frank got up from the table. 'Don't listen to him, Eddie. It's all a load of balls.'

The Unit operated out of premises in Soho Square. There was also a makeshift studio in Blackheath, formerly a school art room, and which, with its painted plywood sets, still resembled one. Together they comprised the home of British documentary film-making, a genre that some viewed as ground-breaking, others thought insignificant and a few considered dangerously left-wing.

Everything ran on a shoestring, nominally under the aegis of the Post Office, whose promotional wing they were, although you would not perhaps be aware of this were you to watch some of the films they produced. Macleod preserved a degree of latitude in that respect: as a form, the documentary – or 'interpretive realism', with the stress falling on the 'realism' – was in some significant part his creation.

Frank came back to the table and sat down with a sigh. 'Christ. Even the Gents smells of herring.'

'Eddie,' Dougie said, 'I'm afraid you're going to have to pop back to London first thing and collect some more stock for us. Will you do that?'

Eddie said that he could do that. 'How many cans?'

'Six ought to do it. No, make it ten.'

'Ten?' said Frank.

Dougie said, 'It would be a pity not to film the church, seeing as we're here.'

'That hulk of a place?'

'It has an angel roof, rather a fine one.'

Frank looked blank.

'Carved angels all along the nave. Fifteenth century.'

'Let me guess,' Frank said. 'Ships' figureheads? Is that the connection?' He was thinking of the worm-eaten specimens in the seamen's museum, which had been a devil of a place to light, and tatty with it. 'Otherwise, even I can't see how you intend to stitch footage of angels into a documentary part financed by the fishing industry and purporting to be about it.'

'You're beginning to sound like McGod.'

'McGod pays our wages.'

'For now,' said Dougie. 'I wouldn't like to bet on who'll be paying our wages this time next week.'

It was past nine and the news, and the pub was filling up, a few couples, a swaggering group of noisy lads and one or two solitary drinkers. The fishing contingent was well represented.

'Once more unto the breach, dear friends,' said Frank, lifting his glass.

'Or close the wall up with our English dead.'

Shakespeare, thought Eddie. Almost certainly Shakespeare.

He watched the two men. They were both wearing what he had come to regard as the Unit uniform: baggy flannels, none too clean, tweed jackets with sagging pockets, stained and holed pullovers. He would have liked to dress the same, but his mother wouldn't let him go out looking like that. Dougie, who could be debonair when he wanted to, had a paisley scarf knotted at his throat like a cravat.

'You've gone quiet,' said Frank, raising his voice over the blare of the bar.

'Mmm.' Dougie traced his finger through the wet rings on the table top.

'I shouldn't waste your time brooding over her. She's obviously married. More to the point, so are you.'

'Mind your own bloody business, Frank.' Dougie drained his pint. 'If you must know, I'm thinking that no one in this country has a clue what lies in store.'

'It's unlike you to make such sweeping statements.'

'I mean it. Unless you've experienced total war, you've no idea what it's like.' A small muscle tightened the corner of his mouth.

'On the contrary, I'd say that thanks to certain elements of the press the public imagination is rather overstimulated in that department. Why else are people killing their pets?'

Dougie lifted his eyes. 'Nothing prepares you for it.' He pushed back his chair.

'Where are you going?' said Frank.

'I'll see you later, back at the digs.'

After the noise and blaze of the pub, outside it was cool and still, the first tease of autumn in the air. Here and there in the lane leading down to the sea a few houses were observing an unofficial blackout in advance of what was daily expected to be enforced with warnings and fines; in most windows, however, a little light glimmered, and glimmered was the word, because electricity had reached by no means all the town's households.

A tang of brine and rotten bait, and a fisherman went past swinging an oil lantern. Further along the front the lighthouse swept its great beam over the sea. A couple came out of the pub into a triangle of light and stood embracing on the slicked cobbles.

Dougie Birdsall had given five months to Spain, a trifle set against the life his friend and colleague Ellis had given. He could no longer remember the name of the village where Ellis had been killed – if he'd ever known it, he'd blanked it out, he supposed. They had fetched up there after a week's march through the maquis in the freezing cold, scraps of burlap wrapped round their boots, hunger gnawing their stomachs, and afterwards he had never been able to find the place on a map, perhaps because he had never been entirely sure where they had set out from, or in which direction they had gone – by then the great cause had become a disorganized horror of betrayal and folly. He had forgotten nothing else about that day, however, and added to the burden of this knowledge was the certainty that others would soon share it.

The shingle sucked and rattled as the tide went out. In the wild, lonely sound he could hear the wide grey skies of these low-lying marshes and trees bent crooked by a wind that blew straight from the steppes across the North Sea. Never before had he been so aware of the country as an island, lighthouses strung along its coast shining their beams over the deep, black waters.

War: now there was a subject, he thought.

3

Late morning, Julia set off in search of the director. After her husband's raised eyebrow the previous evening, she thought it wise to be circumspect, which was why she took pains to keep her tone light and offhand when she enquired in the newsagent's after the whereabouts of the crew. This caution was also something of an acknowledgement that the prospect of seeing the man again was making her heart skip about in her chest like a faulty bit of clockwork and that she seemed to have got dressed with much more care than usual. All incredibly foolish, she told herself. And yet this – what was it? – *anticipation* refused to go away.

In her rather heightened state, colour and detail assailed her on all sides as she went along the street. She was not used to this specificity, the way cobbles gleamed individually, the flaking paintwork at the base of a lamp post, faded posters advertising the summer funfair and the annual ploughing competition, the thud of a cleaver and the heavy scent of blood that trailed across the butcher's threshold, little girls skipping arm in arm in their cardigans. It made her feel dizzy and untethered.

The film crew were smoking and drinking tea in the Rose Café near the lighthouse, where the newsagent had said they would be. All, that is, but one of them. Bracing herself for amused speculation, Julia went up to their table and asked where she might find Mr Birdsall.

'Dougie?' said the man who had been operating the camera the day before. 'He's gone off to sketch in the church. We're just sitting here twiddling our thumbs, waiting for him to tell us what to do next.'

The church. This seemed incongruous somehow.

'Well, to be honest,' said the man, 'we're waiting for more film stock to arrive.'

'I see,' said Julia. 'Thank you.'

'My pleasure. When you find him, say Eddie rang, and they can only spare us five cans.'

Afterwards she would wonder why he wasn't surprised she was searching for the director, why he hadn't asked what business she had with him. Then, remembering his knowing look and how it had raked her up and down, she realized he thought he didn't have to.

In contrast to its looming exterior, its buttresses, intricate finials and carved weathered stonework, St James's was a chalk-white, bare barn of a place inside. Centuries ago, Puritans had pillaged every church along this coast, looting what was valuable and portable and smashing the rest. Here they had removed all the pictorial glass, along with several crosses, banned representations of God the Father and other Popish idolatry, together with the brasses, which were worth something. Legend had it that they had also fired muskets at the roof in an attempt to dislodge the angels, which were otherwise too high to destroy. Some, however, were of the opinion that the small holes that peppered the figures were more likely the work of *Xestobium rufovillosum*, the deathwatch beetle.

Dougie sat sketching in the end pew, breathing in the ancient smell, part damp stone, part a chill ascetic holiness composed equally of dead flowers and unanswered prayers. Above him the angels flew along the tie-beam roof, sinewy, androgynous youths to whom flecks of gold and colour still clung. Their broad outstretched wings – tense, poised for the downbeat – were carved into ridges of overlapping feathers. Once they must have been vivid, even gaudy, bright with life. Even now it was possible to make out that the shields they carried had originally been painted bright red – English red – and quartered with white in a reversal of the flag of St George. Their faces, however, were what held his attention. These were not avengers or comforters. These were messengers interceding between one world and the next, and the news they brought was that life was endurance.

He was thinking that Frank's half-joking suggestion the previous evening had some merit. The angels would not make a bad pairing with the ships' figureheads: they had a similar folkloric quality.

Dougie sketched, looking up at the angels, down at the page. His pencil was quick, confident. It did what it was told, as well it might after all the years of practice he'd put in, everything he had drawn, from a pithead to a woman's bare limbs. There had been a time when he'd thought he'd be a painter. Then he'd married in the belief that love would water the blooms of art and instead marriage had parcelled up that dream and thrown it out of the window, just as it had put out the welcome mat for the grocer's and coal merchant's bills.

Before he'd left London, his wife Barbara had finally agreed to do what he had been urging her to do, which was to go to Canada and take their three little girls with her. *Once upon a time there were three little sisters, and their names were Elsie, Lacie and Tillie; and they lived at the bottom of a well.* His three little girls – Alice, Eleanor (Nell) and Katherine (Kitty) – shared a room in the cramped flat he rented near Primrose Hill, which was all he could afford on his wages. Canada would be good for them. Space, air, proper weather. Most importantly, safety. (After Spain, where he had seen bombs rain down on babies, Dougie did not believe that the government's plans for evacuation would be sufficient to protect children, his or anyone else's, from total war.) Barbara, who had cousins in Toronto and who had spent a year and a half there after leaving school, always spoke of the country as an Arcadia. She would enjoy it, he thought, once she weaned herself off their war of attrition, which was to say the slamming doors, endless anxieties about money and long sulking evenings that their marriage had become.

Which, after all, was his fault, as she constantly reminded him.

Barbara had never forgiven him for going to Spain, not even when the photographs he had taken there had led to his current employment, not the path he'd originally wanted to follow, but one that (just about) paid the grocer's and coal merchant's bills.

He turned a page in his sketchbook and the woman he'd filmed at the beach wandered through his mind, walked around and made herself at home, as she'd been doing approximately every three to four minutes since he'd woken up that morning. Rather than ignore her, as he had been trying without much success to do, this time he let her stay and took a good look at her.

Julia passed through the lychgate, went up the path and pushed open the west door. She had absolutely no idea what she was going to say. How she was going to say it. What she should do with her hands, which had suddenly become extraneous, unrelated parts of her dangling at the ends of her arms.

She came into the church and he was there in the back pew, head bent, drawing. The next moment he had risen to his feet and she found herself bathed in his gaze.

'Oh,' she said, as if she had come across him by accident, as if she were one of the flower ladies, come in to do the displays. 'Hello. We meet again.' She felt heat travel up her neck: how provincial, how married, she sounded. (Sounding provincial or married had never bothered her before.)

'We do.' The expression on his face said he'd been expecting her. Which couldn't be the case. Mockery was the more likely interpretation.

'Here.' He reached for his sketchbook. 'Tell me what you think.' They might have been resuming a conversation that had been interrupted.

At that, she was forced to come close to him, to walk across the stone floor, to enter his gravitational pull. To smell his smell of tobacco and shaving soap.

'I'd be glad of your opinion.'

Conscious that turning the pages gave her hands something to do, her eyes somewhere safe to look, it was a moment before she realized how good the sketches were. 'The angels,' she said, glancing up at the roof. 'You know, the way you've drawn them, they rather remind me of planes.' Then, because it seemed like she was criticizing his artistic ability, she backtracked a little. 'What I mean,' she said, 'was that I hadn't realized until now that it was possible to see them that way. Somehow menacing and protective at the same time.' She reconsidered, shook her head. 'No, that's not it either. It's more that they're indifferent.'

Dougie found himself astonished. Physical attraction was one thing; a meeting of minds another. (Dougie was always on the lookout for a meeting of minds.) 'How odd you should say that. It's exactly what I was thinking.'

She caught his eye and looked away. 'Apparently I'm to tell you that Eddie rang and said they could only spare five cans.'

As soon as she blurted this out, she realized she'd given the game away. 'The crew told me where you'd be.'

He smiled. 'I see.'

Now she really was fumbling for words. 'The thing is, I've had second thoughts. I mean to say, yesterday, when you filmed me –'

'You'd rather I didn't use it.'

'How did you know?'

'Your husband beat you to it.' He explained that early this morning when he had asked the vicar if they would be allowed to film inside the church, the vicar had referred him to Richard, who, as churchwarden, was responsible for its upkeep. 'He said I had permission to shoot the roof but not his wife.'

'Oh,' said Julia. Ordinarily she would have found her husband's care for her reputation rather touching. At this moment she felt embarrassed and, to tell the truth, a bit owned.

'I doubt that your husband has much of a legal leg to stand on,' said Dougie. 'And I wasn't going to take any notice of his objections in any case. However, if you feel the same way, of course I must respect your wishes. Which is a pity.'

Julia was no longer sure if she felt the same way. 'I just thought I might look rather foolish.'

'I shouldn't think there's the remotest possibility of that,' he said. 'Or of me filming you in such a way that you did.'

She was watching his mouth. He was watching hers.

'Are you free today?' he said.

'What do you mean?' Julia was unbalanced by a number of emotions, none of which she was prepared to put a name to.

'Have lunch with me.'

'Where?' she said, gazing wildly round the church. What she meant was *where* in a small town could a woman have lunch with a man who wasn't her husband?

He laughed. 'No, not here. Not unless you fancy wafers and communion wine. What's that inn on the high street called?'

'The Angel.'

'The Angel. One o'clock.'

Richard occasionally ate at the Angel. Not today. Today Richard had gone to Ipswich to meet the barrister who might represent Perry Clayton. Even so, she was bound to come across someone she knew, or who knew Richard or had professional dealings with him.

'No, I shouldn't.'

'You owe me that at least. If I'm going to have to lose the footage.'

On the other hand, why would she allow herself to be seen in such a public place if her intentions weren't entirely above board? No one would be that flagrant. In any case, she could hardly suggest that they go somewhere out of the way instead, some hidey-hole. That would be tantamount to suggesting, or acknowledging, something else. Which couldn't be further from her mind.

She nodded. 'All right, then. One o'clock.'

The Angel had no connection with the angel roof whatsoever; in fact, it pre-dated the church by several centuries and had once been the guest house of the local priory, with which it was reputedly connected by a secret underground passageway. Outside, its low, jettied front was punctuated by small diamond-paned casement windows. Inside, it was dark and cool and warren-like, with a number of dim snugs and lounges opening off an exceptionally uneven black-and-terracotta tiled hall. It smelled, and by no means faintly, of boiled vegetables, beer and roast meat.

This was madness, thought Julia, as she came through the door. The same thought had been going round and round her head for the past forty minutes, during which time she'd gone home, freshened her face and checked her appearance in three mirrors. Not once had she admitted the obvious. Which was that in the space of less than twenty-four hours she had lost all control of herself.

She was a little early. The dining room, which looked out over a very pretty, old-fashioned garden, was far from full, and she had the opportunity from the corner table she'd chosen, of the two the waitress had offered her, to establish that she recognized only three of those lunching that day, and that not one of them was more than a nodding acquaintance. Rather than easing her mind, however, this convinced her that the next people to come through the door were bound to be the Batesons, the Murrays, the Whitakers, or any of the other couples with whom she and Richard socialized, at the yacht club and elsewhere.

The next person who came through the door was Dougie. After that, the King and Queen might have popped in and she wouldn't have noticed.

He sat down and gave the menu a rapid, dismissive glance. 'Why don't they serve fish in towns where they catch it?'

She laughed. 'I've often wondered that.'

'I shall have the mutton,' he said, taking in the blackened beams, horse brasses and knowing quaintness. 'It seems appropriate somehow.'

She had the mutton, too. She didn't like mutton.

That lunchtime she discovered that Dougie could get quite drunk on words: she had not expected this in a film-maker, not that she'd ever met any film-makers. He didn't talk down to her, or past her, or at her; he seemed genuinely to relish conversation as a means of exploring ideas. She found this beguiling, infectious. Seventeenth-century poets, farm machinery, pigeon racing in working-class Yorkshire households, Shakespeare, the light in the south of France, the irrigation systems of the fenlands, the difference between gouache and oils (how they dried, how they were worked, what they cost), the latest in sound-recording technology. Even making a film about fishing took on a new light when he put it into the context of documenting the kind of working life that was generally overlooked or distorted.

Despite this outpouring, he was a good listener. There was always room for what she had to say, which was more and more as lunch went on.

'So you're a Londoner,' he said.

'Are you surprised?'

He hid his surprise. 'Why should I be?'

'Well, there's London and there's London,' she said. 'I grew up in the sort of area people call a village – at least the sort of people who have never lived in one. My father's still there.'

It was so easy to confide in him. She wasn't conscious of shaping the facts or misrepresenting them, yet his interest seemed to make her more interesting to herself. Her uneventful suburban childhood, her awkward schooldays, her abandoned studies – four and a half troubled terms at the Royal College of Music – became a new and more compelling narrative in the retelling.

'A Londoner *and* a pianist.'

'Yes.'

'Mmm,' he said. 'I'm no musician, but I've always thought film shares a similar form. They're both bound by time, for example.' He paused, fork in air. 'There's a piece I particularly like. *"La Cathédrale engloutie."* Do you know it?'

Julia nodded, delighted. 'I do, and I play it. Often.'

'I should like to hear you play it.' He smiled to himself at this fresh conjunction. 'What made you give up your studies?'

I met the handsomest man I had ever seen and fell in love with him

32

might have been an answer. It was the one she had given her mother at the time.

They had both left most of their food. She pushed her plate a little way away. 'I wasn't good enough.' The words came out of her mouth and surprised her.

'Oh? Was that what they told you?'

'They didn't need to.' Julia stared out over the garden with its brick pathways, dappled grass and orchard trees, fruit heavy and ready to fall. 'I never seriously thought I'd pass the entrance. You get accepted at a place like that and you think you've arrived. Or, at least I did. Then you realize it's only the beginning. A little later you discover that others are much better than you and, more to the point, that they have what it takes.'

'Talent?'

What a personal question. Yet Julia was shocked at how willing she was to answer it. 'Yes, in a sense. When you're very young, you don't appreciate that your own talent might have a ceiling until you bump your head on it.'

'You didn't match up to their standards.'

She smiled. 'It was worse than that. I didn't match up to my own.'

She had never spoken of this to anyone before, or even admitted it fully to herself. What was doubly surprising (and at the same time oddly natural) was that this man had brought it out of her.

'So you got married instead and made your mother happy.'

She shook her head. 'You don't know my mother. She's dead now, but she had a rather thwarted life, I think. Sometimes I wasn't sure whether I was doing it for myself or for her. She was hugely disappointed when I gave up.'

'I married young too,' he said. 'Although my motives were rather different from yours, I imagine.'

Married.

She didn't know why this news should have surprised her, or upset her to the degree it did. The waitress came to remove their plates and enquire about pudding, and Julia sat plucking away at her napkin.

'I suppose your wife doesn't understand you.'

'My wife would say she understands me too well.'

'Does she?'

'Well enough to know we're better apart. She's agreed to go to Canada with our little girls for the duration.'

Children, too.

'Perhaps we should ask for the bill,' she said.

'Must you go?'

'Yes. Yes, I must.'

The implication was clear. He wanted more. He expected more. She realized, with a swooping feeling in her stomach, that before she had learned he was married she had been on the point of giving it to him. And what did that say about her?

When they came out of the inn into the brilliant sunlight, she thanked him, said goodbye and almost ran in her haste to get away.

4

At the sink Harry ran the taps. Water gushed out. The old dog pricked up his ears, then settled back into his basket with a sigh. 'Has he been out?' said Julia, coming into the kitchen.

'Had a little snuffle round the garden.'

'Any joy?'

Harry shook her head. 'I've got the mop handy.' The spaniel had been having accidents lately.

Julia sat down at the scrubbed deal table where her son was eating his breakfast. For the past two days she had been conscious of a feeling of uncertainty or restlessness, as if someone had been sandpapering her nerve endings. It would be the coming war, she thought. She wouldn't give in to it. 'Lovely morning again,' she said.

'Windy,' said Harry, turning off the taps. 'Where's your games shirt, Sunny Jim?' she said to Peter. 'I can't find it. It needs to go in the wash before you go back to school.'

No answer.

'Peter?' said Julia.

'What?'

'Don't say "what?", darling. It isn't polite. Harry asked you a question.'

'Sorry, Madre,' said Peter. 'I didn't hear.'

'Where's your Aertex? Harry needs to wash it.'

'It's in my trunk.'

'No, it's not,' said Harry. 'And it's not under your bed either.'

'Perhaps it's in my tuck box.'

'What's your Aertex doing in your tuck box?' Julia glanced up, caught Harry's eye and shrugged.

Peter didn't know what his Aertex was doing in his tuck box. He didn't know whether his Aertex *was* in his tuck box. Like many schoolboys, those possessions that weren't actually in his pockets at any given moment tended to come and go of their own accord. 'May I get down?'

'Finish your toast first,' said Julia. 'Crusts as well.'

Peter chewed his crusts. 'Are you going to Bury today?'

'Don't talk with your mouth full. You know that I am.' She was going to Bury to equip him for the new term.

'You can always buy me another one there.'

'That's not the point,' said Julia. 'You should look after your belongings.'

Harry plonked down the teapot. 'Chance would be a fine thing.'

Julia consulted her list. Blazer, socks, two school shirts. Aertex?

'Finished,' said Peter, indicating his plate.

'All right,' said Julia.

He headed for the back door.

'Where are you off to?'

He scuffed his toe on the floor, then looked up. 'Nowhere in particular.'

'Don't slam the door,' said Harry to the slamming door.

Julia was under no illusion where Peter was going. Off to the harbour to watch what he could of the filming.

She knew, because Dougie had mentioned it at lunch, that they were filming this morning beyond the mole. He'd offered Sam Binns three pounds to take them out in *Mon Amy* and she'd told him with a laugh that, firstly, he'd offered too much and, secondly, he'd offered it to the worst skipper in town. To which he'd replied it was a pity she couldn't take over the budgeting because he was useless at it and always overspent. With that memory came an involuntary image of his hands.

In normal times, Bury St Edmunds, with its cathedral, guildhall and Abbey Gardens, and its two rivers, the Lark and the Linnet, was a typical East Anglian market town, part medieval, part Georgian, the fringes Victorian and none of it lively. Lately that had changed. War was here, or close by, in a way it wasn't at home. Many windows were criss-crossed with tape. Outside the Salvation Army headquarters a terrier lifted his leg on a pile of sandbags.

When Julia made her way from the bus to Buttermarket the narrow streets were clogged with raw recruits from the training camp outside of town, along with one or two flight officers from the airbase at Mildenhall. One lad, moving off the pavement to allow her to pass, was wearing a uniform so large it seemed to move independently of him. They could have weighed him for it, her father would have said.

Whittle and Son, the outfitter for Peter's school, was busy with mothers, all of a certain class, all wearing a certain sort of hat, the same sort of calculation in their minds: leave it as late as possible after the summer growth spurt. You couldn't call the atmosphere festive, yet it was in its way seasonal. Tickets were issued in strict rotation. Clearly there was a system, which wasn't to say your needs would be served, merely that every appearance would be given that they might be.

'St Barnabas?' said an assistant.

'Crossfields,' said Julia, handing over her list.

The assistant – a man in his early fifties with lines of grey hair combed over his scalp – ran his finger down it.

'Two sizes up, I thought, for the blazer.'

'Two sizes, madam?'

'He's grown.'

The assistant inclined his head. 'Might I suggest three?'

'Three?' said Julia, thinking of the recruit she'd passed in the street. Peter would never forgive her if she bought him a blazer to drown in. 'He doesn't grow that fast.'

The assistant said, 'In view of the present emergency, we are recommending parents take a longer view.'

'Are you,' said Julia.

'We anticipate that the demand for cloth by the services,' said the assistant, 'will perforce cause a shortage for schools.'

'Oh.'

'I am also afraid to inform you,' said the assistant, 'that the Plantagenet games bags are currently out of stock. Shall we send one on to Master Compton care of the school when they come in?'

'Yes,' said Julia. 'That will be fine.' Throughout this entire exchange she realized, with a jolt, she had been simultaneously thinking of Dougie, as if he had set up residence in a parallel groove in her mind.

Abbey Gardens was crowded. She came through the gate clutching the parcel of Peter's uniform and saw the fine weather had filled the benches and green spaces: mothers, babies, shop girls on their lunchbreak, old men, a smattering of khaki, small boys peering into freshly dug trenches.

When it was warm, you never remembered what it was like to be cold. You remembered shivering, putting more coal on the fire, getting out of bed in the morning and finding the floor icy under your feet. But these were descriptions of cold, not the reality of it. Similarly, she imagined, they would look back on these last days of peace and be unable to recall what they felt like.

It was two hours until the next bus back. The sun was shining. She had her book, and a ham roll she'd bought in the bakery, the necessary ingredients for killing time, yet she found herself too restless to sit and carried on walking down the avenue of limes.

The bells of the Norman tower began to ring and the air filled with tumultuous changes, structures of sound. At intervals on the smooth turf stood the ruins of the old abbey, lone piers of mortared stone shaped by time into giant human forms, the blurred suggestion of heads on top of bulbous weathered trunks. A man raised his hat to her. A child cycled past.

By and by, she came to the river. The Lark, a tributary of the Great Ouse, was sluggish and shrunk by the summer, overhung by drooping willows and red-stemmed dogwood. Small insects hovered.

On the bank was a couple, kissing, oblivious of her approach. Both were young, barely twenty, and unremarkable enough. The girl had rather thick ankles; the boy had brilliantined hair and rosy ears that stuck out. Yet the urgent sweetness with which they clung to each other pierced her. She stopped and stood watching them, unable to tear her eyes away.

It could only have been seconds before they sensed her presence, broke off their embrace and turned their flushed heavy-lidded faces in her direction. No one spoke. Then abruptly she went back the way she had come, past the ruins, up the avenue of limes, past the chatting mothers, the babies, the small boys, the old men soaking up the sun, the shop girls folding their sandwich wrappings. She had never understood temptation before – how it carried on mocking you after you thought you'd sent it packing, how it left behind loss.

You little fool, she told herself. You have a husband and a son. You have a home. You aren't lovesick and twenty. She came out of the park.

Harry was making toad in the hole for supper and Julia wondered whether she had managed to buy any flour – they were running low and, like sugar, it was one of the things that was flying off the shelves as war approached. Perhaps she should try to track some down herself, just in case.

And that was when she saw him, standing on the other side of Abbeygate Street by the insurance building.

Him.

The coincidence seemed extravagant, fictitious, laughable.

She stepped off the pavement. A squeal of tyres, a blaring horn and the parcel of Peter's uniform flew out of her hands. The car, which had missed her by inches, screeched to a halt a little way down.

'Are you blind?' said the driver, leaning out of the window. His hat fell off. He got out of the car to fetch it and shook it at her. 'Next time, look where you're bloomin' well going.'

Julia put her hand on her heart, which was racing. 'Sorry, my fault.'

The car drove off. Rooted to the spot – she had no choice, as her legs had stopped taking instructions – she watched him head towards her. Midway across the road, he retrieved her parcel.

'Are you always so careless of your personal safety?' said Dougie.

She stared at him. 'What are you doing in Bury?'

'Right now, I'm buying you a drink and making sure you drink it. You know,' he said, 'compared to London, this town has no traffic to speak of. I shouldn't think a car comes past here more than once an hour. It takes some talent to get yourself under it.'

'I didn't get myself under it.'

'Fortunately.'

They began walking back towards Buttermarket. He had a grip of her elbow. But this didn't exactly steady her up. She stole a glance at his face, then looked away. What was it about the arrangement of these particular features that had such an effect on her? Why did his mouth, his voice, drive every thought from her head? He wasn't handsome, like her husband, yet he made her husband's handsomeness seem pointless.

'I thought you were filming,' she managed to say.

'Too windy.'

'It's not that windy, surely?'

'It is when you've got a camera that weighs two hundred pounds in a boat with a shallow draught and an operator who's capable of being seasick on a duck pond.' They passed the outfitters. 'You were right about the skipper, by the way. We didn't even leave the harbour. No point wasting stock. We've little enough of it.'

'Wasn't there anything else you could film?'

'You sound like my crew.'

'Sorry.'

'To tell the truth, a lot of filming is waiting.' He glanced at her. 'You're shaking.'

'Sorry.'

'Try not to apologize quite so much.'

She allowed herself to be steered into a pub, sat at a table and bought a brandy. He watched over her as she sipped it.

'Better?'

'Yes, thank you.'

The pub, whatever it was called – the George, the Prince Arthur, the Duke of York – something royal in any case, was one of those frowsty places with brown ceilings, brown mirrors and dull brass. She was the only woman drinking in it.

'Last orders,' said the barmaid. 'Last orders, ladies and gentlemen, please.'

'What *are* you doing here?'

He set down his pint. 'Looking for you, among other things.'

Looking for her. Could that be true? It seemed less believable than coincidence. 'How did you know where I was?'

'Your son told me.'

'You asked him?'

'He volunteered the information. You've had to buy him a new Aertex, I gather.'

'Time, please,' said the barmaid, ringing a bell.

'I don't understand,' said Julia. 'You can't have thought you would just fetch up here and find me.'

'Dearest,' he said, 'I did. Admittedly, I nearly killed you in the process.'

'*Time, please*,' said the barmaid.

'What now?' said Julia, 'dearest' pounding in her ears.

'Now I'm going to drive you home.'

It wasn't his car, he was at pains to explain; it was on loan from the Unit. Outside: battered. Inside: rather a tip. Decayed apple core in the footwell. Papers, maps, books on the seats.

'Oh,' he said. 'Throw the jacket in the back.'

Dougie drove erratically, speeding up and slowing down when you least expected it. He shot blind corners and lingered by clear

41

level crossings; he overtook when he shouldn't have done yet daw-
dled in the wake of a cart so as not to spook the horse that was
pulling it. Soon enough they neared the coast, evident in the bright
reflected uplight over the high hedgerows, the sense of an imminent
expanse just out of sight. When they turned on to the road that ran
straight through the marshes down to the town and the silvery blue
sea lay in view, he pulled the car over on to the verge and stopped.

He had barely spoken since they left the pub. Now he turned to
her. 'What happens next is up to you.'

'What do you mean?'

'I understand why you ran off the other day.'

She nodded.

'And I won't press you. But you must know one thing.'

She stared ahead.

'I should very much like to take you to bed.'

If he had told her he loved her, couldn't live without her, said
what they said in films, in books, she would have got out of the car
and marched home across the marshes. The truth, spoken plainly,
was what stunned her.

The windscreen was speckled, smeared, with dead insects. She
looked through it and at it, shifting her focus from the far to the near.
Somehow from the first moment she had seen him she had known
it would come to this. She had known it as she knew her own name.
'Where are you lodging?'

The town didn't boast many guest houses; it had few visitors. There
was a down-at-heel hotel, the White Sands (doubly a misnomer,
for there were no sands, white or otherwise) and rooms to let here
and there, chiefly above the pubs. Most of the crew were accommodated in these, which was handy enough for what they liked
doing best after work. Dougie shared digs with the camera operator in an old fisherman's cottage on the front near the lighthouse.

They were renting it from the postmistress, he said, as they
pulled up in the cobbled lane and got out of the car.

'Yes,' she said, 'walkers and birdwatchers stay here sometimes. But mostly it's empty.'

'Frank's a birdwatcher, funnily enough. He's spending the afternoon down at the estuary doing just that.' He opened the door for her and they went into the hall. Ahead were uncarpeted stairs.

Afterwards, she remembered the aching distance between them, how charged and alive it was, how much she wanted the feeling to last for ever and how much she didn't. But who made the first move she could not say. They were apart one moment, the next they were together, dissolving whatever separated one person from another.

He took her face in his hands, kissed her hair, her ears, her neck. Then he found her mouth. The world fell away.

What sort of kissing fed hunger with hunger? There was no end to it. She drank in the way he tasted, drank in his smell. Her hands drew him to her, the nape of his neck, the small of his back.

'Darling.' He pulled back to look at her. 'Darling.' The expression on his face was naked and tender as he led her upstairs.

A small featureless room, bright afternoon sunlight, dusty floorboards, clothing, papers, books strewn about. They came through the door, and there was a shocked, plummeting moment when she realized what she was doing, then they were clutching at each other, unbuckling, unbuttoning, and she knew she had been waiting for this her whole life.

When they fell on the narrow bed his weight on her was a homecoming. The contours of his body met hers. His skin met her skin.

'Open your eyes,' he said.

She opened her eyes.

'That's better. Now I can see you properly.'

Then he entered her and she gasped at the wet welcome she had made for him.

★

43

A little later they were lying entangled in the bedclothes. He traced her profile, down the bridge of her nose, across her lips to her throat. 'So beautiful.'

She shook her head. 'No.'

'A Modigliani, that's what you are.'

Modigliani? But then he was kissing her again, running his hands over her body, his wonderful warm hands, and she lost all sense of where he started and stopped and where she did.

When Frank returned to the cottage a little after six, Dougie was sitting smoking in the tiny front room. Like the rest of the cottage, it was furnished, sparsely, with oddments. Some of the furniture was too big, some of it was too small; none of it would have been easy to shift at auction.

'Stone curlews, a pair of marsh harriers and a bittern,' said Frank. 'Not bad.' He slipped the strap of his field glasses over his head and set them down on a table with a bad leg. 'Might we have a little illumination, do you think? Or is that not included in what we're paying for this tip?'

Dougie chucked a box of matches at him. 'Oh for London,' said Frank, lighting the oil lamp perched on the narrow mantelpiece. 'Oh for the Tottenham Court Road.' He replaced the smoky glass sleeve over the flaring lit wick. 'And how was your afternoon? Satisfactory?'

'I went to Bury.'

'Did you.'

'And then I came back.'

Frank sat himself opposite in a frayed basket chair. He was a large man, and it was a tight fit. 'Tiring, was it?'

'What do you mean?'

'You look completely fagged out.'

'Thanks,' said Dougie. 'Any news?'

'We're not at war yet. Eddie almost exposed a can of footage. And the trawlerman you were talking to earlier said he'd take us out on Sunday, but he wants the same money as you promised the

44

other bugger, the one with the useless boat. Plus a little bit more, seeing as it's the Lord's Day.' A creak of wicker. 'You're not listening.'

'Of course I am.'

'Had any supper?'

'Not hungry.'

'Pub?'

'You go. I'll be along later.'

A brief flash as the lighthouse beam swept over the cottage and glared right into the corners of the room and under the furniture. After dusk, you could time yourself by it.

'Oh, I get it,' said Frank, tilting his big head on one side like a coquette. 'Now it comes to me. It's not tiredness, is it? It's freshly fucked.' *Post coitum omnia tristia sunt*, he thought.

Dougie put out his cigarette in a scallop shell overflowing with stubs.

'You had her, didn't you? The fishwife *manqué*. Quick work, I have to hand it to you.'

'What a way you have with words.'

'I'd say that was more your department.' Frank got up from the chair, and for a moment it was touch and go whether the chair would get up with him. 'Was it worth it?'

'Stick to your birdwatching, Frank.'

'Oh, I shall. Much less bother.'

5

Julia carried a tray into the garden. Saturday afternoon and, in the absence of Pye, their unreliable gardener, Richard had cut the grass and sat on a white-painted cast-iron seat mopping his forehead.

'What a good job you've done,' she said.

'Not bad, is it?' He brushed clippings from his gardening trousers.

She set down the tray on the white-painted cast-iron table and poured from the jug. Gulls wheeled overhead.

On the lawn, Peter was practising his cricket strokes, whacking the ball into the shrubbery and keeping up a running commentary. 'Oh, well played, Bradman,' he said. 'Well played.' In this he was aided by pale Simon Beeston, a boy who lived two doors down, who was bowling, and badly. Before Peter had gone away to school, they had been friends. She was unsure of the exact status now.

'Boys,' she said, 'there's lemonade here, if you'd care for some.'

Julia was at sea. Everything was the same and everything was different. Within the shell of ordinary life, structured and orderly – her husband in his gardening trousers, the fresh smell of cut grass, her son pretending to be a famous Australian batsman – was a strange new landscape where all the signposts were missing.

Her skin was alive; her blood sang. The world was so highly coloured it hurt to look at it. But the physical manifestations were nothing compared to the swell of emotions that threatened to pluck her up and dash her to pieces. There wasn't a single waking moment when she didn't long for Dougie – his voice, his touch, his mouth on hers – with an intensity that might equally be pleasure or pain. Mixed with that desire, bound up with it, was an appalling guilt at what she had done, and the gnawing fear of discovery.

'Julia, are you listening?' said her husband.

She blushed. 'Sorry. I was miles away. What were you saying?'

'The evacuees,' he said. 'It doesn't reflect well on us. We should have taken one. Two, even. We've plenty of room.'

The evacuees. She'd seen them earlier on the high street with their host families, the brown luggage labels that said who they were tied to their coat buttons, an air of bargain basement about them.

'I wasn't in, Richard.' She handed him a glass of lemonade. 'You can't expect Harry to give such an undertaking on our behalf.'

Thwack. 'And Bradman scores his century.'

'At any rate,' she said, 'I gather they're all housed now.'

'That's not the point.'

Julia smiled to herself: the point would be principle. 'You mightn't have found it agreeable on a daily basis. They've come from the East End. Quite rough and ready, by all accounts.'

Richard took a sip of his lemonade, made a face. 'Did Harry sugar this?'

Briefly she laid a hand on his shoulder. The impulse behind this was a great surge of pity. A curious thought occurred to her, which was that she would have liked to ask his advice on how to cope with her own betrayal of him.

And it wasn't once now, but twice; and it would be three times if today went as planned. Yesterday when the billeting officer had called round she'd been with Dougie.

He had been sitting by the window, sketching, talking. She had been curled up half dressed at the end of the dumpy little sofa, feeling every minute of the past hour in the heat of her skin and the looseness of her limbs.

Smoke curled upwards from his cigarette. 'Don't move.'

'Why?'

'I'm trying to draw you.'

'I thought you were drawing the view.'

'I am.'

His attention exalted her.

Dougie said, 'You moved.'

'Sorry.'

'Stop apologizing, Sinclair.'

Sinclair was her maiden name, one of the many details of personal history they'd so far exchanged. A little unusual for an endearment, perhaps, but she couldn't imagine one that would have had a greater effect on her. 'May I see it?'

His answer was to lean across and kiss her. 'When I finish.'

Finish? she thought. She didn't want this ever to end.

The week before her wedding, her mother had given her an awkward little talk up in her bedroom about what she called the 'trying side of marriage'. Accepting that men had needs – omitting to say what those needs might be – was a small price to pay for marital harmony and the eventual blessing of children. One just had to get used to it.

The trying side of marriage had not proved trying at all. Once the honeymoon flush had died down and the shyness sorted itself out, she had found it rather cosy, like having a cup of tea when you really wanted one. But this wasn't tea, it was wine. It didn't quench thirst, it created one.

Julia collected the glasses, put them on the tray and checked her watch. Almost three, which was when she had arranged to meet him. You could stop this madness, she thought. You could stop it right here, right now.

'Peter,' said Richard. 'Let Simon have a go batting. It's only fair.'

The boys changed sides and effortlessly Peter became a famous English fast bowler. 'And Larwood takes another wicket.'

Richard stood and surveyed the garden. 'That pampas grass is dreadfully untidy. I think we should dig it up and get rid of it.'

'I'm not attached to it.' She picked up the tray. 'Popping out to the shops for a bit.'

'Right you are.' He smiled. 'By the way, that colour suits you.'

Indoors, Harry was turning out the scullery, humming and clattering. The dog was in his basket and the cat was curled up illegally on a pile of clean laundry. On the table was a letter from her father, which had arrived in the second post.

The letter ran to several pages of Basildon Bond and included an appended diagram on graph paper of the Anderson shelter he was constructing, with measurements. Her father, a retired accountant, was a reliable correspondent of minutiae.

Julia set the letter aside to read later, brushed off the uneasy feelings it aroused in her: the nagging suspicion that she had failed her father too. Then she reached for her shopping basket, a fluttering bird caged in her chest, its wingbeats, tiny heartbeats, almost unbearable. Ten minutes and she would be with him.

At that instant screams came from outside, followed by the sound of her husband shouting for her.

She dropped the basket and rushed to the back door just as Harry came haring out of the scullery. In the garden, Richard was bending over their son, who was stretched out on the ground. It was Simon, unscathed, who was doing the screaming.

All mothers know that bringing a life into this world gives a hostage to fortune, just as all mothers learn that a working knowledge of the medical dictionary is not enough to avert disaster, for trouble, when it comes, will always choose the moment when you are looking the other way and will take the form you least expect. It will also, thought Julia, hurrying to her son's side, choose the worst possible time.

'What happened?'

'I'm not precisely sure. I was putting the mower away,' said Richard. 'Simon, will you *please* get a grip.'

'I didn't mean to,' said Simon, the screams subsiding to sobs. 'I didn't mean to.'

Harry said, 'He's out cold.'

Julia knelt down on the grass. Her pulse drummed in her ears. How small he looked, how pale! 'Where's all the blood coming from?'

'Try to keep calm,' said Richard. 'Head wounds always look

worse than they are. Harry, fetch the first-aid box. We'll have to take him to the cottage hospital. He doesn't seem to want to come round.'

The cottage hospital, on the outskirts of town, was an Edwardian brick building that resembled a slightly inflated pair of semi-detached houses. They parked in front. Richard gathered up Peter from the back seat, where Julia had been holding his limp body, and ran with him indoors. They were all splattered with blood.

It seemed to take hours. In the green-tiled waiting room, the clock ticked away. Richard stood by the window, from where he issued reassurance, both in words and in the silence of his back. Julia sat twisting her cold hands.

This was her punishment, she knew. Don't let my child die, she said in her head. I'll do anything, but don't let my child die. Don't let him be maimed or broken.

When the door of the waiting room opened, she jumped out of her seat. 'Mr Compton?' said the doctor. 'Mrs Compton?'

Peter had come to half an hour ago, he said, and was making sense. A trifle dazed, as one might expect, but his vision was not blurred, which was a good sign. The gash had needed four stitches and would probably leave a small scar. 'A little lower and he would have lost the eye. A little more power behind the bat and we'd be looking at something rather more serious than concussion. Even so, I'd like to keep him in tonight as a precaution. Always better to err on the safe side.'

'Thank God,' said Julia. 'May we see him?'

'Peter?' she said, coming into the consulting room with its surgical smell of rubbing alcohol and disinfectant. Relief washed over her.

He opened his good eye. The other, beneath a bandage that swaddled half his forehead, was swollen shut. 'Mummy.'

'Mummy' turned her stomach to water. She sat down on the edge of the examining couch. 'How are you feeling, my love?'

Peter was white as a sheet. 'I've got a beastly headache.'

'I expect you have. Nasty bump.'

He struggled to raise himself up on the pillow. 'May I have a drink?'

She turned to the doctor and he nodded. 'Here you are,' she said, raising a beaker to his lips. Even these were greyish.

The back of his hand flitted up to his dressing and a little water dribbled down over his chin. 'Am I going to be very disfigured?'

'Not at all,' she said, her mouth twitching at the corners, her heart leaping up. 'There may be a little scar.'

'Simon's a rotten cricketer,' said Peter. 'He wouldn't make the second eleven at my school. Even if we had a tenth eleven he wouldn't make it.'

'I expect he wouldn't,' said Julia. 'What happened?'

'I was showing him how to bat. He kept missing the ball.'

'But not your poor head.'

'You must have been standing right behind him,' said Richard, from the other side of the examining couch. 'That wasn't particularly sensible, old boy.'

Peter said, 'I think I'm going to be sick.'

Twenty, thirty, forty minutes, and she still hadn't appeared. Dougie tried to apply himself to the chits from the shoot. McGod always wanted to see the figures before the footage. As usual, they refused to add up. He felt around in his pocket and pulled out a note and a handful of coins. Not enough to make up the difference.

In the primitive kitchen, he took one of the bottles of ale Frank was chilling in the sink. The label, slimy to the touch, slid off under his fingers into the cold water. The bottle-opener wasn't in the drawer or anywhere in its immediate vicinity.

Fifty minutes. He was unsuccessfully trying to lever off the bottle top with a combination of brute force and a blunt knife when he thought he heard a knock on the door. No one was there.

An hour. What had happened to her? Had she been found out? Had she changed her mind?

Dougie went from room to room. The cottage was small; it

didn't take long. He thought about going for a walk on the beach, then dismissed the idea – or deferred it for when he might need its bracing consolations. Something about Julia, something he couldn't put his finger on, had got to him. What's more, he was taking no steps to defend himself against it; on the contrary, to all intents and purposes he was welcoming it with open arms.

As he welcomed her, when she eventually arrived around half past four. 'Ah,' he said, after she told him what had happened, 'the old cricketing accident excuse again. How is he?'

On her way over to the cottage, Julia had pictured a cooler reception, considering how late she was. She had half expected not to find him there at all. Either possibility would have made what she meant to do easier. Now, his evident relief at seeing her, his arousing smell of tobacco and shaving soap, his nearness, was an electric-bar fire on her skin.

'He's a little shaky.' She might have been talking about herself. 'I came –'

'Wrong tense.' He touched her face. 'But we'll soon see to that.'

'No,' she said, drawing away. 'I came to tell you –'

They hadn't got much further than the hallway.

A rap on the door. 'Mr Birdsall?' Another rap. 'Mr Birdsall?'

'Oh God,' said Julia. 'It's Mrs Coveney.'

'Go upstairs,' Dougie said. 'I'll get rid of her.'

The postmistress was perched on the doorstep like a little tame robin, bright of eye yet ready to fly off, or to peck. 'Mr Birdsall, I do hope I'm not disturbing you.' She peered into the hall. 'I heard voices. I thought you might have a visitor.'

'I was reading a script.'

'A woman's voice,' said Mrs Coveney.

'I play all the parts,' said Dougie. 'What can I do for you?'

She tilted her head. 'I was wondering if you will be wanting to stay another week? If so, terms would be favourable.'

'Thank you, but no. We're leaving tomorrow,' said Dougie. 'Now, if you don't mind, I'm rather busy.'

But Mrs Coveney was not the sort to pass up the opportunity to snoop on what she regarded as interestingly irregular lives. It took a good few minutes before she could be persuaded to go, which was not before various excuses had been advanced in an attempt to gain access, each more obvious than the last, ranging from a pressing need to inspect the paraffin heaters 'should the night turn chill' to a sudden anxiety about towels.

'You can come down now,' said Dougie, calling up the stairs. 'The coast is clear of enemy shipping.' He went into the front room. 'That was tiresome,' he said when Julia came through the door. 'It's obviously not our day today.'

'No.'

'What's the matter?' He studied her face. 'You look like the world's ended. She didn't see anything.'

'You're leaving tomorrow.'

'So that's what it is. I thought you were going to say you wanted nothing more to do with me.'

That had been her intention, which she now realized she could have accomplished simply by staying away. 'Is it true?' she said.

'Yes,' said Dougie. 'Macleod wired this morning. He wants us back in London. Or rather he wants the camera back.'

She sank down at one end of the sofa and stared round at the tawdry seashell pictures and the model boat – very handmade – on the windowsill. No doubt intended to impart cheer, a holiday mood, their effect was the opposite. 'Why didn't you tell me?'

'I was going to. But, as you may have noticed, we were interrupted.'

It occurred to her that after all she didn't have to say anything. She didn't have to put an end to it: it had put an end to itself. She began to feel everything was hopeless. 'I suppose I'm just a conquest to you.'

'You're showing a surprisingly damp side of yourself, Sinclair,' said Dougie. He sat down beside her, fished about in his pocket and passed her a handkerchief.

'Don't you possess anything that's clean?' she said, blowing her

53

nose on it. 'I'll never see you again.' Whether this was a statement of fact or intention, she wasn't sure.

Dougie said, 'Remind me one day to teach you the rudiments of logic. And while I'm at it, I'll furnish you with a railway timetable.' He opened his sketchbook, wrote a few lines and tore out the page. 'Here's where to reach me.'

She stared at the paper. The address was in Soho Square.

'Your turn.' He handed her the pencil.

'Whatever for?'

'Don't be fatalistic.' He took her face in his hands. 'Did you think it would stop here?'

She laid her head on his shoulder. 'I don't know what I think any more.'

'Then don't think. It's a great mistake to do too much of it.' He murmured into her hair. 'We're filming tomorrow morning. We won't leave until later. See if you can get away after lunch, if only for a short time. Will you try?'

She found herself nodding.

'In a few weeks Barbara and the children go to Canada, which will make things easier. That's not long to wait.'

Barbara, thought Julia. The wife had a name.

Sunday morning and, down on the mole, half the population of the town was watching a film camera and associated cabling and equipment being loaded on to the back of the *Bawdsey Belle*, the men cooperative and arguing by turns about the right way of doing things, the women taking an unaccustomed back seat, patting their hair, striking decorative poses and giving their best profile. Children ran about. Their thin high shouts echoed across the harbour water.

Dougie clambered on board. 'How are your sea legs this morning?' he said to Frank.

'I didn't have breakfast.'

'Sensible precaution.'

'I do try to keep everyone's best interests in mind.'

You wouldn't think it would be hard to shoot the sea at sea. They filmed a few reverse angles from ship to shore: that was straightforward. But whenever they tried to get a clear shot of an open expanse of water, which Dougie was determined to have, something bobbed into view. Once it was a pleasure boater, who waved his pipe cheerily from the tiller of his dinghy, another time a dark grey vessel, a minesweeper, loomed up on the horizon, and then gulls, resting on the water, flapped up directly over their heads, crying and screeching.

The gulls did it. Dougie lost his temper all over the boat. Then, soon after, he got the footage he wanted and everyone was happy. 'Cut,' he said as Frank rushed to the side and retched.

'What's the matter with your man?' asked Joe Seddon, the skipper.

'He gets a bit queasy,' said Dougie.

'No swell to speak of.'

'We can head back now.'

'I could kiss you for that,' said Frank, returning and wiping his mouth.

'Do and I'll make sure we stay out all day,' said Dougie.

When they puttered past the mole around eleven, the harbour was deserted. 'Where's the welcoming party?' asked Frank. Not a soul was about.

They were tying up and starting to unload the equipment when the siren sounded, low at first, then rising to a mournful wail. It was as if all the streets and houses in the town were voicing their distress.

'We seem to be at war,' said Dougie.

'You missed the broadcast,' Harry said.

Julia came into the hall, unpinned her hat and stripped off her gloves. 'No, they had a wireless at the hospital.' Behind her, Richard brought in Peter as if he were a consignment of china.

Peter said, 'Hitler is a rotter.'

'Just look at the state of you,' said Harry. 'You'd think you'd seen action already.'

This pleased him, Julia saw. However, he took no persuading to go upstairs to bed, where he lay propped on pillows, the bandage askew over his eye. 'Will I be better by Tuesday?' Tuesday was when he was due back at school, a date he anticipated as much as she dreaded.

She tucked him up. 'We'll have to see what the doctor says. You gave us all quite a fright.' A stab of guilt there, a twist of the knife. She had no sooner bargained for his life than she had let down her side of it.

'I was brave, though, wasn't I?'

'Very,' she said.

'You know, Matron can always change the dressing.' He touched the dressing. 'She's rather an expert at those sort of things.'

Clearly he was desperate to show off the bandage.

'Let's not worry about that right now. Would you like me to read to you?'

'No,' he said faintly. 'Hospital was quite exhausting.'

Julia doubted that Peter would be going back to school before the stitches were out. That gave her at least another week with him. But as she went down the stairs her mind was focused on another departure.

'I would feel happier,' said Richard later that evening when the news was over, 'if Chamberlain weren't leading us into this. If we must be in it, we're going to need someone who at least has an appetite for it.'

They were having a drink in the drawing room after dinner. The blackout was up, the walls had closed in. Everything was deadened. 'Have you made this stronger than usual?' said Julia.

'No, I always make them the same.'

That afternoon between bouts of nursing she had managed to slip out for long enough to meet Dougie. Outside the cottage, Frank had been packing the car.

'Chin up, darling,' said Dougie. 'Write to me. I'll write to you.'

She nodded, and saw that he was already somewhere else. It

struck her then that she knew him in one way but not in most others.

Now she was sitting in the stuffy lamplight, feeling a great sense of anticlimax. He would be gone now, she thought. Gone back to London, to his wife, who had a name. Tears pricked at the back of her eyes and began to trickle down her face. Everything was so confusing.

'Come, Julia, we knew this was on the cards.' Richard reached over and patted her on the knee.

'It's the shock.' She blew her nose on the handkerchief Dougie had given her the day before.

'Good heavens,' he said. 'Where on earth did you get such a grubby article?'

She got up from her chair. 'I think I'll go to bed.'

'Good idea. I'll be up shortly.'

Richard arranged papers in his study, sorting them into piles. He cast his eye over the terms of a will, the seventh he'd been asked to draft in as many days, and slipped it into his briefcase. Out in the kitchen, he heard the dog whine in a dream. His brother stared out of his photograph, always twenty-two, always uniformed, clean-shaven, alive. The responsibility of defence settled on his shoulders. Around him the household slept.

6

There were tea chests on the landing, suitcases by the front door and everywhere in the flat that strange dislocation that occurs when objects vacate their places and thereby leach their meaning: when you take a look at something you have spent years not seeing and think, what's that for? Do I need it? Do I want it? And because familiar objects need their familiar places to make sense of themselves, often the answer is no.

The war was a month old. Barbara and the children were taking the train to Liverpool tomorrow, from where they would sail to Canada. Dougie was sitting in the bay window at the dining table he used as a desk between mealtimes, staring at the blackout. Wind shivered and rattled the sashes, which didn't fit properly. He could smell bonfires and drains.

'What are you doing?' said Nell, coming into the room. Nell was five.

He put down his pen and turned. 'Writing a letter.'

Nell stood on one foot and picked her nose. 'Who to?'

'A friend.'

The letter was to Julia. He remembered telling her they hadn't long to wait. Yet every day felt like a year. Being apart from her was driving him mad.

'Is your friend a dog?' said Nell.

'No,' said Dougie.

'Because dogs are good friends. Mummy says so. Mummy says we can have a dog in Canada.'

'Does she?' said Dougie. 'Actually, I am writing to a cat.'

'Are you?' said Nell.

'Yes, I am writing to George.' George, a large tortoiseshell, was lying on the table with his paws tucked under him. He looked like a tea cosy.

'You don't have to write to George, Daddy,' said Nell. 'He's right next to you.'

'Oh, so he is,' said Dougie. 'Hello, George. Well, then, I am writing to a bat.'

Nell shook her head. 'You are silly, Daddy. Bats can't read.'

'Shouldn't you be in bed?'

'I shall write to George when I'm in Canada,' said Nell, who couldn't read or write. 'Because he might get lon-er-ly. I won't tell him about the dog, though.'

'Best not,' said Dougie.

Barbara appeared in the doorway. 'Come along, Nell. We've an early start tomorrow. Have you done your teeth?'

'Daddy is writing to a bat,' said Nell.

Barbara gave him a long look. 'Yes, I expect he is.'

'Who is she?' asked Barbara.

'I don't know what on earth you're talking about.'

'No. Of course you don't.'

'Please, Barbara. Not now. Not on the last night.'

'Quite,' said Barbara. 'You could have waited.'

She wore clothes well, his wife. Even on the little housekeeping money he was able to give her, she made herself as elegant as it was possible to be in the shabby environs of Primrose Hill. After all this time he still didn't know how she did it, although he knew her mother paid for the West End hairdresser.

Barbara went round the room, mechanically tidying. She picked up a jersey of Alice's, a pair of Kitty's tiny socks, and gathered them into her arms, hugging them close. 'I feel sorry for you. I don't think you have the capacity for happiness.'

It was odd, thought Dougie, because he could have said the same about her. He lit a cigarette. 'You might have a shipboard romance, you know,' he said. 'Think of it. See if you can get yourself invited to the captain's table. You'll find yourself among a better class of person.'

'Are you drunk?'

'I've had a drink.'

The flat was too small for them. The kitchen was off the half-landing, the two bedrooms were upstairs and the bathroom was shared. This room was a catch-all. Here they ate and rowed and Dougie worked in the bay window when there was sufficient peace and quiet, which was rarely. The alcoves beside the chimney breast were stuffed with his books, double shelved. On the walls they'd painted ochre when they were first married were his paintings, hot little oils, vivid little gouaches, singing out of their background. Over the mantelpiece was a paler ochre circle with blurred edges.

'Where's the Arnolfini mirror?'

'I've packed it,' said Barbara. 'It's in one of the tea chests.' The tea chests were full of those possessions – hers and the children's – which they weren't taking to Canada but didn't want to get rid of. She had arranged to store them at her parents' house.

'I like that mirror.' Similar to the one in the Van Eyck marriage portrait, it was the eye of the room. Fish eye, banker's eye, sorcerer's eye. He didn't remember how he knew such terms for convex mirrors, but he did know them. Once facts stuck themselves to the flypaper in his head, they tended to stay there.

'My brother gave it to me.'

'Your brother gave it to you as a wedding present,' said Dougie. 'Correct me if I'm wrong, but I assume that means it belongs to both of us.'

'Well, unpack it then, I don't care,' she said. 'The movers aren't coming until next week. That leaves plenty of time to retrieve it, even for you.' Barbara often complained that he was slow at getting round to things, which was true up to a point. He was slow at getting round to things that she wanted him to do.

Two thoughts crossed his mind. The first was that he wondered what they had ever seen in each other or, rather, he wondered why they now saw each other so differently. The second, which followed

60

on from the first, was sadness that their marriage had come to this relentless picking of scabs and point-scoring. (He chose at that moment to forget Spain, some of the women who had followed Spain and, more particularly, the one to whom he had been writing earlier.) 'I'm sorry, Ba.'

'For what?'

'For everything.'

'Everything?' said Barbara, heading for the door. 'Well, I suppose that just about covers it. I'm going to bed. You'll arrange a cab?'

'I said I would.'

The next morning there was no room for him in the cab, which was stuffed to the gills with luggage. They said their goodbyes on the pavement. Alice, eldest, grave and tam-o'-shantered, climbed into the back seat with three-year-old Kitty, who had her thumb in her mouth. 'Be good,' he said to Nell.

'I will try,' said Nell. 'But I am only five. It may be easier when I am six.'

Dougie lifted her over the kerb and handed her in alongside her sisters. You weren't supposed to have a favourite child, but he did. Kitty was too young to notice this. Alice wasn't.

'Well,' said Barbara. She was wearing a fox fur whose smell of mothballs warred with her usual scent and won.

'Safe journey.' When he kissed her cheek she flinched. 'Send me a wire when you arrive.'

'Of course.'

'Captain's table, remember,' he said.

'Goodbye, Doug.'

The cab rattled away, coughing exhaust. He looked back at the house and could see Mrs Tooley, their downstairs neighbour, staring at him out of the window. She hadn't put her teeth in yet. It was that early. He crossed the street and went into the park.

From Primrose Hill on a fine, clear day you could see all of London laid out at your feet, or most of it that mattered. The panorama stretched from the docks in the east well beyond the Houses of Parliament by way of St Paul's, across a descending swathe of green dotted with trees and lamp posts, a domesticated urban countryside that was hedged round by terraced streets and criss-crossed by paved paths. This morning, mist was clinging to the lower slopes and hollows and the sky hadn't yet decided which colour it wanted to be. Leaves were falling.

Dougie often walked through the park to work. Prosaically, it saved Tube and bus fares. Creatively, it cleared his head and put other ideas in there, along with the possibilities – or the delusions of grandeur – that all good views inspire. Today, he came down the hill blind, as if in flight from himself.

Last night he'd woken in the small hours, gasping in the strangle-hold of a 'Franco'. A year or so ago, the nightmares had been more common; the year before that they had come by day without warning, slipstreamed him into a hideous parallel world tasting of cordite and dust. This was the first Franco for months and it was a bad one.

He never slept afterwards and had learned it was pointless to try. So he'd got up, gone downstairs and smoked two cigarettes in the claustrophobia of the blackout, staring at the pale ochre circle over the fireplace. Then he went to look for the Arnolfini mirror.

He found it in the second tea chest, loosely wrapped in news-paper under a packet of letters and a canteen of silverware which had also been a wedding present. (He had never liked the cutlery; it was falsely ornate.) These past days there had been something fevered and careless about Barbara's packing and he saw at once that the mirror was broken, not shattered, but sufficiently dam-aged to spoil it. It was with a wry kind of disgust, or a sense of irony, that he wrapped it up again and put it back in the wooden crate.

The letters he flicked through in the weak hall light. They were all from him and dated from the period immediately before their marriage. Some of the phrases he remembered; evidently, he had remembered them well, because he had repeated a few in the letter he had written that evening, which bothered him less than perhaps it ought to have done. He replaced the packet, resting the canteen on top to weigh it down. Then he had gone upstairs, climbed into bed beside his wife, who had her back turned, and lay unsleeping, unseeing, until the birds began their rusty chorus of unoiled wheels.

Now in the park his memories of the Spanish war threaded through the purposeful ugliness of the present one. Waterlogged trenches, dug before Munich and half fallen-in, ran this way and that, an anti-aircraft gun emplacement crowned the top of the hill and the slow, drifting blimp of a silvery barrage balloon bobbed cartoonish over their road.

At the bottom of the hill, nestled among shrubbery, was what his children called the Squirrel's Postbox, its top now daubed with yellow gas-detection paint. Into it he threw the letter he had written to Julia, suggesting they should meet (and describing what they might do when they did), and heard it make some sort of hollow connection with the interior of the cast-iron drum.

No bombs had fallen. No enemy troops had landed on the beaches or parachuted down from the skies. The war was happening a long way off in unpronounceable Polish places. You didn't hear gunfire on Oxford Street. What you did hear was a clumsy, clanking sound as bureaucracy ground into gear. This was the British way. All the clerks in Whitehall ordered new stationery in green, buff and plain and set about devising acronyms.

When Dougie arrived at Soho Square, people were huddled round the noticeboard, on which was pinned the latest directive from the recently formed Ministry of Information (MOI).

'What's a PO235?' said someone.

'I don't know, but apparently it replaces the CN507.'

'That's all right then.'

Dougie brushed past.

'McGod's in a mood, just to warn you,' the post boy said.

Macleod had been in a mood ever since they'd shut the cinemas at the outbreak of war, when they'd also shut the theatres, the concert halls, the football grounds and the zoo.

'Makes a change,' said Dougie, going up the stairs.

In the eighteenth century, 21 Soho Square, where the Unit was based, had been a brothel catering to the gentry, infamous for sensational tableaux involving candles that lit and extinguished themselves, dancing skeletons and chairs that tipped their unwary occupants through concealed trap doors, frissons which all added to the pleasures of the flesh. Nowadays, such mechanical trickery was long gone, along with most of the interior detailing, the building partitioned, altered and refashioned to suit a line of work that depended on creating other illusions. The exception was Macleod's office, a light and pleasantly proportioned room on the first floor with a view of the leafy square. Here, if you could not precisely imagine aristocratic shenanigans, you could at least imagine aristocrats. Macleod had done his best to democratize his surroundings with a regulation steel desk and filing cabinets.

'Douglas,' said Macleod as he entered the room. 'Take a pew.'

Dougie took a pew. He'd thought he was early, but Harold Travis and Basil Meers were already there. Travis was Macleod's latest protégé. Basil Meers, a tall, thin, stooping man who looked like a heron, was the Unit editor. They nodded hello.

'I see there's been another directive from the Ministry,' said Dougie.

'The Ministry,' said Macleod, 'couldn't direct its way out of a paper bag.' He crossed the room and shut the door. 'Which brings me neatly to the reason I convened this meeting. I cannot disguise the fact, gentlemen, that we're at risk of closure.'

'They'll open the cinemas soon. They'll have to,' said Basil Meers.

'That's not the point,' said Macleod, resuming his seat. 'The point is, when they do, what will they show?'

'Propaganda,' said Dougie, lighting a cigarette.

'You want to give up those filthy things.' Macleod reached round to open a window. The noise of London blared in. 'But you're quite right. It's hard to make the case for our kind of film-making in present circumstances. And Christ knows I've tried.'

'Our' kind of film-making was very much Macleod's kind, which they all understood, as did everyone who worked for him. Filming real people in real places doing real things: briefly put.

'Truth is the first casualty of war, is that what you mean?' Dougie picked a shred of tobacco off his tongue. 'Surely you don't think we should take a leaf out of Goebbels' book.'

Macleod permitted himself a smile. It sat uneasily on his face, which was built to be pugnacious. 'Far from it. Truth is the best weapon we have. The question is whether they'll let us tell it. But first we need to make them sit up and take notice. As things stand, I've thirty-seven on the payroll, not counting Blackheath, and most of them idle. That's years of expertise going to waste.'

Macleod hated waste almost as much as he hated pen-pushing.

'What are you suggesting?' said Travis. He had an open boyish expression that made him appear younger than he was.

'I'm suggesting you make a suggestion.'

Dougie said, 'How about something along the lines of common purpose?'

'Explain.' Macleod adjusted the yellow woollen tie that poked out over the top of his Fair Isle jumper.

'Nothing like war to show you how dependent we all are on each other.'

'Factories? Filling sandbags?' said Travis. 'That kind of thing?'

You didn't want to underestimate Travis, thought Dougie. He cottoned on fast. 'It won't be just the services who win this.'

'Glad you think we're going to win,' said Basil Meers.

'We have to,' said Dougie. 'So we will.'

Macleod sat pulling at his lower lip. 'All right. Put it down on paper and get it to me by the end of the week. No dilettantish, artsy-fartsy Cambridge nonsense. I want a simple breakdown. Something we can bang out quickly. Preferably without involving the War Office.'

The meeting was over. Dougie was halfway out of the room

when Macleod gave him a nod. 'I saw the rough cut of the fishing film yesterday.'

'It needs more polish.'

'It's absolute shite. You didn't get the shots.'

'You're talking about Grimsby. We had a bit of bad weather up there.'

'I'm talking about the footage of the trawler,' said Macleod. 'I don't know where the hell you filmed it. What I do know is that one minute fish are swimming around somewhere in the sea and the next they're in the boat. We don't see the nets hauling them up. We don't see them caught, which some might say is the point of fishing. Without that shot you haven't got a sequence. It doesn't hang together.'

The judgement rankled, because it was true and Dougie knew it.

'You want to sit in with Meers, watch him cut. That'll show you what you can and can't do in the edit.'

Basil Meers was the last person Dougie would have asked for advice. 'I don't think he cares for my work.'

'Precisely,' said Macleod.

For the rest of the week Dougie fizzed with frustration, his least favourite frame of mind. In his cubbyhole on the second floor, a tangle of pipes and peeling paintwork for a view, he sat in front of a blank piece of paper and felt like punching a wall.

Time pressed heavily on him. He told himself he didn't want to let the side down. The truth was he didn't want to let himself down.

Home was no better. Having the flat to himself and all the peace and quiet he wanted of an evening ought to have made things easier. Instead, there was something dispiriting about the place with the children gone and perversely he began to think that their noise was the counter-irritant he needed in order to concentrate. A brief note came from Barbara to say they had safely embarked, along with a number of bills that she normally dealt with. Not a word from Julia. He tried to remember what he'd written in his letter. Perhaps he'd come on too strong – or left it too late.

Friday morning, he arrived early at the Unit and went up to the third floor.

'Dougie,' said Basil, when he came through the door of the cutting room. 'What can I do for you?'

The telegram arrived around eleven.

7

It was only when Julia boarded the train that the full realization of what she was doing hit home. Compartment doors slammed up and down the length of the carriages. A guard shouted. It was still not too late to get off, to retrieve the case she had stowed on the brass overhead rack. It was still not too late to turn back.

A whistle, a hiss of steam and a jolt. Across the compartment, a middle-aged woman in a tweed suit and squashy hat raised her eyes from her newspaper.

The train began to move. Julia pressed her gloved hands down on to the hard oblong of the unopened book in her lap as if that would quell her panic. What if there was a crisis and Richard tried to reach her? What if he telephoned her father and discovered she wasn't there? What if she came across somebody she knew?

That morning, packing her weekend bag, making arrangements with their housekeeper, returning her husband's goodbye kiss, accepting spending money from him, along with the warm wishes he sent her father, she had been driven by an imperative that seemed to exist outside herself, something that had a life and a will of its own.

The imperative or impulse had taken her all the way to the nearest town served by the branch line, to the post office, from where she sent Dougie a telegram, and to the railway station, where she bought her ticket. To the waiting room, where she had waited, and to this compartment, whose only other occupant was now slipping sweets from a twist of paper and pencilling in answers to a crossword puzzle. The bulbs in the lamps were blue, one more novelty of a war that wasn't behaving like one. A poster screwed behind a sheet of glass advertised the Continent via Harwich.

What was she doing?

The train began to pick up speed. She stared through the window at the flat familiar landscape, the isolated stands of trees, the gulls swooping over the brown ridged fields, landing and alighting, landing and alighting, the boy cycling up to a halt, and the green lorry parked by the dusty roadside. The signal boxes and level crossings flew past. Nothing settled her. A speck of grit blew into her eye and she extracted it with the tip of her finger.

Perhaps if she had grounds, an excuse, to behave this way. If there had been ill treatment, something to complain about. But there was nothing to complain about except there was nothing to complain about.

'Oh!' she said, and only realized she had said it out loud when the tweedy woman opposite raised her eyes from her puzzle and frowned a question.

'Sorry.'

Then she could hear him say, 'Stop apologizing, Sinclair,' and began to tremble.

And yet there was still time, she told herself. Where the branch line met the main line she could always change trains and turn back. She could always go home.

Those first few days after Dougie had gone back to London, Julia had often found herself at her desk, picking up her pen and putting it down again. Scratching the nib on the blotting paper, making chicken-feet marks, filling in circles with drips and blots. What was the point in writing? He would forget her – he had forgotten her already.

Picking up her pen and putting it down again. It was wrong. She was married, she had a son. There was nothing to say. It was over, and some distant part of her that she couldn't quite reach breathed a sigh of relief.

Peter went back to school, with his scar and gas mask. Julia played the piano a lot. She played 'La Cathédrale engloutie' and imagined Dougie listening to her. After a time she could not hear his imagined comments on her playing; she was forgetting the sound of his voice.

The letter came just when she'd given up expecting it. You don't really know anybody until you read what they're like on the page. Dougie on the page seduced her all over again. Such was the power of a good prose composition.

'My own Sinclair, I miss you terribly,' he wrote. 'Your skin is like silk, did I tell you? I want to fuck you so badly I can't think of anything else.'

That letter was in her handbag, memorized. The train sped along. She saw Peter in hospital, his head bandaged, water dribbling over his chin. She hadn't heeded the warning. No doubt the gods would find some new and uniquely terrible way of punishing her for what she was planning to do. Wouldn't it be best to turn back?

A little way outside Colchester the train came to a halt in a siding. No announcements were made. Five, ten minutes of inactivity and the tweedy woman put her head out of the window of the compartment door, then sank back in her seat declaring that the unexplained delay was typical of the way the war had disrupted the timetables.

'We wait here any longer,' said the woman, 'and I'll miss my connection.'

Julia had been wondering whether the train had sensed the opposing forces inside her, pushing forward, pulling back, and stopped itself on purpose. Now, with the woman's fretting, her anxious checking of her ticket and watch, she felt as if something was about to be taken from her before she had the chance to seize it.

The woman shook her head. 'I'm sorry, you must excuse me, I'm on edge. My daughter's expecting her first any day now.'

She produced a photograph of a young woman with fluffy hair, and Julia admired it.

'They say she takes after me.' The photograph was tidied away. 'Are you going far?'

Was she? thought Julia. Exactly how far was she going?

A clank, and the train got underway again. 'About time,' said the woman.

They were moving, slowly. 'London,' said Julia, over the noise. 'I'm going to London.'

'Oh, do take care in the blackout, won't you?' said the woman. 'There've been so many accidents, one hears.'

Richard had said the same that morning.

Then all at once the madness was back, the driving, relentless imperative, and she marvelled at its power to override her better judgement, to mow everything down in its path. She would deal with the gods later.

'It's not the gods you have to worry about, Sinclair,' said Dougie. 'It's the mortals. They're much more dangerous, by and large.'

They were sitting in a small Soho restaurant run by a Hungarian who had greeted Dougie like a long-lost brother or comrade-in-arms. The walls were crowded with pictures and on each table was a little lamp with a pink shade which flattered all the faces in the room. The tables were very close together, so that the waiters in their long white aprons had to perform balletic manoeuvres to serve the food and pour the wine, which they did with a kind of mocking deprecation of their own performance that only served to highlight its consummate skill. This wasn't her London, thought Julia, gazing round at the other diners, many of whom were in the services and not all of them English. At the next table was a Canadian pilot.

Earlier, when she had arrived at Liverpool Street, she'd noticed the same prevalence of uniform, just as she had breathed in the city smell of dirty wet pavement. Dougie had been waiting for her at the barrier. Now his thumb was pressing against her palm and she was flooded with an enormous sense of well-being and the extravagance of hours to spend with him. No past, no future, no fear on either account. She was conscious only of a long exhalation into a limitless present tense.

'What a lovely lady,' said Viktor, the Hungarian restaurateur, coming to enquire after their meal. 'You are a very lucky man.'

'Luck has nothing to do with it,' said Dougie.

'Luck has everything to do with it, my friend,' said Viktor.

'Do you often come here?' said Julia, when Viktor had taken his professional solicitude to another table. By which she meant, do you often come here with your wife?

'Sometimes, if I'm going to be staying late at the Unit.' Then he began to describe the difficulties he had been having at work, how he couldn't see his way clear on this new film and, lightly, jokingly, how it was all her fault for putting him through hell. 'The telegram was a nice touch. I'll say this for you, you do keep me on my toes.'

'I'm sorry,' she said. 'I know I should have given you more warning.' But more warning would have meant more thought, and it wasn't thought that put her on the train or kept her there.

'Don't apologize, Sinclair,' he said, with an amused look. 'Indecent haste is perfectly fine by me.'

In fact, the telegram had given him quite a fright. In the short interval between learning that it had arrived at the Unit and him opening it, his mind had had time to picture enemy torpedoes and his children in a lifeboat cast adrift on the mountainous waves of the North Atlantic, the lifeboat sinking, Nell in her little orange buoyancy jacket going under.

Viktor returned with brandies and the compliments of the house.

They drank their brandies. 'Tell me more about your film,' said Julia.

As he did, she could sense an unwinding in him. This pleased her.

Dougie lit a cigarette. 'You mustn't indulge me,' he said to Julia, after a time. 'I'm frightful at talking shop.'

'They also serve who only stand and wait.'

'What did you say?'

'That's what it's about, isn't it?'

He exhaled. 'Yes, that's exactly what it's about.' He shook his head and smiled.

'Listen to this.' Dinner was over and they were at his flat, a place Julia registered as one of alien smells, colours and urgencies, of both danger and safety, impressions only heightened by the fact they'd kissed all the way back in the cab.

'"Tea for Two"?' she said, picking up the record sleeve. A little banal, wasn't it? A little Lyons Corner House? And here she wondered, with a slight sinking feeling, whether she had misjudged him and he was not quite so extraordinary after all. As if she had discovered he wore dentures.

'Art Tatum.'

'Who's he?'

Dougie lowered the needle. 'I heard him play at Ciro's last year. As a pianist, I'd be interested in your opinion.'

A scratching sound as the needle went round the disc. Then the opening bars burst out and all thoughts of Lyons Corner House went clean out of her head.

What *was* this?

She had never heard anything like it before. The music swept her up and turned her inside out. She felt it in her spine, on the soles of her feet, in her itching finger-ends. It was joyous, joyous, joyous.

When it stopped, she said, 'Play it again.'

If anything, it sounded even better. This time what she heard was a whole new vocabulary. An exuberant teasing playfulness that pushed you forwards, sideways and all round the harmonic houses. Dizzy cadenzas cascading up and down the keyboard over a strutting, striding rhythm. She was stunned. It was like listening to a melody in three dimensions.

Dougie was watching her face and when he saw how the music affected her, he smiled. 'This is how you make me feel,' he said. 'You are very jazz, Sinclair.'

'Funny that,' she said. 'I was thinking the same about you.'

'Again?'

She nodded. Then they were circling, twirling round the room, laughing and bumping into the furniture.

It was dark. A moment of dislocation before she remembered where she was, marvelled at where she was, then her hand reached out to the other side of the bed and found it cool and empty. She got up and fumbled about on the floor, found a shirt – his shirt – and put it on.

Downstairs, a light was burning. He was sitting at the table in the bay window, writing. A cat, hunched on the back of an old cracked leather club chair, swiped a paw at her arm experimentally.

'You're awake.'

Dougie turned. 'I've been awake most of the night, as you can't have failed to notice. Come here.'

She went across to him and leant over his shoulder.

'They Also Serve' was written at the top of the page. Underneath was a scene-by-scene breakdown. 'Your doing,' he said, pulling her round on to his lap.

'You would have got there without me.' She was thrilled.

'I wouldn't care to bet on it.' He kissed her ear. 'What do you want to do today?'

She laughed.

'Apart from that,' he said.

'Apart from that, listen to the Art Tatum.'

He smiled. 'You'll wear it out.'

All weekend, wherever they were, however they were occupying themselves, Julia felt as if she were carrying a large brimming bowl of water from one side of a room to another: this was happiness and she didn't want to spill a drop. (Happiness was a more complicated emotion than she had thought, remarkably close, at times, to its opposite.)

Evidence of Dougie's family was everywhere in the flat: in the tea chests on the landing, in the spill of face powder on the chest of drawers in the bedroom, in the three small cots next door with its nursery wallpaper. She tried not to see these, or dwell on them, or mention them.

At the same time, she kept coming up against all the ways in which Dougie was a stranger to her. While this novelty enticed and excited her, it was also daunting. Julia had grown up and married into a world of antimacassars, of gloves and hats and table linen, of wallpaper, doilies and coasters. Of things you put over things, lest real life come in direct, messy contact with you, or vice versa. Dougie, she was beginning to understand, did not live in this world; he barely acknowledged it. The paintings on the walls said this, so did the stain in the kitchen sink, which was the shape of Africa, and so, too, the dead flowers decaying in a vase of stinking water. Most of all, the books on the shelves, on the table, under the bed, many of which sprouted torn slips of paper slipped between their pages. There were other concerns here, and they had nothing to do with appearances.

Equally unsettling was his part of London – what her father would have called a 'rough area'. It wasn't the East End, a district that had infested her imagination since childhood with amorphous dread, but it was a far cry from the suburb she'd grown up in. Evenings spent drinking in public houses were rare experiences for Julia; an evening spent drinking in a public house frequented by inebriated poets and Irish working men who sang Republican songs was a shock to the system. Along with her Hungarian introduction to Soho, she felt as if she had spent the weekend in a foreign city. It was but one of many ways she had lost her bearings.

'Next time,' said Dougie, 'I should like to hear you play.'

They were standing under the Great Eastern war memorial at Liverpool Street Station, waiting for her train to be announced. The anonymity of a busy railway terminus surrounded them, all the strangers coming and going, no one caring who they were. Above arched a vaulted glass roof supported by cast-iron girders through which the fading sunlight slanted.

Julia tucked away 'next time' like a present to unwrap later. 'How do you propose to do that?' she said. He didn't have a piano.

He lit a cigarette. 'I'll think of something.'

'Let me have a puff,' she said.

He put his cigarette between her lips. 'That's four puffs and counting. I'm afraid I'm a terribly bad influence on you.'

'You are.'

'Have you got the disc?' he said.

'I do. It's safe in my bag.'

The station clock, which had been telling her the same time whenever she glanced anxiously at it, chose that moment to rush forwards. The tannoy blared and the barrier was opened. Dougie had bought a platform ticket and followed her to her carriage.

'Steady on, squire,' said a sergeant, climbing on board with his kit bag. 'Give the missus a chance to breathe.'

She cried all the way home, despite the fact she was rather relieved to be going there.

8

Peter was home for half-term, unidentified stickiness in his tuck box, Aertex shirt gone missing again. 'Do you want mustard in your sandwich?' asked Harry. '"Mootard", as the Frenchies say.'

'No,' said Peter. 'Mustard is foul.'

'"No, thank you,"' said Julia.

'No, thank you,' said Peter. 'Shall I tell you a joke?'

'Go on.'

'What did one wall say to the other?'

'I give up,' said Julia, sitting herself down at the kitchen table. 'What did one wall say to the other?'

'I'll meet you at the corner!'

Julia laughed because he found it so funny. 'Good joke.'

'I read it in my comic,' said Peter. 'Do you want to hear another one?'

'Perhaps after lunch,' she said. 'Your scar wouldn't show, you know, if you didn't sweep your fringe across like that. I swear it's redder now than when you went back to school. Does it bother you?'

'No.'

Mothers, thought Peter, hadn't the first idea. His scar was a badge of honour and much admired for its many and varied fictitious causes. He wasn't going to hide it away.

Richard, who had been working at home that morning, came into the kitchen.

'Sandwich, Mr C?' asked Harry.

'Thank you, no,' said Richard. 'I'll have a bite at the Crown later.' He handed Julia a letter. 'This came for you in the second post. I must say, Marjorie's quite the correspondent.'

'Yes, she is,' said Julia, leaving the letter lying by her plate and trying not to look at it. It was from Dougie.

That morning she had woken up determined to put a stop to it, as she had woken up on other mornings with the same resolution. Dougie's timing was uncanny. She didn't need to read the letter to be drawn right back to him. His handwriting accomplished that all by itself. It didn't seem to matter how often she decided there wouldn't be a next time when the next time was all she could think about. Along with the last time, its details now blurred smooth by too much remembering.

On the other hand, why should she assume that he wanted there to be a next time? One weekend wasn't much to go on. Perhaps he was writing to tell her it was over. A man like that – there would be other women. Wouldn't there? Yet – 'my own Sinclair' – how could that be true? Now her fingers itched to open the envelope.

'Who's Marjorie?' said Peter.

'Sorry, darling, what did you say?'

'She's an old college friend of your mother's, whose husband is in the forces,' said Richard. 'Your mother is being a great support to her.'

'Not really.' Julia took the letter and got up from her seat. 'She just needs a bit of hand-holding.'

'A violinist, isn't that right?'

'Viola,' said Julia. 'She plays the viola.' Marjorie Askew: whatever had become of her? she wondered as she went out the door.

Peter didn't understand how hands could be held with letters. His letters, which they were made to write on Sunday afternoon after chapel, were equal parts requests and boasts. Those he received from home asked too many questions. That was the long and short of letters.

Late afternoon in the drawing room, and the light was going. Soon it would be time to black out the windows, to shut out the sea views. From the kitchen came the smell of baking.

Here was the thing, thought Julia, putting on the record. How do you make *that* from *this*?

This was the sheet music of 'Tea for Two'. On the page was the melody, the notes, the key signature, the tempo. Simple enough. Child's play. Yet on the gramophone, what was being done to the melody, the key signature, the tempo, was of a different order altogether.

A pity she hadn't been at the club with Dougie when he'd seen Art Tatum. She'd have liked to have taken a good look at his fingering. But she knew that what she was hearing was nothing as simple as dexterity. What she was hearing was speed of thought, the ability to expose harmonic relationships and create new ones. The inventiveness dazzled her.

When the record finished, she tried to reproduce what she had heard. It was hard. Harder than Rachmaninov, harder than Liszt. Even Liszt, they said, could not always play Liszt.

The front door opened and closed.

'Peter?' she said.

Richard came into the drawing room. 'Not your usual repertoire,' he said.

'No,' said Julia. 'It's jazz.'

'Is that what you call it.'

That was ungenerous of him, she thought. 'You're home early.'

He sat heavily in his chair. 'Yes.'

She turned on the piano stool. He was staring at the floor, his hands braced on his knees. Her heart skipped. 'What's the matter?'

Did he know? Had she been found out? She glanced at the bureau where she had sat reading Dougie's letter earlier – 'When can you get away again?'; and where she had written her reply – 'Soon, soon, I promise'; but the desktop was neat and clear. Caution was second nature now.

'Perry Clayton,' he said.

She had forgotten all about Perry Clayton. 'I thought the trial was next month.'

'There won't be a trial.'

He raised his eyes. His expression was beaten, hollow. 'He's hanged himself in his cell.'

'Oh no!'

'I'm afraid so.' Richard took a deep breath and pinched the bridge of his nose. 'The governor rang me this afternoon. There'll be an inquest, of course, and a few rapped knuckles, I suppose. He used the bedclothes.'

'I'm so sorry, Richard.' She knew how much effort he had made to ensure that Perry Clayton was properly represented and what a point of principle this was for him. 'I'm so sorry.'

'A waste of a life. *Two* lives.'

'He was guilty, though, wasn't he?' she said.

'Yes,' Richard said. 'Yes, he was.' He got up, crossed the room and stood looking out of the window. 'The last time I saw him he was full of remorse.'

'You couldn't have predicted this.'

'Couldn't I?' he said. 'You know, his wife never once visited him. Sometimes I think passion is a terrible thing.'

Passion was a terrible thing. It tore you in half. Julia had never felt divided against herself before. The pain was physical, insupportable at times.

Some days she tried to walk it out of herself. But this did not work. In one direction, a walk might take her past the Martello tower, where she had first laid eyes on Dougie; in the other to the cottage where they had first made love. She saw these points on the shingle coast as hallowed ground, glowing with meaning. When the postmistress rented the cottage out to a pair of elderly brothers, she felt the desecration keenly.

One bleak Sunday afternoon in mid-November, when she could stand it no longer, she took her distress to Fiona. It was risky, she knew. Yet, of all people, she thought her friend might be sympathetic. That she might be entertained was also a distinct possibility, which she would just have to deal with.

Fiona lived down by the green in a Regency house with smart paintwork, arched windows and fine glazing bars. If dogs could resemble their owners, so too could houses.

The unburdening proved easier than Julia expected. Once she started, staring at the striped wallpaper, it all came out in a stammering rush.

There followed a little silence. Then Fiona said, 'I suspected something was up.' She smoothed her skirt. 'Drink, darling?'

'Please.'

Fiona went over to the sideboard and busied herself with bottles and glasses. Her mind was reeling. Never Julia, she thought. Never her dearest friend. Never in a million years.

She remembered that time a little while ago when she had caught sight of Julia in the street looking like someone had given her the most enormous present. Her immediate assumption was that she was anticipating a happy event and wasn't yet ready to share the news. Then, lately, with Julia so distracted, she had put the change of mood down to miscarriage.

The truth was beyond her wildest imaginings. This was precisely the sort of foul behaviour she'd once been on the receiving end of, a fact that Julia seemed to have forgotten about.

'I just don't know what to do with myself,' she was saying from the sofa. 'It's driving me insane. I've never felt like this before.' Julia was clearly of the opinion that no one had ever felt like this before.

'Lemon?'

'Please.' Julia paused. 'I'm sorry, I didn't know who else to turn to.'

'What are friends for?' Fiona handed her the gin and sat opposite. 'Let me be sure I've got this absolutely straight. This man you spent the weekend with in London is the same one who filmed you that day on the beach?' Fiona had it absolutely straight; she was only buying time to compose her reactions.

Julia bristled a little. Her friend might have been talking about any Tom, Dick or Harry who whistled under their breath when you went past. 'He works for a government film unit. Quite high up in it, actually.'

Fiona lit a cigarette. 'I see.'

'I know it's wrong,' Julia said, helping herself to a cigarette, 'and I keep meaning to put an end to it, then another letter comes. He writes the most wonderful letters.' And here, remembering the language of the letters, she flushed to the roots of her hair.

Fiona, tapping ash into the ashtray, noted the flush and the smoking.

'Don't worry,' Julia said. 'I'm not a complete fool. I don't leave them lying about. They're quite safe where I've put them.'

'I'm glad to hear it,' said Fiona. 'Does he have a wife?'

'She's abroad.'

'Children?'

Julia, whose confession had momentarily lightened her distress – even saying Dougie's name aloud was a relief – now found her distress deepening to a trough. She reached across to touch her friend on the arm. 'I don't want to hurt anyone, least of all Richard. You do see that, don't you?'

Fiona, shrinking back, disguised her revulsion with a cough. She might have been listening to one of her husband's heartless little home-breakers burbling on in their heartless little fashion. All those horrid little secretaries.

'This isn't sensible, darling. I do hope you realize. You are play-ing with fire.'

'I know,' said Julia. 'That's what I keep telling myself.'

'Then put a stop to it before things get well and truly out of hand.'

Part of the reason Julia had sought out her friend was to be given precisely that advice. Now she had been given it, she found she didn't want to hear it. 'I wish it were that simple,' she said.

How Fiona endured that afternoon she was unable to say. After Julia left, she poured herself another drink and sat numbly drink-ing it. For the first time she had experienced the inequality of friendship and she didn't like it at all.

It was three weeks later. On account of the war and the blackout, the yacht-club Christmas dance had been scaled down and shifted earlier in the day to a buffet lunch: there would be no dancing.

The clubhouse was a low building clad in white boarding perched on a short pier down by the estuary. Fiona was a little late. This was intentional: parties made her miss her husband badly. Geoffrey had always been the life and soul. She came into the noisy, overheated room and almost turned back again.

Tired paper chains were looped between race photographs and display cabinets and taped snowflakes were uncurling from the misted windows. By the door, a group of men in brass-buttoned blazers were discussing, with all due male gravity and well-judged equidistance from one another, the recent Soviet invasion of Finland and advance on the Mannerheim Line. Others were talking boats and how much they missed them. She threaded her way through the crowd and spotted Julia over near the drinks table, next to Alan Bateson, the club president.

'Mrs Compton tells me she is teaching herself to play jazz,' said Alan Bateson when she joined them. He had a ruddy, weathered face and the unshakeable confidence of a prize-winning helmsman. Many of the trophies in the display cabinets had his name on them. 'I call that very enterprising and quite possibly a little fast.' He seemed on the brink of winking, or bottom-pinching.

Julia laughed. She was animated and glowing. 'No, I didn't say I was teaching myself how to play it, I said I was finding it very difficult to play it.'

Gazing round the room, sipping her sherry, Fiona sensed a sharpening of male attention in Julia's direction, and not only from the Alan Bateson quarter. Sensing it too, his tiny bird-like wife came up and claimed him.

'Jazz?' said Fiona, steering her friend to a quiet corner. 'You might as well hang a sign round your neck.'

'Saying "pianist"?' said Julia.

'You know what I'm talking about.' If Julia was sending out such signals in public, thought Fiona, the Lord only knew what she was letting slip in the privacy of her own home.

Julia, who had been enjoying herself – so far as someone who disliked sailing could enjoy herself at a yacht club – was brought up short. 'I thought you understood.'

'I understand the risk you're taking, which is more than you appear to.' Fiona lowered her voice. 'You don't know how lucky you are. Men like Richard aren't ten a penny. You're putting your whole world in jeopardy. Can't you see that?'

Her whole world, thought Julia, looking round the room. The Batesons, the Murrays, the Whitakers, Major Lees, Reverend Weir, the Burroughs, the Huntleys, that odd braying woman in the funny hat whose name she had forgotten. Was this her whole world? It wasn't, not if Dougie wasn't in it.

'What happens if this man gets you pregnant? Have you considered that?'

Julia flushed. Dougie used protection.

'Listen to me, darling,' Fiona said. 'Men wander. They can't help themselves. It's different for us. We're not free agents. We have our homes and families to consider.'

'Ladies?' It was one of the young sea cadets, handing round the mince pies.

Fiona waited until he had moved out of earshot. 'Just because you got away with it once, it doesn't mean you'll get away with it again.'

'I have done.'

'When?'

'Last weekend.' Julia was in no mood to be lectured. If she wanted to be taken to task for cheating on her husband or warned about the risks she was running, she could do those jobs herself, and better than anyone else. 'Stuffy, isn't it? I'm going outside for a bit.'

A few minutes later Fiona was thinking of leaving when Richard came over, with the mild air of abashment with which he usually approached her. 'Good turnout.'

'Yes,' said Fiona. 'Remarkably good.'

The sea cadet came past again and Richard helped himself to a mince pie. 'Where's Julia?'

The poor lamb, thought Fiona. 'Gone out for some air.'

'Quite a chinwag you two were having earlier.' He bit into the pie. 'Gosh, this is hot.'

He couldn't have heard anything. Could he?

'Oh, we were just discussing the usual. The trials of mother-hood. The trials of Christmas shopping – especially in wartime.'

'Ah,' said Richard. 'I can't speak for the trials of motherhood but so far as Christmas shopping is concerned you should think about a little jaunt to London. Julia went to town last weekend, with remarkable success.'

'Yes,' said Fiona. 'She did say.'

The sky was indigo and cerise, with greenish streaks on the hori-zon. You had these skies sometimes on late-winter afternoons and for the life of her she couldn't remember what the fishermen made of them, what they were supposed to herald or foretell. (There was no one more superstitious than a fisherman.)

Unnatural, she thought, leaning on the railing outside the club-house, listening to the lapping water, smoking a cigarette.

'Nothing natural about nature,' Dougie had said, the previous weekend. 'The Fauvists knew this.'

The Fauvists?

They had gone along to an exhibition of modern British art at the National Gallery. All the treasures – the Titians, Rembrandts, Raphaels, Van Eycks – had been shipped out of the museum for safe-keeping. Great grubby tidemarks on the walls announced their illustrious absence. The exhibition, which was small, had been thrown together in a room off the main entrance.

'I don't know whether these artists should be flattered or dismayed,' said Dougie. 'On the one hand, I suppose they should be pleased that the MOI have drafted them in to fill the cultural vacuum in which we find ourselves. On the other, it does rather suggest they're expendable. No one's hiding these works in Wales.'

'I like this one,' said Julia.

They had stopped in front of a still life, the forms fractured, re-assembled.

85

'Why?'

'It reminds me of your paintings, for a start.'

She had forgotten her gloves and they were holding hands in his coat pocket, the same coat that later at a bus stop he was to open and wrap round her, to scandalized glances in the queue. Or perhaps it was the coat, not the gesture, that was shocking: it was an alarming shade of orange.

'It's like jazz,' she went on. 'It's not elaborating on something simple for the sake of it. It's a kind of exploration, an investigation.' She turned to him. 'Pulling something apart is a good way of putting it back together again, don't you think?'

'Yes, Sinclair,' he said. 'I do.'

'You seemed to enjoy yourself tonight,' said Richard, getting under the covers.

'It was all right,' she said. The party was over and the doubts were back, the terrible guilt, the fear. They ate away at her like wild animals. They wouldn't leave her alone.

A squeak of bedsprings. 'I think I'm going to have to move the boat somewhere drier. Alan said those sheds on the north side aren't sound.'

Her throat tightened. 'Richard, do you love me?'

He turned over in bed and put his arms around her. He smelled of clean pyjamas. 'What sort of question is that?'

His embrace was comforting and familiar. So was his love-making. When it was over, she wondered, as she had on previous occasions, who she was betraying now. Tears seeped out of her eyes and fell.

No more weekends in London, she told herself. No more Dougie. No more tug of war in her head. Tomorrow she would write and put a stop to it.

'Not more snow,' said Julia, coming into the kitchen. Big white flakes drifted past the window. It was late January and the entire country was in the iron grip of the worst freeze in years.

'A farm cart's broke its axle on the Whitmarket road,' said Harry. 'And, to save you asking, we're out of sugar. Mr C had the last of it on his porridge this morning.'

'Oh.'

Somehow the bad weather made rationing, which had just come in, doubly punishing. Julia could not remember a time when there had not been sugar in the sugar bowl. She wondered how Peter was faring: he liked his tea sweet and his cakes sweeter. But the school would have some way of dealing with it.

She sat at the table and turned over the pages of Harry's *Picture Post*. Gay girls in their skating dresses posed on the frozen Serpentine. In London, Dougie was ill with bronchitis. Next week, if the trains were running, he was going to Birmingham to film a factory that made fuselages.

She hadn't seen him since that weekend before Christmas, but she hadn't stopped writing to him. The other night she dreamed that he had turned up unannounced on her doorstep to claim her and Richard beat him to a pulp. Halfway through the assault he turned into Perry Clayton. She woke drenched in horror.

There had been other dreams, too, dreams of a sexual nature, which put a shamed warmth in her body for the rest of the day. Were there other women as brazen as her whose minds pictured penises? Particular penises at particular angles?

'How are you getting on with the socks?' Harry said.

'The socks?' Julia closed the magazine. 'Oh, the socks.'

These were intended as a donation to the Red Cross. Two hundred thousand troops of the British Expeditionary Force, Marjorie's fictitious husband included, were now stationed in Belgium and France, strung out along the Maginot Line. All in need of footwear.

'Not well.' Julia eyed the tangle of khaki wool. 'I think the socks might have to become a scarf. There aren't any corners in scarves.'

Harry wondered, not for the first time, how a pianist could be all thumbs.

'Popping out for a bit,' said Julia.

Smoking again, thought Harry. Mr C wouldn't be pleased, but it was not her place to tell him.

'Smoking?' said Richard. 'You?'

He'd come across her puffing away at the bottom of the garden beside the shed, where he'd gone in search of the shovel to clear the front path.

She dropped the cigarette on the frozen ground.

'It steadies my nerves.'

'I wasn't aware you suffered from nerves.' He shook his head, more in sadness or disbelief, it seemed, than anger. 'I suppose you've picked this up from Fiona.'

'Quite possibly,' said Julia. She gazed around the garden, which was inches deep in snow. 'There will be a lot of damage after this winter.'

'Yes,' said Richard. 'I'm afraid we must reconcile ourselves to some losses.'

A loss came soon enough. The dog died. Harry found him the next morning, stiff in his dog basket.

Julia sat at the kitchen table and wept into the wood grain. Perhaps she cried a little too much.

'He had a good life,' said Richard, patting her shoulder. 'A long life.'

The dog was older than their marriage. Julia put her handkerchief away. 'Peter's going to be very upset.'

'Peter will take it on the chin,' said Richard. 'Poor old thing,' he said, looking at the dead dog in his dog basket. 'He can't have found these last months much fun.'

'What are we going to do with him?' Inappropriate hilarity bubbled up in her.

'Good question,' said Richard. 'The ground's frozen solid.' In the event, they wrapped him in a blanket and stored him in the shed until the earth was soft enough to dig.

★

The thaw, when it eventually arrived towards the end of February, coincided with the worrying news that Marjorie was suffering from a bad bout of bronchitis. 'She sounds very poorly.'

'Does she smoke?' said Richard.

'I've no idea.' The inadvisability of smoking had become quite a theme of late. 'I think she could use a hand. Can you spare me for a while?'

'Of course,' Richard said, bashing the egg in his eggcup. 'Stay as long as you need.'

'I may have to be away for my birthday.'

'Not to worry.' He smiled to himself. 'I'm not promising anything, but you might find a little surprise waiting for you when you get home.'

9

Since Julia's first visit, the flat in Primrose Hill had shed all traces of family life. The tea crates were long gone, and so was the spill of powder on the chest of drawers. In the children's room, the nursery paper had been painted over, the three little cots had been shifted into the attic, and Dougie had set up a study for himself. Downstairs the furniture had been rearranged. Overall, the effect was more atelier than home and hearth.

'I'm afraid I had to give him your address.'

Dougie came across from one of the shelved alcoves, where he had been searching for a book by Jung he wanted to show her, in a continuation of a discussion they'd been having about the symbolism of the Tarot. He sat down on the arm of her chair and brushed the hair back from her cheek.

'What have you told him?'

'I said I'm staying with a friend who's been ill and that we have a lot of catching up to do.'

He laughed. 'That's one way of putting it. What's this friend called?'

'Marjorie.'

'No,' he said, shaking his head. 'I'm sorry. I don't like the name. I'll be a Madeleine or a Marion, but I refuse to be a Marjorie.'

'Luckily Richard doesn't suspect anything,' said Julia.

He got up abruptly. 'I don't like the name Richard either,' he said, and went back to the shelves, where he stood pulling out one book after another and shoving them back into place as if they annoyed him.

She was going to respond, but thought better of it.

Then he turned. 'What do you want, Sinclair?' The nickname came with none of its usual amused tenderness.

'What do you mean?' A pulse beat in her throat. 'This is all I want. To be here with you.'

'Do you?'

'Isn't it obvious?'

This is where he asks me if I'm still sleeping with my husband, she thought.

'I haven't seen you for months,' he was saying. 'Have you any idea how hard that's been?' His illness (Marjorie's illness) had left him thinner than ever.

'Of course I do,' said Julia, still uneasy. 'It's been hard for me as well. But let's not worry about that now. We've a whole week to look forward to.'

'A whole week,' he said drily. 'You should come with a ration book.'

Now she was in London, now she was with him, her birthday was neither here nor there. She knew his was in August and had the date circled in her diary. Those first times back at the cottage, when she had told him when hers was, he'd laughed. 'Pisces!' he'd said. 'How delightfully appropriate.' These were some of the inconsequential personal details that had seemed so significant at the time. Six months later, he showed no sign of remembering and she decided not to remind him; it would be tantamount to asking him outright to buy her a present or flowers, or spend money on her that he didn't have, or perhaps didn't want to spend on her.

Nevertheless, on the morning of her birthday, which was Friday, she was disappointed when he told her that there was to be a showing of the final cut of *They Also Serve* that evening and a party at a club in Wardour Street afterwards. The timing could have been better, she thought. But she was not about to tell him what day it was now or insist he miss the screening on her account; she had always found the kind of wheedling and manoeuvring that some women went in for false and demeaning. (It was also the case that she had never had to wheedle for anything; whatever she wanted or needed had always been provided.)

'Don't worry,' she said, watching him dress. 'I'll meet you afterwards if you want, or see you back here later. But of course you must go.'

'I intend to,' he said, 'and I'd very much like you to come with me.'

She hadn't expected the invitation and wasn't sure she welcomed it.

'What's the matter?' Dougie paused in the act of buttoning up his trousers. 'Not all of them bite.'

'They know your circumstances. They know you're married.'

'They're my work colleagues, Julia,' he said, 'not my moral guardians. What we do here is none of their business. Besides which,' he said, bending over to give her a kiss that tasted of mouthwash, 'I want to show you to yourself.'

'You mean the footage?' She was alarmed. 'But you promised you wouldn't use it. Anyone might see it.' Richard might see it, she thought.

'Don't be cross.' A half-smile. 'I couldn't bear not to. I've had nothing else to remember you by this winter.'

Julia had never been inside the Unit. Dougie had pointed it out to her once and had told her the story of the building's colourful past, little else, so she didn't know what to expect when she arrived that evening. Through the pedimented entrance was a squarish hall where a number of people were talking, overspills from the room on the left where the main gathering was.

This was overwhelmingly male; perhaps four or five other women out of sixty or so. The atmosphere was collegiate, the smell industrial, the surroundings institutional. Dougie was embedded in a group in the far corner of the room, animated, gesturing and oblivious of her arrival. She went over to a trestle table by the blacked-out windows and accepted a weak gin from a plump, pimply lad who was serving the drinks. Then a person she did recognize, Frank the camera operator, came over and began to talk to her about Dougie, which was the one topic they had in common, apart from the topics everyone had in common, namely the war and the weather.

Frank was concealing something or other behind a large man's affability. 'You'll be pleased when you see how he's used the footage he shot of you. It's slotted right into place.' He gave her a sidelong glance.

She didn't plan on seeing the footage. She planned on putting her hands over her face when the time came. 'Who is he talking to?'

Frank blew out his cheeks. 'The short bloke is Quentin Cheeseman, a big noise in the MOI and between you and me a complete and utter ass. The stroppy-looking person is the boss, Macleod, and next to him is Travis, who shot some of the film. The tall one is Basil Meers, the editor. You want to watch out for his wife.' Frank nodded in the direction of a woman in a busy print dress on the fringes of the group, who was burrowing away in her handbag. 'Sylvia's a great friend of Barbara's.'

Another sidelong glance, this time more calculating. 'You been in London long?'

'About a week.'

From across the room came Dougie's shout of laughter.

'Good to see him back on form,' said Frank. 'He's been seventeen kinds of miserable all winter. And Dougie miserable you *don't* want to know.'

After that, he introduced her to a few others, whose names and jobs she found hard to keep track of, then people began to drift towards the stairs and the lift, heading for the screening room. Dougie materialized by her side and draped his arm round her shoulders, which attracted attention. He was excited, yet underneath she sensed tension, wound tight like a spring. He'd had a haircut.

'You look wonderful,' he said.

'Thank you.'

'I haven't seen that dress before.'

This amused her. He hadn't seen most of her dresses.

'Mmm. And smell wonderful, too.'

'*L'Heure Bleue.* I bought it this afternoon.'

'*L'Heure Bleue,*' he said. 'My favourite time of day. Good choice. It suits you.'

The film was short, under half an hour, and its tone was established at the beginning with a line or two of commentary that made reference to the previous war. 'And now we must fight again.' Ordinary men and women filling sandbags, distributing gas masks, marshalling chattering schoolchildren through alien streets, raising barrage balloons on long anchored cables, joking in canteens, working on production lines, standing and staring out over the sea beside 'our old island defences' (her!), peering in shop windows, putting up blackout, hurrying into a shelter as a siren wailed a false alarm.

It wasn't what you'd call propaganda, not exactly. The real world, with all its shadings and uncertainties, was too present for that.

The lights came up. 'Did you see yourself, Sinclair?'

But he was soon surrounded and she never got the chance to answer, or to tell him how proud of him she was.

The Paradiso in Wardour Street was a hot, noisy basement with midnight-blue walls and a silver-foiled ceiling. When they came down the stairs, 'Begin the Beguine' was crackling on the gramophone. The bar was a hatch at the far end, where a tired, heavy-lidded blonde in a tight dress took pleasure telling people she couldn't serve them the drinks they had asked for and sold them warm champagne at extortionate prices instead. Around the perimeter of the room were a few tables. No one sat at them, although some people sat on them, which led to breakages. A far cry from the yacht club, thought Julia.

Macleod had gone home after the screening. Now others arrived, girlfriends, wives, guests, some dressed up, some dressed down, one of them a man in pink trousers who clearly 'batted for the other side', as Richard would have put it.

Dougie was buoyed up. When he introduced her to Travis and Basil Meers, she had the sense he was showing her off, and not in the way a man normally showed off a woman but in the way a man showed off a valued colleague. This acknowledgement that she was in some sense part of their endeavour excited her.

'And this is Mr Cheeseman,' said Dougie. 'He's the man from the Ministry.'

'Pleased to meet you,' said Cheeseman. He was short, balding and had the habit of raising himself on the balls of his feet when he wanted to get a point across. This was in most sentences.

Julia asked him what he thought of the film.

Cheeseman inclined his head. 'It has a good deal of merit. Perhaps it's been a little long in production, however. In wartime one must respond rather more quickly to events.'

The production delays that had beset the film had been the MOI's doing. Chiefly these had centred on the script, with the Ministry insisting on inserting chunks of wordy exposition into the voiced-over commentary, in the 'public interest', which Dougie had battled to take out again.

'It was Miss Sinclair who came up with the title,' said Dougie. 'And the title was what gave us the shape.'

Julia smiled to herself at how he had unmarried her.

'Milton,' said Cheeseman. 'Very good.'

He might have been praising a schoolgirl for a Latin declension, or having her hat on straight. Julia, who knew about the script wrangles and was feeling mischievous after champagne, said that she thought the commentary was admirably restrained. 'It treats the audience as adults, not children. In fact, you almost didn't need it at all. We're all so sick of being hectored in leaflets.'

Cheeseman gave a quick, tight smile. 'It is always interesting to meet a woman with a mind of her own.'

'Pompous ass,' said Dougie, after Cheeseman had left. 'And, what's worse, it looks like we're going to be working for him rather than simply answering to him. But at least we're still in business for now. Do you want to go home?'

She nodded.

'I'll get your coat.'

★

95

In the Ladies, Julia realized she was a little tight. She splashed water on her wrists, glimpsed her flushed, happy face in the mirror, then went into the lavatory and drew the bolt.

Behind the door, she heard a couple of women come in, the swish of their dresses, the snaps of their handbags and powder compacts. A hiss of atomized scent.

'Did you see her?'

'I did. On the screen and in the flesh.'

'And what did you think?'

'Well, say what you like about Dougie, he's got good taste,' said the other.

'Oh, she's pretty enough,' said the first. 'But Barbara, now Barbara has style.'

'If you admire that kind of thing. She's always seemed rather brittle to me.'

'Is it any wonder? What the poor love has had to contend with over the years would try the patience of a saint.'

The powder compacts were snapped shut.

'Yes, I've often wondered how she stands it.'

'Oh,' said the first, 'he strays, but he's like all men. He only strays so far. He knows which side his bread is buttered on.'

There was a shove at the door. 'Never mind. Let's go back. I can wait.'

Julia came out of the lavatory. In the mirror her eyes were huge dark pits.

They went home in a cab. All the way she stared out of the window at the zebra-striped wartime city, black streets faintly lit here and there by shaded torches and hooded headlamps that picked out the white cautionary banding painted on kerbs and bollards and lamp posts.

Barbara had style, did she? A wife might be in Canada, but she was still a wife. And what about the other women she'd had to 'contend with'? Who were they? How many had there been? Did they have style too? She obviously had none.

'I think you've had a little too much to drink,' said Dougie, as they came into the flat. 'I'll make us some supper.'

The flat was cold. The fire was unlit. She huddled in one of the club chairs and kept her coat on. The cat threaded itself through her legs: they had reached an uneasy truce, she and the cat. Downstairs, she could hear Mrs Tooley, who she'd now met twice and hadn't liked on either occasion, riddling out the grate. Outside, a shrill whistle and the distant sound of a train.

A few minutes later Dougie appeared with a couple of plates. She put away her handkerchief. It was his evening and she wasn't going to spoil it. But she felt like spoiling it.

'Something wrong with my scrambled eggs?' he said.

The eggs had the texture and consistency of small bits of rubber. 'You're a better film-maker than chef.'

'You can talk,' said Dougie with a smile. They ate out most evenings, because Julia didn't know how to cook; she only knew how to instruct cooks. He remembered her asking which days his char came and being surprised when he couldn't stop laughing.

'Basil was quite taken with you.'

'That's nice.' Unlike his wife. Julia was almost certain it had been Sylvia she had overheard in the lavatory.

'He thought you were perceptive.' As did Dougie, surprisingly so: the comment she had made to Cheeseman about the film not needing a commentary had set his mind fizzing.

'Yes, and I do know my Milton.'

'What's the matter?'

She shook her head. 'Nothing.'

From the twin of her chair Dougie said, 'Sitting separately is a bore.' He came across the room, took her plate and put it on the floor. Then he reached into his pocket, drew out a small box and placed it in her lap. An address in High Holborn was scrolled in gold letters on the top.

She looked up. 'What's this?'

'Open it,' he said, perching on the armrest.

She opened it. Inside, on a velvet cushion, was a brooch, about an inch in diameter, a circle of garnets set in gold. The dark red stones were like little pinpricks of blood.

'Happy birthday, Sinclair,' said Dougie.

She burst into tears.

He held her, waited out her crying, then drew her coat aside and pinned the brooch to her dress. 'Leave him. It's a waste for us to be apart. Can't you see that?' He wiped her face with his handkerchief. 'People fall in love every day. You have to stop feeling guilty about it.'

She traced her finger round the circle of stones. Love. It was his first mention of the word.

IO

Peter was worried his mother was sick. Ever since he'd come home for the Easter holidays, she hadn't been herself. There was a strange look on her face all the time. She wasn't paying any attention to him. As an only child, he wasn't used to being ignored. She wasn't paying any attention to the new puppy either.

Mothers did die. They died in books, and they died in real life.

Last term, Oulton's mother had got sick and the first time Oulton had known about it was when he had been summoned to the headmaster's study to be told she was dead. The news had got round Plantagenet. It wasn't supposed to, but it did. Afterwards everyone avoided Oulton and pretended not to hear him crying. You weren't supposed to cry in Plantagenet. They cried a bit in Windsor, but Windsor was a wet sort of house and always came last.

Peter wondered if they would avoid him too if his mother died. They probably would. He began to dread going back to school and being summoned to the headmaster's study. He could picture it. The cups of tea and the niceness.

These days his mother was always playing the piano and what she played was always sad. When he was younger she had tried to teach him to play but he wasn't good at it. The notes wouldn't sort themselves out. He was good at cricket and maths. He was bad at geography, but that was because they had a rotten teacher, Mr Beadell, who threw chalk at them when they got a capital wrong.

'Going out now,' he said, over the breakfast table.

His mother was reading a letter. The new puppy was scratching herself in the old dog's basket, which was surrounded by newspaper.

'Going out now,' he said again.

99

She looked up and smiled, but the smile was not in her eyes. She didn't even ask where he was off to. 'Have a nice time,' she said.

The puppy whined. Julia picked up the small warm round body, opened the back door and set her down outside. Wet brown eyes beseeched hers. Mabel: her birthday surprise. Not you, too, she thought. Don't you reproach me.

She closed the door and had a sudden yearning for her mother, her thickened arthritic knuckles, her dry *papier poudré* skin, the voice that still came out of the mirror to issue judgements. 'Patent is dreadfully common.' 'I do think a little colour at the neck brightens the face.' 'You could do anything if you put your mind to it.' She wanted her mother so badly, but she didn't want to hear what she would have had to say to her.

'Julia, would you mind playing something else?' said Richard, coming through to the drawing room from his study. 'You've played that piece three times.'

'That piece' was Chopin's 'Raindrop Prelude'. She rested her hands on the keys. 'Have I? I'm sorry.'

'It's hard to concentrate.'

'Of course. I don't know what I was thinking.'

The 'Raindrop Prelude'. One day during the week she'd spent with Dougie they'd happened to be passing the Bechstein showroom in Wigmore Street, and he'd insisted they go in. 'I'm assuming you have no strong objections to German instruments,' he'd said as they went through the taped-up plate-glass doors with their bronze handles.

The assistants in the showroom had fussed around; sales were down on account of the war and there was a surplus of stock. The first piano she tried had a split case.

'How do you know?' said Dougie.

'You can hear a buzzing.'

Dougie said, 'I can't hear a buzzing.'

'There is a buzzing,' said an assistant, nodding.

The second piano was all right, as far as it went. But the third one sang. She had sat down then and played the Chopin, a piece she had known by heart since girlhood. The sweet, sad truth of it, the drumming rain, had borne her away and, when she came back to herself, there was a little ripple of applause from the assistants and a stout woman in a felt hat who had wandered in from the street.

'You are a constant source of amazement,' Dougie had said, shaking his head.

Now she became aware that her husband was staring at her from the doorway.

'What's the matter?' she said.

'You're wearing that brooch again.'

'Am I?'

'Where did you get it?'

'I told you the other evening. Marjorie gave it to me when I was in London by way of a thank-you. It used to belong to her mother.'

For Richard, most instances of wrongdoing were as banal as the motives that lay behind them. It was an occupational hazard of his profession that you became a little jaundiced in that respect. If he had little to do with out-and-out criminality on a daily basis, other mortal sins were well represented in his filing cabinets: greed, envy, muddle and stupidity – weaknesses of all kinds.

A little jaundiced he might have been, but he was more than capable of seeing past the surface of things: in his working life he had to be. Lately, however, he had found himself forced to exercise this skill where it had never been required before, which was to say at home. His wife was behaving oddly.

Julia was a devoted mother. There was no doubt about that whatsoever. Yet this Easter, Peter came home and the sun failed to shine for her. Her attention was elsewhere. There was a great deal of moping and piano-playing. In short, she was behaving exactly as she usually behaved in the first week or so after their son went back to school – what Richard called her 'blue period'. For one of these to coincide with the holidays made no sense at all. It was as if the calendar had gone topsy-turvy.

And who could ignore a puppy?

But it was a conversation he had with Fiona that finally solidified his disquiet into suspicion. The week after Easter he ran into her on the high street. Later, he wondered if she had been waiting for him.

Richard was a little wary of Fiona. She was Julia's friend, and women talked to one another. Then there had been the way Geoffrey had repeatedly made a fool of her over some secretary or another, which struck him as unsavoury.

Julia always laughed about how elliptically Fiona spoke, as if her thoughts were racing on ahead and it was up to you to join the dots. It was the same on this occasion. After a meandering preamble he couldn't quite follow, she made the odd suggestion that he should take Julia away on holiday.

'A little break. Before they stop us from going anywhere. I think it would do her the world of good to be spoiled a little,' said Fiona. 'I don't know whether you've noticed, but she doesn't seem to be herself lately.' She glanced to one side. 'In my experience, getting away on your own, just the two of you, can be just the ticket.'

Richard was bemused. Why should Fiona concern herself with their holiday arrangements? Then on the way home, somewhere between the florist's and the greengrocer's, he joined the dots in a different fashion and the floor fell out of his life.

In my experience. Fiona's experience of married life, as he understood it, was one of repeated betrayal.

Jazz. Smoking. That brooch. To cap it all, the way she was behaving to Peter. Singly, perhaps explicable. Together, perhaps a pattern. A nasty little worm in his brain suggested that Julia's trips to London might be part of the same picture.

Suspicion is torture to those who keep their minds in order and their emotions well in check. Suspicion demands evidence. Sunday afternoon, when his wife was out, Richard went looking for it.

He found nothing in the little bureau she used as a desk, except his own self-loathing in searching it. Nothing in the canterbury where she kept her sheet music. Nothing in her wardrobe or under the felt-lined tray of her jewellery box. Each successive location a sickening reproach to his lack of faith in her.

He was on the point of lifting up the mattress of their bed – something Julia had once said about Fiona's daughter hiding her diary had sprung to mind – when he sat down on it instead and applied his mind to the problem.

If I were Julia, he thought, where would I put something I didn't want anyone else to find? Where is off limits to me, to Harry, to Peter? Where would none of us dream of intruding on her privacy? (And yet all the while, as he was asking himself these questions, he was convinced there was nothing to find, could be nothing to find. Of course not, because she was his dearest wife and he loved her.)

He got up from the bed and went over to the wardrobe again, where he turned out all her hatboxes and shoeboxes. Nothing but hats and shoes.

On her dressing table beside the jewellery box was a bottle of perfume, *L'Heure Bleue*, which she had brought back from London. He unstoppered it. She always smelled of it nowadays.

And that was when the back of his mind told him where to look.

The bottom drawer of the dressing table on the right-hand side was where she kept what he described to himself as her 'women's things'. He eased the drawer open, as if to shield his own ears from any proof of what he was doing, and could almost taste his disgust.

'Modess' said the blue-and-white packet. It was half full of sanitary towels. 'Modess' said the blue-and-white packet underneath. It was stuffed with letters. Letters from Marjorie.

'I did warn you, darling,' said Fiona. 'Repeatedly.' Rain trickled down the Regency windows with their fine glazing bars. 'You should have listened to me and put a stop to this months ago.'

Julia, trying to square circles in a pretty chintzy sitting room with striped wallpaper and amusing cushions, cried into her teacup. She had said nothing to Fiona about the conversation that she'd overheard in the club; that would mean lifting the rock under which she'd buried it.

'I love him so much. So much. What am I going to do?'

'Are you sure this is love, darling?'

'What else could it be?' said Julia.

Fiona lit a cigarette. 'Lust, for a start.'

Julia didn't want to hear this. 'He wants me to leave Richard.'

Fiona shook her head. 'Are you completely mad? You hardly know the man.'

'I didn't say I would,' said Julia. 'But I'll lose him if I don't find a way of being with him more often.' Here she was being somewhat disingenuous. If her week with Dougie had taught her anything, it was that she could no longer stow him into a compartment that she opened whenever it took her fancy and kept closed the rest of the time. She blew her nose.

It wasn't that she had any difficulty imagining what it would be like to live with him. Over the past months, she'd entertained that fantasy often enough to taste it and feel it and find space for her clothes in his wardrobe. Her imagination was even powerful enough to bring Peter along with her; she pictured Dougie teaching him about filming and chess. What was unthinkable was the rest: the shame, the scandal, the pain she would cause Richard. 'Oh God, I just don't know what to do.'

Fiona understood the loss her friend was dreading. It was the same loss that drove her even now, five years since Geoffrey had died, to sleep with his jacket on bad nights, although it had long ago stopped smelling of him. But losing a husband of many years was one thing, losing a lover you shouldn't have taken in the first place quite another. 'Sometimes, darling, I do want to shake you.'

Avril, Fiona's younger daughter, bounced into the sitting room in a horsey way, took in the scene over the teacups and backed out again in a manoeuvre worthy of dressage.

'Does Richard suspect anything?'

'He hasn't the first idea.' Through blurred eyes Julia stared out of the blurred window, crumpling her handkerchief in her fingers.

Fiona reached across to grasp her hands. 'Then listen to me. It's not too late to put this behind you. By some miracle, so far you've not been found out. Put a stop to it here and now and go away for a few days with Richard. Just the two of you. Make a fresh start.'

It was the same advice she had given Richard, a suggestion she had made, she told herself, entirely for Julia's benefit. What Fiona did not admit to herself was her growing fear that she might be discarded too, passed over for a ridiculous affair that was bound to end badly. Now, whenever they saw one another, which was less frequently, another person was in the room, breathing in all the air. In other words, Fiona was both jealous and lonely.

'Promise me you'll think about it.'

Julia nodded. There were no answers, she thought, no comfort anywhere.

It was Monday night, a week later, and Harry had roasted a chicken for 'the last supper' before Peter returned to school. (Meat rationing, recently introduced, had enforced a scaling down of the tradition from beef: even the chicken had not been easy to come by.) Julia came into the dining room and flinched at the sight of the bird sitting plump and brown among its trimmings. She had lost her appetite and all track of time. The occasion dismayed her on both counts.

Richard pulled out her chair. 'Thank you,' she said, then nodded at her son across the table. 'Isn't this lovely?'

He nodded back, his hair slicked, his face shining clean.

'I feel as if I've hardly seen you this holiday,' she said, shaking out her napkin from its bone ring and smoothing it on her lap. 'Have you enjoyed it?'

Peter did not know how to answer this. 'Yes, thanks.'

Harry brought in the gravy boat and a dish of peas. Richard slapped the knife against the steel and carved.

'Just a little for me, please.'

Peter's eyes flitted to her face.

Moments passed when no one uttered a word. If Julia had been fully present, she might have noticed the silence and said something to fill it. But Dougie had found his way into the dining room and was taking up all her attention.

Harry swung through the door to collect the plates. Julia's, with its pushed-around food, she registered with a disapproval that came out as a clatter of cutlery and crockery that clearly said: 'waste'.

'I've baked a cake, if anyone's the slightest bit interested.'

'How could we not be interested in your cake, Harry,' said Richard to her departing back.

Harry returned with the cake, which she set down. 'Don't blame me if it's not as light as maybe. I've had to stretch the sugar and all sorts.' She paused. 'These are the last sultanas left in England.'

They ate the cake out of duty, although it tasted no different from others they had eaten for pleasure.

'Well, you're all packed,' Julia said to Peter.

'Thanks, Madre.'

'Thank Harry. She did it mostly.' She got up and pushed back her chair. 'I'll come up and say goodnight in a while.'

'Where are you going?' said Richard.

'Out for a bit. I have a head.'

'It's raining.'

'It doesn't matter.'

Julia was sitting at her dressing table brushing her hair when Richard came into the bedroom. Over the months, she had schooled herself not to betray the whereabouts of Dougie's letters by so much as a glance at the drawer where they were hidden, but she felt their existence as heat emanating from it.

'How was your walk?'

'Wet.' The halyards clinking and clanking, the black, deserted cobbled streets, the salty gusts funnelling up from the harbour rocking the creaking pub signs.

Richard's eyes met her mirrored ones, like a hairdresser. She had the sense he was waiting for something.

'Did you say goodnight to Peter?'

'Of course. Why do you ask?'

'You didn't seem to take very long. Didn't you read to him?'

'Not tonight.'

'Whore' crouched in his head like a toad.

The next day they woke up to find the war had stopped pretending it wasn't one. Reports came of the German invasion of Norway and Denmark, no less sudden, no less shocking for the measured tone of the BBC bulletin. Within a matter of hours, swastikas were flying in Copenhagen.

Only Harry, in constant communication with the astral plane, was not surprised. The spirits had warned her about it, she said; like all such warnings she received from the other side, these tended to be announced *post facto*.

The evening broadcast was over. Richard switched off the wireless and poured himself a drink. A second drink, and a large one, Julia noticed. This was unusual. So was the way he knocked it back. Harry had gone to bed early, but not before checking underneath it. The bad news was telling on them all.

Even Peter, she thought. That morning, when they were packing the car with his trunk and tuck box, he'd made a terrible scene, stamping his feet like a two-year-old. Then, when they had pulled up outside the school, he'd sat in the back seat in his over-large blazer, arms folded, refusing to get out.

'Come on, old boy,' Richard had said. 'Don't be daft.'

'Mummy,' said Peter.

She turned in her seat to give him a pat. 'Hurry along, darling. Your father needs to get back to work. Be good, and I'll see you soon.'

On the way home, they drove past an old man walking along the road, red-faced and crooked, carrying a bunch of flowers in a shaking hand. The incongruity of age and blooms would have intrigued Dougie, thought Julia, saving up the image to describe to him.

Now, she thought, her eyes staring unfocused at the blackout as if it were a blank cinema screen where he might appear, all she wanted to hear was what he was making of these invasions; on no real foundation, she had the sense that talking to him would make the news easier to bear. All the conversations she had these days, all the meaningful ones, were with him: in person, on the page or in her head.

If this is the case, she thought, surely it means I should be with him. Surely this tells me where I belong. But just as she reached the brink of a decision, she shrank from it.

It was raining again. Water coursed down the gutter, a desolate sound. When she turned her gaze back to the still, lamp-lit room, she saw that her husband was watching her. Instinctively she rose from her seat to go upstairs, where her face could not be read.

'Sit down, Julia,' said Richard.

'I'm tired, darling, I'm going to bed.'

'Sit down.'

Something is not right, said her body, which began to tremble and chill. 'Richard, please, it's been a long day.'

'*Marjorie*,' he said, his eyes hard like marbles. 'Let's call her by her real name, shall we?'

The walls bulged in and out. The floor pitched and tipped.

'I don't know what you mean.'

He intercepted her at the doorway and caught hold of her wrists.

'What are you doing, Richard?' Her mind was chaos.

'"D" for David, is it? Or "D" for Dick? Let's have a name for this "D" who writes such filth to you. This *director*.'

The letters. Oh God, she thought, he's found the letters. And it was clear that he had read every word of them.

'Please let go.'

'Name him.'

She named him.

'Oh yes, now it comes back to me. Birdsall. How ridiculous.'

She began to cry.

'Tears, Julia? Or would you rather I called you Sinclair?'

'Please, Richard, you have to understand –'

'Spare me the squalid details.' He was still clenching her wrists. She could feel her bones under her skin. 'I've had a bellyful of those.'

'When did you find them?' Her voice cringed.

'What difference does it make?'

She saw then what she had done, who she was in his eyes. The two lives she had been at such pains to keep in separate compartments snapped together and became one.

'How could you do it?' he was saying. 'Didn't I give you enough? Didn't I provide you with a roof over your head, a family, everything you could possibly want?'

'I'm so sorry, Richard. I'm so sorry. Please don't shout.'

The shouting went on, repetitively.

'Do you take me for a complete fool? Seven months you've been carrying on with this man behind my back. Seven months!'

She tried to pull her hands free. 'Mayn't we talk?' She wanted to explain that she had been unable to help herself, that she had not chosen to fall in love, that she had been unable to choose to fall out of it. 'I didn't want to hurt you, Richard, I didn't, I truly didn't.'

'You disgust me.' He pushed her away so roughly her head hit the door jamb.

You could hit your wife, you could beat her: it was permissible and commonplace. Yet this small act of violence stunned them for what they had provoked in each other. Underneath lay scenes of smashings-up and melodrama, and it was no comfort to her that she had placed them there.

'Get out.' His face was white. 'Get out of this house! I never want to see you again!'

Time collapsed. She ran from the room right into Harry, the housekeeper's look of bewildered dismay, hair net denting her forehead, as sudden and clear as a snapshot in her mind. Shock propelled her up the stairs, where she snatched at things without knowing which things she was snatching at. Shock flung her down the stairs and into the rain.

London, 1944

Peter was building a Meccano railway on the stairs. It was wonky and rattled. He tightened the bolts.

He was running down the beach with the dog. She tried to follow him, but her feet wouldn't move.

From above came a narrow probing beam of light. Someone called. She heard their thin cries.

The planes were coming closer and closer. A rumble of engines. Crashes and bangs. Whines and whizzes. Shrieks and thuds.

Dust trickled down her throat and choked her.

She was playing the piano. Her fingers hurt. The piano made crashes and bangs.

She was carrying a piano down a London street. It was heavy.

She was pinned. The light went out.

There has to be a way out of here, she thought.

II

Chalk Farm Road. Grimy, down-at-heel, not a green field in sight. The sort of joke that London's long history told repeatedly.

Laden with laundry and shopping, mindful of her handbag and whether its clasp was done up (it was), Julia headed back in the direction of the Underground. It had been cloudy all morning; now the sun came out.

This did little to improve the view. She was not a casual visitor to this part of town any more; she was no longer a tourist, with the tourist's arm's-length curiosity about how the other half lived and private relief that clean, quiet lodgings in a better district were waiting once she had done with being intrepid. Which meant, however uncomfortable the thought might be, that the view was in some sense her view.

She came past the workingmen's hostel, a dirty grey building with terracotta exhortations under the roofline interspersed by low reliefs of sooty sunflowers. As ever, it struck her as both ominous and contaminating; contaminating because to set eyes on it was to somehow imagine yourself in it. Further along, knowing children armed with sticks swarmed out of a yard chasing a dog with a bald tail.

The pavement was crowded near the Tube entrance and tram stop. People were shouldering past each other, chatting, smoking, checking their appearances in shop windows, some smiling.

'The British way of dealing with a crisis,' Dougie had said.

Pretend it's not happening, thought Julia, averting her eyes from the headline on the placard, blocking her ears to the newsvendor's cries. 'Dutch surrender! Dutch surrender!'

Five minutes later she was turning into their road – Dougie's road – and resting her eyes on the wide smooth greenness of the park. It was a relief to be home, if this indeed was home, which she supposed it must be, as nowhere else was. She went up the path and let herself in.

At the back of the passage came the creak of a door and a scuffle along the cracked encaustic tiles.

'Miss Sinclair?' The 'Miss' stressed. It was Dougie's downstairs neighbour.

Julia made for the stairs and sped up them as fast as her burdens would allow. A brass rod rattled loose and she caught her heel, where she always caught her heel, in the worn bit of frayed carpet near the landing. The laundry toppled out of her arms.

'Miss Sinclair?'

Too late.

'Yes, Mrs Tooley,' she said, massaging her ankle. 'What is it?'

The woman was wearing a stained floral overall and men's slippers. From above, you could see the chalky line of her centre parting where the black dye had grown out.

'You had a bath this morning.'

Two and a half tepid inches in a stained tub with chipped enamel. 'Yes,' said Julia, over the balustrade. 'I did.'

'And yesterday.'

'What of it?'

'Them geysers don't like it if you fire them up that often. They been known to blow.'

'Have they?' Julia hunted around in her handbag for her latchkey.

'Another thing,' said Mrs Tooley. 'You want to stomp of an evening, you go down the dancehall. Some of us find it hard enough to sleep these days.'

'Thank you for telling me,' said Julia. 'I'll bear it in mind.' She unlocked the door and went into the flat.

Inside she was greeted by a tang of paint, the dead used air of extinguished cigarettes and, more distantly, a library scent of old bindings and printed paper. Her trunk, which she had retrieved a fortnight ago, remained half unpacked on the landing. It was well over a month since her husband had thrown her out, and Primrose Hill was taking some getting used to. Everything was.

At times like these she felt a profound disorientation which love was doing nothing to alleviate. Richard she did not miss, so she told herself repeatedly – how could she, when it was Dougie who made her blood sing? Yet during the hours when she was alone, her marriage, the solidity of it, could not be forgotten so easily. Nor could the guilt.

Her instinct was to play her mood out of herself – Schumann would have done the trick, Beethoven would have been even better – but her instinct was like some sort of phantom limb, because there was no piano. Instead, she went upstairs, threw the laundry on the bed and took her shopping into the kitchen.

A stack of cups and plates sat on the Africa stain in the sink. The cups were a shabby sort of brown inside. She didn't understand why this should be so. It wasn't as if she didn't wash them. How dreary it was doing dishes. You did them and then you had to do them again.

She scrubbed the potatoes with a wooden-handled brush worn flat in the middle. (Was there some knack to perking up the bristles?) Then she unwrapped the plump blue-black fish and placed them on a plate with a dish on top, as the cat was showing an interest.

Half past four said her watch. She should do the washing-up. Or dust? But dusting never seemed to make any difference; the rattling sashes, loose in their frames, saw to that. The ancient carpet sweeper was useful only as a form of indoor exercise. Instead she went along to Dougie's study and pushed open the door.

Here was the source of the paint smell: a small canvas propped on a splattered easel in the corner, a little essay of fractured planes that didn't know what it wanted to be yet. What dominated the room, however, was a large felt-covered panel, rather like a substantial blackout blind, tacked up on one of the walls that flanked the window. On it were pinned drawings, scraps of illustrations torn out of magazines, newspapers, leaflets. At first sight you might think the arrangement was random. Look closer, and you saw the method in it. The curve of a woman's spine that echoed the swell of a hump-backed bridge, an advertisement for male support garments next to an escape artist trussed in his chains, a suite of images where a theme was teased out, looping up from a skipping rope via a washing line to an acrobat on a high wire.

He'd been working on it the previous evening when she'd poked her head round the door to say she was going to bed. 'What are you doing?' she'd said.

'Just keeping my eye in. Why don't you come and have a play?'

'It's rather late.'

'It's not that late.'

'I didn't get much sleep last night.'

'I'm well aware of it.' He drew up a chair for her, patted the seat.

'You are a hard taskmaster.'

'It's not my fault you inspire me.'

'Do I really?' she said, sitting down.

'Oh, you stimulate me in all sorts of ways,' he said.

In the end they had sat there for ages, fiddling around with torn paper, as absorbed as if they were completing a jigsaw on the prom deck of an ocean liner with land nowhere in view and nothing else to occupy their time, or like children who had invented a private game before tea which made no sense to anyone but themselves. Occasionally their hands would brush and Dougie would glance at her, wearing an expression she could not identify.

He pinned a scrap up on the board. 'Yes, yes, that goes better.'

'How about this?'

'No, let's leave that aside for the moment.'

'And this?'

'Ah, excellent. Echoes the Brâncuși.'

'Isn't it funny,' she said, 'how you can change the way you read an image just by putting something different next to it?'

Dougie shook his head. 'Sometimes, Sinclair, you say the most surprising things.'

In the light of day, as Julia stood tracing the connections on the board, it all seemed foolish. What was the point of creating anything – anything at all – when the world was hell-bent on destroying itself? When countries fell, armies retreated and refugees were machine-gunned as they fled? Better get a gun yourself, better fire it. Better still, get a tank.

Something Dougie had told her the other day insinuated itself into her head, something that someone who knew someone in the War Office had said, which was that there were rumours in high places about a negotiated peace. (She remembered, not so long ago, wishing she could discuss the news with him. That was before she discovered he had sources of information that supplemented the official broadcasts in ways that did not always make for reassuring hearing.)

'A negotiated peace?' she had said. 'What does that mean?'

'Essentially, jackboots in Whitehall,' said Dougie. 'In which case, Sinclair, we'll have to head for the hills and set about bomb-making. The Highlands, for preference. I've never liked Wales. Too wet in one way, too dry in another.'

At that moment, a noise distracted her and she went to the window. Down below in the narrow untended garden, she saw Mrs Tooley digging a hole under a laurel bush, heard the spade ring against stones. Then she saw her pick up a bundle wrapped in what looked like an old hearth rug and bury it in the ground.

Back home around the start of the war, there had been some talk of the vicar interring the candlesticks and communion plate. He had settled for locking the church instead. She wondered what Mrs Tooley was keeping safe from invaders. Fear was a taste on her tongue.

'Mackerel,' said Julia, setting down the plates.

'I can see that,' said Dougie. He had returned late from the studio and in the abstracted mood that told her he hadn't left it behind.

'The potatoes are a little overdone,' she said, 'and also a little underdone. I'm not quite sure why this should be. But I've given you the best ones.'

She sat down and pushed her damp hair back from her face. At least the fish were all right, nicely browned. She'd caught them just in time. There were only a couple of black bits.

'Mrs Tooley buried her valuables in the garden this afternoon. Well,' she said, with a false lightness – the British way of dealing with a crisis – 'I'm assuming they were her valuables. Unless they were body parts.' The woman seemed to her a likely murderess.

He was staring at his plate. 'You made this yourself.'

'I did,' she said. 'Although the peas, of course, are tinned.'

'Naturally.'

She forked a potato, which shot across the table. 'How did it go today?'

Dougie prodded his mackerel.

She retrieved the potato and ate a mouthful of peas, which tasted reliable, predictable. 'I collected your shirts. But I'm afraid they lost a handkerchief.'

She understood now that she had formed a wrong impression of his attitude to cleanliness. Scruffy clothes, dirty jerseys and so forth: these were what he wore on location, which made a kind of practical sense, although she suspected there was more to it than that. Otherwise, he was particular, not to say fastidious, about his collars and cuffs. Socks, not so much so.

'Julia,' said Dougie, 'did you clean these?'

'Of course,' she said. 'I washed them under the tap for ages. Some of the skin came off, but I don't think that matters.'

He prodded his mackerel again, which oozed. 'That's not the kind of cleaning I meant. You're supposed to remove the guts before you cook them.'

She stared at the fat fish on her plate.

'How on earth did you not know that?'

She waited for him to laugh off this mackerel debacle the way he laughed off her singed toast and her tinned meals – 'Canned Cuisine' was what he called them. When he didn't, a slow burn rose in her face.

'You might as well give these to the cat. They're inedible.' He pushed his plate across the table. 'By the way, the reason the potatoes were overdone *and* underdone is because you didn't cut them up into the same-sized pieces. It's basic physics.' He got up from his seat.

'Sorry.' Her smile felt like a guilty dog waving its tail. 'I always was useless at science.'

'Domestic science, clearly.'

That stung. 'Where are you going?'

He fumbled in his pockets. 'Have you any change?'

'Thruppence or so.'

'Thruppence?'

'They charged more for the washing this week.'

'God, Julia!' said Dougie. 'I gave you thirty shillings on Monday.'

'You gave me a pound.'

'It was thirty shillings. I remember it distinctly.'

It was a pound, thought Julia. 'London's expensive. The potatoes were ninepence. I'm sure they shouldn't have been as much as that.' In fact, she was not sure how much potatoes should cost. Until six weeks ago, she had never bought any.

'Money well spent.'

That stung too. 'You know, it would be much easier if we paid on account.'

Light blue touchpaper.

'Have you any idea how hard it is to find the rent every month?'

She had been warned about his temper, and now he was losing it she understood she had been wrong to discount the warning or to imagine it would never apply to her. He began shouting and waving his arms around.

Millions of women made millions of meals every day, ordinary working women eking out their husband's low wages. How could it be so fucking difficult. Couldn't she get a fucking book of recipes out of the library or something. He couldn't go on giving her money hand over fist and have it chucked in the bloody bin.

She stood and scraped the plates. This intransigent flat, which refused to clean itself or look after itself in any way. How was this now her responsibility? 'You cook, if it's so easy!' The words flew out of her mouth.

'Christ!' he said. 'So I'm to work all hours and toddle home to make your supper? Precisely how do you fill your time?'

Good question, thought Julia. She filled her time by waiting for him to come back.

'Standing in queues, for a start!' she said instead. 'Buying lavatory paper – it doesn't replace itself, you know!' (Which had been news to her.) 'Collecting your shirts from the laundry!' Your *fucking* shirts, she had been on the point of saying. 'Where are you going?'

The door banged behind him. Her heart was pounding; her cheeks were flushed. For two pins, she would have run after him and shouted in the street. Rowing, she thought, as a person who was new to the experience, was a bit thrilling, whether or not you had a leg to stand on. Frightening, too, and she burst into tears while the cat leapt on to the table and tore the mackerel to pieces, crunching the bones sideways in its thin needled jaws.

When she woke the next morning a little after dawn there was that jolt of mental correction when she realized she wasn't at home and that the man sleeping next to her wasn't her husband. Dougie had his back turned. When had he come back? Late, she supposed. She got up and he didn't move a muscle.

Down on the landing, decorated outside the kitchen with a slime of what the cat had been unable to digest, she knelt by her trunk and sifted through the remains of her former life. Her hair, grown long, fell over her face and she pushed it back with annoyance.

Clothes (winter and summer), sheet music, a few books, a few records, some shoes, some hats: an edited selection of a much more extensive collection of belongings.

She had returned to the house, not as a thief or ghost but as an unwilling participant in a game of Grandmother's Footsteps. When she let herself in, she had noticed there was a new doormat.

The sound of the door closing had brought Harry to the end of the hallway, where she stood half in and half out of shadow.

'Mrs C.' The housekeeper's eyes slid over her. Her mouth was set in a line, her expression guarded and accusatory.

Years of intimacy, no less warm for their formal basis, were gone, vanished without trace. Until then, it had not occurred to Julia that she might have shattered other loyalties.

'Mr C didn't mention you were coming.'

'I'm just collecting a few things. I arranged it with him.'

'Arranged' sounded amicable. Richard hadn't been amicable. Previously she would have said he had a forgiving nature. But previously there had been nothing for him to forgive.

'I see,' said Harry.

The wordless censure irked her. 'Don't worry, I'm not making off with the teaspoons.'

Or the piano. Richard had made that clear. She had thought it was hers, since she was the one who played it, but it turned out it was his, since he was the one who had bought it.

Harry sniffed and returned to the kitchen, from which direction came the wholesome aroma of a stockpot, its familiarity oddly unsettling.

Julia went from room to room, each indifferent to her inspection. The house hung on her like a dead man's coat. Perhaps it was bravado, or perhaps it was repudiation, but she found she wanted very little; some drawers she barely opened. Yet how spacious it all was, how clean, how orderly.

Harry came upstairs as she was removing a photograph of Peter from its silver frame. It dated from last summer and he was squinting into the sun.

Julia, conscious of scrutiny, put the photograph into her handbag. 'The negatives are in my desk drawer. He can always have another print made.' On impulse, she wrenched off her rings, the gold band and the solitaire, and dropped them on to the glass top of her dressing table, where they spun.

'Terrible vibrations in here,' said Harry. 'Terrible.' Lunch was not offered.

Eventually the trunk was packed, labelled and its carriage paid for. Before Julia left the house, seeking a more tangible talisman of her son, an old jumper or shirt perhaps, something that had his grubby-knee boy-smell, she tried the door to his bedroom. It was locked.

Now she sat on her heels running her fingers over the photograph. Part of what had been 'arranged' between her and her husband was Peter. Peter was to remain in ignorance of what she had done and where she had gone. Peter must be protected. To that end, she must continue writing to him as if nothing had happened, sending the letters care of Richard, who would forward them on with the right postmark. (Presumably after reading them.)

If this was a form of domestic censorship, it was one to which she had submitted without protest. Better than the alternatives: her husband telling his own version of events or, worse, her having to account for what to any nine-year-old must seem a desertion. He was much too young to understand or make sense of it all.

How keeping Peter protected from the truth was going to survive the half-term break was a problem they had left unexplored. But here the war had stepped in and solved it for them. As the situation in Europe worsened, boarding schools up and down the country, Crossfields included, cancelled all holidays for the foreseeable future, deeming it too dangerous to send children home, especially those who lived in main cities or coastal areas. Their own hostilities could therefore be concealed behind the exigencies of a much greater conflict. While none of this made her separation from her son any easier to bear, it did recast it in the light of the kind of rupture many families were enduring. After all, as Dougie kept reminding her, his own children were five thousand miles away.

'I suppose I must buy you a train ticket.'

She started and looked up.

Dougie, hair sticking up in some directions, flattened in others, had pulled on his trousers but was not wearing much else. (He didn't believe in dressing gowns or slippers, which were bourgeois.)

'Oh, are you throwing me out too?'

'Julia.'

She swept up her things and began stuffing them back in the trunk. 'It's hardly surprising. I can't cook, I can't clean, I can't keep house. I am unacquainted with the physics of potatoes. I'm obviously no use to you whatsoever.'

'Julia.' He made a move towards her, stepped in the cat sick and lifted his bare foot in disgust.

She slammed the lid of the trunk and sat on it. 'Why, I can fritter away a whole pound in five days.' Her gaze challenged him to disagree with this. He didn't. 'And, according to that foul woman downstairs, whose foul son creeps about spying on me, I take too many baths. Although I do pay for them. Admittedly with your money.' The geyser was coin-operated.

He ran his fingers through his hair until what was flat was upright, and vice versa. 'What's Kenny been doing?'

'He looks up my skirt.' She got up from the trunk, twisted her hair into a knot and made to brush past him.

'You can't blame him for that.'

'God!'

They stared at each other.

'I have a filthy temper.' He said this in the way you might say 'I'm five foot eleven' or 'My middle name is William.'

'I find I have a temper too.'

A half-smile. 'I daresay you didn't need one before.'

Their faces were inches apart.

'I can't give you the kind of life you're used to,' he said. 'But I had imagined you wanted a different one.'

'Perhaps not quite so different.' Tears pricked.

His finger traced the curve of her cheek.

'Where did you get to last night?'

His answer was to take her to bed.

A week went past. The Germans were in France, the BEF was cut off with their backs to the Channel, and they were having a party. A bottle party.

'What's a bottle party?' said Julia.

'Democratic,' said Dougie. 'And cheap.'

'There hardly seems cause for celebration.'

'Sitting on our own by the wireless won't change anything. Don't put your hair up tonight. I like it loose.'

The idea of hosting a party without Harry to make the cheese straws and preside over the drinks table dismayed her. As did the alarming people who came with their democratic bottles of Beefeater's and Bass. Film people like Frank and Basil, whom she knew. Painters, talkers, writers, whom she didn't, including a woman she kept catching sight of here and there throughout the evening who had a memorable if not an altogether pretty face and who always seemed to be staring at her.

At one point, handing round sandwiches, she found herself jammed in a corner with Frank's sister, a plotter in the Wrens, and a man with a wall eye who was holding forth about Norway, how the campaign had all been about controlling the supply of iron ore (with statistics), which was why losing it was such a disaster.

'Disaster, yes, but not solely nor primarily for that reason,' said Frank's sister, who was what Julia's mother would have called sturdily built and her father would have called opinionated.

'Do enlighten me,' said the man.

'Anchorages in fjords. Safe harbours out of the range of our reconnaissance. Control of the North Atlantic. Hitler means to starve us. If he doesn't invade us first.'

'Sandwich?' said Julia.

The man with the wall eye said no and moved away.

'Bad loser,' said Frank's sister. She held out her hand. 'Mattie. I don't think we've properly met.'

'Julia,' said Julia.

'So I've heard.' Mattie gestured at the blackout blinds. 'Dougie's doing, I take it. The end of civilization as we know it.'

The blackout blinds were covered in chalk drawings. Fragments of classical temples, triumphal archways and broken columns were set in a plane of severe perspective out of which grew stunted trees, their roots cracking through a pavement that tapered to an inexorable vanishing point. A lone female nude surveyed the blasted landscape.

'Yes, he spent all last night working on it.'

'Are those your breasts?' said Mattie. She had a full-throated, rounded voice, rather pleasant, if a little booming.

'I've no idea.'

'Here's betting they are.'

'Rather Paul Delvaux, don't you think?' said a young man who was threading his way over to them through the crowded smoky room, one arm held aloft to save his drink from spilling.

Paul Delvaux: Belgian surrealist, thought Julia, whose art education was now considerably advanced.

'Florian!' said Mattie. 'Have a fish-paste sandwich. They are really rather remarkably good if you're absolutely bloody famished.'

'Thank you no, darling.' Florian had cheekbones that looked like they were carved from marble, a flop of dark hair and a plump defined mouth. 'The only fishy substance I can tolerate is caviar.'

'Oh do stop pretending to be posh,' said Mattie. 'It's jolly irritating. Every bit as bad as my brother passing himself off as one of the proletariat. What do you pretend to be, Julia?'

Julia, who could not imagine where this was leading, said without much conviction that she didn't pretend to be anything. She was about to exercise the hostess's right to circulate when Dougie appeared and absently caressed the nape of her neck.

'Florian,' he said, 'where's Bernard? Is he putting in an appearance later?'

'No,' said Florian. 'He's in mourning for France.'

'Why?' said Julia, alarmed. 'Has France fallen?'

'Not that I've heard,' said Dougie.

'He should mourn a bit closer to home,' said Mattie. 'The way things are going.'

'Still,' said Florian, 'he mourns, on the chaise longue.' He mimed mourning for France on a chaise longue.

The corner of Dougie's mouth was twitching. 'That's a pity. I was hoping to introduce him to Julia. She's a pianist.'

'A pianist,' Florian said. 'How extraordinary.'

'I'm a little out of practice,' said Julia. 'I haven't got a piano at present.'

'Bernard has a baby grand. You must come and play it.'

'Bernard is a composer,' said Dougie. 'A very good one.'

'If you like a racket,' Mattie said.

'Not a racket,' said Florian. 'Atonal.' He turned to Julia. 'What lovely long stretchy fingers, darling. Tell me, do you play jazz at all? We dote on it. Or are you of the classical persuasion?'

Julia shook her head. 'Jazz is beyond my stars. I can't get the hang of it.'

'Don't be so hard on yourself, Sinclair,' said Dougie with a smile. 'There are no female jazz musicians that I can think of. Singers, yes, but not musicians.'

Some sort of commotion reached them from the other side of the room. It was Kenny and a few of his pals.

'How did they get in?' said Julia.

'I invited them,' said Dougie. 'Excuse me.'

Florian went after him.

'Surprisingly antediluvian these leftists,' said Mattie. 'There's a girl at my digs who plays boogie-woogie like a dream. Nonsense to make out it's anything to do with testicles. She'd teach you, if you asked her nicely.'

Breasts, testicles – whatever next? Julia came from the sort of family who said 'white meat?' and 'dark meat?' when carving a bird, to avoid the anatomical terms. At that moment she noticed that the woman with the memorable face, whose features were all individually a little too big for beauty, was still staring at her. 'Who is that person?'

Mattie followed her eyes. 'A glutton for punishment, among other things. Caro should have known better than to come.'

'What do you mean?'

'Nothing.' She glanced at her watch. 'Well, I'd better be off. My shift's in an hour. What line of war work are you in?'

'None at present.'

'*None?*'

'I've only been in London a month or so.' Six weeks, but still.

'In a month or so there might not be a London. Oh, look,' Mattie said, pointing at the blinds, 'the end of the end of civilization as we know it. All the chalk's come off.'

So it had. The drawings on the blinds were smudged and obliterated to head height. Someone began to sing *La Marseillaise*.

The next morning, a Saturday, they slept late. Julia rose first and went to make the tea. Briefly, a rumour of disquiet reached her from the previous evening, a trickle of water down the back called Caro. This was followed by another – something that Frank had said towards the end when he was drunk, something about Macleod leaving.

Then she collected the post.

'Fish-paste sandwiches,' said Dougie, propping himself against his pillow. 'How breakfasty.'

Julia set down the tray.

'What's the matter?' he said.

'Nothing.'

'Out with it.'

'I've heard from Richard.'

'Oh? And what does Adolf have to say for himself?'

She handed him the letter.

He read it through twice, then drew her across to him and kissed her forehead. 'I think it's time we found you a lawyer. One you're not married to.' He lit a cigarette and passed her the packet.

The letter, typed and undoubtedly carbon-copied, expressed in formal legal language Richard's intention of suing her for divorce and custody of their son, citing Mr Douglas Birdsall as co-respondent.

'It could be worse,' he said, casting it aside. 'He could have begged you to come back.'

'Would you have begged me to come back?'

'Obviously,' he said.

Divorce, co-respondents, petitions. Christ, he thought.

12

The Fitzroy Tavern was on the corner of Charlotte Street and Windmill Street, a big spit-and-sawdust sort of place, a bohemian haunt since the twenties. The Dog and Duck in Soho was where the Unit drank. Frank would be there, as he was most days. But Dougie didn't want to see Frank, or anyone else from the Unit. They were all twiddling their thumbs, shooting a bit of footage, fiddling about in the studio – everyone, including Travis. *They Also Serve* had not led to much, except a few training documentaries along public-information lines – *Keeping Rabbits for Extra Meat*, that sort of thing. Macleod had left and they were rudderless without a producer.

'And what are you having, my good sir?' said Pop, behind the bar.

'Pint of mild.'

'Right you are.' Pop leant on the tap, wheezing a little. 'Haven't seen you for a while.'

'No,' said Dougie.

'Andre's in,' said Pop. 'You'll find him at the back. Or not, as it takes you.'

'Cheers.'

Dougie had no desire to see Andre Masclin, who was a man of many projects and few completions. Instead, he took his pint to the front, where the engraved Victorian windows were further obscured by blast tape. Giddy times he had spent here in years past. Delia Krug had danced naked on a table. Then there was that odd chap who ate glass. Roaring nights, with the declaiming poets and artists and artistes and all the other riffraff London turned out of its pockets. This had been at a time when he had thought nothing of spending whole weeks in front of a blank canvas. Which was pretty much where he was now.

But his strongest memory of the Fitz was the day after Nell had been born. It had been a difficult delivery and she a bawling red scrap of a thing; Barbara touch and go there for a while. He had come from the Middlesex Hospital across the road to wet the baby's head, feeling the redundancy of the by-standing father, the guilt of the husband, and found himself in tears. You could cry in the Fitz. It was allowed. Everything was.

'Birdsall.'

Dougie glanced up and saw that Masclin was making his way across the pub in his direction. His heart sank. He was not in the mood for the man's particular brand of self-deception.

With his bluish-white skin and hooded eyes, Masclin was one of those people who don't look especially mammalian. He was clutching a tattered sheaf of pages and was accompanied by a man in his early forties who was vaguely familiar.

This turned out to be Julian Embry, an actor turned producer-director working under contract to Gaumont-British.

'Don't believe I've had the pleasure,' said Embry when Masclin introduced them. 'But I've heard of the Unit, of course.'

Embry had a suave sheen to him that wasn't altogether due to money, or health or good looks, although he was evidently in possession of all three. Dougie would have taken an instant dislike to him had he not already disliked him on principle – the principle being that he was in features.

Nor did he warm to the man when names, both industry and household, were dropped in a masquerade of complicity intended to convey dominance. (It was at this point that Dougie found it necessary to stand, if only to demonstrate a height advantage, and to lean back against the table and light a cigarette with a weariness that was real.)

'Tell me,' said Embry, 'how are you documentary chaps getting on without Macleod? I hear the MOI obstructionists did for him.'

'He was never happy behind a desk.'

'Quite,' said Embry.

Masclin asked Dougie what he was working on at present.

'Nothing' would have been the honest answer. 'This and that' is what he said. In any case, the question was merely an invitation to ask one back.

When he didn't, Masclin obliged. It appeared that the tattered sheaf of pages was a script he had written. *Up the Garden Path* was 'some way into development'.

'It's a comedy,' said Masclin.

'I should imagine it is,' said Dougie.

'At times like these,' said Masclin, 'the public needs to be entertained.'

Embry made a show of checking his watch. 'Ever thought of jumping ship, Birdsall? Diving, as it were, into the commercial sector?'

'Why should I do that?'

'It pays better, and we don't suffer as much interference.'

'No,' said Dougie. 'Not my kind of film-making.'

Embry shrugged. 'Each to his own. Call me old-fashioned but personally I prefer telling stories.' He handed Dougie a card. 'If you ever change your mind, do get in touch. We're always looking for people who know their way round a camera.'

This was an insult and was taken as such. After the pair of them left, Dougie sat tapping the card on the table, until its lower edge grew damp and wavily distorted in the wet rings on the table top.

Pop came by to collect his glass and began to talk about Dunkirk, as most people did that week in June, given half the chance. 'Marvellous boys.'

'Marvellous.' Dougie'd seen the newsreels; who hadn't? Grimy faces leaning out of carriage windows, thumbs up. Mugs of tea and sandwiches. What remained of their forces and the French, the numbers daily rising to a tally no one had dared hope for.

'They've got wards full of them across the road.'

'Have they?'

'Still,' said Pop, glancing at Churchill, pinned up behind the bar beyond the optics. 'Wars are not won by evacuations.'

'No, indeed.' Dougie reached in his pocket for his notebook.

★

128

Matron's black lace-ups squeaked down a long greeny-grey linoleum corridor on the second floor of the Middlesex Hospital,
turned sharp right, then left by a scabrous light well giving on to
dull brickwork sprouting buddleia. Her starched cap had sharp
upturned wings.

'Your credentials, Mr Birdsall, may have got you this far,' she
said, pushing open a door and waiting for him to pass through.
'From here on, the well-being of our patients is *my* concern. We're
very busy and very understaffed. As one might expect.'

'Of course.'

'Ten minutes. No more.'

The ward stretched ahead, the high-level windows blacked out
with paint. It was late morning the following day, and stifling. The
smell hit him first: sweetish, close, with an undertow of butcher's
shop, overlaid with carbolic. It was only then that he registered the
sounds coming from the beds ranged to either side, some of which
were screened.

It was clear to him as soon as he went through the door that this
had been a mistake. But he was not about to admit as much to
Matron nor turn his back on the men whose eyes were now following him as if he were a doctor, come against the odds to put things
right. He would take the full ten minutes he had been allocated.

A porter pushing a gurney disappeared round the back of a
screen and a few moments later reappeared with a shrouded body
laid out on it. One of the nurses, carrying a bedpan, whispered to
Matron in passing, 'Private Greenwood.'

In the middle of the ward was a long table laden with biscuit
tins, frilled cakes sashed in ribbon and bottles of champagne. It
looked like a display at Fortnum's. 'The public has been most
generous and appreciative,' said Matron, seeing where his eyes
were straying. 'If a little ill-informed.'

None of the men, propped up in the beds or stretched prone,
groaning or silent, seemed interested in or capable of eating and
drinking. One of them was being fed through a straw inserted into
a hole in his face. Bullets could go anywhere. Jaws, noses, heads,

shoulders, hips, backs, cheeks, chests. Penises, he thought, and other unseen places. There were many amputees. Many multiple amputees.

Everywhere, the brisk steps of nurses as they pulled wheeled screens across, fetched linen, water and drugs. He counted four of them. There were perhaps two dozen white-painted iron beds in the ward, all occupied, save now for the late Private Greenwood's. Halfway down on the left-hand side, a middle-aged woman sat reading to a soldier with bandaged eyes, like a mother telling her child a bedtime story.

One nurse, holding a bundle of soiled dressings at arm's length, advanced across the ward, looking as if at any moment she might break into a run that would take her clean out of the building into Mortimer Street.

'Sister?' said Matron.

'Matron.' The nurse stopped in her tracks.

'What is it?'

'Have a look.'

The dressings were crawling with maggots.

'What do I do? There's more of them.'

'Leave them. They clean the stumps.' Matron turned to Dougie. 'Seen enough?'

His response was to ask her if he might talk to one of the men. She checked the watch pinned upside down to the bib of her uniform and then led him to the bedside of a sandy-haired young man missing both arms below the elbows. 'I've a visitor for you, Private.'

The boy turned his head on the pillow. He had very clear blue eyes. His name was Atkins and he came from Tottenham.

Dougie sat down on the hard edge of a hard chair and explained he was a film-maker working for the government, recording the war.

'Nice life, I expect,' said Atkins. 'Can you do it with no hands?'

Across the ward, the middle-aged woman was still reading to the soldier, her voice rising and falling. Reading was easier than finding something to say.

'Joke, governor,' said Atkins. 'Your face. Now there's a picture.'

Dougie said, 'You could do it with no hands. Some of it, anyway.' He tapped his head. 'You do a lot of it up here.'

'That rules me out, then.' Atkins laughed. 'Thick as two short planks, I am.' He struggled to lever himself upright on bandages damp with yellow and pink. 'Where's your camera?'

Dougie had nearly brought a crew with him. He shuddered to remember that now. It was a pity that Macleod was no longer around. He wanted to tell him that there was such a thing as too much truth. 'I'm not filming today.'

'Can't say I blame you. This is hardly what folks want to see, is it? We're no oil paintings.'

Atkins, thought Dougie, underestimated his own intelligence. 'What happened to you, Private?'

'Gangrene is what they say. I don't remember nothing about it. What I remember is they strafed us just as we was approaching the port. Then I didn't get off the first day, not the second day neither. And the sea was that filthy.' He winked. 'Do us a favour. Scratch my nose, would you? I'd do it myself, but it's not the same with the dressings.'

Dougie bent across and scratched his nose.

Matron reappeared. 'Time's up, Mr Birdsall.'

'He's a film-maker,' said Atkins.

'So I gather,' said Matron.

A film-maker under false pretences, thought Dougie.

'Don't you worry about me, sir,' said Atkins. 'They're going to fix me up good and proper. Artificial limbs – they can do wonders with those. I'll be right as rain, you'll see. I'll be able to smoke and everything.'

Matron ushered Dougie to the door of the ward, as if he might run away and hide under one of the beds like a recalcitrant child seeking to prolong playtime.

He paused at the door to collect himself. 'Are they all like him?'

She softened. 'The morphia helps. We may need to reconsider the dose.'

When he went out of the hospital into the glare of the street he remembered that this was the day Julia was seeing the lawyer.

Julia was so nervous that she had to ask several times at the porter's lodge before she was capable of taking in the directions she was given. The solicitor's office, a suite of panelled rooms, two of which contained clerks, typists and files, was three floors up on the eastern side of one of the austere eighteenth-century brick squares that comprised Gray's Inn. (Richard would have killed for such premises, she thought. His own office was above a funeral director's.) The view from the window was of a tree in full leaf, a London plane, one of those hardy survivors. She found it useful to focus on.

Mr Gore-Finlay had a reputation for successfully representing wives in difficult divorces. He filleted the facts out of her in a matter of minutes.

'How would you describe these letters your husband found?'

She hesitated.

'Let me put it another way,' said Mr Gore-Finlay, who had a hawkish face and a forensic manner. 'Should they be read out in court, would the judge gain the impression that you and the co-respondent were friends, that you were conducting a harmless flirtation, or . . .'

'No,' she said, with a scorching blush. 'They go some way beyond that.' A breeze rippled the leaves of the plane tree. 'A long way.'

He was taking notes, his pen scritching across the paper. 'And where are the letters now?'

'In my possession.' The Modess packet was one of the few things she had taken with her on her night flight from home.

Mr Gore-Finlay said, 'All of them?'

'Yes.' Come to think of it, she didn't know. 'I'm not certain.'

'It might be useful to establish that. No other evidence that you know of? A private investigator's report? Witnesses?' The solicitor went on to explain that, since adultery was regarded as a quasi-criminal offence, a high standard of proof was required. The petitioner had to satisfy the court beyond all reasonable doubt that it had occurred, with dates, if possible. 'You haven't, for example, left your signature in a hotel register somewhere?'

'No.'

At that moment a siren sounded. The door opened. 'Sir?'

'What is it, Miss Hodges?'

'The siren, sir.'

'False alarm, I expect. So many of them these days.'

Miss Hodges closed the door.

'Where were we?' He put down his pen. 'Oh, yes. In my experience, wives rarely stray when all is well with the marriage. Have you any cause for complaint? Has Mr Compton been unfaithful to you or been cruel to you in any way?'

'No,' said Julia. 'My husband has always been thoroughly decent to me. He's a solicitor.'

'That's a pity.' Said with no trace of irony. Mr Gore-Finlay paused, gave her a level gaze freighted with she knew not what. 'Now, Mrs Compton, I'm afraid I must be somewhat indelicate. Did marital relations take place between you and your husband at any time after he discovered your adultery?'

Could a blush blush? It could. 'No, not after.'

'Certain?'

'Quite certain.'

Scritch, scritch went the pen.

'You may wonder why I should need to ask you such a distasteful question,' he said. 'The answer is that there have been cases where a husband has been refused a divorce because he did not desist from marital relations with a wife he knew to be adulterous. This can be viewed as condoning the offence.'

For the first time, Julia understood that Richard was now her opponent.

The solicitor referred to his notes. 'You are no longer living in the matrimonial home.'

'No. I am living with Mr Birdsall.'

'The co-respondent.'

'Yes.'

'Is it your intention to marry, should the divorce go through?'

Until the solicitor asked the question, Julia had been keeping from herself how much she wanted this to happen, and the degree to which a future where she was Dougie's wife was alive in her mind. Mrs Dougie Birdsall – she tried on the name like a schoolgirl marrying herself to a boy she had a crush on at the back of her homework diary.

'Mrs Compton?' Pen poised.

'We haven't discussed it yet. Mr Birdsall is married. Although,' said Julia, anxious not to paint too grim a picture, 'he and his wife are separated.' This stretched the truth somewhat.

'Mmm.' Mr Gore-Finlay drew the papers together. 'Well, Mrs Compton' (how she wished he would stop calling her that) 'there are two courses of action open to you. Firstly, defend the divorce and hope that your husband has nothing more material to place before the court than his recollection of your letters.'

'Unlikely,' said Julia.

'I think so too,' he said. 'As someone more than familiar with the legal system, he is bound to have his ducks in a row, if you forgive the colloquialism. The other option, of course, is not to contest. Washing one's laundry in public can be very upsetting.'

'I don't mind about the divorce,' said Julia. 'It's Peter I mind about.'

'Unfortunately the two are very much connected.'

Julia was remembering the pantomime over Peter's recent birthday – his tenth – which had appalled her. 'Their' present was an Everyman edition of *Robinson Crusoe* chosen by Richard: was the irony of the castaway story deliberate? 'Is my husband likely to be awarded custody?' She almost didn't want to know the answer. Her heart thumped around in her chest.

'There is nothing quite so hard and fast about it.' The solicitor went on to explain that she might be lucky and the judge might take a broader, more tolerant view of human frailty, might be of the opinion that children are best kept with their mothers, or at least shared with them, whatever the failings of those mothers. On the other hand, she might find that the judge regarded a wife's infidelity as symptomatic of moral unfitness. 'Even so,' said Mr Gore-Finlay, 'there are always visiting rights to play for. And these can be generous.'

A terrible thought struck her. 'Could I be prevented from seeing my son at all?'

He capped his pen. 'It has been known for petitioners to apply for such orders. However, even if they are granted, they apply only until the child reaches the age of majority. They do not last a lifetime.'

The all-clear sounded and the sun danced in the leaves. Neither was cause for relief. Julia thought she had prepared herself for the worst. She hadn't. A shadow came over her mind, and settled there.

'A final word of advice,' said Mr Gore-Finlay, rising from his desk. 'It would be better if you kept away from your son until the case comes to court.'

'Why?'

And here Mr Gore-Finlay made a reference to Solomon and the two warring mothers. 'Judges dislike seeing children used as ammunition in their parents' battles.'

'Peter's at school.'

'That's much the best place for him while the two of you sort out your affairs.'

The first thing Julia did when she returned to Primrose Hill was to work her way through the Modess packet. Although it was ages since she'd read the letters, she had many of them by heart. This was why it didn't take her long to realize that one was missing. *I want to fuck you so badly.*

'Oh dear,' said Dougie later.

'It seems I am a quasi-criminal.'

'Well, that makes two of us,' he said.

'Richard's very good at planning. I always forget that about him.'

Her head was resting on his lap, her eyes staring at some indeterminate point on the floor. She turned to examine him upside down. The reverse skyline of his beaky nose. 'I can't allow that letter to be read out in court.'

He wasn't keen on the prospect himself. 'We'll cross that bridge when we come to it.'

She sighed. 'It's going to be so expensive.'

'I dare say it will be.'

She levered herself upright. 'Would you be able to help me out, do you think?'

'Julia,' he said, 'I might not have a job next week. I barely have one now. It's about as much as I can do to feed us and put a roof over our heads. But there's nothing to stop you from looking for work.'

'Doing what?'

'I don't know. Teaching piano?'

'I don't have a piano!'

Out of nowhere a row blew up. Over the course of the next hour and a half it blew them all around the houses before dropping them, exhausted, right where they had started.

'Borrow from a friend, then,' said Dougie. 'That friend of yours – what's she called? – isn't she well off? Or ask your father for a loan.'

'I can't do that,' said Julia.

13

Plevna Avenue, north-west London, was a broad street where late-Victorian villas minded their own business behind trimmed privet hedges. The semi-detached house where Julia had grown up was two doors down from the junction with Inkerman Road, off which ran Raglan Street and Alma Terrace. They liked their battles and sieges and generals, those nineteenth-century street-namers.

Julia went round the side of the house and was confronted by the implacable bulk of an air-raid shelter. All the flowers were gone, as was the swing which she and her brother had fought over. In the beds were tender vegetable seedlings. She was early. Half past three; her father would still be with the Rotarians.

The key was under the terracotta pot beside the back door, where it always was. When she let herself in she was unnerved by the smells of her childhood. She left her things in the kitchen and went into the dining room.

Here her father had set up a command centre worthy of Whitehall. On the far wall, Fountains Abbey had been taken down and in its place was a large coloured map of the world stuck with flags. Soviet hammer-and-sickles in the Baltic states. Italian tricolours strung along the Alps. Swastikas all over Europe. The flag stuck in Paris made her flinch – France had fallen the previous week. As a visual summary of their island isolation, of imminent invasion, it was unsparing.

She wondered where her father had found or bought the flags, and then she noticed on the sideboard the paper, paints, pens and pins he had been using to make them, which struck her as typically frugal, but also almost unbearable. Guilt washed over her at the industrious way he had been combating his loneliness.

Her father arrived on the dot of four, as she was setting out the tea things. 'Julia,' he said, removing his mackintosh.

Even by his standards, this was far from an emphatic greeting.

'Hello, Dad.'

He nodded at the tray. 'Cakes.'

'Shop-bought, I'm afraid. Not Harry's.'

A thin smile. 'I hope you didn't pay over the odds.'

They had their tea in the sitting room. Nothing about it had changed in twenty years: the same Victorian balloon-backed chairs upholstered in gros point, the same herbaceous wallpaper, the gate-leg table with its 'don't touch' cargo of Royal Worcester figurines. 'Well, it's all looking very ship-shape in here.'

He grimaced. 'Not for much longer. Bridie's leaving.'

'Oh.' Bridie was her father's daily and the sticking plaster that allowed her to countenance him living alone. 'Where's she off to?'

'Factory.'

'You'll find someone else,' she said.

'I doubt it.'

A little silence fell and in it she could hear her mother's absence. Her father had loved her mother, there was no doubt about that. But she had been a woman whose need to be understood was at least as great as her need to be loved, and he had never quite succeeded in doing this. Julia had understood her, which is why she had been able to hurt her. And now, she thought, she would hurt her father, too, with a bombshell delivered in person.

'Have you heard from Michael?' she asked, to delay the moment. Michael, her elder brother by four years, was a mining engineer in Durban. (The favourite child, Julia believed, unaware that Michael believed the same of her. Theirs was a prolonged rivalry.)

'Busy, by all accounts.'

'Doris and the girls?'

'Flourishing.'

The conversation staggered to another halt. Julia became aware of the chink of spoons in cups, of cups in saucers. Where were the words she had rehearsed? Gone.

He said, 'If you're going to ask me for money, the answer is no.'

'I'm sorry?' said Julia, a pulse beating in her throat.

'Richard paid me a visit a while ago. He warned me you might well come begging.'

'What do you mean?'

'You know full well what I mean.'

Her mouth dried. She had a clear picture of her father and her husband discussing her in this very room, the accountant and the solicitor, the two thoroughly decent men; they had always liked each other. It filled her with dread, and something much more slippery. 'Whatever he told you, you must understand –'

'I don't want to hear any more about it.' Her father looked at her with the coolness of a stranger. 'You made your bed, you must lie in it.' A dusky colour rose in his face, as if prompted by the word 'bed' and all that it implied. He got up from his seat and went to stare out of the sitting-room window through the gauze of its net curtains, the blackout blinds drawn up under a floral pelmet.

'Please, Dad, I need your help,' she said to his back, which had disgust written down the length of it.

No answer.

'Richard wants custody. I can't allow that.'

'Thank God your mother's not alive to see this,' he said. Then he turned. 'I must say, I find it inexcusable that when you needed a smokescreen for one of your illicit encounters you should tell your husband you were visiting me.'

On the doorstep she cried, offending all the net curtains in the street. On the train she cried, causing a rustling of newspaper.

'I can't believe Richard would do that.' Julia was steadier now, but only just.

'Why are you surprised? These highly moral men have no grey areas.'

The blackout was in place and Dougie was drawing little sketches for Nell. George the cat had joined the Local Defence Mouse-cat-eers, the Home Miaow, and was armed with a frying pan and cricket bat to defeat the Nazi rats parachuting down from the London skies.

Today another leaflet had been pushed through the letterbox: 'If the Invader Comes'. They were to keep calm, that was the gist of it. 'If', Julia thought, was the authorities' way of saying 'when'. The Germans were twenty-one miles away.

'Isn't Nell a bit young to understand this?' she said, peering over his shoulder.

'Oh, Barbara will explain it to her.'

Julia winced at the name of the wife. Thin blue airmail envelopes arrived from her at irregular intervals. She knew where he kept them; in fact, she'd read them, searching for clues about this other woman, searching for evidence that the marriage was over. All she had learned was a great deal about life in Toronto, where Barbara had an administrative job in provincial government. It sounded dull.

She began pacing up and down. 'Richard always seems to be a step ahead of me. I don't like it.'

'Sinclair,' said Dougie, putting down his pencil. 'He's a lawyer. You need to prepare yourself for more of the same. You should have put your father in the picture weeks ago. That way he might have been more sympathetic.'

'I doubt it.' Another circuit of the room. 'What am I going to do?'

'Something will turn up.'

'Yes, Mr Micawber.' She was regretting leaving her rings behind: that had been a gesture she could ill afford.

He reached for her and pulled her on to his lap. 'Why are you dressed as a governess?' He fingered the collar of her suit jacket.

She rubbed her nose. 'These are my tidy clothes.' The idea had been to look as little like a harlot as possible.

'Well, make yourself untidy,' he said, releasing her. 'We're going out on the town.'

'What's the occasion?'

'I've something to tell you.'

★

'This Sancerre is very good.' Dougie mopped his mouth.

Julia gazed round. The grill room was bright and dark, mirrored and panelled, populated by officers and their wives or girlfriends. 'Stardust' tinkled on the piano. She wondered what Dougie had to tell her that could only be said in a hotel – an expensive one. He'd ordered lobster.

No row, she told herself. Don't bite the hand that takes you out to dinner, even if it doesn't pay the legal bills. 'Stardust' became 'Melancholy Baby'.

'Is something the matter?' said Dougie. 'You look like you're in pain.'

Julia realized she was flexing her fingers and stopped. Whenever she heard a piano it made her hands hungry.

But she was saved from having to explain this by the entrance of a brunette in a silver lamé gown who made every head turn and chatter die on lips. The woman was halfway across the room when she was apprehended by a hotel functionary of some kind and escorted out.

'No better than she should be' was Dougie's amused observation.

She had never consciously noticed him noticing another woman before, not with such evident relish. 'What do you mean?'

'She's a prostitute.'

'Now there's a job I could do.'

'Don't be cynical, Sinclair. It doesn't suit you.' Dougie put down his glass. 'Shall I tell you my news?'

'Go ahead.'

The Ministry was moving them to Denham, he said. Studios just outside London, where the film units for the army and the air force were already located.

'You should see the resources they've got – the equipment, the labs. One could be in Hollywood.'

Dougie was tearing a bread roll into smaller and smaller pieces (he did the same thing with bus tickets). 'And they've finally found us a producer. Chap called Hugh Trevelyan. Cambridge, a little before my time. I met him this afternoon. He used to be a screen-writer, done a bit of editing and directing, too.'

'Agreeable?'

'Kindred spirit.'

It was nothing short of miraculous, Dougie thought, given that it had been Cheeseman who had done the choosing.

The lobster arrived with fuss and finger bowls.

'There's a script he'd like me to take a look at.' Dougie cracked a claw.

'I'm to have a free hand and as much stock as I want. Worth celebrating, don't you think?'

'Will it mean more money?' Hope flickered into life: it was a rationed commodity these days.

'Try being a little more enthusiastic.'

'I'm sorry.'

'Don't you understand how important this is to me?' He gestured at the room with his crackers. 'Take a look around. What do you see? Uniforms. Most of them wondering why I'm not in one. This is my chance to make a proper contribution.'

'I know, it's very good news. I'm pleased for you.'

'Money isn't everything.'

It is when you haven't got it, she thought.

A little later, shellfish and Sancerre had done the trick. They played the Face Game.

It was one of Dougie's theories – one of many – that if you paid attention you could spot faces from art, from history, all around you every day. Archetypes. Throwbacks. And the famous – whose faces, after all, were not copyrighted. The librarian with the high forehead and pale, hooded eyes who looked like a Renaissance con-tessa, the eighteenth-century squire behind the counter at the post office, the Roman sentry punching tickets on the tram. And scores of Ronald Colmans. 'They do seem to pop up everywhere.' She, of course, was a Modigliani, which she had learned was a compliment.

'Over there,' said Dougie. 'Velásquez.'

She turned and saw a sallow-skinned, long-faced woman with fine black eyes.

'Bang on.'

'Your turn,' he said as the waiter refilled their glasses.

The waiter had one of those complexions that was both doughy and ruddy, and an unfortunate haircut.

'Bruegel,' she said, when he had gone. 'He only wants a jerkin and hose.'

Dougie bit his lip. 'So he does.'

'Third table from the window: Brunel.'

'Hang about. You're not giving me a go.' He squinted over her shoulder. 'Mmm, no side whiskers.'

'True, but he is smoking a cigar.'

'He is. Bonus point. You're too good at this.'

Julia twiddled the stem of her glass, spilled a little. 'The astrologer in the *Daily Telegraph* says we're to expect the invasion next Tuesday.'

'I've never believed a word I read in the *Telegraph*,' said Dougie. 'And I'm not going to start now.'

'Perhaps if we're invaded I won't need a divorce.' More wine was spilled.

'Time I got you home, Sinclair.' Dougie signalled for the bill.

'Will we be invaded? Do you think?'

'Anything's possible. Although, thanks to Churchill, I think a negotiated peace is looking less likely.'

They were standing waiting for a taxi when Brunel and his party came out of the hotel. One of them advanced up the queue to tap Dougie on the shoulder.

'I happened to notice that you and your companion were staring at my friend.'

'Were we?'

'Quite rudely, I'd say. I'll have you know he brought his entire battalion safely out of France. Not a man lost.'

'In which case, I should very much like to shake his hand.'

'We were merely remarking on his resemblance to Ronald Coleman,' said Julia.

'Yes,' said Dougie. 'We thought it quite striking.'

On the way home in the cab, her head lurching on his shoulder, Julia calculated that the evening had cost half of what she owed the lawyer.

There was a thudding. It came from inside her skull and from beneath the floorboards.

Julia opened her eyes. This was a mistake. The light hit her like a blow. Dougie had already left – for Denham, she remembered, as if through a fog made of iron filings – and the blackout had been taken down.

Thud, thud, thud.

Her first thought was that the invasion had come and there were Germans at the door. Her second thought was that it was the milk-man wanting payment (his bill was weeks overdue).

Her next thought was that it was Mrs Tooley hitting her broom handle on the ceiling to announce a visitor. Which it was.

'Coming!'

The visitor, making her way up the stairs in a hat worn at an angle that spoke of years of pinning headgear just so, was Fiona. She drew level, drew breath, hand on heart – pure theatre: there were not many stairs, nor were they steep.

'Don't tell me. You happened to find yourself in the vicinity.'

'Darling. I thought I'd left it long enough.'

Only later did Julia wonder what her friend meant. 'Long', as in since they had last seen each other? Or, as in long enough after daybreak for any respectable person to be up and fully clothed?

As it was, she was only too conscious of her dressing gown, tangled hair and bare feet. Beyond her, the shabby, unaired flat. The den of iniquity.

'Aren't you going to ask me in?'

Julia opened the door further and beckoned her to come through. 'I'll go and get dressed.'

When she returned, she found Fiona standing in the middle of the sitting room taking in the paintings on the ochre walls, the bursting bookshelves, the overflowing ashtrays, the cat attending to its toilet. Her eyes – habituated to pretty views and amusing cushions – flitted here and there, her curiosity a pungent perfume.

'Won't you sit down?' Julia removed a stack of newspapers from one of the club chairs.

Fiona considered for a moment, then perched on the edge. 'You must love this man very much.'

'You've no idea.'

'Oh, I think I've an inkling.'

'How about some tea?' said Julia.

'That would be wonderful. You clearly could do with a cup.'

Julia brought in the tray and apologized for the biscuits. 'They're rather stale, I'm afraid.'

Fiona said, 'Where's the piano? Upstairs?'

'Richard won't let me have it.' Julia set down the tray. The teapot slopped and the lid chinked. 'He wants a divorce and custody of Peter.'

Fiona, clearly resisting the urge to pour, allowed her cup to be filled, but not before noting its interior brownness. 'Gosh, that's grim.'

'And expensive.'

'Are you quite well, darling?'

The aspirin Julia had swallowed in the kitchen, her mouth held under the gushing tap, was having no effect and a vein in her temple pulsed spikes of pain into her skull.

'I've no regrets, if that's what you're asking.' This was mostly true.

Fiona's hat was very smart. Her linen dress too, the pistachio colour flattering rather than bilious, as it would have been on most people.

'I'm glad to hear it. I've been so worried about you. Just that brief note to say where you'd gone and why, then nothing for weeks.'

'Sorry. I've been a bit distracted.'

'Haven't we all?' said Fiona. 'Defence Area, Invasion Area, Restricted Zone – they can call it what they like, but it's no picnic living on the front line, let me tell you. They've mined the beach and put these ghastly concrete cubes like giant sugar lumps all over it.'

Julia's attention drifted. 'Picnic' and 'beach' had been enough to remind her of the day she'd met Dougie, a day she often revisited with a kind of wonder at life's strange accidents.

Fiona talked on. The evacuees had been sent packing. Major Lees had constructed some sort of dug-out in the woods on the high ground beyond the church, fully equipped with tins, camp beds and whatever weaponry he'd been able to commandeer – bottles in socks and pitchforks, mainly. 'It's supposed to be hush-hush, but everyone knows about it.'

If Fiona knew about it, thought Julia, this was understood. Had the censor been listening, he would have clapped his hands over his ears by now – or over her mouth.

Had she heard that Richard had formed up a detachment of Local Defence Volunteers?

She had not heard. A pause. 'How is he?'

Fiona gave her a look she had last seen on the face of her chemistry teacher returning a D-minus homework. 'How do you think?'

Julia felt heat travel up her face. Her head pounded. 'I still don't understand what prompted him to go looking for the letters.'

'Don't you?'

'Did you tell him?'

'What do you take me for? I wouldn't dream of it.' There was the noise of a train and the sashes rattled in their frames. 'He was bound to twig at some point, the way you were mooning about.'

Julia stared into her cup. 'Why did you come? It's a long way for a social call. I might not have been in.'

Fiona lit a cigarette and fanned the smoke. After a time she said, 'Ginny's up the duff. Airman. *Trainee* airman. To be honest, I came to town to do a little shopping in advance of the wedding. I admit the detour from Oxford Street might have been a bit of an impulse but frankly we could all be speaking German next week, so I thought why ever not?'

In the light from the window you saw what you normally didn't: the grey hairs among the red, the fine lines around the mouth, the blurred looseness along the jaw. The frock, the hat, the nail polish looked more like armour now.

'I'm going to be a grandmother. Isn't that the limit?'

It would indeed be a blow, thought Julia. 'You'll redefine the role.'

'Perhaps. Toby's a sweet chap, actually. The young know how to seize the day, and who can blame them? I've been thinking "Marmee".'

'I'm sorry?' said Julia.

'Marmee, the mother in *Little Women*. "Granny" is so terribly ageing.' Fiona smoothed her skirt and got up from her chair. 'Well, I'd better be on my way.'

'Must you?' said Julia.

'Yes,' Fiona said. 'The mother of the bride's outfit awaits. Dear old John Lewis. Whatever would we do without it?'

'Quite,' said Julia, who could no longer afford to shop at John Lewis, or any other Oxford Street department store.

At that moment she was overcome by a longing, not for her home – not precisely – but for certain, unremarkable things: a tablecloth edged with a Greek-key pattern, a Wedgwood vase she had liked to fill with early blossom and late chrysanthemums and the toys her son refused to play with any more and which leant crookedly against each other on the top of his chest of drawers – a knitted lamb called Lamb, a painted wooden dog on wheels and his teddy, named by him with a three-year-old's self-absorption, Peter Richard Compton. From another time and place these things asked how she could have abandoned them. The question pressed a bruise in her mind.

When she came back to herself, Fiona was staring at her.

'Are you going to tell Richard you've seen me?'

'Why should I do that?' Fiona drew on her gloves. 'Next time I must meet this man of yours.'

Julia, who could not imagine introducing Dougie to Fiona, said he worked very long hours.

Very long hours, thought Fiona, remembering the 'long hours' Geoffrey had put in with various secretaries at various roadside inns. Men couldn't change their spots any more than leopards could – and a man who was prepared to steal a woman from her husband might well be a man who made a habit of it. 'So long as you're happy, darling,' she said, trying without much success to keep the irony out of her tone.

Distance inserted itself between them. Julia waited for an invitation to the wedding or an offer of financial assistance. Neither came.

14

The airfield was patchily green, overlooked by a stubby concrete control tower, runways pocked here and there with craters, some of which showed signs of ongoing repair. A dense smell of kerosene hung in the air, so heavy you caught a hint of it half a mile away. Makeshift blister hangars clad in corrugated steel sheeting surrounded the site and transport of various kinds came and went, rumbling through the gate and around the perimeter track, throwing up dust. It had been a hot, dry summer and now, late August, the ground was parched. Outside one of the Nissen huts that served as barracks, a flight officer was throwing up into a flowerbed.

'Lieutenant Styles?' said the wing commander.

'Sir.' Styles straightened and mopped his mouth with a handkerchief.

'You've besmirched the lobelia.'

'Yes, sir.'

'We can't have that.'

'No, sir.'

'Hose 'em down.'

The wing commander was explaining the facts of life to Dougie. 'Average age on this base: twenty-three. Average life expectancy: eighty-seven air hours. Most of these lads won't see their next birthday. And don't think,' said the wing commander, 'that I'm a pessimist. These figures come from the Air Ministry and as such are most likely an underestimate. Not something you'll be able to put in your film, of course.'

They came past an orderly mopping out a latrine.

'We're telling a different sort of truth.'

'Wasn't aware there was more than one kind,' said the wing

commander. 'Still, you can spin whatever yarn you like so long as it helps recruitment.'

Dougie was about to deliver his usual lecture on documentary film-making, which was essentially Macleod's with a few elaborations of his own, then thought better of it.

'People seem to think,' the wing commander was saying, 'that what's going on fifteen thousand feet over their heads is some sort of sideshow put on for their benefit. Keeping score, as if it were a cricket match. But these boys are all that stand between us and the abyss. And not just the ones in the air. We're desperately short of ground crew.'

They went round a corner and along a cinder path. On a dead bit of lawn, a group of airmen was sitting smoking in the sun, reading the papers and taking it in turns to throw a stick for a sheepdog.

Twenty-three, thought Dougie. Most of them didn't look a day over eighteen. The only one who did look a little older was sitting apart from the others.

'Jerzy Stanisławski,' said the wing commander, following his gaze. 'Pole. A little too keen, in my estimation.'

'Is that a problem?'

'It can be. A squadron's a team. You don't want mad buggers in it any more than you want glory-chasers. In the air, they've got to look out for one another.'

The dog, tail swishing, fetched the stick. The stick was thrown again. The dog, tail swishing, fetched the stick again.

'Lovely day for it, sir.'

'Indeed it is, Crawford.'

They stood watching the young men in the sunlight for a while and then carried on walking in the direction of the mess hut. 'Do they know the odds?' said Dougie.

'They can subtract. So can their families. I haven't told you any of this, by the way.'

It was Dougie's first meeting with the wing commander. Yesterday they had filmed maintenance crews in one of the hangars patching up planes and this morning WAAFs manning the radio telephones or, rather, one WAAF in particular. She was bound to help recruitment, thought Dougie, remembering her. Women would be drawn to the natty uniform she was wearing and men would be drawn to what filled it.

A Hurricane came in to land and taxied to a stop at the end of one of the runways. The base's current status was 'Released'. 'Released' was a step below 'Available' and two steps below 'Readiness', steps measured in hours and minutes, not days. They rotated the airfields in and out of action to give the pilots time to rest a bit and train, and to save fuel and wear on the engines.

But this raised questions, thought Dougie. For such a strategy to stand a chance of success, they had to know when the enemy planes were underway, where they were heading and in what numbers. And they had to know these things fast – it took six minutes for a Dornier or a Messerschmitt to cross the Channel, or so he had been told. The script he was shooting made a great deal of lines of communication feeding from sector to sector into central command. Some of the more hysterical newspapers talked about death rays.

When the engine noise subsided, Dougie said, 'One thing I wanted to ask you, sir.'

'Fire away.'

'Detecting the enemy – does it really all come down to ground observers with field glasses? I was thinking in particular about cloud cover. Visibility, and so on.'

'Were you.'

'The script's a little vague on that point.'

The wing commander smiled to himself. 'Let's keep it that way, shall we?'

They reached the mess hut. Dougie's crew – electricians, camera operator, focus puller, key grip, lighting technicians – were making adjustments to their equipment, taping cables, moving track. An arc light had been set up to shine through the window. Fixed to the front was a blue gelatin filter that would simulate a summer's evening. The idea of the sequence was to show fliers relaxing off duty.

'All this monkeying about,' said the wing commander, straightening his tie. 'I'd no idea. Good job we're stood down at present.'

Dougie held open the door. 'They wouldn't let us film otherwise.'

'I should think not.'

In the mess hut, Frank was looking through the camera and motioning at the clapper-loader.

'I hope you know your lines, sir?'

This was not a question to ask a wing commander. 'Word perfect,' he said.

Dougie said, 'Don't look at the camera.'

The airfield was one operational centre; the studio was another. Denham was a vast complex. Seven sound stages, a dubbing theatre, metal, carpentry, paint and plastering workshops, canteens, vaults, dressing rooms, offices and changing rooms for extras, all powered by the largest diesel-run generator in the country, distributing enough electricity to serve a small town via aluminium bars routed in underground tunnels. Along with a water tank the size of a lake for mocking up sea battles and a huge lot for open-air filming.

The cutting room was in the converted stable block of the original estate, next door to the film laboratories. It smelled of pear drops from the acetate they used to cement the clips together. On the walls were hooks, and from the hooks were suspended lengths of developed footage, their tail ends gathered into black cotton bags on the floor. Smaller lengths of film were spiked around the perimeter of the trim bin.

'And was he?' said Basil Meers. 'Word perfect?'

'He knew his lines all right.'

Tony, Basil's assistant, came through from the labs with a can of developed footage.

'I hope that's the sequence in the mess,' said Dougie.

'Half,' Tony said. 'The other can will be ready in about twenty minutes. They've had a rush job on Handel.'

Basil threaded the film into the Moviola and switched on the projector. They watched in silence until the film spooled out, flicking.

Dougie began pacing and smoking. 'I told him not to look at the camera.'

Basil swivelled round in his chair. 'He's not an actor.'

'Clearly,' said Dougie. 'It's an awful performance.'

'Which is all to the good.'

'Is this a theory of yours?'

'It's something I've observed,' said Basil. 'You want to stay on a face that recognizes the camera is there. That self-consciousness can't be faked. But I think you might be missing some shots.'

Dougie stopped in his tracks. 'Have you any idea how hard it is to film on an airfield? Planes landing and taking off and so forth?'

Tony, sitting at the splicer, raised his head, scenting a row.

'Keep your hair on,' said Basil. 'Let's see what's in the other can.'

What was in the other can confirmed Basil's suspicion. A number of key shots were missing.

'I'll never get permission to go back and reshoot,' Dougie said. 'Besides which, there isn't time. Can't we try it a different way?'

'What other way did you have in mind?'

'Montage,' said Dougie, with the sense he was pushing out a little boat into a very rocky sea.

All afternoon, frame by frame, they hunted for connections, for clashes, for echoes and chimes. At the end of it they had a sequence that worked.

'Montage,' said Dougie, quoting Eisenstein, 'is the nerve of cinema.'

'Montage covers a multitude of sins,' said Basil. 'You're good at it.'

It was still light when they left for the day. Double Summer Time. The sky was a kind of pearly magnolia colour flushed with faint blue and pink, as if it were trying to pass itself off as porcelain. 'How's Barbara?' asked Basil as they walked down to the station.

'Learning to waterski.' Dougie paused a moment to light a cigarette.

'That's enterprising of her.'

'She's already mastered the winter sports.' He exhaled and threw the spent match away. 'I thought Canada would suit her, and it does. She's always had a bit of an outdoorsy side.'

'And Julia? How's she?'

Dougie admired Basil's impartiality, misreading it as approval. 'She's looking for a job. Without much success. She needs money for the divorce.'

A couple of boys cycled past, whooping. 'Can't you help her out?'

'Have you any idea how expensive it is?'

They went on a little way without speaking. But Dougie was unable to keep quiet for long, any more than he could keep still. Some sort of mechanism in him, a wind-up one probably, made this impossible. 'The trouble with the job hunting is that apart from playing the piano her skills are limited. I've never met anyone less domesticated in my life.' He smiled. 'I thought women were supposed to pick these things up at their mother's knees.'

'Still burning the saucepans then.'

'She must be the only person who's pleased when they put something else on ration or there's a shortage in the shops. It narrows down the options.'

'Poor you.' Basil liked his home comforts.

There were compensations, Dougie thought.

They came past the goods yard and went round to the station entrance. No railway signs these days, no road signs either; none since Dunkirk. All painted over or taken down so the Germans would have to ask for directions.

The London train was in. They found an empty compartment and got on.

'Well, if she's serious about finding work, they're looking for people at Sylvia's outfit.' Basil slammed the door and pulled down the leather tab to open the window. The light was beginning to go.

Sylvia's outfit was the Institute of Labour Management, located in Lancaster Gate. Dougie was unclear what they did there. Something to do with labour management, he supposed.

'No use, I'm afraid. She can't type.' Though why not, thought Dougie? Typewriters, pianos. They both involved keys. He flexed his fingers the way he had seen Julia do.

A hiss, a clang and a jolt and the train got under way.

'She wouldn't have to type,' said Basil. 'It's clerking in the main. Anyone remotely literate and numerate would suit. Can she spell?'

'Beautifully.'

'Then she's already streets ahead of most of the girls and half the broken-down old boys they've got kicking around the place. Shall I put in a word?'

'What about Sylvia?'

Sylvia's allegiance to Barbara is what he meant.

'They wouldn't be in the same department. Sylvia's been promoted again.'

'Good for her.' Sylvia – now there was a capable woman. Just not someone you'd particularly want to go to bed with.

Then all the way from West Ruislip to Marylebone Dougie carelessly talked about his suspicions that they had some new way of detecting the enemy.

She must have dozed off. A scratch of the key in the lock and she was instantly awake. Dreams – dreams of Peter running down the beach – tumbled away.

'Sinclair,' he said. 'You're still up.'

'I am.' She disentangled her numb limbs from the chair, dislodging the cat.

'Good.' He held out his arms; she walked into them and was reminded of that time in the bus queue when he had wrapped his coat round her. He smelled of drink and tobacco and another sweetish, soapy scent she couldn't identify.

'You've done up your shirt buttons all wrong,' she said.

He peered down at them. 'Christ, so I have. No one said all day.'

'You've been at the studio, then, have you?'

'Yes,' he said. 'And I went for a drink afterwards. If that's quite all right with you.' He pulled away and re-buttoned his shirt. 'I think I might have made a bit of a breakthrough this afternoon.'

'That's good.'

He was about to elaborate when something in her expression stopped him. 'How about you? Any bites?'

'None.' The notice she had placed in the classified columns of *The Times* had brought no replies. If there were Broadwoods, Bechsteins, Steinways left in London, there were no children learning to play them.

'Well, there may be something else in the offing. Basil –'

The telephone rang.

'Don't bother answering it,' he said. 'People should know better than to call so late.'

The telephone carried on ringing. They both stared at it. It sat on a little shelf whose slope testified to Dougie's shortcomings as a handyman.

'Something might have happened.' To Peter, she meant.

But before she could move, he had snatched up the receiver. 'Hello? No, no, it isn't. I'm afraid you have the wrong number. Bloody exchange,' he said.

Julia was not a fool. The buttons done up wrong, the sweet, soapy scent, the phone ringing at eleven o'clock – she knew she had grounds for suspicion. The difficulty was that she had compelling reasons not to act on them. All she could do was bury them under the rock with the others. It was getting crowded down there.

15

Julia came out of the Tube at Lancaster Gate, half walking, half running and, turning her face upwards to the sun, was blessed by it. Outside the kiosk on the corner by the station entrance the tobacconist was sweeping up fallen leaves and glass splinters, unlikely conjunctions of this London autumn. The swish of the dead leaves and the shirring of the swept glass had their echo in the smell of charred wood and something earthy or medicinal, plaster or brick dust perhaps. These days, everywhere and everything reeked of dead houses, dead streets, particles of the pulverized city on the soles of your shoes, settled in the seams of your clothing, in your hair. A reminder, should you need it, that one morning it might be someone else doing the sweeping, someone else noticing the sweeping.

Thirteen (lucky for some) Leominster Gardens was the second turning on the left. The stuccoed building, five storeys high, was still standing. You never knew, not from one day to the next, and not knowing gave everything a weight, a meaning it did not altogether warrant. This was certainly true of the Institute.

The Institute was tiered, which was to say the men who made the decisions and communicated with the Ministry commanded the large airy rooms on the first and second floors, and those – chiefly women – who administered the decisions, informed the decisions with paperwork and privately queried the decisions among themselves occupied the hastily partitioned, cramped rooms on the top floors. Down below, the basement was equipped with camp beds and other temporary arrangements for firewatchers and those working late after the sirens had gone and unable to get home.

When she pushed open the door and went into the vestibule Mr Keyes was waiting in his booth. ('K-E-Y-E-S, I'm not a commissionaire for nothing.') He handed her a pen to sign the register. 'You're late.'

She scrawled her signature. 'Bad night.'

'Yes, well, we've all had a bad night.'

She headed for the staircase.

'Miss Sinclair?'

'Yes?' she said, her hand on the banister.

'Miss Plume hasn't come in today.'

'Oh.' Miss Plume was the senior clerk and her supervisor. She had never been known to be anything but early, even after the worst night.

'Just so you know.'

'Has she telephoned?'

'Not as yet.'

Going up the stairs, pausing from time to time to note another raw gaping site through the taped-up landing windows, she wondered whether Miss Plume had been detained or, as it were, detained permanently. War sprouted such euphemisms: the rash of 'suddenly's in the death notices, for example. No doubt they would find out one way or another.

They were living through history, that's what everyone said. But history had banished every tense except the present. Nights, which used to mark out one day from the next, were as continuous as the waking hours – or else oblivion.

When Julia reached the fifth floor and Records Office G (Midlands East), which was no more than a cubicle, she found a pile of flimsies waiting for her in the cardboard box lid that served as her in-tray. Birmingham, Wolverhampton, Dudley, Solihull, Walsall, West Bromwich, Coventry: reports of production days, manning levels, unofficial walk-outs. She had expected to be as inept a clerk as she was a housekeeper. She had expected to chafe against the monotony. Instead, she found the dogged sorting of the right pieces of paper into the right folders, the right folders into the right files, the right files into the right filing cabinets – and their subsequent retrieval when requested by some denizen of the lower floors – as soothing and comforting as it was apparently pointless. Amid chaos was order. After the raids, sweeping up.

'You're late,' said Mr Slater, who shared the cubicle with her and was one of the few males on their floor. He liked to tell people he had failed his medical owing to a heart murmur. Julia had heard him announce this to complete strangers, post boys. The truth was, he was well over the age of conscription and not wearing it well. 'Bad night?'

'A bit.' Between two and almost four: a lot.

'We had a right pasting. Third time in as many days for Kensal Rise. But then, there is the gasworks.' Mr Slater scratched the end of his nose with a finger that wore a rubber sorting aid. 'Miss Plume's not in yet.'

'I know.'

'John Lewis has gone.'

'You're joking.'

'Burnt right out,' said Mr Slater. 'To think I was there only last week purchasing collar studs.'

At ten to one, Bea Justin (Records Office E: Midlands West) put her head around the door. 'Lunch?'

They lay on the grass in Kensington Gardens, their sandwich wrappings packed away. There had begun to be a chill in the ground. It came through their coats, spread out beneath them. In the flower-beds grew rows of cabbages.

'God, I'm dead,' said Bea. 'All in. Do you think anyone would notice if I stayed here for the rest of the afternoon?'

'Miss Plume would notice.'

'Mmm,' said Bea, and the unspoken thought hung between them.

Like the calming effect of filing, Bea had also been unexpected. Until they had met in the ladies' cloakroom on Julia's second day in the job, she had not realized how much she had missed female company.

Bea had an easy open manner and the free-limbed unconscious physical grace you associated with girls who spent their summers on tennis courts, girls on whom even school uniform could not do its worst. (Julia, whose prettiness had been late arriving, had not been that sort.) She was twenty-four and engaged to a serviceman stationed in Egypt – or 'Auntie Edna', in their code to circumvent the censors. Giles had terrible sunburn and didn't think much of the Pyramids. 'A heap of old rubble.'

In return, Julia had told Bea about her true marital status, about Peter and about Dougie (who caused consternation at the Institute, where personal calls were forbidden, by ringing up pretending to be an undersecretary). Bea, who was essentially practical-minded, received such information with equanimity. Her loyalty to her fiancé, in her mind absolute, she regarded as in no way compromised by the occasional liaison she'd allowed herself since his departure. ('Only as far as the bra, that's my rule.')

'Do you ever get the feeling,' said Bea, staring up at the innocent sky, 'that you're hallucinating? I mean,' she went on, 'actually seeing things?'

'Yes,' said Julia. 'Sometimes.' These days she felt permeable.

Bea sat up, sneezed and blew her nose. 'Do you? I do. I saw a rabbit on a roof the other day. Except it was a corner of a tarpaulin.' She fished around in her bag. 'Here, I thought we could share this.' She produced an orange. 'Old Baines saved it for me. It's only a little bit off.'

The citrus tang released by Bea's fingers digging in the peel was heaven. Never mind the unclouded night that the sunshine forewarned, not now. They sucked at the segments.

'Your reorganization of the incoming chits was remarked upon,' said Bea, wiping her mouth with the back of her hand. 'I shouldn't wonder if you weren't kicked downstairs, the way you're going. I've worked here for eighteen months and never thought of that.'

Julia shrugged. 'It just seemed sensible.'

As if in one mind, they got up and shook out their coats, put them on and headed back to the Institute.

'Come out with us this evening,' said Julia. Now, this was not sensible, but it was what they did: as often as they could, they went out and enjoyed themselves – 'seizing the day', Fiona would have called it. 'We're going to a supper club in Greek Street, well below ground, no windows. Really, you'd never know what was going on up top.'

They crossed the road, dodging two or three as yet unfilled holes from a bad night a couple of weeks ago. 'I'd like nothing more than to meet this chap of yours.' Bea smiled. 'He sounds like a hoot. But I promised Susan I'd mind the fort. She's on duty tonight.' Bea lived with her sister, a volunteer warden, whose husband was on the minesweepers and whose children were in Wales.

'Hello, all's right with the world,' said Bea as they came up to the fifth floor. '*Voici la tante de ma plume*. Right as rain and as large as life.'

Miss Plume was holding forth.

In addition to being the senior clerk and supervisor of the fifth floor, Miss Plume was a monologist. Every morning she had a compulsion to recount, with bus numbers, times, refreshments taken and wished for, sirens sounded, all-clears passed, everything that had happened to her since the previous evening. Julia had not been at the Institute long enough to know whether the raids had brought out this tendency in Miss Plume or merely worsened it. Whichever was the case, in her attempt to dramatize her experiences, she made the nightly bombing seem as ordinary as the wet afternoon of half-day closing. This was a considerable achievement.

So it was understandable that the monologue on this occasion was an account of her unexplained absence that morning, which turned out to involve a mislaid umbrella, the lost-property office at Victoria Station and a night spent sheltering in the Underground, after which, contact with 'some very unwashed people' had necessitated a tiring and much diverted journey home to her flat in Swiss Cottage in order to decrease the risk of communicable disease. 'Imagine my dismay,' said Miss Plume, 'when I discovered the telephone was out of order. You must all have been frightfully alarmed.'

Someone asked if she had retrieved her umbrella.

'Of course,' said Miss Plume. 'I have always found the Lost Property office to be most efficient.'

'They ought to put her on the wireless,' said Mr Slater, applying his rubber sorting aid to a stack of flimsies. Flick, flick, flick. 'She'd soothe some nerves.'

By late afternoon, work tailed off in all the Records Offices, except Records Office A (Greater London), which was only to be expected. Elsewhere in the partitioned rooms, people began to anticipate the night.

In Julia's case, anticipation took the form of heading off to the Ladies and changing out of the clothes she wore to work and into the frock that Dougie liked.

'Where do you think you're off to?' said Mr Keyes, when she made her way downstairs after the siren sounded.

'Out.'

'In this?' The night roared, the building shook, the sky burst into fragments.

'I've got to meet someone.'

'You'll meet your Maker if you aren't careful. Be a good girl. Go down the basement. It's a heavy one. He'll wait.'

Pedro's was packed. It seemed that the whole West End was here; and if not here, then in similar places close at hand. These were the people who chose to stay when they had the option not to, who kept houses open among so many dust-sheeted and shut up. You might suppose this to be a show of solidarity with those Londoners, by far the majority of the eight million, who had no choice but to remain and be bombed. You might even be told so, with the sort of pride that flew the flag of humility. But that would not be the whole story, for no truthful account could omit the fact that many were having the time of their lives.

'Waiting for someone?' said the blonde, arching her eyebrows.

Dougie reached across to light her cigarette. 'A friend. She's a little late. And you?'

They were both sitting alone at tables for two.

'Oh, I often toddle along of an evening. See who turns up.'

A distant, thundering sound.

The blonde caught his eye. 'Don't you just love this?' She stretched an arm to the ceiling and the creped flesh underneath it wobbled. 'So thrilling, don't you think?'

'That's one way of looking at it.'

The blonde laughed. 'It's the only way of looking at it.' There was something sultry about her mouth and the whisky notes of her voice. 'Let me guess what you do,' she said.

'You won't.'

'Try me.' She swivelled around in her chair and studied him in the guttering candlelight. 'You're not in uniform.'

'True.'

'You're young enough to be called up, but something tells me you're exempt.'

'Also true.'

'I wouldn't say you were a civil servant.'

'You flatter me.'

'Clearly not a vicar.'

Dougie laughed. 'I'm very glad to hear it.'

'Cultured accent, dishevelled dress, general air of superiority.' The blonde pressed her fingers to her temples, in a dumbshow of thinking. 'Oh, I've got it. BBC.'

Dougie was amused. 'May I buy you a drink?'

'I'd be delighted. But first you must tell me if I'm right.'

He signalled to the waiter. 'Another Scotch?'

The waiter brought their drinks. 'I'm a film director,' said Dougie.

'Really,' said the blonde, touching her hair.

He had her full attention, but she did not have his, because at that moment he spotted Julia across the room.

★

Julia came downstairs into the gathering chatter and saw Dougie clinking glasses – 'Cheers!' – with a woman whose impressive cleavage swelled from the front of a tight black bodice: 'all her goods in the shop window', her mother would have said. Her mind made one of those instant dismissive calculations: too old and brassy, surely. But Dougie was laughing.

She wove her way between the crowded tables. He waved and stood up.

'My friend,' he explained to the woman. Out of the corner of his mouth he said, 'You look beautiful,' as Julia squeezed past him with a rustle of skirts.

'Some friend,' said the blonde, with a laugh.

'Am I interrupting something?' Julia was confident, now she was closer, that her first instinct had been right. No threat. *Well* past forty. The hair colour out of a bottle. In the humid basement, a line of sweat beaded the woman's upper lip, which bore the faint trace of a bleached moustache.

'Who was that?' she said later, when the woman had left.

'No idea. But I was about to be devoured.'

She smiled. 'I'm sure you would have handled it.'

'That reminds me. Is Kenny still being a nuisance?'

In the dark under-stairs cupboard where she sheltered with the Tooleys on bad nights, Kenny's wandering hands had been lending an added vexation to the business of staying alive.

'Oh, he's scarpered. I haven't laid eyes on him since he got his call-up papers last week. And before I forget, I'm afraid the ceiling has come down in your study.'

Something clandestine about the autumn evenings, something snatched and liable to fall through at the last minute and with no notice, gave these encounters in the raids the tenor of an affair – their affair when it had first begun. It was obvious others felt the same, obvious in the dark fumbled streets charged with fear and sex.

A few distant thuds, then a much nearer one, broke conversation. Oil bomb in Marylebone, said someone, who had deputized himself to go out and ask a policeman. Then talk resumed, and things were as before: not hectic perhaps, but wholly alive and present.

It was not true what Julia had told Bea. She imagined that nowhere in the city, except on the deepest Underground platforms, could you forget what was happening up top. So far as a shelter was safe – the Institute basement, for example, the under-stairs cupboard at Primrose Hill, the tunnels at Denham – the supper club was safe enough. But this was to ignore what harm a basket of incendiaries landing on the roof might do – thanks to the porter Mr Keyes and his drills, she was now fully informed in that regard, along with everyone else in her department. Pedro's, while maintaining a certain pre-war style in the quality of its refreshments, had no visible fire exit.

They held hands across the table and talked about their work. Or, rather, since Julia's work did not lend itself to conversation, they talked about Dougie's.

They were together so little. The last time they had spent any length of time in each other's company had been ten days ago, a Sunday, when they'd packed up the paintings, the early Birdsalls, and most of his books and taken them to be stored in the attic of his producer's house in Hertfordshire. 'I paid twenty-five guineas for this,' Dougie had said, laying a first edition of *Alice's Adventures in Wonderland* in a tea chest as if he were putting a baby to bed. A month ago, before the bombing began, the knowledge that he possessed such a valuable book – a book which, if sold, might fund a divorce – would have inspired her to hit him round the head with it. But at that moment his possessiveness seemed perfectly reasonable. People were losing everything.

'To think a little bad weather used to make us miss shots,' he was saying. 'Considering what's coming down from the sky these days, a force-nine gale would be a piece of cake.' He shook his head. 'You know, when I stumbled across this collagey way of working in the summer, I thought I was making a virtue out of a necessity. But it turns out to be much more expressive than that.' His new film was about the bombing.

'You didn't stumble across it,' said Julia. 'It's the way your mind works. Have you heard anything from the MOI?'

'Yes, unfortunately. We have to cut the sequence we shot in Poplar, cut it right back. They're worried it shows too much damage.'

Mere mention of the sequence he'd shot in Poplar ambushed her with retrospective fear. On the first night of the Blitz – what had seemed at the time the catastrophic beginning of invasion – they had watched London burning from the top of Primrose Hill, the sky pulsing red in the east as if the sun had decided to set in the wrong direction. She later learned that while they were standing there Frank was filming the blazing docks from the riverbank near Greenwich. The same impulse to bear witness now sent Dougie to locations where he stood every chance of being a casualty of the next bomb that fell. 'But isn't the point to show how well we cope? Isn't this aimed at the Americans?'

'Exactly. And if the point is to show how well we cope, I should have thought you'd need to see the scale of what we're coping with. All the same, it seems I've gone too far. God knows,' he said, stubbing out his cigarette, 'how they decide such things. However, they very much liked the tea-making in the mobile canteen. And the plucky kid. Everyone likes a plucky kid.'

'They should trust your judgement. They must know you see things you can't film. That doesn't mean you aren't telling the truth.'

'Doesn't it?' An example of his self-censorship sprang to mind. It was the Middlesex all over again. You might talk about limbs being lost, as if they might turn up down the back of the sofa, or limbs blown off, as if in a high wind. But the leg retrieved from the bomb site in Poplar by the Heavy Rescue sifting through a smoking, shifting pile of rubble that used to be three terraced houses was the actuality: no flesh below the knee, nothing except a loose flap of skin and gory splintered bone, the foot gone, blasted to buggery. A bloody skein of dangling veins flapped about as the body part was covered in sacking and laid on a stretcher alongside an assortment of humanoid gobbets.

Other things, too. The people who had been killed by bits of other people, for example. 'Now heads is heavy,' the rescue worker had told him. 'Ten pound or more. You don't want to be hit by one of those.'

Then there were the vermin who had crawled out of the wood-work: the ones who pinched the rings off dead fingers, who whisked away roof slates stacked by the kerbside, who looted bombed shops, who raped in the shelters, who knifed black-market rivals in dark wharves and alleyways or conveniently bludgeoned burdensome wives. He had been told so many similar stories by members of so many defence squads, by policemen, firemen, ambulance drivers, wardens, that it would be idiotic, or wilfully blinkered, not to believe at least some of them.

'Do you know,' he said, 'demolition men are notorious for thiev-ing? They stuff their overall pockets with silver and whatever else they can lay their hands on. Apparently they view it as compen-sation for the danger of the job.'

'That doesn't surprise me, I'm afraid,' said Julia. 'War was never going to turn us into a nation of saints.'

'I suppose not.'

Julia said, 'Besides, if you filmed such things, the Germans would use it as propaganda.'

'There is that.'

She was watching his mouth. He was watching hers.

'Shall we go?' he said, his thumb circling in her palm.

They went upstairs, pushed through the thick blackout curtain that hung limp inside the club entrance and came out on to the street. Outside things had quietened down a bit. The guns were silent, although the imprint of their heavy sound still hung in the air. Searchlights fingered the black sky. Shrapnel clattered on a Soho roof and rattled into a gutter.

There in the dark they turned to each other, and in the hunger of their kiss was their first kiss, laced with experience.

'Later,' she said, knowing full well you couldn't depend on there being a 'later' and not wanting him to stop. He didn't. She didn't.

Instead he steered her down an alley and had her up against a wall.

'Good evening?' said Bea, the next day.

'Yes, thanks,' said Julia, turning her face away. Her hand reached round her back, under her blouse, where the wall had scraped her.

'Did absence make the heart grow fonder?'

'Doesn't it always?' It had been another person who had had sex in the street, thought Julia, another person who had enjoyed it, although 'enjoyed' did not begin to convey the blind urgency she had felt. Such was her present dismay that already in her mind another story was being written, where Dougie had been the sole instigator of this quite shameful and outrageous act – an act worthy of ten divorces – and her transgressive pleasure had played no part in it at all.

Late October, the thirty-second night of continuous bombing. A bad night.

Julia was in the under-stairs cupboard with Mrs Tooley and George. The guns were pounding away on Primrose Hill, but they didn't bother her any more. She could sleep through the guns. Once she put her head on the pillow, she was out like a light.

What bothered her was what they were hearing now: swoosh, swoosh, *swish*, followed by thud, thud, *thud* as bombs dropped nearer and nearer. A gap, an enormous THUD and the house shook on its foundations, wobbled like a milk tooth. You couldn't shut out the noise. Nor could you contain it. You became it, and it became you.

'Did you turn off the gas?' said Mrs Tooley when she could make herself heard. Dirt, or some loose constituent of the house, trickled down underneath the stairs.

'I did,' said Julia.

'Have you got the torch?'

'I have.'

'Mind you don't go switching it on, then. We'll need the battery when they come to rescue us. We'll need to shine a light, show 'em we're here.'

They had spent all or parts of twenty-three nights in this under-stairs cupboard, five on the trot one week. On each occasion Mrs Tooley said the same thing and on each occasion it felt like the first time she'd said it.

George scrabbled in his basket, meeping.

'You want to get rid of that cat.'

'He's not mine to get rid of.' Julia had become attached to the cat. She talked to the cat.

Early on in the Blitz, she and Mrs Tooley had discovered the one thing they had in common, aside from, or rather related to, the desire to stay alive: an aversion to public shelters. The local shelter where Mr Morton, their warden, urged them to go on a nightly basis was a surface shelter, and they'd all heard about those. 'You'd be a sitting duck, I tell you that for nothing,' Mrs Tooley said. Julia agreed. The Tube didn't appeal either. You had to queue early to secure a spot and her job ruled that out. Besides which, she had a horror of its stinks, latrines, unwashed bodies, the stale, claggy odours of the refreshment trains, and of shifting for herself among large numbers of strangers.

Say what you like about Mrs Tooley, but she was no longer a stranger.

It seemed to Julia that in the matter of sheltering, where and when, they all clung on to the illusion of choice, because choice suggested that you had some control over your destiny, and that decisions could be made by applying reason to evidence. Yet she knew this was not the case. The first time you decide to go down the shelter, the shelter takes a direct hit. The first time you decide not to go down the shelter, you're killed in your bed. Hundreds of chance decisions, hundreds of ways chance could catch you out. You couldn't second-guess them all. The best you could do was pick a place where you didn't mind waiting for death.

Swoosh, swish, swish. Thud, thud, THUD.

The walls pulsed with the blast wave. A shudder, a roar, then a sound like someone kicking a tin trunk down the stairs.

That was near.

Safe as houses.

Except houses weren't safe any more. They were killers, versatile killers with many methods up their sleeve. Flying glass from the windows. Dodgy ceilings. Gas explosions. Burst water mains. Heavy furniture that toppled over and sent you flying into the next world. Mr Morton, the cats' meat man in a former life, had told them of the wife two streets away obliterated by her own cartwheeling dining table, a table she hadn't finished paying for yet. In the next breath, the boy whose wardrobe had fallen over him like an upturned coffin and saved him when the ceiling came down.

'If you can't face the Tube,' Dougie had said, 'promise me you'll sit under the stairs. It's the strongest part.' She'd seen this for herself. Who hadn't? Those peeled-away doll's houses, fronts off, roofs off, and still the stairs clung on, connecting floors that were gone, connecting nothing with nothing. Didn't mean you'd be dug out, though. Didn't mean you wouldn't be trapped by the rubble. Didn't mean you wouldn't burn to a crisp.

Didn't mean Dougie wouldn't either, wherever he was.

'How's your boy getting on?' said Mrs Tooley, a few hours later.

'Fine, by all accounts,' Julia said into the dark. 'He likes school, which is just as well, considering he has to stay there. At least, he likes everything about it except lessons. And the food.'

A chuckle. 'Bet you miss him.'

'Yes, I do,' said Julia. The bombing had brought one benefit. It had allowed her to delude herself that war was all that separated them. Peter's latest letter was in her handbag, and her handbag was at her feet beside her respirator. *Dear Madre, Could Harry send a parcle, the food is drettful.* Day boys from Birmingham were now billetted at Crossfields: the school was full to bursting.

'Still, he's well out of this.'

'He is,' said Julia. 'Have you heard from Kenny?' This was pushing things, she knew, but they had arrived at the stage when confidences seemed in order. It was either that or plan your own funeral.

'He's with my sister.'

'Where's that?'

'Over the water,' said Mrs Tooley, with grim satisfaction.

Ireland, thought Julia. A low drone of planes sounded overhead.

Shells fired from the anti-aircraft emplacement on the top of Primrose Hill shrieked on the ascent and exploded at some altitude. Then came a sound Julia dreaded more than any other, the cascading rattle of incendiaries.

Mrs Tooley had heard it too. In the dark sloping cupboard, musty, cobwebby and black-beetled, Julia sensed a different quality of attention, the working of a tongue around toothless gums.

'The roof,' said Mrs Tooley, 'do you think?'

'We'd best check.'

No answer.

Julia put out a hand she couldn't see and with it touched some yielding, uncorseted part of Mrs Tooley. 'If it's the roof, it'll take two of us to deal with it.'

Another cascading rattle.

They plunged from the cupboard and ran up the dark stairs. At the top, weak wavering torchlight located the ladder placed in readiness under the roof hatch, alongside a shovel and a pair of buckets filled with sand.

'Something's burning.' Julia grabbed a bucket, climbed the ladder and opened the hatch.

White light, eye-aching. Two of them, two brilliant magnesium lumps, were burning in the roof space, one under the eaves. A haze of smoke stung her eyes.

'Pass me the shovel,' she said to Mrs Tooley. 'Hurry.'

They called it a drill because they drilled it into you. Wardens, leaflets, cigarette cards.

Inching from joist to joist, crouching under the smoke, she shovelled sand over both bombs until they were covered. Then she scraped up the particles of burning metal as fast as she could and dropped them into the bucket.

She handed the bucket down to Mrs Tooley and shone the torch around the attic. The skeletal shapes of the children's cots. One, two, *three* holes in the roof. There was another one somewhere.

It didn't take long to find it. When she pushed open the bedroom door she saw the bomb had burned through the ceiling and landed on the mattress. The fire was beginning to catch, flames licking the ticking.

The guns started up again, and the thuds. The banshee whines, the ack-ack ack-acking away, the shrieks and the roars and the clangs and the clatters.

She worked quickly, fetching the second bucket, dumping sand on the incendiary and scraping up the burning bits under the bed. Then she sent Mrs Tooley for the blanket that was soaking in the bath and threw it on the mattress. The bed hissed and steamed.

As soon as the fire was out Julia took both buckets down the stairs, switched off the torch and opened the door. Overhead, raking searchlights. Shrapnel hissing, clanging everywhere. She left the buckets in the street.

'You get all of it?' said Mrs Tooley, back in the cupboard.

'Let's hope so.' It was only then she was aware that her heart was hammering.

While Julia sheltered in an under-stairs cupboard of her own choosing, Dougie was a few miles away, crouched alongside Frank on a flat, narrow strip between the leaded slopes of a valley roof. They were filming.

'Over there,' said Frank. 'Land mine, don't you think?'

'Possibly. Judging by the scale of the fire.' The fierce Fauvist colours – the lurid greens, blood reds, sharp yellows – the sheer gaudiness of the Blitz: this they could not capture. 'How I wish we had Technicolor.'

'Do me a favour. Those cameras are the size of a fridge. It was hard enough getting the Newall up here.'

And if they could not reproduce the colours, nor could they begin to suggest the smells. Down by the docks the other day had lingered the stench of burning resin, tar, spice: an unholy, industrial, commercial stink. Tonight, a damp heavy fug of cordite hung over Soho Square.

A starburst over to the east, then the rumbling chunter of impact. Searchlights caught the planes, masses of them, engines thrumming, black shapes with wings outstretched against the lit-up sky. Each bomb blazed a path for the next.

'Bastards,' said Frank, passing him the hip flask.

The angel roof, thought Dougie, taking a swig. What had Julia said that day back in the church? Not menacing, not protective, but indifferent. As indifferent as God. You would have to be to destroy indiscriminately, to know that you must be killing women and little children, the elderly, the sick. Schools, churches, hospitals had taken direct hits – another crump nearby and he wondered about the Middlesex.

'Are we done?' said Frank. 'Because I for one am beginning to feel rather uncomfortable up here, even with the tin hat.'

Shrapnel was pinging around the place. They packed up, rapped on the roof hatch and handed the camera down into several pairs of unseen hands. This took a while.

Back at street level, they paused in the doorway. 'Thanks,' said Dougie.

'Always happy to oblige.'

Dougie lit a cigarette. 'I couldn't let them shovel in that appalling newsreel footage.'

'Oh,' said Frank, 'I quite agree. Worth risking your life not to have them shovel in that appalling newsreel footage. Where are you off to now?'

'Home.'

'In this? You'll be lucky.'

'I worry about Julia sitting through it on her own.' Or as good as, he thought, remembering Mrs Tooley.

Frank said, 'I expect she worries about you out here filming.'

'She would do if she knew.'

In the event, Frank was right. He couldn't get home. It was too late for the Tube to be running. On the roads were no taxis, no buses; the only vehicles ambulances, fire-pumps, hose-laying lorries, mortuary vans, careering past on their way to incidents. He hadn't got much further than the blasted caverns north of Oxford Street when a warden blew a whistle in his face and more or less marched him into Goodge Street Station.

Every shelter had its own character. Some were still and sober, temples of waiting and silent prayer. Some were busy with darts, card games and knitting. Others were as lively as a barrelful of monkeys: at Aldwych – or was it Bank? – there was reputedly a conjuror who did tricks while his accomplice picked your pockets. Goodge Street Station, where there wasn't so much as a square inch of platform left unclaimed, had a musical bent. He found a spot to prop himself up by the lift shaft and listened to 'One Man Went to Mow' echoing along the tunnels.

The mornings were the worst. Dougie could stand the clamour of the nights because they roused a kind of *Boy's Own* excitement in him which he understood to be the way he dealt with fear. The determination of the rescue squads in the face of the nightly onslaughts and the comradeship in the shelters also brought out a kind of pride that was part fierce patriotism and part a sense of wonder at what the human spirit could take. But mornings were desolate. The next day when he came out of the shelter at Goodge Street amid the clearings-up, he had the sense that he was moving through memories of the dead, or that he himself was the one being remembered, that he was someone else's memory. He felt weightless.

In the Lyons Corner House where he went for breakfast he was gripped by the sudden dread certainty that Julia was dead. He saw the house at Primrose Hill, a pile of rubble like so many others, and her lifeless body underneath it, bundled up in the cupboard under the stairs. When he lit a cigarette his hands were shaking.

It was early, and there were few others in the teashop: one or two customers on their own like him, and a couple of women murmuring at a table near the entrance, their hats touching. The waitress came with his tea and a bun so stale you could have bowled it. Beyond the steamed windows an army lorry juddered past, new recruits in their battledress off to training camps, their young half-shaved faces half asleep.

From the phone box on the corner he rang the flat. There was no answer. A chill settled inside him and he decided to walk for a bit, see if he could walk the feeling away. The house in Primrose Hill loomed in his mind. He formed the notion that if he went back before he got through on the phone he would find no one and nothing there. This was nonsense: the lines were always going down. But everyone was superstitious after their own fashion these days. Everyone had their way of crossing their fingers.

All around, the streets were a maze of diversions. Each morning London had to learn new routes, flush its traffic through its own damage as best it could. Buses churned down side roads and, everywhere, the rumble of rubble being shifted and cleared.

The raids had been going on for long enough now that you could distinguish new ruins from old. The old, stuck all over with little paper Union Jacks, already beginning to soften a bit, to acquire a sort of historical aspect; the new, raw and ragged. This morning, Holborn was a mess, blocked off, and the rescue squads were busy, digging, calling at intervals, watched by a small crowd of rubber-neckers.

He stood a moment, wondering which of the familiar buildings had been bombed. The insurance headquarters? The music-hall theatre? That little parade of shops where he had bought Julia the garnet pin? It was hard to get your bearings, marshal your memory, when whole streets were gone.

'Gone'. That implied a vacancy, a vanishing act. What he was seeing and smelling was deconstruction, where the parts occupied more room than the formerly whole. How buildings came to pieces told you how they were put together.

It was always the same. Up above, the rakish angle of caved roofs, exposed joists, purlins and rafters; down below, the everlasting pinkish brownish whitish dust, churned into sticky mud by the fire hoses. Floors sandwiched together. A litter of bricks, half bricks and what held the bricks together; the slithery slope of blasted timber, planks over planks; wires, twisted pipework and fallen guttering. Laid bare the stage sets, or doll's-house rooms, a flapping curtain snagged on a hook, lavatory tiling, a panelled corridor leading nowhere, family photographs lined up on a mantelshelf above a floorless room. Here and there in the rubble something recognizable: a typewriter with paper fed through the carriage, a tailor's dummy, an umbrella stand fashioned from an elephant's foot. The city a surrealist's landscape, where trees wore clothing.

Tin-hatted men were swarming over the wreckage, peering into holes and cavities, their boots scrabbling for purchase. 'Quiet!' and an arm would go up.

The stillness was a wound in itself.

Oh my London.

He turned north towards Bloomsbury, into the austere pattern of Georgian streets around the British Museum, each door-case, each fanlight seeming to shimmer on the brink of loss. The eighteenth-century mind, which he admired so much for its enquiry, its industrious reason, its codifying of what was beautiful and useful, and not least for its honest vulgarity, was nowhere more present than in these threatened, coal-blackened squares. It began to rain.

As he walked, he could not tell the difference between what he had shot and what he was seeing, what he remembered and had recorded and what was presently laid out in front of him. 'We Can Take It,' read the slogan on the back of a salvage van.

★

176

The all-clear. They came out of the cupboard, stretched their numb, cramped limbs, all pins and needles, and looked at each other as if surprised to discover their voices were attached to bodies. Every morning that same astonishment, the same dizzying fall away into separateness after the same dark closeness of smell and sound and fear. It was almost a kind of embarrassment.

Mrs Tooley said, 'Turn on the gas, will you? I'll set the kettle to boil.'

Mr Morton, the warden, called by in his tin hat to check them off his list and tell them number thirty-nine had gone and the back of number twelve in the next road. UXB in the park; they wanted to watch out, keep away from the taped-off parts. 'They're softening us up for invasion. That's their game, all right.' He handed them a bottle of milk.

'Where'd you find that?' said Mrs Tooley.

'On the doorstep.'

Julia was sitting on the stairs drinking her tea. The usual glorious release of morning was missing; she didn't know why. Instead, she felt gritty inside and out, her head swimming. She thought she should ring the Institute, tell them she'd be late, then she remembered it was Saturday and she didn't have to. Only the senior staff worked Saturdays. 'Number thirty-nine?' she said. 'Is that the one with the green door?'

'Brown door. Second on the right past the turning,' said the warden.

'The Connells,' said Mrs Tooley. 'Rough lot.'

The warden said you mustn't speak ill of the dead. He shook his head. 'All six of them, including the gran.'

'Being dead don't make them any less rough,' said Mrs Tooley.

The warden noted details of their incendiaries for his report, then paused halfway out the door. 'You use a stirrup pump?'

'Sand,' said Julia. 'They've sold out of stirrup pumps.'

'You done well,' said the warden. 'I shouldn't think one in four would have had the sense. Perhaps,' he said, 'not one in ten.'

Julia said it was nothing; she'd been taught how to do it at work.

'You can teach people until you're blue in the face,' said the warden. 'That doesn't stop them sitting around on their backsides waiting for someone else to do it for them.' He nodded. 'You saved the house, you know. And probably your skins and all.'

Julia was surprised. She supposed she had. What she'd done she'd done without thinking, just as she would have pushed Peter out of the way of an oncoming car purely on instinct.

When he had gone, she thanked Mrs Tooley for the tea and made to go upstairs. Her feet didn't seem to want to connect with the treads. Her feet didn't seem to be at the end of her legs.

'You want to have a wash. I should,' said Mrs Tooley. 'You need a penny or two for the geyser, you just ask.'

Julia nodded.

Mrs Tooley said, 'Your man's wife, her that went. I'd like to see her deal with them bombs the way you did. Some people haven't got the stomach for this.'

Julia barely made it upstairs before she was sick in the lavatory. She ran the taps in the basin, but the water was off. So she leant over the bath, where the wet blanket had been soaking, and rinsed out her mouth. You filled the bath and the kettle before the sirens went. Most times, it was the only way you had water in the morning.

The phone was dead.

George, released from his basket with the all-clear, eyed her from his usual perch on top of one of the club chairs, tail flicking. Nothing else was as usual. Denuded ochre walls where the pictures had been, emptied bookshelves, a coarse film of dirt sprinkled over everything, and the last of the windows gone. She went to fetch the dustpan and brush to sweep up those jagged splinters that had fallen indoors, not out. Days later, an odd glint would catch her eye and she would find another lethal shard lurking by a skirting board.

The bedroom was worse than she expected, the mattress damp, blackened, with a yawning cavity in the middle down to the springs, the blanket ruined and pillows ditto. It smelled foul. She was so tired she briefly considered hauling the children's cots down from the attic until she realized how foolish that was. Instead, returning to the sitting room, she cobbled together the seat cushions of the club chairs, undressed, wrapped herself in her good coat and lay down on them while the cat curled itself at her feet, on her feet and between her feet, until it had made itself quite comfortable thank you.

War made strange bedfellows, thought Julia, thinking not of the cat but of Mrs Tooley. War made strange beds.

Two hours later, the telephone woke her. It was Dougie. 'Sinclair. I've been trying to reach you.'

'The phone was out of order.'

'What was under water?'

'I said the phone was out of order. We had a bit of a fire.'

The operator: 'One minute, caller.'

'Where?'

The line was bad. She had to shout. 'In the bed.'

'Your side or mine?'

She laughed. 'Where are you?'

Dougie said, 'On my way home.'

He was elated. Julia was alive, he was alive, they were both alive. What did they say? *You don't die a day sooner than you're meant to.* Others would not have survived the night, but they had. A form of rebirth propelled him out of the phone box and on to the pavement. That was when he noticed where he was. Lamb's Conduit Street. He had meandered round in a circle.

A degree of normality was returning after the raids. People walked past, engaged on errands or private business. The sun came out. He lit a cigarette and watched a young woman coming along the street towards him.

'Is it working?' she said, indicating the phone box.

'All yours,' he said, pulling the door open for her.

My God, how lovely she was. Stupendous eyes. Great legs.

'Bad night,' he said.

Her stupendous eyes brimmed a little. 'Frightful.' She stepped past him into the phone box and the door closed behind her.

A few minutes later she finished her call and emerged. 'Oh. You're still here.'

'I was wondering if you'd have lunch with me.'

A wan smile. 'What makes you think I have lunch with strange men?'

'Dougie Birdsall,' he said.

Her name was Imogen Watts and, yes (after some charming prevarication), she supposed she might accept his invitation; she was quite shaken up, she had to admit. There was nothing like the Blitz, was there really, to break down the barriers between people.

This unoriginal sentiment made him smile inwardly. But she was so very, very lovely to look at. And now the elation had worn off, there was that familiar chafing sensation that someone was waiting for him in a place they both called home.

'There's a nice place round the corner,' he said. 'I'm assuming you have no strong objections to Italian restaurants?'

'Let's hope it's still standing.' Her smile was a little stronger, as if she had instructed herself to be brave.

'I came past it earlier.'

I have been faithful to thee, Cynara! in my fashion. That absurd line of Dowson's echoed in Dougie's head. Unlike Barbara, who had always been able to tell what he had been up to as soon as she heard the scratch of his key in the lock, Julia lacked the nose for betrayal. Or perhaps it was her eyes she kept shut. Whichever was the case, he led Imogen Watts up Lamb's Conduit Street towards Luigi's with the deeply reassuring sense of the danger that safety bestowed.

16

'Good Lord,' said Dougie. 'Half the BBC's here.'

And most of the Unit, thought Julia.

It was New Year's Eve and they were at Bernard's house in High-gate.

A rumble of conversation filled the room; smoke wreathed under the ceiling. Despite the number of people and the occasion, this wasn't a hectic dancing on graves; the mood, if not entirely sober, was sombre.

For good reason. The big raid on the City two nights ago had cut a wound deep in the national psyche. The destruction of buildings had become commonplace, not so the destruction of architecture. The morning after, there had been a leaden few hours when no one knew if St Paul's was still standing or whether they could bear to carry on if it wasn't. Then word began to spread that the cathedral had survived, against all odds, and this morning there had been a photograph in the *Mail* to prove it.

Dougie had been trying to talk his way past the cordons all day, with no success. None of his friends in the rescue services would let him anywhere near the worst of it. The entire area was a haz-ard. Fires were still burning, blackened remains of buildings still toppling as snow fell.

Now as they made their way through the crowd she was con-scious of glances in his direction, admiring and curious. More than once she heard the murmured words *London Pride*, which was the title under which his Blitz film had been released. Overnight he had become somebody. Yet her pride in his achievement was tempered by an anxiety that from now on she would have to defend her claim on him against all comers.

Bernard had been a somebody for some time. They found him

in the blacked-out conservatory, standing next to a concrete mermaid with a concave back from which sharp leaves grew. He was at the centre of a small, rapt, tweedy group, all male, talking about a work in progress, a 'sonic poem very much inspired by the nightly cacophony'. It was an inner party, a salon within a salon. Flapping a hand and mouthing hello to acknowledge their arrival, Bernard moved to the baby grand and dashed off a few thunderous dissonant chords to the accompaniment of shrieking twangs on the piano strings produced with a pair of pliers.

'These fragments, these fragments,' he said, returning.

'Most powerful,' said a man with deep grooves in his face.

'Ben thought so, when I sent it to him.'

Ben would be Britten, thought Julia.

'Although of course he is a raging pacifist,' said Bernard. 'The sort who would welcome invaders with open arms and furnish them with hot-water bottles and tickets to the Hippodrome.'

'It's easy to be a pacifist in New York,' said Dougie.

Bernard pointed at Dougie with his pipe stem. 'This is the man who made the film that's been such a great success at the American box office.'

Heads turned.

'Dear boy,' said Bernard, 'a little bird told me Roosevelt had a private screening. Is it true?'

Julia sensed a hesitation on the 'Roosevelt'. She felt sure Bernard had been about to say 'Franklin' or perhaps 'Frank'.

Dougie said he didn't know whether or not it was true.

'Artistically, I thought the film most original,' said Bernard. 'All the visual links you were able to make, the connections. One sees such odd things these days, one needs an entirely new vocabulary.'

Dougie, visibly flattered, began to talk about film language.

Florian came into the conservatory with a couple of young naval lieutenants. 'Your film, Dougie,' he said, his hand on his heart. 'I've seen it five times. It doesn't half buck one up. Oh hello, Julia, darling, didn't notice you there.'

Stranded on the edge of the group, a dotted outline of a person, Julia felt simultaneously invisible and exposed. At that moment through the drawing-room door she noticed a young woman with a heart-stopping face standing in front of the fire. She had black hair amateurishly chopped around her jawline and was wearing a holed red jumper, a pink silk shirt and a pair of men's pinstriped trousers. Something had happened to clothing lately. You were no longer shocked to see people in the street in their pyjamas or dressing gowns, or in whatever they had been able to snatch up on the spur of the moment. This was different, this was a pose, thought Julia, surprised at the animosity that flared like a lit gas jet. As if sensing the ill-feeling, the girl turned and stared in her direction, a long level look, then resumed the conversation she was having with a BBC type in a sleeveless Aran jumper and horn-rimmed spectacles, one earpiece held in place with sticking plaster.

It was getting on for midnight.

'Do you mean to tell me you have no windows?' said Netta, Hugh Trevelyan's wife.

'It's impossible to get them boarded up,' said Julia. 'There's such a shortage. And no point in getting them glazed, of course. Supposing, that is, one could get them glazed.'

'But you must be absolutely perishing in this weather.' Netta had a broad thinking forehead and large practical hands. Before her marriage, she'd been a commercial illustrator working in advertising, but she'd given that up to have babies and sit on local committees. A lynchpin of the Chorleywood WVS, Julia understood.

'We wear our coats. And sometimes blankets.'

Netta shook her head. 'Oh dear, no. That is too bad. You must both come to us. We have plenty of room.'

Julia said, 'We're hardly bombed out.'

'Neither of you can possibly function under such circumstances. Let me speak to Hugh.'

Someone had turned on the wireless and there was that moment of forced suspense, before the fake renewal of the New Year. Julia looked around for Dougie but couldn't see him, and when the time came to sing 'Auld Lang Syne' she found herself holding hands with Sylvia and Bernard's housekeeper, Mrs Railton. It was at times like these – dates on the calendar with memories indelibly stamped on them – that she missed Peter most. *Should auld acquaintance.*

Afterwards, Sylvia handed her a handkerchief, in the manner of a bus conductress punching out a ticket.

'Sorry.' Julia blew her nose. 'Thanks.'

Sylvia was addressing the middle distance. 'That system you devised has made quite a difference this past month, with the raids on the industrial towns. I have drafted a memo recommending that the same procedure be adopted across the Institute.'

'Have you?'

'I must confess I was surprised. You have a flair for this sort of work.'

A flair for filing? 'It just seemed straightforward,' said Julia.

Where was Dougie? she thought. Then she saw him through the drawing-room door, out in the hall, talking to the girl with the chopped black hair. 'If anyone else talks about huge doll's houses with their fronts ripped off, I am simply going to scream,' said the girl in a clear, carrying voice. 'It's such a bloody cliché.'

Sylvia followed her gaze. 'Not the easiest of men, I imagine.'

'Who was that person you were talking to just now?'

'No idea,' said Dougie as they went out into the snowy night, the stinging flakes falling unobserved, but not unfelt. After the warm, crowded house it was bitterly cold and deathly still. Only criss-crossing searchlights probing the skies from Hampstead Heath disturbed the darkness.

From Highgate back to Camden it was a long way downhill. They turned out of Bernard's road, she slid on the ice and he put a hand under her elbow to steady her up.

'Netta's terribly concerned that we have no windows,' said Julia, huddling in her coat. 'To the extent that she's invited us to move in with them.'

There was a short pause, when she imagined him turning the idea over in his mind. This surprised her: she had thought he would dismiss it out of hand. Did she want him to dismiss it out of hand? She wasn't sure.

'Well, it's much nearer Denham. And it wouldn't be difficult for you to get to work either. They're on the Tube and the main line into Marylebone.'

Footsteps came past; a man's, by the sound of them. Across the road, a door opened on a blare of New Year sound, then thudded closed again.

'What do you think?' he said.

'I can't say the idea of being somewhere warmer and cleaner isn't appealing.' She tried to make this sound indefinite, fence-sitting.

'Company for you, too, when I'm at the studio or away filming.' He was conscious of letting out a breath, relieved that she was prepared to entertain the notion, which had not sprung to Netta's mind unaided. Lately, the feeling of responsibility, of placing Julia in unnecessary danger simply by virtue of where he had chosen to live pre-war, had been weighing on him. In his mind, she had been dead under the stairs any number of times.

'The children wouldn't bother you?' The Trevelyans had two boys and a girl under eleven, all in boisterous rude health, with pets.

She could hear his smile in the blackout.

'You mean more than the raids and the guns? No, I doubt it.'

Warmth, cleanliness, company, convenience. Somehow this cataloguing of advantages was not as persuasive as it might have been. The flat in Primrose Hill, which had once seemed so intransigent, now stood in her mind as some sort of emblem of their love and life together.

'We'd lose our privacy. At least to some extent.'

She imagined it being rather like putting up at a bed and breakfast where one knew the proprietors. And proprietors of bed-

and-breakfast places were always a bit snoopy, whether you knew them or not.

'"The grave's a fine and private place, but none, I think, do there embrace,"' Dougie said. The dim light of his shaded torch picked out a bomb-damaged patch of pavement, which he steered her around. There was that sudden familiar earthy smell mixed with a nauseous stench of gas and effluent, a kind of reeking cavity in the air, which told them more than the pavement had been damaged. He remembered someone telling him about a block of flats in Stoke Newington. A direct hit in the middle of the building had trapped over a hundred and fifty people deep underneath the shattered floors, where they had drowned in sewage. No one had come out alive. To drown in shit: he gagged at the thought.

They came past Kentish Town Station, identifiable by the white 'S' for shelter painted outside. There were more people about, more voices, a little off-key singing.

'You wouldn't mind moving, then,' she said.

'I can't help but feel we're chancing our luck staying where we are,' he said. 'It would be nice not to worry about you any more than is strictly necessary.'

Here was the second-guessing again, thought Julia. The reasoning that led you to flee from danger right into its open arms. 'I suppose it would be sensible.'

They walked the rest of the way home in silence, a rare enough silence in Dougie's case, a puzzled one in Julia's. It seemed to her in these first minutes of the New Year – a year likely to bring invasion or worse – that he was bestowing on her as much safety as it was in his power to give. And safety was not a quality with which she associated him.

The dome of St Paul's was Darwin's forehead. He dissolved the two smooth hemispheres into each other in his mind, then carried on sketching.

A week later, the area around the cathedral was still smouldering, wisps of thin grey smoke rising in the air, as if from camp fires. A light snow fell, white on black, and immediately melted. They were near St Lawrence Jewry, or what remained of it. An arched window framed in stone was latticed, cross-hatched, all the panes gone. High up to either side were chipped and shattered memorials, busts, festoons, garlands, inscriptions. Down below, the strong diagonals of wreckage and cracked tomb lids, where the burning steeple had crashed down. Below that, unknown vaults held the fire's fierce heat.

A stage set, he thought, trying to capture the geometry, to compose what he was seeing. He had his Leica slung over his shoulder; he could have taken a photograph, but what he wanted was not reportage, it was the telling response of the human eye. It was more truthful.

There had been a time, some weeks ago, when he had found the loss of a London landmark supportable, set against the loss of hundreds, thousands, of ordinary London homes and lives. No longer. For before him, behind him, to either side, were the graves of eight Wren churches, churches that had sprung in all their intelligent beauty out of the ashes of London's last great fire, along with Wren's masterpiece, the cathedral.

What, all my pretty chickens and their dam?

Not the dam, thank God, thought Dougie. He rubbed his eyes and bent his head to his drawing. Not the dam.

Julia was perched on a hillock of rubble a short distance away, trying to work out where her father's accountancy office had been. She remembered visiting the premises as a schoolgirl, along with her brother, up two floors in a sooty Victorian building off Moorgate, a place stuffed with ledgers that had smelled of tired paper and polished wood, with a swimming dim light from green Holland blinds. The telephonist had always given them peppermints from a bag she kept in a desk drawer, shushing her lips as she did so. Now, H. W. Peters & Co. was some part of the obliterated scene in front of her – which part, it was impossible to tell.

Fore Street was closed. Cheapside and London Wall were sealed off. Not that they resembled streets any more.

She had spoken to her father twice since she had seen him in June. The first time was in September, soon after the beginning of the Blitz, when she realized he didn't have her telephone number; the second, on Christmas Eve, when she had been badly missing Peter's heart-sick anticipation of his stocking. On each occasion he had said that he was as well as could be expected and rung off as soon as possible.

The ruins swarmed with people. They popped in and out of view from behind the few standing walls, scrabbled up and down, clustered in small groups, pointing. One of them was waving.

'Mattie?' said Julia.

'Well remembered.' Mattie scrambled up the side of the hillock, panting. She was in civvies, which suited her less than her uniform, being dowdier and less tailored. Dougie looked up from his drawing.

'I saw your film,' said Mattie, clutching her hat on her head. 'You're developing quite an eye, aren't you? Rather different from Macleod's.'

'That's the general idea,' he said. 'But thank you.'

'I thought it most impressive. The sequence in the raid was thrilling.'

'Frank's the best cameraman there is.'

'You mean he puts his neck on the line when you ask him to.'

Dougie glanced at Julia, then began to pack up his drawing materials. 'A reserved occupation,' he said, 'doesn't guarantee safety. Nor should it.' He got to his feet and said he was going to move a little further away, see if he couldn't get a better view of St Paul's.

Julia watched him go. 'They didn't actually shoot that bit in the raid,' she said to Mattie. 'It was newsreel footage.'

Mattie snorted. 'That sequence was filmed by my brother from the roof of Soho Square.'

'What do you mean?'

'Did you not know?'

Julia shook her head.

'Did Dougie not say?'

'No.'

'Well, you want to ask him,' said Mattie. 'He was there too.'

Julia felt a hand squeeze her heart. Moving to Hertfordshire wasn't going to prevent that from happening in the future.

They stood for a while and watched men working on the remains of a building; to the left, cranes lifted blackened girders in slow-swinging arcs. Shouts, and then a charred wall came down as if in a dead faint. Onlookers, hundreds of them, raised their eyes to the sky, the crump of the falling masonry bringing to mind a different kind of drop.

Bomb tourists, they called them.

'Do you think they laid on a coach?' said Julia.

'It's human instinct,' Mattie said, winding her muffler round her throat. 'They only want to see for themselves what the papers won't tell them.'

'You mean they come for the truth?'

'Isn't that why you're here?'

Julia did not reply. She was here because Dougie was here, because she had hitched her desires to his. She was here because it was a way of spending a day with him, which was a rare enough occurrence.

Mattie stared into the distance. 'I was christened at St Bride's and, ever since I was a little girl, it was always where I planned to be married.' She turned to Julia. 'Do you know it?'

'No,' said Julia.

'The steeple is tiered, like a wedding cake.' Mattie's gloved hands shaped the tiers of a wedding cake. 'That part's still standing. Everything else is burned out.'

Julia often fooled herself into thinking that she didn't judge the appearance of others – in adolescence, her own had been nothing to write home about and even now her good looks seemed like the trick of the light in a mirror, on the point of vanishing. But there was no getting away from the fact that Mattie strongly resembled her brother, in a way no woman would want to. It was hard to imagine her as a little girl – she was so much her own unvarnished present self – much less a little girl with romantic ideas in her head. Ponies and gymkhanas, perhaps, not bridal veils at St Bride's.

They set off, walking – slipping – in the direction Dougie had gone, stones and loose dirt cascading under their feet, threatening to reveal at any moment disinterred skeletons, dry bones rattling to the surface from the many ruined churchyards, or to drop them into some concealed, heat-blasted cavern.

The landscape was as desolate as a battlefield and with about as many distinguishing features: part of a wall here, an empty shell there, no more. You imagined snipers on what rooftops remained, tank treads lurching, grinding over the debris, chewing it up and spraying it out, multiple black dots of invaders peppering the skies. For surely this was the prelude.

Mattie tripped on a shattered tombstone and narrowly avoided falling over. 'It's the wilful neglect that makes me furious,' she was saying, recovering her foothold. 'The stupidity. Leaving these buildings unattended over the holiday. Shutting them up without so much as a caretaker in attendance. We bloody asked for it.'

'It was no one's fault the tide was low.' At the height of the inferno, the mains had burst, the hoses had been unable to suck up water from the river mud and the pumps had run dry.

'They jolly well should have anticipated that possibility and constructed a reservoir. Not a single aspect of this war has been properly thought through. Not evacuation, not shelters, not anything.' Mattie turned to her, her breath a cloud in front of her face. 'Do you ever feel that you want to fire a gun? Repeatedly?'

'I can't say I do,' Julia said.

Mattie shook her head slowly from side to side. 'Are you quite certain you're fighting the same war as I am?'

There was an element, an undercurrent, of hostility in the question that Julia did not like, and it was echoed in the embattled expression on Mattie's face, which suggested that should she get hold of a gun she might use Julia as target practice.

*

The three of them went and had tea. There had been nothing to eat or drink in the City since the raid, no water, no gas, but Mattie knew a café at the top of St John's Street near Sadler's Wells. It turned out that Dougie knew it too. When they reached it, they found it 'more open than usual', as the saying now went. One of the plate-glass windows was gone; the other heavily taped. It was crowded with rescue men dressed in grimy overalls, with filthy hands and faces, as blackened as coalminers'. One recognized Dougie, and he went over to speak to him.

It was a scruffy place: cracked linoleum, peeling walls, days'-old, curling sandwiches in a glass cabinet. A stopped clock on the wall sat above a poster of Frinton-on-Sea, and a framed, slightly askew photograph of Anna Pavlova as the Dying Swan hung beside a pair of miniature ballet shoes in a nod to the location.

Julia ordered at the counter and carried the mugs over to their table by the taped-up window. Mattie was writing in a notebook.

'Diary?' said Julia.

'Something like that.' Mattie put the notebook away.

'I've got a job,' said Julia, sipping her hot chocolate. It had a thin, rather granular taste. She explained about the Institute of Labour Management.

'It sounds like filing.'

'It is filing.'

Mattie, Julia thought, was the kind of person who was always going to find her lacking. Or perhaps she hadn't got the hang of Mattie's bluntness. Or perhaps her bluntness was ordinary rudeness. Turning in her seat, she saw that Dougie was still talking to the rescue men. Then, when she thought about going over to give him his tea before it went stone cold, she saw the girl with the chopped black hair come in, the girl from New Year's Eve.

This time she was wearing a long black greatcoat, which she had belted tight at the waist, leather riding boots and a soft grey beret. Her lips were scarlet. Her cheekbones – how had she previously overlooked the cheekbones?

'Probably a dancer,' said Mattie.

191

'Who?' said Julia, pretending not to have noticed the girl, or to have experienced the same instant dislike she had felt the week before. Which play, film, or novel did she think she was in now? *Anna Karenina?*

The young woman with the chopped black hair – and the cheekbones – went over to the group of rescue men and began talking to Dougie.

'You can always tell dancers,' Mattie said. 'They have a way of holding themselves. A certain carriage of the head, a springy spine.' She drank her tea. 'You needn't look so alarmed. I wouldn't have said she was his type.'

'I've no idea what you mean,' said Julia, who did not care to have her mind read so easily.

A siren wailed. Then a distant thud. People looked up, calculated the distance and remained where they were.

Mattie was talking about the East End, whether Julia had been there, and if not, why not. 'Everyone should see it, even sheltered creatures like you. It's devastating.'

'I'm sorry?' said Julia. Preoccupied by the girl with the chopped hair, watching her as a cat might watch another slink into its backyard and through the bushes, her animosity like a living thing, she had caught the 'sheltered' too late to refute it with her bomb story. And she was rather proud of her bomb story.

Dougie came over to join them, put his Leica down on the table, took a sip of his tea and made a face. 'They lost two members of the squad in the raid. One of them was a chap called Briggs. A chap I filmed.' He lit a cigarette. 'They wanted to know if I would go to the funeral.'

'You should,' said Julia.

Mattie said, 'Are they expecting you to shoot it?'

Out of the corner of her eye, Julia saw the girl hovering around the counter, pulling a compact out of the pocket of her greatcoat, dextrously applying powder.

'Who's she?'

Dougie turned his head and shrugged. 'Her? A pain in the arse. She saw my film and now she wants a job.'

'Are you going to give her one?' said Mattie.

'Not up to me,' said Dougie.

Mattie snorted. 'Is that so?'

'She was at Bernard's party,' said Julia. 'That's a bit of a coincidence.' She waited for Dougie to say that there was no such thing as coincidence, but he didn't.

Another thud, closer by.

'Did Julia tell you we're moving?' said Dougie as they came out into the street and headed for the Angel. People were already queuing up outside the Underground station, clutching blankets, deck chairs and bedrolls, concertinas and birdcages.

'No,' said Mattie. 'She didn't. Where to?'

'Hertfordshire. Hugh and Netta's place.'

'You surprise me, Douglas. I had you down as a stayer.'

They parted at the barrier. Mattie's direction was south towards Embankment; theirs was north.

'Poor old thing,' said Dougie.

Down on the platform, a few families had already marked out their patch, bedding rolled up the curve of the grubby tiled wall, thermoses at the ready. An elderly man in a homburg was smoking and playing Patience, slapping down the cards as if he had something against them. A gust of dead air blew down the tunnel as a train approached.

Julia said, 'I thought she was doing her level best to be unpleasant.'

Dougie waited for her to mind the gap, then stood next to her, his Leica swinging from its strap. 'Her fiancé's plane came down over the Channel last month. They'd known each other since they were children. She's heartbroken.'

London, 1944

There has to be a way out of here, she thought. There has to be somewhere.

Out of here.

The sky was rising and falling. Beams slanted. The ceiling was missing.

Something shifted, tilted, gave way. A cavity opened up, a vacancy. From above came a narrow probing beam of light.

Someone groaned; something moved.

She smelled gas. The light went out.

There was no breath in this place. There was nothing to see. The walls walled her in.

I am trapped, she thought. Panic rose in her throat and choked her.

She was playing the piano. Her fingers hurt. A little tune, a little starling tune, lifted off the keys and flew away over her head. Up, up, to the narrow probing beam of light flew the starling.

17

The Trevelyans' place in Chorleywood was a brick-and-flint Victorian farmhouse with a slate roof which had been enlarged to the side and the rear sometime around the turn of the century. Together with a ramshackle barn and various slumped, huddled outbuildings, where Belgian refugees and Norwegian sailors had been accommodated in fleeting tenures (Netta collected people), the house sat on high ground in about an acre of garden. This adjoined a meadow, which in turn gave on to the village common, with beech woods beyond.

Inside, it was unassuming. Furnishings went together as if they had chosen themselves – the books conferring in the bookcases, the thin rugs creeping over the floorboards, the Windsor chairs with their dodgy rungs ranged around the dining table all said this. As did the dog hairs and dusty fingermarks.

The same companionability, however, did not always extend to the occupants. Small wonder. They had not gone to live in a bed and breakfast; they had gone to live with a family.

It was a Sunday in mid-July. Half past ten, and the air was thick and brooding. 'Not English, is it?' people had been saying all week, fanning themselves, flinging windows open wide. Julia, leaving the dim cool house to go and meet the train, was inclined to agree. She could remember summers when the only spell of hot weather could be guaranteed to coincide with school sports day. Since the war, seasons had become oddly seasonal.

The direct route to the station was by the lane that led to the main road, a journey she made every weekday morning and evening to and from work. Today, with time to spare, she set off the long way, which meant heading down the garden in the direction of the meadow.

Deep in snow when they had arrived six months ago, branches bare, the garden's well-composted productivity and wire hen-run now made her father's digging for victory, or what she remembered of it, look like someone playing about with a window box. To either side of a mossy brick path was Eden. Runner beans were setting at the top of their ridged supports, lettuce, carrots and onions were cropping, the boughs of espaliered apple and plum trees were already dotted about with small hard fruits ready to plump and ripen. They all worked here, weeding, hoeing, watering, even Dougie when he was around. For good reason: it fed them.

At the end of the brick path, she opened the gate and went into the meadow. The sun was hot on her bare head; the long grass swished at her bare legs, stems catching between her splayed toes in her flat sandals. From the brambly hedgerows twined through with honeysuckle came a rustling, like someone sifting sweets in a paper bag at the cinema. Bees drowsed in and out of the red campions and field scabious. Overhead swallows skimmed, from a distance their tiny shapes, bent wings and curved tails as precise as if they had been cut out of thin sheet metal.

'Pink, pink, pink,' warned a blackbird. 'Pink, pink, pink.' A tabby tail – George's – stalked through the tall grass.

Paradise, and she was miserable.

After Camden, she had found herself dropped into a rural idyll that her mother, who had longed to escape from a suburban village to a real one, would have adored. ('Chestertonian', Dougie called it.) This initial impression had been subsequently reinforced by silent nights, intact windows and everywhere the evidence of good, practical housekeeping of the bread-making, sock-darning and hearth-sweeping sort. There was even a piano, which, after she had arranged for it to be tuned, was playable.

What more could she want? In the first few weeks, freed from a dull heavy bomb anxiety whose pervasiveness was apparent only after she had left it behind, she had felt a fluid sense of possibility. Every morning she woke with the giddy prospect of life stretching ahead of her, the Blitz a bad dream.

This feeling had worn off in due course. Instead, all through the remainder of a hard winter, all through spring and into summer, she had walked the tightrope of the paying guest, which entailed making many fine judgements about how much help to offer and of what nature.

Other adjustments were involved. Hugh had a way of clicking his jaws; she wondered how Netta could stand it. The collie, Tinker, was barking mad. And the children were not so much boisterous as bewildered by the extent to which they found themselves striving to conform to their parents' separate and contradictory expect-ations, which led to misapprehensions, gouged thumbs, clashed chords and dented pride on an almost daily basis.

Every evening after the children went to bed, Netta worked on the Diaries: one each for Nicholas (eleven), Matthew (nine) and Louie (seven), illustrated in pencil and coloured inks, with events of the day fictionalized almost as soon as they had happened. 'Louie catches her first fish – it's a whopper'; 'Nick and the scrap-metal drive'; 'Matthew's sailboat – all his own work – launched on the village pond'.

Julia could understand the hungry hands – Netta, the illustrator, needed to draw, just as she needed to play. And Netta drew well, if what she drew was less than truthful. Tears, moods, pettiness went unrecorded, such as the morning Nick stole Louie's toast and her retaliation was to sink her teeth into the soft flesh of his upper arm, or the occasion Matthew conducted a scientific experiment on the squealing guinea pig, or any time when the children were being themselves, being children. Nor had the vomiting bug that hopped visibly around the family in late spring merited an entry. Yet the greatest fiction, in Julia's opinion, was that the Diaries were for the children's benefit. She supposed all family albums were the same: hers was, even if it was no longer in her possession.

Naturally there were also adjustments on the other side. By now, Julia was used to the state in which Dougie left a bathroom. 'A word,' Netta had said to her one morning, and showed her the bristles in the scummy sink, the bunched, sopping towel, the unflushed loo, much to her embarrassment. Julia thought less of him for that, perhaps unfairly, since all that had changed was that his careless untidiness had found a wider audience.

Netta's sensible view of war was that it required a postponement of desire for the greater good. It was her stock answer: to children wanting new toys or comics, to volunteers who took objection to their place on a rota, to Chorleywood shoppers complaining in queues about rations and shortages and showing each other dismayingly small lumps of cheese.

In Julia's view, the postponement of desire was a euphemism. What they all felt was the chafe of frustration. The itch of coming into a room and finding it occupied, the itch of always presenting certain aspects of yourself while hiding others. Yet, compared with what many people were going through, there was nothing whatsoever to complain about. Then why wasn't she happier? Why wasn't she grateful? The answer was Dougie.

She walked across the meadow, brushing clouds of midges from her face. The ground was stupefied by heat into benign passivity. Sweat trickled under her thin, cotton clothing and evaporated along her salty forearms. A pair of finches perched a yard apart made a music stave of the telephone wires. Clambering over a stile, she came out on the main road near the shady station approach.

Joe Coram was cycling up the hill. The Corams were their nearest neighbours. The elder son, Ian, was in the forces, and Joe was counting down the days until he could belabour his mother's heart in a similar fashion. 'Morning, Mrs Birdsall,' he said, pumping at the pedals, his face red as a beet, his hair darkened with sweat.

'Morning,' said Julia, wincing inwardly at the marital status Netta had awarded her to save village gossip.

'I hope we'll be seeing you at the match?' This afternoon, Chorleywood was playing the Unit at cricket.

'Of course.'

When she reached the platform Bea was waving to her from the end of it.

★

'I do miss the church bells,' said Netta. 'Sundays aren't Sundays without them. More lettuce?'

Bea helped herself to more lettuce from the dish offered. 'This is wonderful, Mrs Trevelyan.'

'Please call me Netta,' said Netta.

Nicholas got up from the lunch table and paced around the room in the over-large cricket pads he had been wearing all morning. 'Sit down, Nick. You haven't finished.'

'Mum! It's getting late. The match . . .'

'Sit down. We have a guest.'

'We always have guests,' said Louie to Bea. 'We have had guests for a long, long time.'

'Where's Dad?' asked Matthew, the middle one, the quiet one.

'Land of Liberty, with Dougie,' said Netta, handing round the curried vegetable turnovers.

In response to Bea's puzzled expression, Julia explained this was a local inn. Like all English villages, Chorleywood offered a wider choice of public houses than its population would appear to warrant. Although it was twenty minutes' walk away, in an outlying area known as the Swillet, Land of Liberty, Peace and Plenty was Dougie's preference on the grounds of its name alone. He had plans to film it for the same reason.

'I don't want to go to the match,' Louie said. 'The burn people might be there.'

'They won't be,' said Netta.

Louie frowned. 'They might.'

A few miles away was an RAF hospital. Once, back in the spring, a party of injured aircrew had come to the village – not their idea of an outing, one imagined. People had turned away from their shiny puckered faces, missing eyelids, ears and noses; not so Louie, who remembered them well, especially when she was tired.

'Have you been bombed?' said Louie to Bea.

'*Louie*,' said Netta in a warning voice.

'Julia was bombed,' said Louie. 'By incense.'

Bea controlled her twitching mouth. 'Julia is much braver than I am.'

Julia shook her head no. 'Bea stayed. I didn't.'

'But you go to London every day,' said Louie.

'That's different. I come back at night.'

And in so doing had avoided multiple terrors of the kind suggested by the dull, red glow they had sometimes seen from the end of the garden, or those recounted to her at the Institute in weary morning-after voices. The bombing was over – for London, for now – but the truth was, she had escaped much of it.

Once, she had thought nowhere was safe. Since the move, she knew different. Safety – relative safety, for safety could never be guaranteed – might be found at the end of a Tube line in the high woods of Hertfordshire. There was always a choice, and choice always came at a price.

'I have never been to London,' said Louie. 'I shall go when the war is over and meet the little princesses.'

Matthew looked up from his plate. 'But you have been to London, Louie. We went to the zoo.'

'That was before I was born,' said Louie. 'As I distinctly remember.'

'Take your plait out of your mouth,' said Netta. 'Pud? Bea has very kindly brought us cherries.'

'There were pips all over the platform this morning at Marylebone,' said Bea. 'Everywhere's got them all of a sudden. Two bob a pound.'

Nicholas said, 'We've got them here, too. Ours are free.'

'*Nicholas*,' said Netta in a warning voice.

'"Sing to the Motherland! O party of Lenin!"' said Nicholas. 'I know all the words to the Soviet national anthem. We were taught it at school.'

'How clever of you,' said Bea.

'Later,' Louie said to Bea, 'I shall play you my best piece. It is called "Over the Hills and Far Away". It is quite tuneful.'

Although not the way she played it.

★

The cricket match was already underway when Julia and Bea reached the common. The pitch was on the north side near the church, whose steeple was just visible, and as they approached the players were slow-moving white shapes against a backcloth of greenery. A thwack and scattered clapping.

A timeless sight, Julia thought, as she and Bea picked a shady spot to sit. Or at least one that went to the heart of the national character. She had always found cricket dull; now, she was surprised to add it to the long list of things worth fighting for. At closer quarters you saw what you couldn't make out further away: both sides were composed almost entirely of older men and young boys. A generation was missing, and some would not be coming back, including Eddie Grogan, who had once worked with Dougie, killed this past May in Crete.

The Unit team had won the toss and Hugh was batting. There had been some discussion about whether he should play for the side he worked with or the side where he lived; in the event, the Unit was a man short, so it was left to Nicholas to represent the Trevelyans on the Chorleywood eleven.

That Hugh's loyalties remained mixed could be seen by the way he lobbed the ball straight to Nicholas and let himself be caught out for three. Netta left off mending a deck chair, stood up and clapped – for both husband and son, one imagined. Her short-sleeved blouse revealed purplish calluses on her elbows.

'So which one is Dougie?' said Bea.

Julia had talked about Dougie so often she had almost forgotten that Bea had never set eyes on him. As she pointed him out on the far side of the pitch, she could see the effort her friend was making to square what must be by now quite a detailed mental impression with the beaky-nosed, tow-headed reality.

'The one who's reading?'

Julia nodded. Sometimes she thought that it had been the opportunity to reclaim his library that had been the deciding factor in Dougie's decision to move. Their room, in the side extension Netta called 'the annexe', was so stacked with books brought down from the attic that you had to zigzag as if you were a convoy avoiding a wolf pack to navigate from one side to the other.

'Batsman or bowler?'

'All-rounder.'

'Of course he is.' Bea squinted into the distance, her expression unreadable. 'Is he still as busy as ever?'

'Busier.'

'Working on another film?'

'He's always working on another film,' said Julia. 'It's just that some of them don't happen. I'm sorry he didn't make it to lunch.'

Bea turned and smiled. 'All the more for me.'

Thwack! and the ball soared over their heads and landed a short distance beyond the boundary, puffing up chalk dust from the dry ground. Bea went to pick it up, then chucked it back at the bowler – Mr Willis the butcher – in a fluid, accurate throw. He caught it one-handed and rubbed it on the top of his thigh, the red-dyed leather leaving streaks on his whites, the way lamb's hearts and other disappointing cuts leaked on his ceramic trays.

'That was impressive,' said Julia.

'I used to play with my cousins,' Bea said, sitting herself down again. 'I was a proper little tomboy.'

Julia plucked handfuls of grass and remembered the evening she and Dougie had met at Pedro's and had sex in the street afterwards. You couldn't love a little, she was thinking. Passion was never piecemeal. Yet lately she was finding that the more she grasped at it, the more she craved it like a drug, the more it slipped away through her fingers. Since the move, the longest time she and Dougie had spent together had been back in April, when he had had another bad bout of bronchitis, and an illness that had worried her at a distance over a year ago had tested her patience at close quarters: he was not a good patient.

Nowadays, those evenings when he returned for supper he had a new confidant in Hugh, his boss, producer and fellow Cambridge graduate. Those evenings when he was late, he took himself off to the barn to settle his mind painting by the light of an oil lantern, and she would wake in the early hours to the smell of turps in the bed and the sound of snoring – she didn't remember him snoring before. And then there were those evenings, which were many, when he did not come back at all.

She had not expected it to be like this. She had not expected to occupy an obscure maiden-auntish position in the household while he buried himself in work. She had not expected to feel as if he had tidied her away into a lifeboat while he continued to expose himself to danger.

A row might have cleared the air, but they couldn't in all decency row in someone else's house, not the way they rowed. Instead, there was sulking, on her part, and sometimes his.

'Penny for them,' said Bea.

'I was thinking I almost miss the Blitz.'

'You are joking.'

'Not entirely.'

Bea shook her head. 'There's no pleasing some people.'

By four o'clock, the Unit side were 163 all out, Dougie having made a respectable thirty-five before being caught by the vicar. Tea was served on trestle tables Netta had borrowed from the church hall and cost one and four a head, proceeds going to the Red Cross. Children ran around in the heat; elderly people drooped in deck chairs, wearing precautionary cardigans. The urn was efficiently manned.

If war seemed remote in Chorleywood, confined largely to the wireless and the newspapers, you didn't need to scratch far beneath the surface to discover that the considerable energies Londoners had lately devoted to staying alive were here deployed in any number of volunteering fronts. Every cottage was an industry. Nothing went to waste, not even waste. Netta, who was chief instigator of the greater proportion of these local activities, had recently been appointed 'Food Leader'. Her recipe for 'Kidneys Louisiana', which used carrots inventively, had appeared in the local paper.

Bea devoured a sandwich. 'I warn you. Now I know how well you eat here, you'll never see the back of me.'

'You're welcome to come whenever you like,' said Julia. In another part of her mind, she was wondering when Dougie, who was talking to Hugh about Stalin's scorched-earth policy, was going to get around to noticing their existence.

Nicholas in his over-large pads came past with his bat, Louie trailing after, chewing on her plait. Matthew – 'Matthew the Mysterious' – was nowhere to be seen, which was the intention. All the children had inherited Netta's broad, thinking forehead and Hugh's mousy hair. Nicholas had picked up a Roman nose from somewhere. As he practised his strokes, with a concentration that did nothing to conceal his nerves, she felt a strange, fierce tug.

Julia had never doted on a baby who wasn't her own; she was not one of those women who loved children in general. That was why she had failed to anticipate how painful it might be for someone in her circumstances to live with another family. Those sad little deaths she had experienced each term when Peter went back to school, the inching withdrawals she could sense in him each holiday, were nothing set against this present lack that promised a gaping hole in her future. It was getting harder and harder to hide the truth from herself, to tell herself the war was the only reason he was living safely in one part of the country while she was living safely in another. It was getting harder and harder to sit on the sidelines and watch Netta enjoy what she might never again experience.

Nicholas dug his bat into the dry ground, swung it. 'What do you think?'

'Cracking,' said Julia. 'You'll smash it over the boundary.'

'I should say so,' said Bea.

A cabbage white flitted about like a piece of tissue that had escaped the scrap-paper drive.

'Thanks,' he said, reddening.

On the pitch the players were taking up their positions.

'Where have they put you in the batting order?' said Dougie, who chose that moment to put in an appearance.

Nicholas said, 'Tenth.'

'Tail-ender. Good man.'

Then Dougie turned to Bea and introduced himself.

'Oh, I've heard all about you,' she said. 'I gather you're quite the all-rounder.'

'Jack of all trades, master of none,' said Dougie.

You don't mean a word of that, thought Julia.

Dougie studied Bea, narrowing his eyes. 'Are you by any chance a tennis player? Yes?'

Bea smiled and looked uncomfortable.

Forget the Face Game, thought Julia. Someone ought to teach you how to read the human heart.

Frank bowled the first few overs of the next innings, dismissing the openers on the village team, an insurance salesman called Mr Ashton and the butcher Mr Willis. Netta packed the tea things away and the chink of china blended with the odd ripple of clapping from deck chairs. A child cried and was hushed.

Bea yawned.

'Are you bored?' said Julia. 'Do you want to go back?' Cricket, which might be worth fighting for, was not necessarily worth sitting through.

'Oh no,' said Bea. 'It's quite pleasant here, don't you think? Ever so relaxing.'

The heat had eased off a bit and a breeze rustled through the trees that surrounded the common. In the outfield, Dougie failed to put his book down in time and missed a catch.

'How's the divorce coming along?' asked Bea.

'Slowly,' said Julia. 'It's taking much, much longer than I thought.'

A few months ago, after writing to her solicitor several times and getting no reply – telephoning, ditto – she had gone along to his premises in Gray's Inn to discover it in ruins. Mr Gore-Finlay and his clerks had escaped with their lives, but not with their files, and she'd had to go through the whole exercise again in the cramped quarters he now shared with another firm a few buildings away, this time with nothing to rest her eyes on: the plane tree, that London survivor, had not survived the bomb.

It was getting on for six o'clock, the shadows under the trees damson-coloured, when Nicholas, the youngest player on the pitch, stepped up to the crease. After the early dismissals, Joe Coram had put on 73 and Chorleywood were now 160 for nine. Three more runs for a tie; four to win. All this and more was resting on an eleven-year-old's narrow shoulders. In his head, he was at Lord's: this was plainly visible.

Dougie was bowling.

'Watch out, here comes the famous all-rounder,' said Bea.

'Wide!' said the umpire.

Dougie ran up again.

A ferocious ball. The bails flew off the stumps.

Around the pitch there was silence.

'Out,' said the umpire.

'Golly,' said Bea.

As she came up the path to her front door, Netta could hear music sounding out of the open windows. Rachmaninov, she decided. An unaccustomed half a shandy had left her receptive to it. The poor Russians! The poor, poor Russians! The Germans were bombing Moscow. Inside, she tripped over Nick's grass-stained cricket pads and went into the sitting room. Immediately, Julia lifted her hands from the keys.

'Don't let me disturb you,' said Netta.

'I'm out of practice. Mangling the fingering.'

Not that excuse again, thought Netta, who considered it rather poor that Julia could not be prodded to play on village occasions, would not touch the pub piano. She hadn't the nerve for performance was Netta's conclusion. Or else it was the arrogance of false modesty. Lights should not be hid under bushels but spread around so all could benefit, in her view.

The mood of the music seemed to have got into the room, charging it with melancholy. A family home was no place for melancholy, thought Netta, closing the shutters and drawing down the blackout blinds on the dimming summer night. In normal circumstances, she would have lightened the atmosphere with the quick burst of a dance tune, but she no longer felt in complete control of her own wireless.

Instead, she switched on a table lamp and reached for the cigarette box on the mantelshelf. She smoked twice a year, and this wasn't one of the occasions.

'Netta, I'm so sorry about earlier,' said Julia, who had not gone to the pub but had stayed behind to wash up, as the only route to martyrdom that had been available to her at the time.

The first draw on the cigarette went straight to Netta's head and she carefully stubbed it out so that someone else could have the use of it later. 'Don't worry. He must be feeling contrite. He bought a round.'

The joke did not travel, not even the short distance across the room.

'I don't know what possessed him.'

Dougie's performance on the cricket pitch had not surprised Netta. Whenever they sat down with the children to play cards or a board game, he failed to lose in the gracious and disguised way adults were meant to. She had put Monopoly away for the duration.

Well, she thought, even *artists* – Hugh's word, not hers – have their blind spots, their clay feet. To save Nicholas's feelings, the catch would go in the Diary, she thought, not the bowling out. In such a way, she guided her children's memories.

As Netta moved about the room, straightening the rug, touching the familiar in the spirit of domestic luck, she had the strong suspicion that something else was bothering Julia. A mother herself, she put two and two together and came up with Peter. Peter represented a problem to her, and a problem of the worst sort, the sort she had not yet been able to solve.

Secure in her own marriage, she had no objection to divorce for those whose marriages had broken down. In fact, she thought it sensible. (It was also sensible to allow those villagers who were less broad-minded than she was to think that Dougie and Julia were married to each other.) The terrible cost that divorce exacted from erring wives was a different matter. Suffragist aunts, one of whom had had her health broken in prison, had instilled a strong sense of fairness in Netta. Daily, she observed the price Julia was already paying for behaviour many men dismissed as peccadilloes and for which they routinely expected to be forgiven.

Now, in the sitting room, she communicated all of this to Julia in a long sympathetic look, fingering a cushion fringe. 'Did Bea get off all right?'

Julia nodded.

'Did she remember to take the onions?'

'She was incredibly grateful for them.' Onions were now so rare in London they were given as raffle prizes. 'Netta?'

Netta paused in the doorway.

'I just wanted to say how grateful I am that you took us in. I know it isn't always easy.'

'Don't mention it.'

'You've been very accommodating. Especially considering our living arrangements are far from conventional.' Julia gave a quick, tight smile. 'My father treats me as some sort of moral contagion. Most people would, if they knew.'

Netta came back into the room and perched on the arm of the settee. 'How likely is it that you will lose custody of your boy?'

Julia turned on the piano stool, met Netta's eyes then looked away.

'I think you should visit him and explain what's happening.'

Julia shook her head. 'I can't do that. They'd use it against me.'

In her gentlest voice, Netta said, 'If I were you, I should worry less about the court and more about what Peter thinks.'

In the barn, the oil lamp flicked shadows up old crumbling walls that smelled of animal and dung. Under her feet was hard beaten earth. 'Dougie?'

'I thought you'd gone to bed.' He was standing in front of a painting, squinting at it. 'I suppose you're going to take me to task for bowling Nick out.'

'It wasn't very kind of you.'

He dabbed at the canvas. 'You don't do boys any favours by wrapping them up in cotton wool.'

Or by humiliating them, she thought. 'I didn't come to talk about Nick.' She sat down on the edge of an old wooden cart. 'I want to go back to London. I want *us* to go back to London.'

He turned, brush in hand. 'Whatever for? I thought you liked Twaddles.' (The house was called Traddles – Hugh had a little trouble pronouncing his 'R's.)

'How would you know? You're always somewhere else.'

'Julia,' he said, wearily, 'I can't be on the 5.15 every evening. That's precisely why it's good for you to have company.'

'I don't want Netta's company, nice as she is. I want yours.'

She watched him smear the colours around on the thin sheet of plywood he used as a palette, mix a dot of alizarin crimson with a dot of zinc white. On the canvas, a horse's nostrils flared.

'Please. This is important to me. It doesn't have to be London. Perhaps we could find a cottage nearby. A place of our own.' A place where she was not prompted every waking moment to explore the agony of life without her son.

Dougie sighed. 'You know as well as I do that moving is not going to alter how often I can get home. I'm sorry, but I simply don't understand why you have suddenly taken such an objection to an arrangement that has suited us perfectly well for months.'

Julia started to explain how difficult it was to live with another family when something rose in her throat and choked her. It was the truth asking to be voiced.

'You're seeing someone, aren't you? That's why you're never here.'

'*Seeing someone?*' He threw down his brush. 'Oh, for God's sake, what on earth has got into you tonight? When would I find time to do that?'

The explosiveness of his response and the form it took told her everything.

'Is it that girl from New Year's? That girl in the café at Sadler's Wells?'

'I haven't the first idea what you're talking about! Which bloody girl? There is no bloody girl!' It happened to be true at the moment, he thought, with the righteousness of the falsely accused. 'What proof do you have?' He was shouting now. 'None! Because there isn't any!'

Julia did not believe him. But as the row gained its own fierce and fruitless momentum, that certainty was undermined. It was nothing to do with lack of evidence and everything to do with her dread of losing him. How could she lose him? She would have nothing left. Worse, she would face an even more painful truth, which was that she had read him wrong all along and he was not a man worth sacrificing your family for. This was unthinkable in so many ways. It wasn't simply a question of love, or even sex. It was the emotional investment she had made in his work and in her role as his sounding board.

Louie, hot and fretful, heard noises coming from the barn and dreamed the Germans had come with the harsh voices she heard on the wireless.

Matthew slept through it.

Nicholas tossed and turned in his own humiliation and sense of injustice, as itchy as crumbs on the sheets. Afterwards consoled himself with the fact that he would never have been bowled out had there been proper sight-screens.

Netta put out the light on the night table. The blackout flapped unsecured over the open window, disturbing the sultry air. 'They're having it out,' she said.

'So I gather,' Hugh said.

A little later. 'Do you know she hasn't seen her son for over a year? It might as well be a decade for a child that age.'

Hugh said, 'Don't meddle.'

18

'Call in sick today,' said Dougie.

Julia was exhausted. The row had gone on half the night; the rest of it, they'd spent making up. Be careful what you wish for, she thought, pushing back the bedclothes. Not that she was complaining, although parts of her anatomy were. 'I was considering it. But I really shouldn't. I don't like to let the others down, and I'm going to be late enough as it is.'

'Someone else can do the filing for once,' Dougie said. 'Seriously, I need you to come with me to Denham.'

Denham? Julia had never been to Denham before. 'Why?'

He was already out of bed and getting dressed. 'I'll tell you when we get there.'

It was tempting, and she was tempted. She was also intrigued. She called in sick.

Dougie's powers of description were such that the studio was pretty much how she had imagined it. She could have navigated around it quite easily – there were the sound stages, there was the canteen, over there the water tank. Nothing, however, could have prepared her for the sheer physical scale of the place. It was a small city, and busier than most, with traffic of all kinds. 'Where are we going?'

'Hugh's office.'

He steered her over to the main block, once the country house of the original estate. They entertained film stars in the restaurant on the first floor; she wondered if she would meet one. It was all quite strange. She was so tired, as tired as she'd been after a Blitz night, and everything had the dissociated quality of a dream.

That sense of dissociation only intensified when they walked into a bright room on the second floor and there was Hugh, some-one she saw most days at supper, sitting behind a desk piled high with scripts and film cans. If Hugh felt the same, he didn't show it, nor did he indicate by so much as a raised eyebrow that he must have heard a good deal of what had gone on last night in the barn, and afterwards in the annexe. He was perfectly impassive, but, come to think of it, he was generally impassive.

Not so the others. Besides Hugh, there was Basil and a short balding man she recognized as Quentin Cheeseman from the MOI. The pompous ass. The young lad – twenty or so, she guessed – would be Dougie's new assistant director, Sammy Levin. They all stood when she came into the room, questions on their faces.

'What is she doing here?' said Cheeseman. 'We're not in need of a title.'

So the pompous ass remembers me, thought Julia.

'I asked her to come,' said Dougie. 'She's a musician. Hugh and I both agree she might make a useful contribution to this discussion.'

'I hope you haven't told her anything.'

'No, I thought I'd leave that to you,' said Dougie.

Cheeseman turned to Hugh. 'Strictly speaking, she ought to sign the Act.'

Hugh said from behind his desk, 'I think we can waive that formality. I'll vouch for Miss Sinclair personally, if need be.'

'Miss Sinclair,' said Cheeseman, 'I require your assurances that you will repeat nothing that is said to you today.'

'Of course not.' Was she going to be given a job, or parachuted into France?

'And what type of musician are you, precisely?'

Torch-singer, Julia was strongly tempted to answer. 'I play the piano,' she said. 'I'm a little out of practice at present.'

'She does herself a disservice,' said Hugh. 'She is really very good.'

'She studied at the Royal College,' said Dougie.

Cheeseman said to Julia, 'Then it is possible you may be able to help us.' His tone became reverent. 'The Palace has very graciously invited us to film Her Majesty the Queen.'

Basil rolled his eyes, lit a cigarette and twisted his long legs in front of him.

'What he means,' said Dougie, 'is that we asked if we could film her, and they said yes.'

'I don't quite understand what this has to do with music,' said Julia.

'Well, in a way, it's all your doing,' Dougie said.

'Mine?'

'The Lunchtime Concerts. You told me about them, remember?'

She hadn't thought he was listening.

The Lunchtime Concerts were held in the vacated National Gallery; she went along in her lunchtimes as often as she could. The pianist Myra Hess organized them. She remembered sitting with her shilling programme in her lap, her mind tracing the interstices of Bach's 'Prelude in G'.

'Miss Hess will be performing for the Queen,' said Cheeseman. 'And we shall be filming her doing so. The question is, what should she play?'

'You should ask her that, not me,' said Julia. 'She will have her own repertoire.'

'Her repertoire is mostly German, I gather,' Cheeseman said.

'Forgive me,' said Julia, 'but she's Jewish. The Nazis have banned Mendelssohn. Do you think we should stoop to their level?'

There followed a general discussion about the merits of German music versus English music, during which some incredibly ill-informed and silly things were said, not all of them by Cheeseman.

'I vote for Bach,' said Dougie.

'You don't want Bach,' said Julia.

'Why not?'

'It's a little too cerebral. You want to engage people. You want to appeal to their emotions. I would suggest Mozart.'

213

'German again,' said Cheeseman, raising himself up on the balls of his feet.

'Austrian,' said Dougie.

'Same difference.'

'Mozart's "Piano Concerto No. 17 in G",' said Julia, 'would be my recommendation. It's a beautiful piece.'

'Why don't you play us a bit?' said Hugh, clicking his jaw.

Julia looked round the room. There was no piano.

'Sammy,' said Dougie, 'go and see if they've got it in the sound library, will you?'

Sammy shot off. In the meantime, they had tea.

'The way it will work,' said Cheeseman, dipping his digestive, 'is that you'll film Miss Hess first, then, on a separate occasion, you'll film Her Majesty listening to the same piece of music in the same location.'

'That's going to be a nightmare for continuity,' said Hugh.

'Are you saying it can't be done technically?'

'Technically, it can be done,' said Dougie. 'But it won't have anything like the same ring of truth.'

'I'm afraid,' said Cheeseman, 'that there is such a thing as protocol.'

Sammy came back with a case of records and a portable gramophone player.

They listened. Towards the end, there was the little tune Julia recalled, the little starling tune, the song sung by Mozart's pet starling. Who could fail to be moved by it?

Afterwards a silence fell. Cheeseman was the first to break it. 'Tell me, Miss Sinclair, how long do you think it would take for Miss Hess to learn the piece? If, that is, she doesn't know it already?'

Julia shrugged. 'Three weeks, possibly a month. You'll also need two oboes, two horns, two bassoons, a flute and some strings, if I remember rightly.'

'I see.' He set down his teacup. 'Do excuse me. I've a meeting with the minister at thirteen hundred.' He left the room.

Sammy put the records back into their sleeves. Basil got up and stretched.

'You know she's asked for a dais and a carpet,' said Hugh.

'Well, she's a queen,' said Dougie, 'what do you expect?'

'No, it's Miss Hess who's asked for a dais and a carpet,' Hugh said.

'Oh, Sammy will sort it,' Dougie said. 'Won't you, Sammy?'

'If you can tell me how I'm going to lay my hands on that much wood, I'd be glad to,' said Sammy. 'Most of it's going to coffins. As for the carpet, forget it.'

They walked down the stairs. 'That was a bit of a surprise,' said Julia.

'You did brilliantly, Sinclair,' said Dougie. 'I knew you would.'

'So tell me' – she leant into him – 'do I get the job?'

He laughed.

A smell of cooking, rich cooking, reached her nose from the restaurant. She could hear the clatter of serving dishes. 'Well, do I?'

'What are you talking about? You've got a job.'

So that was how it was, she thought. 'I think you owe me lunch,' she said.

'I don't usually have any,' said Dougie. 'The canteen's quite good if you fancy a sandwich.'

They went and had a sandwich. The canteen could seat fifteen hundred and there were almost that many there today, the greater portion extras – 'crowd artists' – sweating in a diverse range of costumes from every notable era of British history. Full-bottomed wigs, crinolines, farthingales, kilts. It was like some mad fancy-dress party.

They squeezed in at the end of a bench. 'I see Cheeseman has lost none of his charm,' said Julia, peeling back the top of her sandwich and recoiling from its pinkish contents.

'Do you remember telling him that a film might not need a commentary?'

'Vaguely,' she said, over the general din of trays, cutlery and chitchat.

'I've been thinking a lot about that.'

'It would be hard to get him to part with his blessed commentaries, I should have thought,' said Julia.

'What I'm wondering is whether you could make the same sort of links with sound as you do with images.'

'Perfectly possible. Composers do it all the time. And, of course, to play music properly you need to hear these things too.'

'Oh?'

'Well, themes, obviously. Leitmotifs. But a lot of it's to do with the intervals, the pauses. In great music the pauses are always right.'

'You mean the tempo?'

'Not just that.' She shrugged. 'I'm not certain I can really put it into words. It's something to do with the underlying structure. You just feel it.'

A group of child actors in Dickensian dress came and sat at the next table, accompanied by a middle-aged woman. One boy looked so much like Peter it was as if she'd taken a blow to the solar plexus. Their row the previous evening had resolved nothing, she thought. Which meant they were doomed to have it again.

19

To keep his nerve, Peter told himself that he was on a mission, an intelligence operation behind enemy lines. Immediately he began to see himself from the outside, from a remote perspective, as if he were watching a film. In fact, he was acting on impulse and might have turned back at any point after he left the school grounds if the least thing had gone against him – if it had started to rain, for example. But it wasn't raining, it was a dry night, warm for October, and there was also a moon – almost a full moon, a bomber's moon – which meant it was bright enough to see where you were going once your eyes adjusted. Although he'd brought a torch, he didn't know how long the batteries would last and he didn't want to waste them.

The fiction got him all the way to Fendlesham, the village nearest school, and some way out the other side into the open farmland that lay beyond it. All this time he came across no one. Then it seemed the fiction had worked a little too well, because the next thing he knew there was the sound of a vehicle and an army truck pulled over by the side of the road just ahead of him. Two soldiers got out. One of them went for a pee. The other, the driver, who was smoking, came over to him.

'Stan, where you going?'

'There's a kid out here,' said the driver.

'So?'

'Just checking he's all right.'

Peter thought about making a run for it; might have done if there had been anywhere to run to.

'What you doing out here in the middle of nowhere?' said the driver. 'Don't you know there's a war on?'

Peter was going to lie, but something about the way the driver spoke to him – easy, matey – changed his mind. Instead, he told the driver that he was trying to get home.

'And where's home when it's at home?'

'Near Whitmarket.'

'How you planning to get there this time of night?'

'Walk,' said Peter.

'Walk?' said the driver. 'Fuck sake – mind my French – that must be a good forty miles.' He threw his fag end on the ground, where it made a little shower of red sparks. 'We can take you as far as Skeen. That do you?'

Skeen was a village close to where he lived, known for its pig-geries.

'Yes, thanks.'

'Hop in.'

'Stan?' said the other squaddie, buttoning up his flies. 'Are you clean out of your mind?'

'Can't do no harm,' said the driver.

The truck was a Tilly. It had a spare wheel mounted on the roof of the cab and canvas covering the rear. Peter made to go round the back. 'No,' said the squaddie, holding the door of the cab open. 'You coming with us, you have to squeeze up front with the riff-raff.'

Peter clambered into the cab, with its smell of sweaty khaki, beery breath and tobacco. 'What's back there?' he said to the squaddie. He pictured guns, grenades, ammunition, bayonets.

The driver and the squaddie exchanged a look. 'Crates,' said the squaddie.

They got under way. 'Lucky for you I been eating my carrots,' said the driver over the dull noise of the engine. 'You could have got yourself killed. Running away from school, are you?'

Peter thought about not answering this.

While he was thinking, the driver said, 'The blazer's a bit of a giveaway, kid, if you don't mind my saying. To say nothing of the cap and the scarf. One thrashing too many, is that it?' 'Frashing' was how he said it.

Corky had once slippered Peter for tipping ink in the cisterns of the Seniors' lavatories. He thought that was fair, all things considered. 'I'm sorry, I don't know what you mean.' He added 'sir', as he had been taught to do.

'I hear them schools is worse than the army,' the driver said.

'Saying something,' said the squaddie.

'My school's all right,' said Peter. 'I'm just trying to get home. My mother's not very well.'

He wished he had not said this the instant he said it. It might make it true. The whole point of this exercise was to establish the opposite.

Then his mother's face flickered in front of him, as it had done on the screen in the gym. She was standing by the Martello tower looking out to sea, her hair blowing a little in the breeze, a smile lifting the corners of her mouth. He remembered the director telling her where to stand and where to look.

The Birmingham boys had accents. In their accents, they said the film was boring, boring, boring. 'Shut up!' Peter had said.

That one glimpse of his mother had been enough to reawaken a fear that had eaten away at him for months and which he had concealed as thoroughly from himself as new boys hid their homesickness, bunching sheets into their mouths. His mother was dying, maybe dead already, and they hadn't told him.

She wrote to him, it was true. But you could write letters in bed, you could write if you were ill, it wasn't like lifting heavy weights or playing games or coming to visit him at school, things that you had to be fit and on your feet to do. Letters could be forged, anyway. He was quite a good forger himself. His mother's handwriting wouldn't be very hard to copy. It wasn't italic or anything like that.

'Sorry about your mum, kiddie,' the driver was saying. 'What's the matter with her?'

Peter cast around for an illness that he didn't mind bringing down on his mother's head. 'I think it's her nerves.'

'Plenty of nerves around these days,' said the squaddie, and the driver laughed.

They didn't talk much after that, which was a relief.

Some while later, maybe an hour, maybe less, Peter nodding off, they turned down a narrow rutted lane bordered on either side with hedgerows that scraped against the side of the truck. 'What's the time?' said the driver.

The squaddie shone a torch on to his watch. 'Coming up for twenty-three hundred.'

'Twenty-three hundred,' said the driver. 'What's that in shillings and pence?' There was a gap in the hedge. He drove the truck through it, backing up in front of a long, low building, and killed the engine. 'You know where you are?' he said to Peter.

'Are we in Skeen?' He rubbed his eyes.

'Just outside. You keep on that lane, and you'll come to it in about ten minutes or so. Then you want to take the left fork by the church. Don't take the right. They got a roadblock on it.'

They all got down from the cab.

'Thanks very much for the lift, sir,' said Peter.

'Left fork, not right, remember,' said the driver. 'Off you pop now.'

Peter set off down the lane, stumbling a little on the uneven ground. He could smell the high, sour-sweet stink of pigs, hear snuffling and truffling, the hoot-hoot of an owl. He was trying to get used to the blackness, unlit now by the dimmed headlamps of the truck, when he realized he had left his torch behind on the seat of the cab.

By the time he returned to the gap in the hedge, the squaddie and the driver had got the doors of the building open and were unloading the truck.

'You're soft, Stan,' the squaddie was saying. 'That's your prob-lem.'

'He didn't see nothing.'

'He might have done.'

'Well, he didn't.'

What they were lugging out of the truck were not crates. They were jerry cans.

At school, Higson the caretaker kept a jerry can in his shed, along with a stash of greasy magazines he thought was well hidden. The jerry can contained petrol – for emergency car journeys, the emergencies having not yet arisen – and not much of it.

From the effort the soldiers were making, Peter could see that these jerry cans were full. There were a lot of them, too.

'You hear something?'

'Give it a rest, Fletch,' said the driver. 'You're jumpy tonight.'

'Wasn't my idea to pick up that tyke.'

'Couldn't help it. He reminded me of my little brother. Trudging down the road like that on his tod.'

'Correct me if I'm wrong,' said the squaddie, heaving another jerry can off the back of the truck 'but your little brother ain't a toff. That kid squeals, and I'll swing for him.'

Peter stole away from the gap in the hedge. Further up the lane, he ran.

Peter didn't know exactly how far Skeen was from home, but Harry, whose sister lived in the village, could walk there and back in a morning, with plenty of time left over for a gossip, and Harry didn't walk fast. He came to the church, took the left fork, and before long he could smell the sea blown on a salt wind across the marshes. A little later, he imagined he could hear it too, then he found himself walking past the cottage hospital where long ago the doctor had put stitches in his head.

The hospital, the cottages, were irregular shapes silvered here and there by moonlight. No one was about on the bumpy, cobbled streets. From unseen gardens came the trilling song of blackbirds.

When Peter reached his house he realized that he hadn't thought the next part through very clearly. If he had imagined anything, he had pictured arriving sometime during the day, spying on his mother through a window or shadowing her around town as she went to the shops. But the lift, which had been good in one way, had created a difficulty he had not foreseen. It was now very late. No peeking in windows when the blackout was up, and nothing to see even if it hadn't been. At this time of night his parents would be in bed.

He went around the side of the house and let himself in the back door. At once, all the smells of home rushed to say hello. School smelled of disinfectant, farting competitions and boiled cabbage – the farts and the cabbage smelled the same, more or less. Home smelled of ironed bedlinen, baking and clean windows.

Harry was snoring in her room off the kitchen. The cat brushed against his legs and almost startled him into speech. Then he tip-toed into the hall, feeling his way around the familiar furniture, holding his breath when he bumped into a chair and its legs scraped on the floor. A whimper came from Mabel. He waited: nothing more. His father always said spaniels weren't much use as watch-dogs.

It occurred to him then, listening to the household sleeping around him, that there was no reason why he shouldn't go upstairs to his own bed. It wasn't as if anyone expected him to be in it. The school wouldn't realize he was missing until the morning, and by then he would know what to do.

The plan put his mind at ease. It also suggested a new plan, which was that he should first find himself something to eat. It had been hours since tea and he was starving. He had been starving before tea too, and as usual tea hadn't done much to change that.

He was discovering how difficult it was to raid a larder in the dark without the aid of a torch when the hall light came on and he heard voices and footsteps coming down the stairs. The voices were low, the footsteps careful.

He had spent so many hours in moonlight, darkness and near-darkness that colour came as a shock. Peering round the kitchen door, the first thing that struck him was the golden wallpaper in the hall. He had never paid attention to the wallpaper before, either in the hall or anywhere else in the house. At school there was no wallpaper, only walls. It seemed to him quite a miraculous sight at that moment, and he thought how strange it was that he had been standing in the hall only a minute before and it had been hidden from him.

Then his father came down the stairs with Mrs Spencer.

Her red hair was the second shock or rather the shock of seeing her in the house so late with his father was muddled up with the colour of her hair.

Mrs Spencer was his mother's friend. What had she been doing upstairs? Visiting his mother on her sickbed? Paying her last respects?

Peter watched his father take a coat from the hallstand – a green coat – and hold it open for Mrs Spencer to slip her arms into. He strained his ears to hear over the wild pounding of his heart.

'You're certain you don't want me to walk you home?' said his father, who didn't look ready to walk anyone home, as he wasn't wearing a tie or a jacket or shoes.

'No need. It's hardly far.'

'I hate this creeping about. It's so underhand.'

'It's a small town – what can we do?' Mrs Spencer reached up to touch his father's face. 'You don't feel guilty, darling, do you?'

'Not in the least.'

'Good. Nor do I.'

Mrs Spencer pulled a scarf from the pocket of her coat and tied it round her head. The red hair was hidden. 'You know, I think it's time you told Peter.'

Told me what? thought Peter. Told me what?

'No,' said his father. 'Children are best kept out of the divorce court. The time to tell Peter is when things are settled.'

'That can't come soon enough for me.'

His father put his arms around Mrs Spencer. 'A year ago, I never thought I'd say this, but I'm beginning to feel Julia did me a favour running off with that dreadful man.'

What dreadful man? Where was his mother? Where had she gone?

'Did us both a favour, darling,' said Mrs Spencer. 'Mmm. You know, I think we're going to be very happy in the bed department.'

'Yes, indeed,' said his father.

She laughed. 'No regrets?'

'None whatsoever. Birdseed is welcome to her.'

She laughed again. They kissed. Then Mrs Spencer left, and his father went back up the stairs and turned off the light.

Peter leant back against the door frame and pressed its ridges hard into his back. His mind tumbled over itself; there wasn't enough air to breathe. There was no going upstairs now. No staying in the house a moment longer, although where he belonged he didn't know any more. He felt his way round the kitchen to the back door and came out numb into the night.

What he had witnessed – what he hadn't been supposed to witness – did not fit the story he had come home to prove or disprove. It made a different story. A terrifying story, where his parents turned out to be people he didn't know, who told lies and were not good.

Peter's childhood had been no more or less innocent than anyone else's. But, at eleven, some things made more sense than they once would have done: the caretaker's greasy magazines, for example, along with private urges and inklings that he kept to himself. This was why it didn't take him long to work out what Mrs Spencer had been doing upstairs with his father. Only later did he realize who 'Birdseed' might be. Then anger came flooding in to curdle his shame.

20

The Lunchtime Concerts were held in a domed octagonal room to the right of the National Gallery's central hall; despite its shape, it had proved to have good acoustics. To the left, approximately the same distance away, was the gallery where the Raphaels had once hung; this had been destroyed the previous October by an HE, and was now open to the elements.

Blackout cloth was draped under the skylights. Sandbags were stacked under the boarded-up windows. Alongside bins of sand were ranged fire buckets, while on the far wall hung a large reproduction of Uccello's *Battle of San Romano*. Up front on a carpeted dais was a Steinway facing rows of empty chairs.

'Your twenty-one-gun salute,' said Frank. 'I hope she appreciated it.'

'What?'

'Bit late now, but you might want to button your trousers.'

Dougie glanced at his flies. 'Oh.'

'Flashing the monarch's a treasonable offence, so I'm told.'

Filming was over, and the cabling, lights and camera were being dismantled and carted away out of the gallery. They were all giddy with relief, Dougie included. He shouted with laughter.

'Do you think she noticed?'

'I expect she's seen it all before.'

'She knows her camera angles, I'll grant you that.' Dougie checked over his socialist principles the way you might pat down your limbs after a fall and found them more or less intact. This did nothing to dispel his sense of triumph.

Frank tilted his big head and said in a cut-glass falsetto, 'What would you like me to do, Mr Birdsall? Shall I hand you the keys to the Tower of London, or would a knighthood suffice? I thought *your* Crown Jewels rather impressive, by the way.'

Sammy Levin came past with a clipboard 'Wasn't she tiny?'

'Well done for getting that carpet,' said Dougie.

Half an hour later, after the cans had been labelled and dispatched, Dougie made his way down the broad stone stairs to the main entrance, his mind buzzing with impressions and possibilities. Although you could not be entirely certain what you'd got until you viewed the dailies, he felt sure that the sequence would cut together well. There would be a nice ambivalence to it: the Queen as a woman of the people, among her people, the golden thread of continuity that bound all of them together on this small, embattled island. Yet at the same time, *Lunch Hour* was beginning to feel constrained to him, too limited in its scope, too descriptive. Classical music, the National Gallery, royalty. The country had other voices, other songs. The country could sing its heart out.

He came out on to the portico and stood looking across Trafalgar Square. Cranes lifted the glinting diagonals of steel girders. Autumn sunshine bathed Nelson on his column, then scudding clouds dappled Landseer's great reclining stone lions with fast-moving patches of shade. Buses rumbled around. Pigeons alighted one minute and flapped off the next. Nothing was still, nothing was quiet. Cries, shouts, footsteps, traffic, the low drone and pulse of the city. An idea itched away at the back of his head: he couldn't reach it to scratch it.

'Mr Birdsall?'

He turned, with impatience, and saw that it was the new continuity girl, Ann Wightman. What a sight she was. Those Charlie Chaplin trousers, that bilious yellow jacket, her butchered hair – he had seen more presentable art students. He had never been of the opinion that beauty should dress itself down, make an absurdity of a gift. Neither had he ever been of the opinion that beauty should know itself beautiful – it made for humourlessness.

'What is it?' he said.

'I wanted to thank you for hiring me.' The words were at odds with her expression, which was not one of gratitude.

He shrugged and headed down the stairs to street level. 'I didn't hire you. Nora did. We were short-handed.' Nora was the production manager, and she'd taken the girl on because she'd a bit of experience working with Embry at Gaumont – reason enough *not* to hire her, in his opinion.

'You sound displeased.'

He was. She had irritated him when they'd first met months ago, and she irritated him now, not least because the sight of her reminded him of Julia's absurd accusations. 'Just do your job, and we'll get along nicely.'

This was meant as a parting comment. However, she failed to take the hint. Instead, to his dismay, her long legs kept pace with him as he walked down the west side of Trafalgar Square, past Canada House, to his stop on Cockspur Street.

A bus came and he got on it. So did she. He went up the stairs; she followed and sat herself next to him. Heads turned in her direction – heads always turned in her direction – and his annoyance grew. At the front, a small girl in a red knitted pixie hat was singing, with hand gestures: 'Woll the bobbin up, Woll the bobbin up. Pull, pull, pull.'

Pall Mall, St James's, Piccadilly Circus. From the vantage point of the top deck, you could better make out the abrupt interruptions to the familiar streets. You could see right down into gaping holes, across forlorn levelled sites invaded with buddleia and rosebay willowherb, or what people had begun to call bombweed. Some, like the little girl in the red hat – 'Wind it back again, wind it back again' – would grow up knowing only these vacancies. Should, of course, they grow up at all.

The little girl sang, 'Point to the ceiling, point to the floor, point to the window, point to the door.'

'All right, Beryl,' said her mother. 'That's enough.'

The cord ding-dinged, the bus stopped and started, and feet tramped up and down the stairs. The conductress issued tickets with a tinny ratchet of her machine.

'Point to the ceiling . . .'

'Beryl!'

The country had other voices, thought Dougie. This isle is full of noises. All of a sudden the idea was there – veiled, but there. He could feel it, sense its shape and weight and edges. He reached for it and –

'You shout a lot, don't you?' said Ann Wightman.

– And the idea was gone. 'What?'

She took a slim silver case out of the pocket of her horrible jacket, flicked it open, placed a cigarette in her perfect mouth and lit it without offering him one. 'Is it because you don't know what you're doing? Or are you simply bad-tempered by nature?'

'I feel obliged to warn you,' he said, 'that while I might have not hired you, I could quite easily have you sacked.'

'I'm not frightened of you.'

There was no prospect of recovering his train of thought now. Even the Queen took a back seat as the bus wound its way through central London. Routes were no longer diverted through side streets to avoid the cordons and craters; even so, it seemed to take ages to reach Marylebone. With a wearying predictability, this proved to be her destination too.

Marylebone was crowded. All the stations were these days, necessary journeys vastly outnumbering unnecessary ones. If he had hoped to lose her among the servicemen and women with their kit bags, returning from leave, going on leave, transferring from one camp or base to another, or the throngs of office workers commuting to and from their wartime occupations, the hope was a vain one. She would have found a way of accompanying him to the Gents, he felt certain.

There was a long queue at the ticket office. 'Denham?' he said, when they reached the head of it.

Ann Wightman nodded.

'Single to Denham, please,' he said to the clerk. 'And a single to Chorleywood.'

He handed her the ticket as they came away from the office.

There was a clanging sound and a long hissing escape of steam. A guard blew a whistle. The tannoy blared.

'I thought you were going back to the studio.'

'What gave you that idea?'

'They say you practically live there.'

'I give you full marks for persistence, Miss Wightman,' said Dougie. 'But I wouldn't want you to labour under any misapprehension.'

She gave him a long look. 'Don't flatter yourself.'

It was no small consolation, then, to find the idea waiting for him on the train. They had barely left the station when it came to greet him and sat opposite, as recognizable as a friend. (The train was crowded, so it had to sit on the lap of an elderly vicar.)

Documentary film-making had a bit of a problem with words, in Dougie's view. Cutting down on them, giving images room to breathe, was all well and good. Yet take this approach to its logical conclusion and you were back in the silent era.

Unless, said the idea, sitting opposite him, what accompanied the pictures was not simply music but the music of sound. Sound in its most everyday form, orchestrated to a pitch and rhythm that married one type of montage with another, that asked people to watch and to listen.

The train clanked, clanked, clanked past a row of terraces, their untidy yards running up to the track, flapping lines of washing collecting soot, Andersons mushrooming out of the ground, all the vulnerability of these pinched times laid bare in the shabby back views. A child shrieked. He opened his notebook on his knee.

'Winchester Cathedral just after a Handel anthem has been played.' The phrase wasn't his. It was Ford Maddox Ford's. *Parade's End*. Not a book whose thesis he entirely embraced, much as he admired its modernism. But the mood of the whole film, as he conceived it, was right there in those few words.

A portrait of the country in sound.

★

Dougie came out of the station and walked down the rustling lane. Sharp, thin bonfire air announced the coming of winter. A moist fungal chill came up from the ground. Nature shifted faster in the country than in the town.

If he could have been sure of his reception, he would have looked forward to discussing this new idea with Julia – not least because it was an idea that had its origins in their conversations. But they rowed so often now and to so little effect – it was Barbara all over again.

Back in the summer, he'd gone to a screening of a film Travis had directed about Bomber Command. Travis was never less than competent, yet Dougie had come away from the screening thinking it a little cold. What had impressed him most about it was the editing, which Basil had done. There was one particular sequence of a Wellington in flight in which a number of rapid, straight cuts reinforced the realism of the filming. Basil later explained that he'd popped a few flash frames in there. 'You don't want it too smooth. You don't want to dissolve. They'd think they were watching a feature.'

Someone, Dougie thought, had popped a few flash frames into his own life. Like that plane in the film, jerking up and down in the sky, losing height and gaining it, he and Julia were no longer continuous, no longer smooth.

The house was quiet. There were no cooking smells, no voices, no childish pelting feet. Only the dog barked somewhere out in the yard.

For a moment he allowed himself to hope that he had the place to himself, or that Julia might be waiting for him alone in their room, as she used to wait for him in Primrose Hill, the flat a tip, the cooking comic, the laundry missing, her hair loose, her face an eager leap of desire. The last time he had seen her, some days ago, she had been ironing. Competently. Once, her complete lack of domesticity had surprised him, annoyed him, even infuriated him; in retrospect, it seemed rather touching and he missed it. In no way did he think this inconsistent. Nor did he pause to reflect that they were only living here at his insistence.

Then he went into the kitchen and found Netta putting up the blackout, her jumper riding up over the waistband of her skirt, revealing a soft roll of flesh. Julia was huddled by the range, clutching an enamelled mug, her face bleak and white. The table was littered with tea things, ashtrays, children's drawings. The airer, let down from the ceiling, was strewn with wet laundry.

What a greeting, he thought. It was like having two wives. Or a wife and a mother. Or, worse, two mothers. 'Hello?'

'They gave you my message,' said Julia, not asking but telling.

'What message?'

'I rang the studio.'

'I wasn't at the studio. I was filming the Queen.'

Her expression did not change.

'Didn't they say?'

Netta came away from the window, seated herself and took Julia's hands. 'Peter's missing.'

21

'How long has he been gone?' said Dougie.

They were alone in the annexe. Julia was sitting on the bed, twisting her handkerchief in her lap, staring fixedly ahead. 'Since Tuesday night. Richard rang me this morning, as soon as he heard from the school. He seemed to think he might be here.' She gave a bitter laugh. 'I keep forgetting he's no reason to trust me.'

'Peter's more likely to be heading home.'

'I'm afraid that's no comfort.'

Moved by her unhappiness, her sudden fragility, he sat down and put his arms around her. It felt like a long time since he had held her, properly held her. 'Of course not.'

'I don't understand. He likes school.' Her voice was muffled on his shoulder.

But she was remembering the last time she had seen him, when he had made such a fuss getting out of the car, and she was thinking of his complaints about lessons and boredom and not enough to eat and wondering whether there was something between the lines she had failed to read, whether he had been hinting at deeper worries, more serious trouble that he might have told her about if she had been in any way present in his life.

'I liked school too,' Dougie said. 'It didn't stop me running away once or twice.'

'Then why did you?'

'I wanted to see how far I could go before I was caught.'

Despite herself, she smiled. 'I can well imagine that.'

There was a knock on the door, they disentangled themselves, and Netta came in with cups of tea. 'I'll just put these down over here,' she said.

Julia nodded.

Netta said, 'Boys are more resilient than you think. You must try to get some rest.'

When she had gone, Dougie dashed the tea out of the window and poured them both a gin from a bottle he kept in a desk drawer.

Julia said, 'This is agony.'

'I know. We just have to wait it out.'

We. Now that was a comfort.

Later that night would seem more remarkable for what Dougie didn't do than what he did. He didn't go off and talk to Hugh, he didn't mention the Queen, he didn't take himself down to the barn and his canvases. Neither did he attempt to soothe her with empty phrases. Instead, while she lay awake, he sat up reading until the calm turning of pages lulled her into a sense of time passing.

The following morning, he was sleeping beside her and she was rearranging the cracks in the ceiling into faces, remembering Peter as a baby, when the phone rang. She got up and pelted from the room.

Netta was standing in the hall holding out the receiver. 'Your husband.'

'They found him,' said Richard, in Richard's voice.

'Thank God. How is he?' Her heart was beating wildly. 'Is he all right?'

'It appears so.'

'Where was he?' *They found him*, she mouthed to Netta. She hardly dared believe such a burden of fear had been lifted from her shoulders.

'In Whitmarket.'

'He must have been trying to get home.' The word 'home' caught in her throat.

'It appears so.'

'Did they say why he ran away?'

'They'll deal with it.'

'I want to see him.'

'I don't think that's necessary.'

'You can't stop me.'

A pause. 'Then I'll tell Mr Rowsome to expect both of us tomorrow,' he said, and rang off.

It was misty when Julia and Netta left Hertfordshire soon after dawn the following day, the sort of thin, grey, autumnal veil that tends to disperse with sunrise, and for most of the morning, as they picked their way through battered outer London suburbs, heading north and east, visibility had been good. Now, as they reached the fenlands, the views out of the car windows softened and blurred. Distance collapsed. It was as if someone were placing sheets of tracing paper over the world. What was ghostly became Gothic, the trees in the fields shapes sketched in charcoal, then pencil, then gone.

Netta felt blindly for the dashboard and switched on the headlamps. 'How much further?'

'I'm not entirely certain,' said Julia. 'We never used to come at it from this direction.' From the low rumble of engines, it was evident they were driving through a heavily militarized area of bases and camps and airfields. As another lorry thundered by, she wondered how she could ever have thought Peter safe, his school a fastness, within such a zone. 'Look, let's stop somewhere. It's getting worse by the minute.'

'I'll get you there,' said Netta. 'Don't worry.'

Netta had arranged everything. She had borrowed the car and the hoarded petrol. Molly Coram had agreed to mind the children. A bean 'medley' had been prepared for the children's tea and was waiting in the larder ready to go in the oven.

Kindness, thought Julia, could at times feel oppressive, somewhat controlling. Fiona would not have been anything like so kind; instead, she might have made her cross – or laugh – and either would have eased the tension. But she hadn't heard from Fiona for months. That visit to Primrose Hill over a year ago had been, she now thought, a casting off.

By the time they reached Ely, which they managed by tailgating an army truck, they were both limp with the strain of concentration and breath-holding. Netta pulled over to a kerbside and rested her head on her hands. There was no question of going on, and they both knew it.

'I must say, your headmaster knows his hotels,' said Netta, taking off her mackintosh and unpinning her hat. 'This is all very agreeable. And we're right next to the loo, which is an absolute bonus. Which bed would you like?'

The room, with its Morris chrysanthemum wallpaper, the cheery little fire newly burning in the grate, the marble-topped washstand, glazed earthenware jug and bowl, was cosy enough. It smelled of toast and other people.

'I don't mind.' Julia went over to the window and pulled the net curtains aside. Fog pressed itself against the glass, a white-out as impenetrable as any blackout. She couldn't see as far as the other side of the street. All the unanswered questions about Peter's disappearance came and went.

'Did your husband make it to the school?'

'No. Apparently he's stranded in Bury.'

'Perhaps it's just as well.' Netta kicked off her shoes and stretched out on the bed nearest the fire. 'A good night's sleep is what you need.'

'You're dreadfully pale,' Netta said the next morning. She stepped into her skirt and zipped it up. 'I wonder how the children have got on.'

Netta had never spent any length of time apart from her children. The previous evening, Louie, Matthew and Nick had been so present in her conversation you almost expected to see them stroll in from the foggy street or roll out from underneath the beds. It was as if the adventure of being away from them could only be conceived as an opportunity to return to their sides.

'Did the airmen keep you awake?'

The bar at the Lamb Hotel, where they had taken their supper at a corner table, had been packed with grounded bombers' crews, whose backslapping bravado had taken on a desperate edge of self-caricature as the evening wore on. ('Pull the beer-lever, publican, there's a good man! Pull the ruddy joystick, sir. Wallop! Wallop! Wallop! Chaps here are *perishing* for pints!')

'Not really,' said Julia.

'Perhaps there might be time to telephone Molly before we leave,' said Netta, peering out of the window. 'Fog's lifted. Nice day for it. Golly, I had no idea we were so near the cathedral.'

As they drove the short distance to Crossfields, Julia stared out of the car window at the brown hedgerows, the stubble fields with smoke rising, the broad views and open skies that the fog had blanked out yesterday. Up ahead was a familiar stand of trees. 'Next right,' she said.

They turned off the road and pulled in through the gates. From the far end of the long gravel drive, Crossfields was a pretty, white Regency building surrounded by pretty, green fields. Close up, the windows had an institutional air about them and the paintwork was peeling. The school could not have been anything other than what it was, except the country house it once had been.

They parked beside the only other car in the drive. This was their old car, Julia noted with a shock of recognition, or rather Richard's (since he had been the one who had paid for it and was the only one who drove it).

'I'll wait here,' said Netta.

'I might be ages. You could visit the cathedral.'

'Mustn't waste the petrol.' Netta reached into the back seat. 'I'll be fine, I've got my book.'

When Julia went through the main entrance, a blend of smells greeted her: metallic, woody, chalky, not washed behind the ears. A bell rang, and she could hear shrieks, banging desk lids and doors.

Then she saw her husband. He was standing under the board in the hall, gazing at the gilt letters that recorded the fallen of the last war, a memorial to little boys who had become big boys and, in due course, names on a casualty list. He would recognize some of those names and be able to put childish faces to them, for Cross-fields had been his prep school, too.

When he turned, it was obvious that he was in two minds whether or not to acknowledge her presence. Then he nodded and fixed his gaze about two yards past her left shoulder. He was in the uniform of the LDV, the Home Guard, and looked well in it.

Well, you've trumped my governess suit, she thought.

Over the past months, Julia had identified a number of things to dislike about her husband, as you come to find someone you've hurt deserving of it. Reminding herself of these sustained her now. The alternative was to submit to the hollow sadness that the sight of him had provoked.

The meeting was held in the headmaster's study, a command post of sorts overlooking the drive. It was noticeably warmer than the rest of the school: panelled, fusty, lined with books that appeared unread or unreadable. In addition to Mr Rowsome, Peter's house-master Mr Lavery was also present. Rowsome's right leg was shorter than his left, and he wore a built-up, hoof-like shoe. Lavery was a fidgety asthmatic. Corky and the Lav, the boys called them.

'First, let me set your minds at rest,' Rowsome was saying. 'Your son is quite well, as you will shortly see for yourselves. A little tired, perhaps, which is only to be expected, but otherwise no harm done. I know you will be as relieved about that as we are.'

Lavery said, 'A grazed knee was the extent of the damage. But Matron soon put that right.'

Ever since Julia had entered the room, she had been unable to keep her eyes from straying to 'Bertie', a stuffed otter mounted on a wooden plinth that stood on the corner of the headmaster's desk. It was wearing a miniature knitted school cap and scarf and was said to put new boys at their ease. It did not put her at ease. Shifting in her seat, she wondered if Matron had also put right the after-effects of the caning Peter had undoubtedly received for running away. 'I gather he went missing on Tuesday night.'

'That's right,' said Lavery. 'He gave us the slip at some point before lights out.'

'In that case, why did you wait so long to inform us?'

Rowsome adjusted the shoulders of his academic gown. 'Boys generally do this for dares,' he said, in a tone he most likely reserved for mothers. 'Usually, they show up hungry and thirsty the next morning, having spent the night camping out somewhere nearby. Once we established that he was not in the grounds or immediate vicinity, we put you in the picture immediately. No need to cause unnecessary anxiety, after all.'

'They're *in loco parentis*, Julia,' said Richard. 'They must deal with these things as they see fit.'

'Anything could have happened.'

'I acknowledge your concern, Mrs Compton,' said the head, 'but you must understand that our boys do have resources to fall back upon. Peter won his Pioneer badge only last month. He will have known how to light a fire and forage, and so on. In fact, he was caught stealing milk bottles from doorsteps.' A wry smile. 'Not the type of foraging that we encourage, of course.'

'Please be assured, my wife and I are very grateful for your efforts,' said Richard, 'and very sorry indeed for the trouble he's caused. There are better things to do in wartime than hare about after boys who should know better.'

It was one thing for the school to present a united front, thought Julia. It was another for Richard to join it – and rope her in too. 'But he must have had a reason for taking off like that,' she said. 'Did something happen to upset him?'

'Quite the contrary,' said Lavery, jiggling his foot. 'The night he disappeared he was in remarkably good spirits. It was Ciné Club that evening, and he does enjoy Ciné Club.'

'All the same, I know my son. This isn't like him.'

'Julia, please,' said Richard. 'It was a stupid prank. He's safe, and that's all that matters.'

'Forgive me for venturing into the philosopher's realm, Mrs Compton,' said Rowsome, 'but to what extent do we really know anyone? In our experience, the boy himself often doesn't know the reason why he acts the way he does. And, in any case, one can't always trust their explanations, which can be rather fanciful. The important thing, which we have impressed upon your son, is that he must understand that the rules are there for his benefit and must not be broken.' On a nod from him, Lavery left the room.

When he returned a moment later, Julia's first thought was that they had brought in a chum or a friend to vouch for Peter's good spirits, his contentedness at school, and then, with the dizzy sense of stepping into space, she realized this stranger was her son. So much for the assertion that she knew him.

Thin bony wrists protruded from the cuffs of a blazer that had been several sizes too big when she had bought it over two years ago. The round boyish face she remembered had new planes and angles. There were dark smudges under his eyes. The child was not gone, yet shaping up within him was the young man he would become.

Her heart turned over. 'Peter!'

For a fraction of a second, his gaze met hers. In it, she saw an odd blend of emotions, overlaid by wariness.

'Have a seat, Compton,' said the headmaster.

Peter sat in the empty chair between his parents and stared ahead.

Mr Rowsome said, 'Would you care to offer your mother and father an explanation for your behaviour?'

A silence.

'Compton?'

'I'm awfully sorry, sir. I won't do it again.'

Mr Rowsome said, 'That's not what I was asking you.'

'I won't do it again, sir. I promise. May I go now? I have lessons.'

Julia laid a hand on his sleeve. He shrank from her. This rejection was more total, less voluntary, than his usual retreat from affection in a public setting. Her throat closed.

The head exchanged a glance with Lavery. 'Lessons can wait for now, Compton.' He got up from his chair. 'You might like to spend a little time with your parents, since they've come all this way to see you. I'll ask Mrs Rowsome to bring in some tea.'

If the headmaster had imagined that Peter would be more forthcoming when he was alone with them, he was wrong. Nothing would induce him to talk about his disappearance or the reason for it. Instead, he kept apologizing, as if repetition could compensate for a sincerity that was absent. He was hiding something – that was obvious. Of course, they were hiding something too. They were hiding the fact that what used to be a family was now three separate people.

In Julia's case, that silence was entirely self-protective. In Richard's, she guessed, it would have more of a legal basis.

After about half an hour of this, Lavery collected Peter, and he went off with evident relief to rejoin those lessons he found so boring.

Julia placed their cups back on the tea tray. 'He's angry with us.'

For a moment Richard seemed to see those words rather than hear them: it was as if they were floating in the air, nothing to do with him. Then he shook his head. 'Don't be ridiculous,' he said. 'He's ashamed of himself. And so he should be.'

'I wonder whether he has felt abandoned, stuck in school all this time.'

A thin smile. 'You would know about abandonment.'

She chose to ignore the thin smile. 'Perhaps this wouldn't have happened if we had visited him.'

'I did,' he said.

'You did what?'

'Visit him.'

She was so astounded she could not speak.

He got up from his seat, went over to the window and looked down on the drive. 'Not often. I took him to a cricket match in the summer. He seemed to enjoy that. One or two other occasions.'

240

'You never told me.'

'Why should I? What business is it of yours any more?'

She was filled with anger so pure it was beautiful. 'And how did you explain the fact that I didn't come with you?'

'That is not your concern. What is important is that he accepted my explanations.'

'I can't believe you would do such a thing!'

'How's the boyfriend?' he said.

In the headmaster's study, tea remains littering the desk and a weak sun struggling in, they seemed like characters in a poor stage play. She was disgusted by her role in it.

'Goodbye, Richard.' She picked up her handbag and headed for the door.

He followed her. 'In future, you might make the effort to see him.'

She stopped and turned. 'I was strongly advised not to.'

'Not by me.' He held the door open for her; but then he would have held the door open for Hitler's wife, if Hitler were married. 'If I were you, I should find another adviser.'

When they returned to Traddles later that afternoon and Netta was subjecting Molly Coram to a military debriefing, down to bowel movements, Julia was surprised to find Dougie in the annexe. Then she saw he was packing.

'You're going away?'

'Just for a few weeks. Blackpool, to start with.'

'Oh.' Her face fell. The day had disturbed her profoundly; she had been counting on the 'we' lasting a little while longer.

'You've only yourself to blame,' he said with a smile. 'When I told Hugh what we were talking about the other night he leapt at it.' He closed his case. 'How did it go?'

'Mmm,' he said, when she finished telling him.

'Peter's hiding something.'

'It'll come out eventually.' He opened his case and stuffed in another book. 'By the way, which film did they show?'

'Which *film*?'

'At the Ciné Club.'

She marvelled at his self-absorption. 'I've no idea.'

The door of the dorm banged open. The Lav came in. 'Pierce, hand me that torch, if you please. Lights out means lights out. And lights out means no talking. All of you, settle down.' He took the torch from Pierce and waited, a wheezing silhouette.

'Any further disturbance and you're all on jaggers.'

'Jaggers' was detention.

The door closed.

Hughes said, 'When they caught you, did they put you in hand-cuffs?'

Peter turned over in bed. 'I don't want to talk about it.'

Running away had won Peter considerable status in the dorm, in his house and in the school at large. Even the Birmingham boys were impressed. This was no cause of satisfaction to him. He wasn't nine with a scar to show off; he was eleven with a deep wound to hide. He didn't suppose it would ever heal over. In the darkness, he poked it, prodded it and made it bleed again.

22

The Caledonian Hotel was across the road from the railway station. Its lounge was elderly and tartan. At the far end of the room, under a drooping branched ceiling fixture, was a deserted dais where a lone snare drum languished. Somewhere a carpet sweeper banged against skirting boards.

Dougie sat writing and drinking tea that tasted of metallic dishwater while an old waiter in a grease-spotted white jacket collected cups and saucers from abandoned tables and piled them on a trembling, shifting tray. Rain lashed the windows.

He put down his pen and sighed. They were over budget and running out of time. The weather wasn't helping, nor was that idiot Rodney, who'd overslept this morning and lost them the shot of the factory workers arriving at dawn because he had the key of the sound van in his back pocket.

A crash came from the direction of the door.

Across the table, where she was working on continuity sheets, Ann Wightman looked up. 'That was an accident waiting to happen.'

Dougie leant back in his chair and studied her. Today she was wearing a pair of plus-fours and a luridly embroidered peasant blouse with a drawstring neck. 'Why do you dress like that?'

'To annoy people like you.'

On closer acquaintance, she had proved no less irritating than when he'd first met her, an opinion now shared by most of the crew. But he had to admit she was competent. 'And what else do you do to amuse yourself?'

'In Rotherham on a wet afternoon? You tell me.'

'Someone once accused me of having an affair with you.' He shook his head as if to convey how preposterous the idea was. But something familiar quickened inside him.

'Who? Your wife?'

'No, my wife's in Canada.'

'How convenient,' she said. 'This person wouldn't live in Chorleywood by any chance, would she?'

'Have you been listening to gossip?'

'Gossip doesn't interest me. I know better ways of spending my time.'

Something in her expression made his blood race.

It wasn't a hotel with any great claims to respectability. Nevertheless, they went up separately. He brushed his teeth and waited. A knock came on the door.

'So amuse me,' she said.

That afternoon, Dougie found himself back at school.

'Not like that, like this,' she said at one point.

Later: 'Not there, here.'

Afterwards, she didn't waste a moment getting out of bed.

'Why don't you stay a while?' he asked.

She began to collect her strewn clothes. 'I'd rather not.'

'Well, you clearly know what you want,' he said with a laugh.

'I find it simplifies matters.'

He propped himself up on an elbow to watch her dress. The chopped hair, the pantomime clothing, seemed different now. Less a dimming of beauty than a particularly effective foil for it. 'Speaking of simplicity, I've been wondering how best to structure what we've shot,' he said. 'Whether to start at daybreak or midnight. What do you think?'

'No idea,' she said, buttoning her plus-fours. 'You're the director.'

'Doing anything nice for the holidays?' said Mr Slater.

'Nothing special,' said Julia, conscious that Netta would have been appalled to hear her preparations dismissed this way. There was to be an 'entertainment' on Boxing Day, a family tradition apparently, for which sets were being constructed and painted, the dressing-up box raided. Dougie remained on location, too busy to write much – or

244

often – except to say when the location changed. Blackpool, then Bromsgrove, now Rotherham. 'Just a few weeks' had become nearly two months. Missing her son and the man she had given up her son to be with, unsure of both their affections, Christmas loomed on the calendar as a date to be got through, or past, or over.

'And you?'

'A little gathering on the day. Quiet otherwise. One hopes,' he added. 'Still, it's arrived early this year, hasn't it? What with the Yanks coming in.'

'Yes, things are really looking up,' said Julia.

'I said as much to Mrs Slater.'

Miss Plume materialized in the doorway, ducking her head under the paper chains. 'Urgent File Request,' she said. 'Your section.' She handed the sheet to Julia. 'Have you seen Miss Justin?'

'No,' said Julia. Earlier in the month, Bea had spent a couple of weeks off sick with the flu that was going the rounds; since then, she had been rather withdrawn and uncommunicative, not herself.

'If you do, tell her I'd like a word.'

'I shall.'

'Solihull,' Julia read, when Miss Plume had left. 'J. C. McKie and Sons. Production levels giving cause for concern. Rumours of strike action.' It was the usual: a flutter in Whitehall working its way into a flap at the Institute.

'Munitions?' said Mr Slater.

'Tank treads.'

'Pending or deep?'

'The Stacks.'

The deep filing, as opposed to the pending filing, was stored on the third floor. 'I'm going to the Stacks. I may be some time' was the usual joke.

'Oh, jolly bad luck,' said Mr Slater.

She made a face and got up from her seat.

'Mind you don't miss the sherry, now. I'm told there'll be a thimbleful each and a nibble of a mince pie if we're good little kiddies.'

'I'll try my best not to.'

'That's the ticket,' Mr Slater said.

You might say that if you weren't winning the war at least you were keeping track of it. The Stacks would say you were wrong. Memos, letters, interdepartmental communications were often answered on the back of the original document to save paper, which made it hard to know which side to file and, once filed, where to hunt for it again.

Every time Julia thought she had got the hang of the way the rooms and their contents were arranged, they seemed to undergo some sort of redistribution in her mind. Sometimes randomness would guide her to the right set of shelves in the right corner of the right room, where the file would glide into her hand; mostly it was blundering about. Hours might pass.

Julia went down a corridor and opened a door in a spirit of methodical frustration. It was the third one she'd tried. Inside she felt round for the pull-cord and tugged it. A weak light flickered on from a single bare bulb hanging from the centre of the dirty cream ceiling. The original steel cabinets that held the records had long been outgrown. Supplementary shelving sprouted between the rows, each addendum announced in typed notices marked 'Aux.', sub-sectioned and numbered. By process of elimination Solihull had to be in here somewhere.

It was. Along with J. C. McKie and Sons, once she had found it misfiled with the 'Mac's. 'Ha. Got you,' she said, tugging out the buff folder and dislodging a quantity of dust.

At that moment, she became aware of two things: the scritching sound of a match being struck and the pleasant, clean smell of it being extinguished. Most people had the sense not to smoke in the Stacks. It was a tinderbox, greedy for fire. A single spark would be enough for the whole thing to shoot up in flames, all the files and dead paper, all the letters inked, typed and carbon-copied. Laid end to end, they would stretch miles.

But she didn't smell cigarette smoke. Instead she heard the sound of another match being struck.

Another match.

Julia put the file under her arm. The room was one of the smaller ones and the shelving and metal cabinets ran the breadth of it. She peered down each row. The fourth stopped a little way short; there was a window on the flanking wall. Down at the end, at the point where the shelving ended, she saw a woman's legs stretched out on the floor; when she ventured nearer, she recognized the shoes.

'Bea?'

No answer.

Bea was sitting with her back to the window. She looked like a marionette whose strings had been cut.

'Bea!' said Julia, squatting down beside her. 'What's the matter? Are you feeling unwell?'

Lately, Julia had been wondering if her friend had come back to work too soon. The debilitating aftermath of an infectious illness, however, did not account for the spent matches that surrounded her. Matches, like safety pins and soap, were some of those odd things that were scarce nowadays. She had been living with Netta long enough to register the waste.

'Do you feel faint?'

'I'm the little match girl,' said Bea. 'See? That's who I am. The little match girl.' She dragged another match down the side of the box and watched the flame burn down towards her fingers.

'Bea?' said Julia, very much alarmed. 'I'll take these, shall I?' The box said 'Buy War Bonds' on it, like everything did.

'No,' said Bea. 'You can't take the matches from the little match girl.' She struck another match. 'A fire would be nice, don't you think? Warm us all up a bit.'

Julia seized her wrists in one quick, fluid movement. 'Drop the matches, Bea.' She spoke slowly, calmly, the way she would speak to a child.

As if the puppeteer had cut the final string, Bea dropped the matches. A small sound escaped her.

'We should get you home,' said Julia. 'You're not well. You're not over your flu.'

'I didn't have the flu.'

Julia put the matches in her pocket. 'You need to be back in bed.'

Bea said, 'I didn't have the flu. I had a geography lesson.'

A geography lesson?

'Isn't it funny, all these foreign names and places we had never even heard of before the war. Like Tobruk.' Bea raised her eyes. 'Like Tobruk, where Giles was killed.'

Tobruk. Libya. 'L' for Uncle Len.

The December afternoon faded in the taped-up window and there began to be a rough equivalence between indoors and out, a dimming, a greying.

'Oh no,' said Julia. She sank down on the floor and put her arm around Bea's shoulders. Listened while the war blew its foul breath in their faces.

He had been killed in the last week of the siege; they didn't know how. They never said, did they? You got no real information at all. When the telegram had come, his parents had caught the train up from Kent to tell her in person. They hadn't wanted to do it on the telephone. She hadn't cried when they told her or made any kind of scene. She hadn't wanted to make it worse for them; it would have been disrespectful. Their loss was greater than hers. But when they had gone, she went to bed and didn't get up for days. It was weak of her, she knew. Other people had bad news and carried on with things. It was just she couldn't carry on with things. She didn't see the point. It was her sister's idea to say that she had the flu. Last week, her sister had called a halt on the flu and told her to buck herself up and get back to work.

'This morning his last letter came in the post,' said Bea. 'It's dated the day before he was killed. Covered in filthy black marks from the censor. Not much of a keepsake, is it?'

'I'm so sorry.' Never had words been emptier.

'All this time, I've been trying to stay safe for him, praying he would stay safe for me. I could have spent every night of the Blitz wandering the streets, for all the difference it's made.' She closed her eyes. 'I'm so tired.'

They sat in silence while it grew darker.

'Let me ring your sister,' Julia said, after a time.

'She's gone to Wales to see the kids for Christmas.'

'Then let me take you home. You need company at a time like this.'

'No,' said Bea, getting to her feet with the awkwardness of someone who has been sitting on a cold floor for too long. 'I'd rather be by myself.' She smoothed down her crumpled skirt. 'But thanks all the same.'

'Are you sure?'

'Quite sure.'

'I ought to warn you. Miss Plume has been looking for you.'

'Has she.'

'Do you want me to put her in the picture?'

'No,' said Bea. 'Please don't. I couldn't bear the pity.' Not Miss Plume's, and not Julia's, this was clear.

When Julia got back to the fifth floor, Mr Slater was fastening up the briefcase he used to bring his sandwiches to work. This fastening of the briefcase (tarnished brass lock, cracked buckled straps) took place every day exactly half an hour before what he called 'home time' and was thus a reliable harbinger of it. 'Marathon session, eh?' he said. 'Did you win?'

Julia put the file on her desk, along with the form requesting it. 'Well, I found it. But they've all gone now, and there's no one to give it to.'

'All right for some,' said Mr Slater. He was wearing a paper hat. 'One day I should like to knock off early, beat the crowds. Here, I saved you a drop.' He handed her a glass with an inch or so of tawny liquid in it. 'You may not thank me for it once you've drunk it. No mince pies, I'm afraid. That turned out to be a canard. But you did miss the carol singing, which personally I should count as a bonus. I've heard cats that sounded better than Miss Plume's attempt at the descant of "O Come All Ye Faithful".'

'Cheers,' said Julia. She drank the sherry, which was not as bad as it had been billed.

Then it really was home time. Mr Slater, putting on his coat, paused in the doorway. 'Happy Christmas,' he said.

'Your hat,' said Julia.

'Oh, I've decided to go without. Mine's getting so shabby and I haven't the points for another.' He frowned. 'Do you think that's letting the side down?'

'No, I mean your paper hat,' said Julia. 'You're still wearing it.'

'Am I?' He felt round on his head. 'Oh, so I am.'

By the time Julia left, the fifth floor was all but deserted. She peered round the door of Midlands West, but Bea was gone. Only Miss Plume, collecting sticky glasses and carbon-copied carol sheets, remained behind. 'Happy Christmas,' said Julia on her way to the stairs.

'Miss Sinclair?'

'Yes?'

'You're friendly with Miss Justin, aren't you?'

'Yes.'

Miss Plume adjusted her spectacles. It had struck her that since Miss Justin had returned to work her heart wasn't in it, and she wondered if Julia might be able to shed any light on the matter. She would not like to take Miss Justin to task unfairly. For a monologist, Miss Plume could be direct when she chose.

For a moment Julia hesitated. 'I hear that this flu is quite difficult to shake off.'

'Perhaps. However, I have noticed that she has been absent from her post for quite considerable periods of time recently. Today, for example, I saw neither hide nor hair of her all afternoon.'

Julia said, 'I can shed light on that at least. This afternoon Miss Justin was in the Stacks with me. Having quite a time of it. We both were. It's such a muddle.'

'I do hope you're right,' said Miss Plume. 'We cannot afford to employ anyone at the Institute who is less than conscientious. Our work here is too important. It seems to me that some young women do persist in seeing the national emergency as an excuse for flightiness.'

Miss Plume must be the only one in the building who thought what they did there was important, thought Julia as she went down the stairs. Yet she would dearly have loved to counter her accusation of 'flightiness' with an explanation of what war did to people.

'Cheer up,' said Mr Keyes, as she signed out. 'It might never happen. Happy Christmas.'

'Happy Christmas,' said Julia.

She came out of the building and stood for a moment under the stuccoed portico between the peeling columns, adjusting her eyes to the dark streets, letting her other senses come into play, senses she would need to navigate safely to the station. There wasn't much traffic, it was true, but you could not rely on whatever traffic there was seeing you. You wouldn't want to die by accident when so many were trying to kill you on purpose.

Behind her the door squeaked open. 'Oh, good, I've caught you,' said Mr Keyes. 'Telephone.' He winked. 'It's the undersecretary.'

It was Dougie, saying he was back and would she come and meet him, unless, of course, she was otherwise engaged?

The evening began well. When she elbowed her way into the pub where they had arranged to meet and saw Dougie at the far end of the bar, the here and now of him stunned her all the way across the room. 'Sinclair!' he said, waving, and the anxieties of the last two months flapped off on black wings to sit on some other shoulders.

Afterwards they went to have dinner, not at the Hungarian place or the Italian place or any other of the Soho eateries Dougie generally favoured but at a British Restaurant where, for ninepence a head, they queued for faggots and swede. Fresh from Blackpool, Bromsgrove and Rotherham, Dougie was in proletarian mode. As they ate, he talked streams of talk about the filming and how he was thinking of structuring the piece.

'A day in the life seems the best bet, since there's so much else going on,' he said. 'Keep it simple. But I can't decide between dawn to dawn or midnight to midnight, as we did with *London Pride*. The trouble is either way the Queen would be stuck in the middle, which is exactly where I don't want her. That sequence should build to a finale.' He shovelled in a forkful of swede. 'Am I boring you?'

'No, why?'

'You keep looking at your watch.'

'I'm worried we're going to miss the last train.'

'Forget the last train. I've a surprise for you.'

'Oh? What?'

'Finish your supper and you'll see.'

British Restaurants had originally been set up to provide subsidized off-ration food for bombed-out people. The experience was communal. Notices told you to serve yourself and return your plates to the counter when you had finished. Tonight, the faggots were mainly oatmeal. What little meat they contained came from an animal she did not recognize and which possibly didn't exist. The swede was – swede.

'It's sound you're orchestrating,' Julia said, needing little encouragement to lay down her fork. 'So why don't you think about a symphonic structure?'

Dougie gave her a quick smile. 'You're assuming I know what that means.'

'Well, there are various kinds,' she said, 'but the classic form is *allegro*, *adagio*, *scherzo*, *allegro*. From what I've heard about what you've shot, that would mean starting late in the afternoon and finishing there. Which will put Miss Hess and the Queen in the right place.'

'Explain?'

She explained that *allegro* – robust, lively – suited the mood of the filming he'd done in the Blackpool ballroom. *Adagio* was slow and stately, perfect for the night sequences. 'Then you can wake everything up in the morning with a brisk, playful *scherzo* and round it all off with *allegro* again.'

There was a pause, then he shook his head slowly from side to side. 'Sinclair. Whatever would I do without you?'

Julia smiled to herself. Find someone else, she thought. She had known him long enough to appreciate when a meeting of minds more closely resembled a one-way street. All evening, she had wanted to tell him about Bea's fiancé; all evening, he had talked about himself.

'Where's your bag, your suitcase?' she said, when they came out of the restaurant. 'Did you leave it in the pub?'

'All in good time.'

It seemed that Dougie's surprise was to be found three floors up in a mansion block off the Euston Road. He produced a key to one of the flats and opened the door. When he ushered her into the hall, she saw his suitcase open on the floor, half the contents spilling out.

'Go on through,' he said, switching on lights.

In the sitting room, heavy brown velour curtains sagged over the blacked-out windows. The walls were papered in a pre-war design that hurtled green and orange lozenges at each other with some violence. A tubular steel chair sat upright on high moral ground among lesser, slumped furniture. Cigarette burns on the carpet. It was the sort of place, Julia thought, where you might find a corpse in the bath, if there was a bath, which was unlikely.

Dougie lit the gas fire.

As he talked, she understood that the surprise was not in the flat. It was the flat.

Apparently it belonged to a friend of Florian called Archie Pennington, who drove a desk at the MOI but had gone to spend the holidays with friends in the country. (Florian himself, who had turned out to be much older than any of them assumed, had only recently been called up and was driving a far less appealing desk at an army training camp in the north of England.)

'The studio's closed until Monday,' he said. 'In the morning you can pop down to Twaddles and pick up some clothes.'

She knew, without him telling her, that 'some clothes' meant 'that frock I like'.

'Do you like your present?'

'Lovely,' said Julia, wondering if the studio hadn't been closed, how many days he could have spared her. The present she'd bought him, a first edition of Henry Mayhew's *London Labour and the London Poor* recommended by the dealer on Charing Cross Road he patronized, was lying wrapped under the tree, along with the presents she'd bought the children.

'Your enthusiasm overwhelms me.'

'It's just –'

'I know,' said Dougie, putting his arms around her. 'Pretend it's the Ritz. Drink?'

He was giving her exactly what she had once begged him for, thought Julia. A place of their own, however temporary. What she didn't understand was why she was now finding reasons not to want this.

'What about Netta?' she said when he came back into the room. He put the glasses down.

'She's expecting us to be there. Or at least she's expecting me.'

'Julia,' said Dougie. 'Why are we talking about Netta?'

To inject a lighter note, she said, 'I've got a starring part in their Christmas play, for a start.'

Dougie said, 'As what, the Virgin Mary?'

'It's not a nativity.'

He snorted. 'Ibsen, is it? Chekhov?'

'You know what I mean. I live there. I feel an obligation to them.'

They were teetering on an edge. Why was she so intent on pushing them over it?

'But not to me.'

'I didn't say that.'

'Oh, I think you did.'

Some while later, in bed, his arms reached around her. 'Sinclair,' he said. 'Mmm, Sinclair. What do you smell of?'

She turned to him in relief, and laid the length of her body against his.

What followed was a shock to them both.

He had come exhausted to bed before and fallen asleep as soon as his head hit the pillow. They had gone for periods, sometimes extended sulking periods, when they'd hardly touched each other. This – this *failure* – was new. She didn't know any other way to describe the moist soft defeat of it. It was her fault, it must be, and she was fully prepared to take the blame until he jumped to the same conclusion himself.

'Nettafication!' He threw back the covers. 'You're bloody *Nettafied*. How do you expect me to fuck you under the circumstances!' He got out of bed and slammed out of the room.

She lay awake for a long time, while the rock she had placed over the hole where she kept her suspicions worked itself loose. In the morning, she was hunting for her shoes when she found a pair of shell-pink satin camiknickers under the bed, somewhat creased and soiled.

'Are these part of the surprise, too?' she said, holding them up.

'Don't start,' he said.

'I suppose you're going to tell me they're Archie's.'

'How do I know whose they are?'

In the end, they went back to Traddles, where they each enjoyed a miserable Christmas in entirely different ways.

23

'So. Julia,' said Basil, chinagraph tucked behind one ear. 'In or out?'

It was late afternoon in the cutting room, and they were working on the Hess footage. Julia had been in the original pre-Queen audience, and here she was on the Moviola, sitting between two female ARP wardens.

Basil said, 'I say in. She looks like she really hears the music – understandable since she chose it. Have you noticed? True music lovers sit perfectly still. They don't put on a special music-appreciation face, or nod or tap in time to the beat, which is worse.'

Dougie shrugged. 'Whatever you like.'

'A pity to leave her on the cutting-room floor when she's contributed so much to the piece.'

'It's a film, not a bloody thank-you letter.'

Tony, sitting at the splicer, raised his head. They had been tetchy all day, which was hardly surprising, since they'd spent the night working. When he arrived that morning there had been a sea of footage on the floor, three feet deep in places. It was the third week in February and the Ministry was expecting a finished film in a fortnight. Fat chance of that, when the pair of them had spent the morning arguing over a single frame in the Blackpool ballroom sequence, which was to say over one twenty-fourth of a second.

'How is Julia these days?' said Basil.

'Fine,' said Dougie. 'Why do you ask?'

Julia was not fine. Since Christmas, she had been cold-shouldering him. Then there was her son, who had run away again, this time fetching up at her father's. There was to be a reunion of sorts this evening – or a tribunal – and he dreaded the way she would be afterwards, not that he planned to be around to see it. No wonder sleeping with her had become such a washout.

A distant boom.

'What was that?' said Dougie.

Basil took the chinagraph from behind his ear and marked a trim. 'They're blowing up a bomber in Sound Stage 2.' He shot Dougie a quick look. 'Travis is back.'

This was code. Deciphering it, Dougie understood that Ann Wightman was back. He got up and put on his coat.

'How was Norfolk?' Dougie said. They were walking away from the canteen towards the lake. Snow flurried around them, settled on the concrete paths, dissolving only where their feet trod. Under the flat grey light, the low buildings of the studio complex were as bleak and utilitarian as hangars or barracks.

'Even colder than here,' said Ann Wightman.

People in RAF uniforms headed in the opposite direction to the way they had come, seeking cups of tea. Whether these were actors playing the parts of service personnel, or service personnel playing themselves, was not clear. Not one of them, male or female, went past without holding her in their gaze for a fraction longer than was polite. And today she was dressed ordinarily enough. No Russian *shapka*, for instance, just a woollen scarf wrapped high under her chin, snow stars in her hair. Impossible to play the Face Game with this one; she had too many faces and could change them whenever she pleased.

'You left your knickers at the flat,' he said. 'Julia found them.'

'Whoops,' said Ann Wightman. 'Did that give you *un mauvais quart d'heure?*'

'It put a slight damper on the festivities, put it like that. Are you free later?'

'No.' She laughed at his evident disappointment.

'I've missed you.'

She lit a cigarette. 'It's always got to be a grand passion for your generation, hasn't it?'

His generation. He winced. 'I don't know what you're talking about.'

'Passion, romance, love.' Each word was drawled out. 'Isn't that how you justify your adulteries, your bits on the side? For me, for people my age, sex is nothing. One might as well be brushing one's teeth.'

'You fucked Travis.'

'Of course I did. I told you, it was cold in Norfolk.'

He felt a strong urge to hit her. This was oddly arousing. It was as if she were leading him, shackled, into a broader sphere of violence, into the heart of the war itself.

'You're quite the little alleycat, aren't you?'

'Oh,' she said, in a mocking echo of what he had once told her, 'it's just that I wouldn't want you to labour under any misapprehension.'

Plevna Avenue had not survived the previous year unscathed. Julia did not know why she should be surprised to come round the corner and find the corner gone, in its place lumpy ground silently accepting a covering of snow. The Huttons had lived in the corner house when she was a child. Mrs Hutton, who was middle-aged and childless, took her once to Buszards Tea Rooms in Oxford Street – she could not have been more than nine or ten – and she had never forgotten the tiered white wedding cakes in the window or the solid old-fashioned feel of the place with its dark bentwood chairs and potted palms. Buszards had been bombed the previous April, another chunk of her childhood gone. What would anchor memory now?

It was not the last shock of the evening, or by any means the worst.

Her father had said little on the telephone. Unlike the last occasion, she had not even been aware that Peter had gone missing until he had turned up in London. When she rang the doorbell, she wondered whether Richard had been similarly summoned.

Richard had not. Peter was in the kitchen, said her father, leading her into the sitting room, his distant disapproval tempered by what she could only describe to herself as a spring in his step.

The house was not as unkempt as she might have expected, despite the departure of Bridie and the subsequent pounding of the Blitz, although there were certain smells she could not place and which did not belong there. The sitting room was a miracle of preservation, given the window was boarded up.

They sat.

'Second time he's done this, I gather,' said her father.

That was her first inkling of what was to come.

Then he began to talk, fixing his eyes on a patch of carpet about a yard in front of his shoes. And as he talked, she found herself fixing her eyes on that same patch herself, until its worn, dulled reds and blues took on something of a hypnotic quality.

Here at last were answers. Here were facts, divulged to the one person Peter was apparently prepared to trust them with.

Afterwards, she would struggle to remember her father's exact words or the order in which they came out. At the time she experienced each successive revelation like the jack-knifing collision of carriages in a train derailment. Double blows: every one she received herself she received a second time on Peter's behalf.

'Of course, his understanding of divorce is rather limited. Not to mention his understanding of the rest of it. I had to read between the lines, as it were.'

Her father stopped speaking. She heard the tick of the clock measure the silence. Her mind was not silent. Instead, it was filled with clanging, jangling sounds, as if someone were smashing their elbows down on piano keys or sirens were blaring.

'Does he know who I'm with?' she said, when she trusted her voice.

'He knows you're with someone who isn't his father. Isn't that enough?'

She swallowed. 'What was he doing in Whitmarket?'

'Hiding, until hunger got the better of him. We must be thankful he was caught when he was. I hate to think . . .' Her father broke off, rubbed hands callused from gardening along his trousers. They made a rasping sound. 'At least the experience taught him to be prepared. This time he cashed in the postal order I sent him for Christmas and took the train.' For the first time that evening he looked at her directly. 'Did you know Richard was carrying on with Mrs Spencer?'

She shook her head. What had she expected? That he should wait around while she held him in reserve? But Fiona – that pierced her.

'I gather Peter was worried you were dying. He thought that was what the pair of you were concealing from him.'

It was at this point that she began to cry.

'Children always know what the weather is,' her father said. 'Even if they don't know the cause of it.'

She struggled to control herself. 'My solicitor advised me not to visit him. Richard advised himself otherwise.'

'And who advised you to tell me nothing at all?'

'You did,' she said, 'when you washed your hands of it.' Yet in all fairness, she thought, it was the first rebuke he had permitted himself.

He sniffed. 'You had better hear the rest from him.'

This time, when Peter came through from the kitchen, wiping cocoa from his mouth with the back of his hand, she did not see the future young man but the present confused and angry child. From the doorway, he issued statements into the room.

He was not going back to school. If she made him, he would run away again. He didn't want to be at Crossfields any more.

'Peter,' Julia said, aching to take him into her arms, 'I'm not going to make you do anything you don't want to do.'

'Granddad said I could stay here.'

'Did he.'

'He can finish the year at Hurst,' her father said. 'There and back by Tube, tea on the table when he comes home in the evening.'

Hurst, a day school, was her brother's old prep. It was in Harrow, and Harrow was a neutral zone, designated neither to receive evacuees nor send them elsewhere.

'Is that what you want?' said Julia.

'Yes,' said Peter. 'And I don't want to go to St Aubyn's afterwards.'

'We'll discuss that in due course,' said her father.

Crossfields, St Aubyn's. Richard's schools, Richard's choices. Julia was under no illusion that her son's rejection of his parents stopped there. Something that Dougie had said came back to her then, something she should have paid more attention to. 'Do you mind if I ask you a question?'

Peter shrugged.

'Which film did they show at school before you ran away the first time?'

Her father seemed puzzled.

Peter wasn't puzzled. A hard, knowing glint appeared in his eye. 'The one you were in.'

Her heart turned over with a sickening lurch. A lie could be a truth unspoken, and between the two lay shame. She had protected him from nothing. Now, his memories of childhood would always be clouded by what she had done to him; she could think of no worse betrayal.

'May I come to see you once in a while?' Her voice was a whisper.

The silence that followed was the bitterest blow.

'Hop along to bed now,' said her father.

When he had gone upstairs, her father said, 'He'll need time.'

She nodded.

'Let me deal with Richard,' said her father. 'He knows the boy's safe. The school will have told him.'

'Thank you.'

'He is my grandson.' He got up to poke the fire. 'Did you notice his teeth?'

'No.'

'I shall have to take him to the dentist. They've been giving them scouring powder to brush with.' Very carefully, he balanced two coals on the little glowing heap with the tongs.

She left the house soon after and made her way to the Underground, her shaded torch glancing off plump outlines of snow, the external world having altered as much during the past hour as her internal one. The illuminating whiteness she felt rather than saw. What it showed her was herself, displayed on the screen at the Ciné Club, flagrant on the brink of what had seemed so inevitable then.

A fortnight later the film was finished and had acquired a title: *Song of Britain*. There was to be a private screening at Soho Square before its general release.

'I'm not sure if I'll come along tonight.' Julia sat on the edge of the bed, dully brushing her hair. Lately she had lost her appetite for seeing films in which she had played any kind of part. 'Would you mind?'

'Suit yourself.'

On their way to breakfast, the children pelted down the corridor outside the annexe. 'I hate you!' Louie was saying. 'You rotten beast!'

Dougie held one tie up to the mirror, then another. The grey? he thought. Or the red with the stripes? Or was that a little regimental?

'It's Bea's leaving do.'

He turned away from the mirror. 'I said, suit yourself.'

Julia left for work, the children went to school and Netta was out in the garden staking what the March winds had blown down. In the hall, Dougie dialled the exchange.

'Marylebone 357,' said Ann Wightman, when the call was put through.

'It's me. Julia's not coming tonight. She's busy.'

'So I'm allowed to show my face now, am I?' There were

scuffling noises in the background. 'How very kind of you, seeing as I worked on the bloody thing.'

'You know what the difficulty is.'

'Of course. It's called hypocrisy.'

He chose to ignore this. Netta came back into the house, and he lowered his voice. 'Will I see you later? Do you want to meet first and have a drink?'

'No,' said Ann Wightman. 'I'm afraid I've made other plans.'

Bea's leaving party was a small gathering on the fifth floor of the Institute. Nothing to drink or eat but warm wishes all round.

Bea said, 'I can't believe I'm bidding adieu to all this.' Pinned to her blouse was a paper medal Mr Slater had made her, which read 'Distinguished Service Order. For Valour in The Stacks.' At intervals he brought some of their colleagues over to admire its penmanship and wit.

'Yes, how could you possibly tear yourself away,' said Julia.

'Think of me on Monday when I'm swabbing decks.' Bea had joined the Wrens.

'I shall.'

Bea checked her watch. 'Come on, you should go to the screening.'

'No, it will have started by now. Besides, I'm not dressed for it.'

Bea said, 'You look fine. Look, go quickly, before Miss Plume makes a speech. Otherwise you'll be here all night.'

Julia embraced her. 'Please look after yourself.'

'That's not my objective any more,' said Bea. 'It's winning this damn war. I owe it to Giles.'

Julia walked across Soho Square, debating with every step whether she should turn back or go on. Since Peter's disclosure, the very fabric of the building seemed tainted.

Nevertheless, she found herself going through the door. Inside was a crush of people, far more than last time. It was not surprising. Dougie was much better known now.

'So clever the way he's shown us to ourselves, don't you think?' said someone.

'I do agree, he's a genius. A true original. People will be watching this in years to come.'

She said, 'Excuse me' and 'I beg your pardon,' but everywhere were elbows and hands holding glasses and loud voices tuned to their own broadcasts. She had only progressed a short distance into the hall when someone trod on her foot and spilled their drink over her.

'Oh, I am most frightfully sorry,' said the man. (They were all chiefly men: that hadn't changed.) He produced a large, laundered handkerchief and began to mop her skirt, gazing up at her all the while in a roguish fashion. 'I know there's a war on, but this is really quite dreadful booze; otherwise, I would have drunk it and not tipped it all over the front of you.' The handkerchief was blotted pink. 'I think they must have brewed it up in one of the labs at Denham.'

Julia laughed. 'Don't worry about it.'

'You look familiar. Perhaps we've met before.'

'I don't think so.'

'Julian Embry,' said the man, who had a varnish of money and tailoring.

'Julia Sinclair.'

'Julia and Julian, how droll,' he said.

'I assume the screening's over.'

'You haven't missed anything.'

'You didn't like it.'

'Well,' he said, 'I thought there was something almost symphonic about the structure, which was interesting, all things considered.' Damning with faint praise.

'Oh yes?'

'No doubt that was Meers's doing. I don't think Birdsall is at all musical. Meers, the editor, do you know him?'

'I've heard of him,' she said, keeping her cards close to her chest.

'But frankly the rest of it was Birdsall playing with himself as usual. I can't see this going down well in Cleethorpes.' Embry explained that he was a producer at Gaumont. Features. 'I don't know why I come to these things. You know what the documentary boys call us? Lice. Not very nice, is it?'

'No.'

He broke off. 'Ann, darling! I thought he'd banned you from coming.'

Julia turned, and her blood ran cold.

Her.

'Yes, well, he unbanned me this morning. His *other* woman couldn't make it.' Ann Wightman's eyes rested on Julia for a fraction of a moment, then flicked away. 'Have you seen him?'

'He's through there somewhere. Being fawned over, I expect.'

Ann Wightman went off, the crowd that wouldn't shift for Julia parting before her like the Red Sea.

Embry said to Julia, 'Ann was continuity on this. And a bedfellow of Birdsall's in Rotherham, I gather. Awfully squalid.'

A shriek in her ears. 'Excuse me,' said Julia. 'I need some air.'

She fled from the hall and stood outside shaking and gasping for breath, her entire body a silent scream. In the square, bare branches she could not see creaked in the wind. You could expect something – even *know* something – and still have the legs kicked out from under you when it happened. Why was that? Was it because expecting the worst was like taking out an insurance policy that deep down you didn't think you needed? If so, she hadn't read the fine print.

What should she do now? Go back in and confront him? Slink away?

At that moment, Embry came through the door with a third option. 'Oh, there you are. I've got a car round the corner. Fancy a proper drink? It's the least I can do after drenching you.'

A car meant petrol, and petrol meant the black market. She thought of the lift the soldiers had given her son, the jerry cans in the back, the firebomb into which he had climbed, trusting.

'Why not?' she said.

As they drove away from Soho Square, he slapped the steering wheel. 'Of course, it was you in the audience, wasn't it? During the Mozart bit. Birdsall never can resist pointing his camera at a pretty face.'

Later she would wonder what fate had crossed her path with Embry's. It wasn't fate, however, that led her to accept the offer of a drink and where that drink eventually led, which was bed. It was the vicious impulse to cause as much hurt as she had been dealt. Afterwards she realized she'd chosen the perfect weapon for that.

'I gather you went to the screening after all,' said Dougie, taking off his jacket. It was the following evening, they were alone in the annexe and he had arrived home too late for supper, as usual.

'Yes. Sadly, I missed the film,' said Julia. She was hungover, and sore.

'Where did you go afterwards?'

'I could ask you the same.'

Before he could say anything, she hit him. 'Ann Wightman!' She hit him again, hit him until her fists hurt. 'How could you? How could you do this to me? I've sacrificed my son for you!'

He held her off. 'What are you doing? Stop it. You're being hysterical.'

'How long have you been sleeping with her? How long?'

He sighed. 'We've been through this before. I haven't been *sleeping with her*, as you put it. She works at the Unit.'

She was panting. This had not been the plan. All day the possession of proof had given her an eerie sort of calmness. Many speeches had been rehearsed. His replies – contrite, ashamed, begging forgiveness – she had also scripted. Not this incoherent fury that was coming out of her mouth or the lies coming out of his. 'Funny you didn't tell me.'

'Is it any wonder when this is the way you react?'

'There's no point denying anything. I heard all about Rother-ham.'

266

'Then you've heard wrong. These suspicions of yours are getting very wearing.'

She had seen him lose control many times. All their rows had been shouting, screaming, arm-waving slanging matches. She had never seen him this contained. It seemed to her that his insistence on denying the truth, in swearing black was white, was infinitely crueller than his infidelity. Well, she could be cruel too.

'If you must know where I was last night, I went out with Embry. And slept with him. There. You don't like it, do you, when the boot's on the other foot! Now you know how I feel!'

Disgust played on his face, a muscle tightening the corner of his mouth. 'Embry, eh?' he said. 'Good choice, Sinclair. He's got plenty of money. A wife, too, but I wouldn't let that worry you. Tell me, who else in the film business have you had? Frank? Basil? Or are you only interested in directors?'

This injustice broke her, finally. She sank down on the bed and began to sob. 'I wouldn't have slept with him if you hadn't betrayed me.'

'Really,' he said. 'I'm supposed to believe that, am I?'

The row had nowhere to go. That did not stop it from carrying on. On and on it went into the night. Rotherham. Shell-pink satin camiknickers. Shirts done up wrong. Phones ringing at eleven o'clock. Caro, the woman at the bottle party, the glutton for punishment.

At one point, he had escaped to the barn and she had run after him, shrieking and stumbling and crying. Hours later, they were still there.

'I don't understand. How can you care so much about telling the truth in your work and be such a liar?' she said towards dawn. At this stage in the proceedings, it was almost a philosophical question. 'Why can't you admit what you've done?'

'You're insane,' he said, his head in his hands. 'I can't stand any more of this. It's over, Julia. Just pack your bags and go.'

'Where?'

'I don't know and I don't care. Give Embry a ring, I should. You always wanted to go back to London. Well, now, here's your chance.'

'I'm not going anywhere,' she said. 'Besides, you can't throw me out of someone else's house. No more than I can. As much as I want to.'

He couldn't. She couldn't. But Netta could. In the morning she asked the pair of them to leave. They were upsetting the children. She felt sorry for Julia, she really did, but there were limits, and she had reached hers.

24

Maison Dieu. The House Struck by Fire. Ruin, destruction, deception.

At first Julia unleashed her anguish to coincide with the noise of the trains rumbling on the main line out of Paddington, then she stopped bothering. It was around then that she understood she had fetched up in what amounted to a brothel.

Fetched up.

That sounded involuntary, a beaching or a washing ashore, so much flotsam and jetsam from shipwreck. It was not. It was deliberate. She could have afforded better lodgings, but she had chosen not to. She put as little value on herself as she felt valued.

Down the brown-wallpapered passageway day and night came the brisk clip of heels and the heavy tread of shoes. Through the thin walls, thuds and the protesting shrieks and squeals of mattress springs. False cries of pleasure – Oh oh oh oh – and the grunts of pleasure paid for. Sometimes, there was a slap or two and a tumbling about. After, the heavy tread of shoes rapidly walking a shamed, satisfied appetite away.

There was a greasy floral counterpane on the sagging bed, a cheap chest of drawers, one drawer missing a handle and half clinging on to the other, a bar fire that ate sixpences and smelled of singed dust, and a washbasin from whose lime-scaled tap she drank. She didn't unpack her case. There was no need: she didn't get dressed.

Marie, who was one of the working girls, rapped on her door sometimes. She was sixteen or so and hardened, her youth arousing pity, which her hardening kept at arm's length. (Her real name was Joan, she confided, but she thought Marie 'suited her better'.) Once, she brought Julia brandy in a tooth mug. Other times, at

Julia's request, cigarettes from the tobacconist at the corner. She had spots, which she thickly powdered.

Marie went on the streets in the late afternoon, but the trade only really picked up a bit later, she explained. Tuesdays and Thursdays her pimp came round, collected the cash and left his receipts in the purple bruises on her temples and the cigarette burns on her wrists and ankles.

Julia did not go out. She didn't eat – or much – and after a while the hard little knot of her self-rationed stomach dissolved into its own emptiness and the swimming lightness of her head seemed like the most beautiful and finely wrought veil of misery anyone could ever hope to drape between themselves and the great, yawning caverns of misery the world had concealed from her until now.

Grief – and what was this if not grief? – was stupefying, exhausting. No one ever told you that. You could cry yourself to sleep, hiccoughing, nose streaming with snail trails of mucus, as perhaps you had once done as a child after some small monstrous injustice, or you could simply let the grey wash over until lifting your head from the flat dead pillow and remembering your own name was more effort than could be borne.

Yet there were times when you woke suddenly at half past four in the morning, heart hammering, into a perfect lucidity, and all that stopped you from throwing yourself out of the window was the fact you weren't high enough from the ground to be certain of killing yourself. These times were the worst although admittedly the competition was stiff.

It was impossible – logically impossible, it seemed – not to think. Round and round went her thoughts and, each time, each circuit, they bumped into Dougie and what he had taught her.

Each memory was a mine and there were triggers to all of them. Sometimes, in this Paddington boarding house rumbling with trains, a line from Rimbaud would float to the surface of her mind to torment her – *La vie est la farce à mener par tous* ('Life is the farce we are all forced to endure'). Or a scene from one of the many

films she and Dougie had watched together and exhaustively ana-
lysed afterwards; he was very keen on the Marx Brothers.

He was teaching her still. He was teaching her what it felt like to
have a black pulpy hollow where your heart had been torn out, its
edges seared and crisped.

Vagina dentata. And here, the mermaid's purse she had picked up
on the shingle the day she had met him tumbled out of the pocket
of her summer dress, that very first time.

Protect my family.

From what? The war? Dougie was the bomb that had gone off
in her life. He was the explosion. Now only pieces remained.

Every afternoon the organ grinder played in the street outside.
The first time she had taken pity on this poor man living off the
coppers of the poor and thrown coins out of the window. Or perhaps it was self-pity that she had felt. A mistake, at any rate, because
he had been back every day since and she had to keep away from
the window until he was gone. He wore an old dusty topper with
pheasant's feathers stuck in the hatband and a frock coat coming
apart at the seams. No animal beggars, however. A tethered mon-
key or a moulting parrot would have been too much to take. It was
hard enough to hear the jarring, tinny music, out of tune and out
of time: 'After the Ball is Over', again and again and again.

Who am I? she interrogated the mirror, not bothering to make
the 'best face' she had made in mirrors all her life.

Nobody, was the honest answer she supplied on the mirror's
behalf. Not wife, not lover, not daughter, not mother.

Nobody at all. All sense of herself had gone down the rabbit
hole of these other vanished identities. She lacked even the substance to haunt her own room.

Later she was not certain how long she spent in the boarding house.
She remembered watching a fly buzz on the windowsill several
mornings in a row and wondering if it was the same fly; she
remembered the brandy in the tooth mug and the organ grinder.
Time didn't matter. There was so much of it.

Days went by. Sleep, once her friend with the velvet cosh, began to be a problem. The mutations of grief shifted to wakefulness of such a stark and uncompromising variety that it seemed to exist outside herself as a bullying kind of invigilator or interrogator, hoicking her back from the brink of unconsciousness with the painful glare of a bare light bulb shone in the eyes.

A rap on the door.

She broke off a discussion she was having with the wallpaper, which was threatening to become a little heated, and listened.

Another rap. 'Are you there?'

Julia opened the door a crack.

Marie said, 'I heard voices.'

'Have the Germans come?'

'Not the last time I looked.'

'You don't have any more of that brandy, do you? I'm having a little difficulty sleeping.'

'No,' said Marie. She fanned a hand in front of her face. 'Phew. You want to have a wash, smarten yourself up a bit.'

Julia opened the door wider. 'Perhaps you might suggest a few outfits.' She indicated her suitcase, open but still unpacked. The wallpaper quietened at her audacity.

Marie ventured into the room and knelt on the floor. 'This is nice,' she said, tugging out the frock that Dougie had always liked.

'Have it,' said Julia. She went on saying 'have it' until all her best clothes were gone. That felt good.

'Who's he?' Marie held up a photograph.

'I think you'd better go now,' said Julia.

Marie put the photograph back. 'He looks like you.'

'He's my son.'

'Is he dead?' She gathered the clothes in her arms.

'Only to me,' said Julia.

Mattie followed Marie up the stairs. 'She's *here*?'

'I told you she was.'

'Did she ask you to ring me?'

'No,' said Marie. 'You was the only one who was in.' She handed over the small red address book she had taken from Julia's case, although not the money she had taken from her handbag. 'Well, what else could I do? All this carry-on is bad for business. The punters don't like it one bit.' She twisted a finger on her temple. 'If you ask me she belongs in the loony bin.'

'Mattie,' said Julia, opening the door. Frank's sister, she reminded herself. Wren. Plain-speaking. Square-built. Dead fiancé.

'Get yourself dressed,' said Mattie. 'Quickly. I've a taxi waiting.'

Julia went over to the window. The cabbie had switched off the engine and was reading a newspaper.

Mattie said, 'Hurry up.'

Julia came away from the window. 'What are you doing?'

'Good question.' Mattie held up a jumper and skirt. 'Put these on.'

Julia untied her dressing gown.

'I don't understand.'

Mattie eyed her. 'That makes two of us.'

She put on the jumper, then the skirt. Then her shoes, then her coat.

Mattie picked up the dressing gown by one of its sleeves and dropped it in the bottom drawer of the chest. Kicked it shut. A handle fell off.

In the cab, Mattie told the driver to take them to 43 Marlborough Road.

Out of the window the hectic streets changed from poor to middling, from middling to comfortable, then back to middling again. Where were they going? thought Julia: a clinic, an institution of some kind? For she seemed fit for nothing else, and part of her welcomed incarceration, doors slamming, shot bolts, straitjackets.

The taxi came to a stop.

'Where are we?'

'My place.'

*

Time passed no faster or slower at the Marlborough Road flat than it did anywhere else. But a few decent meals and a few baths later, Julia was no longer talking to wallpaper. (Mattie's wallpaper kept its views to itself, unlike Mattie.) She still wasn't sleeping much, but you couldn't have it all.

'He's left me with nothing,' Julia said, one evening during supper.

'Eat your soup,' said Mattie.

'I was an ordinary person before I met him. I had an ordinary life.'

Mattie broke off a bit of bread. 'We're all ordinary. Dougie included.' She paused. 'Dougie especially.'

Julia went on, 'It was as if I was living in a shell and he cracked it wide open. And now –' She fluttered her fingers.

'He must have heard you tapping on the inside asking to be let out,' Mattie said.

'What do you mean?'

'Simply that like most men of his type he prefers to push at an open door, even if it takes a bit of pushing. You talk as if you had no choice in the matter.'

Julia stared at the table. 'I'm not asking for sympathy.'

'I'm not offering you any.' Mattie was aware she had offered much more, which was most of her current leave. 'Look, go back to him, if that's what you want. I gather there's a vacancy. He's sent that continuity girl packing, whatever she's called. Go back to him. On past form, he'd probably have you. You could be another Caro, hanging about for years like a dog begging for table scraps.'

Oddly, the news he had got rid of the bitch was no comfort. 'I don't want to be another Caro.'

'Then you have to be very careful how you represent this to yourself. You will only move on when you are brave enough to admit you played a role in it.'

Later, when Julia lay sleepless in the tiny back bedroom where Mattie had put her up, she understood for the first time that she had tried to pay for happiness with other people's misery. This was how the gods punished you, she finally realized. They made you live with what you had done. If Richard had felt one tenth of the pain she felt now, that was still agony. As for Peter – didn't she owe him a better version of herself? Whether he wanted any version of his mother at all was a different question that only time would answer.

The next day Mattie went back on duty. She was no longer a plotter and now worked office hours for a commander at the Admiralty. Julia cooked a meal and had it ready on the table for her when she came home.

'If this is the best you can do in the kitchen, no wonder he chucked you,' said Mattie, regarding her plate.

Julia's mouth dropped open. Then she began to laugh.

Mattie laughed too. 'So what else did you do today, apart from waste our rations?'

'I enlisted.'

Mattie put down her fork. 'That's the first sensible thing you've said since you came here.'

25

A fortnight after the bombing returned to London in early 1944, Julia was posted to a Heavy Anti-Aircraft (HAA) battery at Mudchute on the Isle of Dogs. When the signal came through she had just come to the end of another training course at Oswestry, all part of the army's ceaseless attempts to mould machinery from human clay. She had been expecting to return to Filey, but one of the many things she had learned over the last eighteen months was not to second-guess the army.

It was bitterly cold and a thick layer of grey cloud pressed down like a dull headache. Julia made her way to the gun site half shouldering, half lugging her kit bags, respirator and water bottle round her neck, comb, cigarettes and travel warrant stuffed in the pockets of her battledress top and trouser pockets. At first she thought there had been a mistake and the transport had dropped her in the wrong place. It was true she had never been to the East End, had never shaken off her childhood dread of it. It was also true that she'd seen enough newsreels to expect damage. But the scale of the devastation her boots were crunching through was beyond her imagination – and well beyond what any censor would have allowed to be shown. She was reminded of the destruction of the City she had witnessed that first winter of the Blitz. Somehow this was worse, not least for the sense of abandonment, the absence of bomb tourists mourning architecture. It was as if an entire civilization had gone into rubble and been forgotten about.

She came past railway arches kitted out as makeshift shelters, isolated terraced streets and truncated sections of terraces, roofless, windowless houses, scorched brick walls, broken heaps of rained-upon furniture and unusable, unidentifiable furnishings. Pubs, churches and shops had not escaped and much of the debris was left where it had fallen. She saw few people. One or two cats slinking, darting about the edges of craters, lots of rats. A bleak haunted place. She later learned they called it the District of the Dead.

The battery comprised four positions arranged in the familiar semicircle on concrete platforms sunk into camouflaged pits, the barrels of the 3.7-inch guns directed skywards over the shipping traffic chugging on the river. It was mid-morning and there was a sentry at each position, field glasses slung round their necks.

The first one, who was furtively smoking, fag tucked into his palm lit end down, told her she would find the duty officer, Lieutenant Woodbury, 'over there', indicating a low sandbagged Nissen hut with a corrugated-iron roof next to a smaller hut with a stove-pipe exiting from one end that was probably the cookhouse. A little way off were other temporary-looking buildings that she supposed were barracks, their walls rippled a little with gun blast. She had seen better and she had certainly known worse. Last winter at an emplacement outside Brighton they'd called Vladivostok they had had to wash in snow and there had been an outbreak of dysentery.

Most of the women Julia had served with and the battery commanders she had served under had been younger than her, so it was no surprise to find the lieutenant was in his early twenties. From the doorway, where she dumped her bags, she had a moment to observe him, note the chin still bearing the livid dints of adolescent acne, the upper lip struggling to sprout a moustache, the square stubby hands shifting through paperwork beside a steaming tea mug. Then he looked up, and she saw his eyes were older than they should have been. There were times when the Face Game returned to her involuntarily and this was one of them. He was the young father, the emigrant in *The Last of England*, she thought, or perhaps a Holbein.

'Sir.'

He returned her salute. 'Corporal Sinclair, we've been expecting you.'

The accent was broad Yorkshire. The army did this: it juggled regions, classes, backgrounds. She had camped, trained and worked with women from Wales, Scotland, Liverpool, Newcastle, the Midlands, the West Country; with hairdressers, teachers, seamstresses, shop girls, farmers' daughters and the occasional deb. She may be in London, but there was no reason to expect a London voice.

He flicked through her papers.

'You're a No. 1.'

'Yes, sir. Since last October.'

'Presumably that was when they gave you the stripes.'

'Yes, sir.'

'Kerrys or Sperrys?'

'Both, sir.'

'Mentioned in dispatches, too.'

She nodded.

'Why was that?'

'It wasn't anything. We were strafed. I remembered to turn off the generator.'

He folded up the papers. 'You'll do.'

The walls were covered with posters: aircraft in silhouette, from the side, the rear, the front, from above. Dorniers, Heinkels, Junkers, Messerschmitts. Recognition was a key part of the training. Their aircraft and yours – you didn't want to shoot down your own side, although on occasion that had been known to happen.

'Corporal?'

'Sir.'

'Your previous postings have been on mixed batteries.'

Of course they had. She didn't know what the lieutenant was driving at. On batteries you always had to have a man to fire the gun. Women weren't allowed to fire guns. Women were only allowed to say when guns should be fired. You might say this was splitting hairs.

'Yes, sir.'

Lieutenant Woodbury gave her a wry smile. 'You'll find we're a little behind the times. Until last month we were male-only.'

These days, male-only batteries tended to be manned by those who were UFM. Unfit For Mixed. Dismay must have shown on her face, because the lieutenant was quick to reassure her that his men were civilized souls, on the whole, and their first draft of ATS girls had settled in well, all eight of them. Unfortunately, however, he went on to explain, the female barracks were not yet completed. Her billet would be with Mrs Hoffmann on Ada Street.

Ada Street? Down here, there were no streets to speak of.

Julia had completed her basic training at Aldermaston near Reading. Those six weeks had been punishing and mindless at a time when mindless punishment had been what she had needed. She had Mattie to thank for that.

The army had no cure for heartbreak. What it could supply was a steady stream of frustrations to take your mind off greater pain for a while. Inoculations and their bruised, feverish aftermath, blisters from route marches, pulled muscles from fatigues, petty humiliations of drilling on the parade ground under the sarcastic Warrant Officer, long, dull Friday nights after the FFI (Free From Infection) inspections, cleaning every item of kit, down to the studs on the soles of your boots and the buttons on your overcoat and uniform jacket. Your toothbrush had to line up in the right direction. Your bedding had to be folded just so. Label showing! Label showing! Your hair could not touch your collar.

She had asked Vera, who had been a hairdresser in Hull before she was called up, to cut hers off.

Vera said, 'You don't reckon the uniform is ugly enough?'

It was an ugly uniform, khaki, itchy. The girls tried their best with it, just as they pinned and rolled the hair that told them they were still female and would have laid down their life to save their lipstick. Julia didn't see the point. She gave in to the uniform and its ugliness.

Nevertheless she felt a pang when feathers of dark hair started falling to the floor. What was she doing? Trying to turn herself into Ann Wightman? But Vera did too good a job for that. Looking in the mirror afterwards, the person she saw was Peter, aged and feminized.

They were endlessly tested, for physical fitness and for nerves under fire. Towards the end of the six weeks they were assessed for intelligence. She had joined up with the vague notion of becoming a driver. So too had many of the others: there were no vacancies for drivers. They found her maths better than most and she was sent to the School of Artillery at Manorbier on the Pembrokeshire coast for the first of many specialist courses.

They were being trained to operate a Kerrison predictor, a Kerry. The first time she saw one she was struck by how much it resembled a movie camera – this great green metal box with its telescopic eyepieces standing on a sprung tripod. It weighed half a ton and was powered by a generator, to which it was connected by a thick cable. Their instructor, a pot-bellied captain with a pencil moustache and a habit of idly probing for earwax, told them that its purpose was to determine the angles of deflection – both lateral and vertical – from a line of sight to a future line of sight so the shell found its target. Or rather shells, since the Kerry was designed to direct the fire of all four guns on a battery.

'Any of you chaps here done any shooting?'

All the chaps here were women. One hand shot up.

'Private?'

'Morrison, sir. Clay pigeons.'

This appeared to amuse the instructor. 'Tell us, Private Morrison, how you bag a clay pigeon. Do you aim straight at it?'

'No, sir. You take a bead and you aim a little way in front of it. That is, a little way in front of where it's going.'

'Why?'

'Because it's moving, sir. It's not stationary.'

'Quite right,' said the instructor. 'Same principle.' He pointed overhead with the stem of his pipe. 'Say the enemy is fifteen thousand feet up. Your shell will take ten seconds to reach him. By which time Jerry is ten seconds closer to his target. If he's flying at 200mph, that's a mile further on. To down a plane, a shell needs to explode within thirty feet of it. You can't judge that by eye.' He slapped the top of the predictor. 'Which is where the Kerry comes in. A few seconds of knob-twiddling gives you your quadrant elevation. All done by gears and gyros.'

He made it sound simple. It was – and it wasn't.

Over subsequent days, sitting in the stuffy classroom, the befuddling summer sun streaming in, flies buzzing and dazing themselves against the windows, she felt like she was back in the school library, chewing her pen, trying and failing to solve a differential equation, or grappling with key signature calculations at college. Up on the chalkboard: azimuth angles, elevation angles, height and range, wind speeds, ballistics. She passed the written tests – just – by cramming the manual and making a couple of good guesses.

The theory was hard; the practice was better. When it was her turn to squint down the 'scopes, her pianist's fingers found it easy to manipulate the dials to keep the target steady on the horizon line. She didn't flinch when orders were barked. Neither did she complain when they were taught how to clean the generator and replenish its fuel supply (which was a dirty job) or how to sluice out gun barrels with boiling water, dry them and oil them (which was another). At this point she would have undergone any amount of training to shoot something.

One warm autumn day in 1942 when she was still at Manorbier, she and Pat Meadows, a friend she had made on the course, had planned a last sea bathe before the weather grew too cold. After work they made their way along the coast, stripped to their underwear and went in – straight in, that was ever their dare. Pat was a strong swimmer, who needed a destination; before long, she was halfway to the rock she used as a distance marker. Julia let the lapping water hold her in the shallows.

That morning she had received a letter from her solicitor enclosing her decree nisi. Thanks to Mr Gore-Finlay and a judge impressed by her army record, she had been awarded joint custody with

Richard. The ruling was meaningless now: Peter refused to see either of them.

She and Pat dried themselves off, shivering. 'That Alan What's-his-face at the dance last night was dead keen on you.' Pat hopped about, shaking sand from her feet. 'I could tell.'

'Was he.'

'You're free now, sweetie,' Pat said. 'Have a little fun.'

Julia wiped her face on her towel. Her lips tasted of salt.

Alan What's-his-face proved to be a better lover than Dougie. That surprised her. He was dull. That didn't.

Straight after Manorbier, she was sent to a training battery down on the south-west coast. This was when she first heard the guns at close quarters. At a distance of twenty yards, where the Kerry was sited, the noise was colossal. Shells jumped where they were stacked and so did the legs of your trousers. But you got used to it, blocked your ears with your fingers and bound your trouser legs with puttees.

They practised aiming at a drogue – a red weighted sail – towed behind a plane on a cable. You had to pity the pilots. Someone told her it was the ones on a charge who were given the job. She had been in the services long enough now to appreciate the elegant irony of that.

Other camps, more training, other batteries, had followed. Some of these postings were livelier than others – there was the occasion when they had been strafed, for example. Most of the work was dull and routine and here boredom was the real enemy.

What relieved the monotony was going to the cinema. This was how Julia came to see *Song of Britain* twenty-three times. All through the remainder of that year it always seemed to be on the programme whatever else was showing. The first occasion threatened to undo all the discipline the army had instilled in her. Pure torture, to see everything she and Dougie had discussed realized on the screen, along with herself, sitting in the National Gallery like the deluded fool she had been. But so much to admire, even love. That cut from Flanders and Allen to Mozart, bang on the beat. Basil's doing, of course. He had a credit. She didn't.

But by the fifth or sixth time she welcomed it. She was not alone in her appreciation. Embry had been wrong. It went down well in Cleethorpes; it went down well wherever it was shown, because people recognized their better selves in it and called it the truth.

Boredom was not a problem at Mudchute. They were too busy, too tired, too edgy for that. For the first time Julia found herself on the front line. Night after night, the bombers came. Night after night found her stationed at the predictor on the foreshore of the Thames, trembling with cold and anticipation.

The Isle of Dogs was not a true island. Bordered by the river to the east, south and west, a narrow strip of land connected it with the rest of the East End – Poplar, Stepney, Whitechapel, Bow – to the north. You might think, with three quarters of the houses destroyed and half the population shifted elsewhere or dead, there was little left to defend. But for German planes crossing the Channel and heading up the estuary, that distinctive loop in the river represented a gateway to the docks in the Pool of London and beyond, to the heart of the capital itself.

The canteen was crowded and smoky. They'd had the usual watery stew, washed down with tea that almost had more substance to it, and Beddoes, the gun layer in B team, was shouting at Julia from across the room.

'What's he after?' said June. June – Private Colbert – was a brunette from Pontefract with large breasts and a complicated love life.

'The usual, I expect,' said Julia.

'Well, he's not getting it from me,' said June.

The women at Mudchute, who were significantly outnumbered on the battery, dealt with this inequality in one of two ways. Some – June included – wore their femininity like a flag and relished the consequences, or appeared to. Julia adopted the opposite approach.

Nevertheless, she was not one of the boys. The men talked to her only in the abstract. She knew their politics, their world view, little else about them. Beddoes, for example, thought these raids were only to be expected, after the pounding they had given Hamburg and, lately, Dresden, which he regarded as criminal. Mason, who was a loader, spoke of the work of the peace, when they would organize collectively for the common good; Sergeant Wooler, too, endlessly. But it was the women who shared the inconsequential happenings of their lives and, in the end, these inconsequential happenings were what mattered. All lives were stories, or else they made no sense.

'Sinclair!' Beddoes was waving his arms, fag dangling from the corner of his mouth.

'What?' Julia cupped her hands behind her ears.

'Give us a tune!'

Banging on the trestle tables.

'Looks like you're on,' said June.

In Julia's old battery it was accepted that piano-playing was her territory. (Wherever you went there was always a piano and the piano was always hired.) When she had arrived at Mudchute she hadn't wanted to tread on anyone's toes, so it was a while before they discovered that they had a better class of entertainer in their midst than Poole, who hadn't much in his repertoire beyond 'Chopsticks'.

For Julia no longer played for herself, she played for her messmates. She played what they wanted to hear. Generally this wasn't Beethoven, although one of her battery commanders had been partial to a little Schubert now and then.

She took her tea mug over to the piano, sat down on the wobbly stool and asked: what should it be?

'"Roll out the Barrel"!'

'"Roll out the Barrel"!'

She laughed. 'Can't you lot think of anything more original?'

But they had already started to sing it – stone-cold sober, they sounded drunk – so she played along to their ragged boisterous voices.

284

It would be 'Lili Marlene' at some point later, 'White Cliffs of Dover', 'Knees up, Mother Brown', 'We'll Meet Again' – and a new one for her, 'Where Does Poor Pa Go in the Blackout?' which was hugely popular, because scatological.

They rolled out the barrel.

'Next?' Julia rested her hands on the keys.

'Your turn, Sinclair.'

'You choose!'

'You sing!'

Julia said, 'All right. But I warn you I'm no Gracie.' She rolled a few chords up and down then began to play what had been a favourite at her old battery.

> *I'm the girl that makes the thing*
> *That drills the hole that holds the ring*
> *That drives the rod that turns the knob*
> *That works the thing-ummy-bob.*

Silence. Didn't they know it? Then it dawned on her that an overwhelmingly male audience might respond differently to the innuendo she and her friends had enjoyed. That she might be inviting attentions she had been at pains to avoid. Oh, bloody get on with it, she thought, and plunged into the second verse.

> *I'm the girl that makes the thing*
> *That holds the oil that oils the ring*
> *That takes the shank that moves the crank*
> *That works the thing-ummy-bob.*
>
> *It's a ticklish sort of job*
> *Making a thing for a thing-ummy-bob,*
> *Especially when you don't know what it's for...*

Laughter. Relief.

But it's the girl that makes the thing
That drills the hole that holds the ring
That makes the thing-ummy-bob
That makes the engines roar.

And it's the girl that makes the thing
That holds the oil that oils the ring
That makes the thing-ummy-bob
That's going to win the war.

'Going to win the war!' A roar. 'GOING TO WIN THE . . .'

Bang, bang, bang! A clanging on a mess tin announced the red warning, come through on the field telephone.

Everyone shot out of their seats, chairs and benches toppling this way and that. Julia rushed from the piano, clapped her steel hat on her head, tugged on her leather jerkin and, over that, her great-coat.

They ran out into the cold night. The sirens began to wail.

'Purple!' came the shout. 'Take post! Take post!'

They heard the bomber before they saw it. A guttural, throaty sound. Searchlights played the sky, caught the plane in their criss-crossing beams.

'Target left!'

Julia squinted down the sight, grasped the clutch on the Kerry and swivelled it eastwards, downriver.

'On!' shouted No. 3.

'On!' shouted No. 5.

Julia released the clutch and the predictor followed the target.

'Bearing 260! Angle 20!' came from Arnott, manning the height-and-range finder.

She wound in the numbers on the red-lit dial.

'Engage!'

Beddoes swung the gun around.

'Fire!' shouted Julia.

The guns cracked and flamed. Shells burst in the night.

There was a piece of the sky that belonged to you. You fired at it and, if you'd calculated the lead times right, the enemy would fly straight into the flak from your barrage. The shells were contact-fused to explode at altitude and fill a volume of air with lethal debris. A single splinter catching a wing, the cockpit or the under-belly of a fuselage would do it. Or not.

Speed was a weapon of war. Every instructor on every course had drummed this into her. The planes grew faster, the airspeeds were ever greater, which meant you had to be faster too. At the beginning of the Blitz, thirty thousand shells were fired for each downed plane. By the following year, it was more like four thousand. Today, the odds were better, the instruments were better, the training was better, but many planes got through.

As did the Heinkel, which jinked, got away. This was the human element.

Another plane came droning behind.

'Target left!'

'On!' shouted No. 3.

Silence.

'No. 5?' shouted Julia.

No answer.

'No. 5? No. 5?'

'On!' shouted No. 5.

'Bearing 249! Angle 20!'

Julia dialled the figures.

'Engage!'

Too late. This, too, was the human element. And another bomber flew on to dump its load.

A gang of feral children lived in the ruins. In the grey dawn, return-ing to Ada Street, bone-weary, ears ringing, Julia saw them scamper away from the standpipe with a clatter of cascading stones and broken bricks. There were a couple of older lads and a girl of the same sort of age, but most of the children were pitifully young. All were thin, dirty and bedraggled. One, who was barely walking, had to be scooped up and carried, her sodden nappy sagging down over a bare red arse. Julia had tried to approach them before, with no success, and she had not been able to discover where they were hiding. The first time she'd seen them she thought her eyes were playing tricks on her and these were ghosts come out to play on the unrecognizable streets where they had been born.

'You get them down here,' Mrs Hoffmann told her. 'They come and go.'

Mrs Hoffmann was a busy, busy, tiny woman in late middle age who wore two spots of rouge high on her cheeks and, every day, the same scarf tied round her head, turban fashion – it was possible she slept in it. She reminded Julia of a wren, because you couldn't imagine how such a big voice could come out of such a little body.

'But who are they? Why isn't anyone looking after them?'

'Julie,' said Mrs Hoffmann. (Julia was 'Julie' the entire time she was billeted with Mrs Hoffmann.) 'You got to understand a thing or two. It didn't take the war to do this, you know. It's always been like this. I've known families on the Mudchute where the head of the household was ten, eleven, twelve years old. Mum dead, dad disappeared, God knows where. They brought themselves up then, they're bringing themselves up now. What you expect them to do?'

Mrs Hoffmann reached into her apron pocket. 'Letter for you.'

She put it down on the kitchen table, which had a chipped enamel top. There weren't two steps between it and the sink. There weren't two steps between the sink and the stove.

'Can't anything be done for them?'

Mrs Hoffmann smiled. Her pencilled eyebrows did not move. 'Manny was the same. It was the filth some of them families lived in that used to upset him, blankets crawling with bugs, I'm talking thousands of them. But show Manny a brick wall and he was the sort to knock his head against it. He'd march them down to the school or the schul or wherever. Once, he wrote to the papers. Never got no joy out of it. Still, his heart was in the right place. Not what you might call faithful, but dead loyal all the same.'

'There's a difference?' said Julia.

'Lovey, you got a lot to learn.'

Manny's photograph was in every corner and on every ledge of every room of the two-up, two-down terraced house. Dead of a heart attack three years ago. 'There's other ways of dying in a war, you know,' Mrs Hoffmann said. 'And natural causes is one of them.' Her son Jacob was a prisoner of the Japs. There had been another boy, too, Benjamin, who'd been born wrong and hadn't lived long. There were no photographs of him.

'Cup of tea?'

'Oh, yes, thanks. I'll make it.'

'You'll do no such thing.' Mrs Hoffmann lit the gas ring. 'You're in luck. It's been off all night.'

Like Mrs Tooley, Mrs Hoffmann had no faith in shelters; unlike Mrs Tooley, she had personal reasons for that. A year ago her niece, Lily, had been crushed to death at Bethnal Green Tube when a woman carrying a baby and bedding tripped on the stairs near the entrance and nearly two hundred people fell on top of her, Lily one of them. Julia had never heard of the incident.

'They hushed it up,' Mrs Hoffmann told her. 'And they cleared it away dead quick, let me tell you. There was hundreds bedding down on the platform that night and when they come up the next morning there was nothing to see. Nothing at all. But we knew about it. We all knew someone caught up in it. She was bombed out four times was Lily. She thought she was safe down there.'

Mrs Hoffmann and her friends told her other things – contrary to appearances, there were others living down here in the ruins. They told her about hiding from the doctor's collector, who would rap on the door first thing Monday morning wanting payment, about the old man who read the newspaper through the bottom of a bottle because he couldn't afford spectacles, about the children who took it in turns to go to school because they had only one pair of boots between them. And they told her about the first day of the Blitz. When Julia had been watching a red glow in the sky from Primrose Hill, Mudchute had been surrounded by burning docks.

'All round it was a ring of fire. The heat was that fierce you might have been in a cauldron. And we thought that was bad. We never knew it would get worse.' The houses had smelled of burned cinnamon and cloves ever since. 'It got in the walls and it's never got out.'

Mrs Hoffmann set down the teapot. 'You want to let it brew. Fresh leaves.'

The teapot was white bone china with violets on the sides and a green handle shaped like a stem. The cup and saucer matched.

Julia said, 'Please, there's no need to go to so much trouble. I'm fine with a mug.'

'No trouble,' Mrs Hoffmann said. 'Second time Lily was bombed out she lost the lot. And she had some nice bits and pieces. That's when I said to Manny I wasn't going to keep my best things in a cupboard no longer. If the Krauts was going to smash them, I'd have the use of them first.'

She filled a hot-water bottle from the kettle and wrapped it in a tea cloth. 'I'll pop this under the covers. It'll be nice and warm when you go up. How long they give you this time?'

'I've got drill at half eleven.'

Mrs Hoffmann shook her head. 'I'll leave you in peace.'

The letter was from Netta. She was one of those people who wrote – and drew – how she spoke. Chorleywood jumped into life from her pages. It was an odd thing, but sometimes late at night or early in the morning, turning the handle of the predictor to train the guns at enemy bombers, Julia had the sense that it was Traddles she was protecting.

Land of Liberty, Peace and Plenty.

When she lived there, she hadn't appreciated it. She had been too bound up in a private life to understand that all lives were public at such times as these, or else they were not real lives, or lives being properly lived.

Julia drank her tea. Next door the small crowded sitting room was being cleaned to within an inch of its life. Through the wall came clinks and chinks of rearrangement, the groan of furniture shifted out of place and back again.

'Sad news,' she read, next to a marginal drawing of a cat with angel's wings floating up to heaven. Underneath, a pictorial map showing the hawthorn under which they had buried George.

Mrs Hoffmann came through from the passage to shake her broom and duster out of the back door. 'Something wrong?'

'A cat I know has died.'

Mrs Hoffmann nodded. 'It's always the little things that get to you.'

Julia went upstairs to bed and buried her head in the flat damp pillow that smelled of burned cinnamon and cloves. No letter from Peter again. For months after she enlisted she had written into silence, a chip of hope sealed in each envelope. At the top of each letter, her army number and present whereabouts. Christmas, and a note came thanking her for the balsawood model-airplane kit she had sent him. A short note. She could hear her father standing over him to make him write it, as she could hear him standing over the ones that followed at infrequent intervals.

When she had leave a few months later, her father reluctantly agreed to her request for them to meet. They had tea near the hostel at King's Cross where she was lodging. It was not a success.

'Too soon,' her father said.

Peter stood a way off. He'd recently had a haircut and the tendons on the back of his neck were prominent, bare and vulnerable.

'Richard married that woman, did you know?'

She shook her head.

'He wrote to invite Peter to the wedding. I must say, I think rather poorly of him for that.'

'Did he go?'

'Of course not. It was term time.'

Peter was no longer at Hurst. He was a weekly boarder at the school where most old Hurstians went. It was in St Albans.

On weekends, she gathered, the two of them filled their time by taking things apart and putting them together again. She remembered this about her father. Some men would sit in a draught and complain about it. Her father would apply himself to weatherstripping.

Spring came, even to Mudchute. The cratered ruins were covered with a fuzz of fresh green growth where weeds had seeded themselves in the cracks and the crevices. Here and there small hopeful flowers peeped out. A lone cherry tree blossomed. The wind blew the pink petals about in a strange shower of delight – the surrealism of it was somehow heroic.

'Sir,' said Julia, saluting. 'You asked to see me.' This came out as a croak. Her voice was going again.

Lieutenant Woodbury had set up an office in one of the bombed houses deemed unfit for human habitation. The house had no roof and not much remained of the upper storey. The staircase led nowhere. On the dank ground floor, semi-cleared, in what must have once been a parlour judging from the peeling remnants of wallpaper, was a steel desk, a field telephone and a battered filing cabinet.

'At ease, Corporal.' He spread his hands. 'Your No. 5.'

'Yes, sir.'

The telephone rang. Lieutenant Woodbury answered it, said, 'Right you are,' and placed the receiver back on its cradle. 'The barrel's on its way. Finally.'

'That's good,' said Julia. They had been waiting weeks for it.

He fiddled with a pencil. 'Poole.'

'Yes, sir.'

'He used to be one of the best. It seems to me he's been letting the side down lately. Would you agree?'

Julia said that Poole's reaction times could be better.

The lieutenant was grey-faced. Acne had returned to his chin, but he'd given up on the moustache, which was an improvement. 'We're all knackered, overdue for rotation. Even so.'

Rotation was the way the artillery regiments maintained combat efficiency. You didn't want the same personnel on a gun position for months on end. Yet Julia doubted whether rotation would help Poole. 'Has anyone checked his hearing?'

Lieutenant Woodbury flushed.

'It could be that,' said Julia, whose own hearing was beginning to worry her.

'Yes,' he said, 'it could.'

That night she was kipping in the command-post shelter when Arnott came in and tapped her on the arm. 'Alert?' she said, snapping awake.

'No.' Arnott had a sallow lined face and a wife and kiddie in Hartlepool. 'We've got a bit of a problem with the generator.'

'Again?'

'Come on, Sinclair,' said Arnott. 'You know how to tickle it.'

The problem with the generator was easy to rectify. She could have done it with her eyes closed, which was just as well, as it was dark.

'You've got to clean it out more often,' Julia said, itching her nose and leaving an oily smear on her cheek that she would not discover until morning. 'The trouble with you lot is you're lazy sods.' She checked her watch by torchlight. An hour had passed. 'You owe me.'

'We'll pay you back,' said Arnott.

'With what?'

'Don't look at me,' said Beddoes. 'I'm spoken for.'

'I want to man the gun,' she said.

Arnott said, 'We were wondering when you would get round to asking.'

'Hop up, Sinclair,' Beddoes said. 'Your steed awaits you.'

Julia clambered up into the gun seat and felt a surge of pure agency.

'Pity it's so quiet,' Arnott said.

What happened next had the quality of a dream. For the first time that night, the sirens wailed. 'Purple!' came the shout. Soldiers sped to their posts.

Searchlights combed the sky.

'On!'

'On!'

'Bearing 235! Angle 15!'

'Fire!' shouted Arnott.

Her foot stamped on the pedal. Flames. A huge explosion in the dark sky.

Lieutenant Woodbury came out of his office as she was heading back to Ada Street. 'I gather you christened the barrel last night, Sinclair. With a kill.'

'A hit?'

'Confirmed this morning. You know I could have you put on a charge.'

'Yes, sir.'

'So we'll credit this one to Beddoes, shall we?'

'How about Arnott, sir?' She had a soft spot for Arnott.

'Right you are, Corporal. Arnott it is. Enjoy your leave.'

26

'I wouldn't have known you,' Bernard was saying.

Ditto, thought Julia. Bernard had not so much aged as deflated – as if the tremendous balloon of self-regard that used to give him such presence had been pricked and all the air had escaped from it. Mattie told her he was depressed and unable to compose.

Julia said, 'It's the uniform, I expect.'

She'd come in her battledress, which strictly speaking should only be worn on the gun site; however there was no one here to report her, only to disapprove.

'Admittedly I'm short-sighted,' said Bernard, 'but for a moment when you came through the door I thought you were a boy.' He extracted a leather tobacco pouch from his jacket pocket and filled his pipe, pushing down the brown aromatic shreds with a nicotine-stained finger. 'Surely the cure for a failed love affair is to find oneself another chap, not turn oneself into one.'

'Now you're being provoking.'

She hoped he wasn't going to talk about Dougie. She could not afford to take a drink from that cup, not a sip. These days she told herself she was an individual only so far as circumstance and context were working through her. Yet sometimes it was hard to give up the sense you had a starring part in your own life, and tonight was one of them. She had known Dougie would not be here. This had not stopped her from imagining what he would have made of her battledress.

It was early evening, and the party was yet to get into its stride. Around the Kensington sitting room were clusters of people, mostly servicemen and women, making the stilted conversation of those who did not know each other well. Beside the fireplace stood a gentleman in wire-rimmed spectacles who was smiling distantly in the way you did when you were pretending it didn't matter that you had no one to speak to.

The flat was Mattie's – or rather it was the flat of her fiancé – and the party was to mark their engagement. Her fiancé, who was also her boss, had the trim, square shoulders and lean back that advertised the work of a good tailor and the quiet authority of someone in possession of a great deal of privileged information. They were to be married towards the end of the year, the date possibly determined by such information. Mattie had found a priest prepared to conduct the ceremony in the ruins of St Bride's – 'after all, it's still consecrated ground' – although you would have thought November might prove a little wet and chilly for an open-air wedding.

Bernard lit a match and puffed on his pipe. 'Once upon a time I seem to remember you weeping over a piano. "Asymmetries", wasn't it?'

'Asymmetries' was one of his pieces. On one of the few times she'd gone to Highgate to practise on his baby grand, he'd bullied her into playing it, then bellowed at her from across the room when she didn't play it properly. 'I don't weep over pianos any more.'

'Oh, I do,' said Bernard, 'I do. Copiously.'

For some reason, this assumption that creative work trumped all other kinds irritated her.

'How are your Americans?' Mattie had told her that Bernard's house had been requisitioned and was now occupied by a number of officers on Eisenhower's staff.

'Very polite, very clean, very large. But they will keep offering me chewing gum.'

She laughed. 'At least they're not likely to be in occupation for long.'

'You have knowledge to that effect.'

'I expect someone here does.'

Julia gazed around at the uniforms – some very senior uniforms indeed. The room itself displayed a masculine notion of comfort, broadly evident as an absence of fuss and the avoidance of any of the brighter colours in the decorator's palette. A couple of good eighteenth-century landscapes hung on the wall – hostages to fortune, you would have thought. She was surprised that places like this still existed in the demoralized dirty city that London had become.

We can't take much more of this, thought Julia. The return of the bombing had not brought about a return of the Blitz spirit. Every face she passed in the crowded streets was pinched with anxiety and resentment.

'Did you ever come to Primrose Hill?'

'Not when you were there.'

'It's gone,' Julia said. Nothing remained of the place where she had once fooled herself into thinking she was happy, the house she had once saved. She had been unable to establish what had become of Mrs Tooley, and this upset her more than anything.

'Why are you surprised?'

The carriage clock on the mantelpiece ting-ting-tinged the hour.

'What a pre-war sound,' said Bernard. 'So decorous, so civilized.'

'Yes, I used to own one like it.'

A little later, after talking to the gentleman in the wire-rimmed spectacles (who was a downstairs neighbour) and a few others, Julia went to say her goodbyes. Mattie motioned to her to follow her out on to the landing. 'I'd forgotten what it's like to give a party. You never have the chance to speak to anyone. Will I see you later in the week?'

People tramped up the stairs.

Mattie said, 'Walter, Felicity. Lovely you could come. Charles is inside.'

'I'll ring you,' said Julia.

'Do,' said Mattie. 'And mind you don't go anywhere near the parks. They're rutting in there every night. It's Rabelaisian.'

The hostel was on Pentonville Road. It was relatively early when Julia returned, and the building was quiet, although the humid smells of talcum powder, scent and sweat lingered as evidence of feverish preparations for nights on the town.

The place had been recommended to her by someone on her old battery. She had stayed here a number of times – it was cheap and convenient for the station. Best of all, it offered the reassuring sense of female solidarity that she had grown to rely upon.

This time, however, she had paid a little extra to have a room to herself. The hostel, unlike some women-only establishments, did not enforce a curfew, which contributed to its popularity. To make the most of their leaves, some of the girls took the tablets popular with aircrews on missions – chemical stimulants that meant you could dance (or bomb) all night. These suppressed appetite too, handy when hunger was otherwise such a distraction. But wakey-wakey pills were not for her. After months on the front line, all she craved was sleep.

The single rooms at the hostel were at the rear of the building. In Julia's, a partition halved the window, which was blacked out with paint, and a narrow bed took up most of the floor space under the disproportionately high ceiling. Pipes banged and she could hear the sound of running water. In the tiny smudged square of mirror over the hand basin she examined herself, ran her fingers through her hair. Perhaps she should let it grow out a little. Perhaps she should put on a skirt from time to time. A little lipstick wouldn't go amiss. Funny, but now that she'd fired the gun and felt that sense of agency, it didn't seem so incompatible with being a woman, not the way she'd come to understand it. She bent down, unlaced her boots, then undid the buttons on her battledress jacket.

Bea was somewhere in the Med: she owed her a letter. Pat Meadows, too, who had mastered the artillery training so well they had asked her to stay on at Manorbier as an instructor. And one day, she supposed, she should get round to replying to Fiona, who had written to offer her the Broadwood. An olive branch, or an unwelcome reminder of a previous wife that wanted shifting, hard to say. She sat on the bed and rummaged in her kit bag for pencil and paper.

She wrote to Peter instead.

It had been about a month since his letters had started coming more often, when they became longer, less forced in tone, when they went so far as to ask what she was doing. The change was as sudden and unexpected as cherry blossom on a bombsite.

She knew better than to rush things. Each word was a careful placing of one foot ahead of the other.

She wrote about her work, as much as the censor would allow. She did not suggest they meet. Since the bombing had returned he was boarding full time at the school in St Albans, a cadet (he had written proudly) in the OTC. His voice had broken (he had written proudly).

She did not ask too many questions. She did not ask how he was feeling or what he thought of her.

The siren went. She finished the letter and some minutes later came the all-clear. It was going to be one of those off-and-on nights. She was thinking about getting undressed and getting under the covers when a light knock came at the door.

The girl had a pale pretty face, a frizz of hair peeking out from under a kerchief. She was wearing mules and a quilted housecoat patterned with tiny pink rosebuds.

Dresden shepherdess, thought Julia. Fragonard.

'I'm ever so sorry to disturb you, but I saw the light under your door. I can't seem to get the electric ring to switch on.'

Down the corridor was a kitchenette where you could make yourself a hot drink or heat up soup or beans.

'It's silly of me, but I'm not very practical,' the shepherdess said.

Then how are you any use to the services? thought Julia.

The siren went again.

'There's a knack to it,' Julia was saying. 'You have to jiggle the plug about a bit.' She pushed open the door of the kitchenette.

Then

27

People fell from the sky. They were angels, falling from the angel roof. They were men, women and children. They were war dead. She understood she was war dead too and reached out to them.

Something shifted, tilted, gave way. A cavity opened up. From above came a narrow probing beam of light. An arm swung over her head. She saw the neat trimmed fingernails on the hand and the rosebud pattern on the quilted sleeve. She couldn't think where she'd seen this before.

Someone groaned. The rosebud arm flopped down. It wasn't attached to anything. It splattered her. She smelled gas. The light went out.

No, she wasn't war dead yet. She woke, knew where she was, sensed it was day. This clarity told her she must struggle.

Her mother told her that she could do anything if she put her mind to it. She put her mind to it and her left shoulder moved a little. She worked her shoulder further and her hand came free.

All this time she felt no pain, which was strange. She rubbed her face with her hand. To rub your face with your hand. It was exquisite.

She tried to move her hips, her legs. They were pinned.

She made a noise. She made another, louder.

There was a patch of sky that belonged to you. You shot at it.

Cherry blossom.

'Over here! I've reached her.'

'Alive?'

'A pulse, just.'

'Can you hear me? Can you hear me?'

She could hear.

'Hold on. Can you hear me? Hold on.'

Pain was a wild animal. Pain was a lion, a tiger, a wolf, biting, tearing.

'I'm going to give you an injection. Can you hear me? She's going into shock.'

She saw Peter. He said, 'Madre.'

28

Porters were packing up for the day, whistling and shouting as they slung wooden crates on to the back of lorries. Around the market the cobbled streets were slippery underfoot with cabbage leaves and squashed fruit. A smell of crushed flowers hung in the warm summer air; sun beat down on dusty awnings.

Dougie turned off Long Acre and walked along Endell Street towards the Cross Keys. He'd spent the morning in a meeting and he needed time to think about what had been proposed to him. Over the entrance to the pub, two sooty cherubs clutched the keys of St Peter as if they were teething aids.

Inside it took a while for his eyes to adjust to the dim light, the red-shaded bulbs, the glints of copper and brass. Market traders in stained waistcoats, flat caps and shirtsleeves squared off in argumentative territorial groups the length of the bar. He took his pint to the rear, sat in a corner and opened his notebook.

The war in Europe was over. The war in the East staggered on. There was peace, of a kind. He'd been asked to go to Germany and film their defeat. The idea was to show the Germans what they'd brought on themselves. As a brief, it was clearer than most. He wasn't certain that it was his kind of film, or whether he had the stomach for it.

When he next raised his eyes, he noticed with a jolt of recognition a familiar stooped figure sitting a few feet away, staring into space. He got up from his seat.

'Mind if I join you?' he said, setting down his pint and pulling out a stool topped in cracked maroon leatherette.

'Dougie.' Something like a smile flickered across Basil's face, then was gone.

Even in the amber gloom of the pub, the man looked ill. His hands shook. His eyes were sunk in hollows.

It had been months since Dougie had last seen him; longer since they'd worked together. A union dispute over working hours had forced Basil's hand around the time when Dougie had been sent to Sicily to film the invasion – a false start, as it turned out, since they hadn't been able to find the money to finance the shoot and all he had got out of it was sunburn. Frank and Hugh had subsequently defected to features. Dougie had spent most of the previous year talking himself into and out of quitting. The Unit was not what it was.

'What are you up to these days?'

Basil fumbled with a cigarette paper. 'The usual. Editing.'

'Whereabouts?'

'Next door.' Shreds of tobacco spilled out of the cigarette paper. His trembling fingers pinched them up from the table top. 'You don't want to know.'

'That dull, eh?'

Basil gave a bitter laugh and shook his head. 'How about you? I saw the diary picture. Fine piece, moving, hopeful.' His voice was flat and uninflected.

'It would have been better if you'd worked on it.'

Basil's eyes met his briefly then shied away, somewhere towards the middle distance, or inwards, which amounted to the same thing. 'Sylvia tells me Barbara is staying in Canada.'

'Yes. I always thought she might.'

'New man?'

'No man at all, it seems.'

'I heard about Julia,' said Basil.

'I loved her, you know.'

'Then you were an idiot to cock it up, weren't you?'

This sitting in judgement was new. 'Yes.'

Basil drained the last of his pint. 'Well. Good to see you.'

A surge of noise came from one of the groups of porters around the bar.

'What is it exactly that they've got you working on?'

A pause. 'You haven't got clearance.'

'I signed the Act years ago, the same as you.'

Next door to the pub was a shop selling theatrical make-up, sticks of pancake, hairpieces, false eyelashes, tap shoes. Basil produced a bunch of keys and unlocked a battered black door to the side. Ahead stretched a dark narrow passage with a flight of uncarpeted stairs at the end. 'You must promise to keep this quiet.'

At the top of the stairs was another door, which Basil also unlocked.

There was the immediate smell of acetate – this was expected – and something else, too, which later Dougie could only describe as the sour scent of despair.

Cans of stock were everywhere, some opened, some sealed with army labels. Basil went over to the bench, brushed aside a few stray trims and pulled up a spare chair alongside his own. 'You'll want to see this sitting down.'

When Basil threaded the film into the Moviola, Dougie noticed that his hands had stopped shaking. Doctor Theatre, he thought. He'd been wondering how he was managing to cut.

Basil pressed the pedal and the sequence began to play. It was a rough assembly. No titles, no commentary, no sound. 'They've asked Hitchcock to do the treatment.'

An orchard, wind blowing through grass, flowers nodding, sunshine.

Barbed wire. A fence. A gate. Iron words written over it.

Fingers poking through the fence, imploring. Fingers that are no more than bone and sinew, thin breakable stalks. What are these filthy striped rags? Whose are these razored skulls?

Barracks. A door is yanked open and corpses spill out. The stench. You can smell it. Rictus grins split their faces into creases of skin.

A woman stands under an outdoor shower, not caring she is naked, viewed, filmed. Lifts her face to the water trickling down.

A man struggles to stand. Collapses.

In a hut, starved children with empty eyes clutch alien toys.

Fat women and fat men shovel dead people. The tangled limbs – the bare waxy tangled limbs – the empty ribcages, the hollowed pelvic girdles over which skin is stretched, taut. Into the pit they go, down into the pit. Down into the pit.

And you know, as you watch, that these are people killed by a truth they cannot help. The simple truth of who they are.

The film ran out, flicking. Little knocks and cries and touches of sound came through the window. Someone shaking out a carpet, a seagull's high scream, the dull, hollow thump of a beer keg being rolled over cobbles.

Basil stilled the flywheel, removed the reel from the Moviola and set it to one side. As soon as he let it go, his hands started shaking again.

'Most of that's Belsen. It was the first one they found. Some commando stumbled across it. The army started filming it as soon as they arrived. Then the War Office brought me in to have a look at what they'd shot.'

Dougie swallowed. 'When?'

'April,' said Basil.

Good God. Six weeks of sitting by yourself in a room on the top floor of a small house in Covent Garden watching hell over and over again.

'The newsreels . . .'

'They don't show the half of it. More footage comes through all the time.' Basil gestured at the unopened labelled cans. 'You've no idea how much of it there is. They keep finding more camps.'

He began to cough. This went on for a while. Then he went to stand by the window, a dark figure against the light coming through the smeared window. 'Well, we all heard the rumours.'

'You mean we're complicit? In *this*?'

Basil said, 'I want to scour out my mind.'

They came out into the daylight. Basil locked the street door, hands shaking like a leaf. 'So.'

'You've cut it like a story.'

'Yes. God help me. Otherwise . . .' His voice faded out.

Otherwise, thought Dougie, you would be numbed, and the anger, the revulsion, the horror, would be lost. And at all costs – at all costs – they must hang on to the anger. They must never forget it.

The shutters were coming down on the Endell Street shopfronts, on the grocers' and theatrical suppliers. The last of the lorries was trundling away from the market. A long line of schoolchildren, topped and tailed by felt-hatted teachers, went past chattering, swinging hands.

'We made a myth,' said Basil.

Dougie shook his head. 'No, we recorded one. There's a difference.'

They parted at Tottenham Court Road Station.

'They want me to go to Germany.'

'Do they.' Basil tipped his hat over his eyes and went down the steps to the Tube.

It was one of those small London squares that used to be so pleasant before the war, a private gated place where nannies aired babies in prams and shy young girls got their first taste of love's great disappointments. Now the gates and railings were long gone and the laurels were leggy and overgrown. The paths were dusty and trodden all around.

He came at the square from Museum Street. There was a huge crater midway along on the eastern side where two and a half houses were missing, the result of a V-1 or V-2, judging by the scale of it. Elsewhere, what bombing had not accomplished, shabbiness had. Splashed in white paint on a gable end was the year-old slogan 'Second Front Now'. The city was spent.

The square was empty except for a tall dark-haired boy and a dark-haired woman. They were walking slowly around the perimeter, the woman leaning on a stick. He could not see their faces but he knew who they were.

She was explaining to the boy why the ack-ack had been able to destroy so many rockets. 'People were scared of them because they didn't have pilots. But the fact they didn't have pilots made them easier to hit. Look.' She drew in the dust with her stick. 'Fixed trajectory. You see?'

The boy said, 'Did you ever hit one?'

'No. I was in hospital by then. But I downed a plane once.'

'Did you? You never said. Did you kill anyone?'

'I don't know. I hope not.'

'Stay here,' the boy said to the woman. 'Lean against this tree. Go on.'

She leant against the tree. It was a mulberry, half its leaves blasted off. Still alive, though.

'Now give me your stick.'

'Please,' said the woman. 'Not today.'

'Give me your stick,' said the boy.

She gave him her stick. He walked a few paces away and stopped. 'Come on.'

'I can't.'

'Yes, you can.' He held out his arms. 'I'll catch you.'

'I'm tired.'

'Come on,' said the boy. 'You can do it.'

The woman stepped away from the tree: first one foot, then the other dragged along behind to join it. She started to laugh. 'I'm going to topple. Then we'll all see my knickers.'

'No, you're not. Come on, another step.'

She took another step. Another.

The boy moved back a pace.

'That's cheating!'

Another step, another.

The boy rushed to catch her before she fell. 'Well done, Madre. Well done.'

She was laughing. 'This is exactly how I taught you to walk.' Then she turned in his direction and saw him.

He thought he had prepared himself. He hadn't. This was a different Julia, looking out of different eyes. This was a person who stood on her own two feet, however unsteadily.

'Hello, Dougie,' she said.

Her lovely Modigliani face.

The boy, who must have known who he was, regarded him with curiosity. He exchanged a look with his mother. 'I'll go queue for some of that dreadful grey bread then, shall I?'

'Yes, thanks. And powdered milk, if you can find some.'

This tact, on both their parts, told Dougie that neither of them thought she had need of protection.

'Do you mind if I sit?'

'Of course not,' he said.

There were no seats, no benches in the square, only an old stone horse trough. She made her way towards it.

'Don't help me.' She eased herself down and perched on the rim.

He sat alongside. He wanted to run his fingers down her damaged leg, to seek out all the hurt parts. She turned her face to the sky and he understood that she was drinking it in, being alive. The sunlight on the garden.

Well, well, she was thinking. Here it was, that old carnal song, the leaping up from flesh to flesh. Desire was a fairground mirror; you couldn't trust it. She knew that now and, like all knowledge, it had been hard won.

'I saw your films.'

'Did you.'

'I liked the Welsh one.'

'I like that one too.'

'"Wales. Too wet in one way, too dry in another."'

'I changed my mind.'

'You know,' she said, 'when I was buried I kept thinking that if I had been at my post I would have shot that plane down. Isn't that strange?'

'Not really.'

They sat in silence for a while. It wasn't awkward.

'I should be going,' she said. 'It takes me a while to get up the stairs.'

'Won't you ask me in for a cup of tea?'

She'd forgiven him. She'd had to in order to forgive herself. But that didn't mean she was under any illusion he would change. His truth was in his work, not in his life.

'No,' she said. 'The flat's a mess. The roof leaks.'

'A roof that leaks in dry weather,' he said. 'That is really quite leaky.'

She smiled. 'Another time,' she said, struggling to her feet and gazing round at the war-damaged square.

She had work to do.

Acknowledgements

During the Second World War, women were called upon to perform many vital roles, not all of which have received the official recognition they deserve. For Julia's experiences on the HAA battery at Mudchute and her training as a predictor operator, I am indebted to first-hand accounts written by Frank Yates, Margaret Ward (née Bennett) and Mary Latham, published on the website bbc.co.uk/history/ww2peopleswar, as well as to Phyllis Ramsden (www.kingscare.co.uk).

Footage shot in wartime Britain by the director Humphrey Jennings still frames our view of the Second World War. Films such as *London Can Take It, Listen to Britain* and *Fires were Started* have earned Jennings critical acclaim as 'the only true poet the British cinema has yet produced' (Lindsay Anderson). I have drawn on Jennings's work and that of the Crown Film Unit in this book. (The title *They Also Serve* was borrowed from a 1940 film directed by Ruby Grierson; *Keeping Rabbits for Extra Meat* is also a real film of the period.)

Invaluable sources have included: *Humphrey Jennings* by Kevin Jackson (Picador, 2004), *Humphrey Jennings, More than a Maker of Films* by Anthony W. Hodgkinson and Rodney E. Sheratsky (University Press of New England, 1982), *Humphrey Jennings: Film-maker, Painter, Poet*, edited by Mary-Lou Jennings (British Film Institute, in association with Riverside Studios, 1982), *Portrait of an Invisible Man, The Working Life of Stewart McAllister, Film Editor* by Dai Vaughan (BFI Books, 1983) and *A Retake Please! Night Mail to Western Approaches* by Pat Jackson (Royal Naval Museum and Liverpool University Press, 1999). Films by Humphrey Jennings are available in a number of different DVD collections.

However, like Julia, Dougie Birdsall is a fictional creation, and his faults are his own.

My great thanks to the renowned documentary film-maker John Krish for sharing his memories of working with Jennings during the war. And to Debbie Postgate for putting me in touch with him.

To Jane Forster, who kept me supplied me with wartime copies of *Lilliput*, and who first suggested firing a gun.

To Paul Evans, Librarian, Royal Artillery Museum, and Major Tim Watts (retired) for setting me straight on military matters. (Mistakes are mine alone.)

My publisher Juliet Annan has been an unerring source of good advice and brilliant ideas – I am deeply grateful for her encouragement, for her keen editorial eye and for suggesting the title. At Fig Tree I would also like to thank Ellie Smith, Anna Steadman and Alison O'Toole, as well as Sarah Day for her copy-editing skills. Special thanks to Alice Chandler, who tracked down the previously unseen cover image.

Anthony Goff, my agent, made many useful suggestions, not least about cricket, and has been an immense help and support, as always. Thanks also to Marigold Atkey at David Higham Associates for her assistance.

I'm grateful to Jenny Hall for her kindness and generosity during a difficult time, to Hilary Arnold, Emma Dally, Celia Dodd, Takla Gardey and Debbie Postgate for unwavering friendship, and to Ann Fischer and Carol and Nick Justin for always being there.

As ever, all love to my children, Katharine and Tom Lazenby, whose ideas and encouragement have been so helpful. Most of all, heartfelt thanks to my brother, Glenn, and to Jocelyn Stephens. You both know why.